About a Vampire

"Remember, no matter how crazy this sounds, I'm not crazy. You are safe with me. I would never harm you. Ever. I promise you that."

"Okay," Holly murmured. But really, the more he said that, the more worried she got. It was the old, "The lady doth protest too much." But in this case it was a man doing the protesting. The more he assured her that he wouldn't harm her, the more anxious she got that he might.

"Right . . . so, you see . . ." He paused again and then warned, "I'm just going to tell you flat out."

"Okay," Holly said.

"Right." He nodded, and then added, "It's going to sound crazy."

"Okay," Holly repeated, not at all surprised. She was already beginning to think there was something wrong with the man.

"So here goes," he said, and then blurted, "I'm a vampire."

By Lynsay Sands

LYNSAY SANDS

ABOUT A VAMPIRE

AN ARGENEAU NOVEL

AVONBOOKS

An Imprint of HarperCollins*Publishers*

This is a work of fiction. Names, characters, places, and incidents are products of the author's imagination or are used fictitiously and are not to be construed as real. Any resemblance to actual events, locales, organizations, or persons, living or dead, is entirely coincidental.

AVON BOOKS
An Imprint of HarperCollins*Publishers*
195 Broadway
New York, New York 10007

First Avon Books mass market printing: October 2015

One

"Crap," Holly muttered, staring down at the sheaf of papers she'd just stepped on. The small disc stapled to the top corner told her that it was the paperwork for one of their clients. It included the burial permit, the coroner's certificate, the application for cremation and the coversheet with the client's name and info . . . and it should have been given to John Byron when he arrived to start his shift at 4:30 that afternoon. Obviously, it hadn't. This bundle must have fallen off her desk at some point that day.

Holly continued to stand there for several seconds, simply staring at the bundle. She didn't even remove her foot, because once she did, she'd have to do something about it . . . like take it to the crematorium . . . and she really didn't want to go down there. Not at this hour. Making the trek during the day was one thing, but it was just past midnight now. She'd have to make her way through the graveyard to get to the building that housed the chapel;

the columbarium, where the urns rested; and the crematorium, where the bodies were stored and waiting for their turn at the retort.

Retorts is what the owner of Sunnyside Cemetery, Max, had called them when he'd given her the tour the day she'd started. He could call them what he liked, but *retort* was just a fancy word for the oven where they burned the bodies.

Shuddering at the thought of the coffins shelved in the cooler, Holly closed her eyes briefly. A popular game here seemed to be to freak out the new worker with tales of the "ovens." Jerry, the day technician, and John, who took the evening shift, as well as her boss, Max, and even Sheila, the receptionist, had all told her one horrific tale or another. But the most memorable was John telling her how the coffins burned away first and the corpses sometimes sat up inside the oven, muscles contracting in the heat and mouths agape as if screaming in horror at their doom. That image had stuck with her, convincing Holly she really didn't want to be cremated. In fact, she'd decided dying was to be avoided at all costs if possible.

Sighing, she opened her eyes and peered at the papers, wishing she could pretend she hadn't seen them. After all, in the normal course of events, she wouldn't have found them until morning. She shouldn't be here now except she'd got home after work, made dinner and looked for her purse to get her blood tester to check her sugar levels, but hadn't been able to find it. Thinking she'd probably left her purse in the car and not wanting dinner to get cold, she'd decided the blood test could wait. Of course, by the time dinner was finished, she'd forgotten all about it . . . until she was brushing her teeth before bed. She'd been halfway done when she'd remembered.

Pulling on her trench coat over her pajamas, Holly had hustled out to the car in her slippers to retrieve her purse . . . only it hadn't been there either. That had stymied her briefly, and she'd stood in the cold garage for several moments, trying to think where it might be. She'd had it at work when she'd paid Sheila for lunch, Holly recalled. She then tried to bring up a memory of slinging it over her shoulder as she left work, but instead remembered that her hands had been full of tax forms and receipts . . . no purse. Holly hadn't noticed at the time because her car keys had been in her coat pocket.

After wasting another few minutes debating whether she could just skip testing that night, she'd slouched with resignation and got in the car to drive back to work. Missing one test once in a while wasn't that bad, but skipping two in a row wasn't good. Besides, the cemetery was only a ten-minute drive from her home. It simply wasn't worth risking a diabetic coma.

Of course, Holly thought now, if she'd realized that coming back would mean having to make a trek through the graveyard—in her pajamas no less—she might have risked the coma.

Grimacing, she bent and snatched up the papers. There was nothing for it, she would have to drop them off before heading home. Otherwise, the cremation wouldn't happen until tomorrow or the next day, which could be a problem depending on when his service was scheduled to take place.

Clasping the papers firmly in one hand, Holly slung her purse over her shoulder with the other. But as she headed out of the office, she couldn't help thinking that life would be a lot easier if she were a little less conscientious. Being a responsible type person was really a pain in the ass at times, she thought as she stepped outside and dug her keys out of her pocket.

The funeral home key was easy to find despite the dark night; it was on its own ring. It was also shiny and new, though that was hard to tell in this light. She'd only received it last Friday. It was now Monday. Why did a brand-new and temporary employee have a key to the company? The answer to that was simple enough: because her coworkers weren't as conscientious and responsible as she was. During her first week there, Max hadn't shown up much before noon even once, and Sheila, the receptionist who also happened to be Max's daughter, had been late three times. The apple really hadn't fallen far from the tree with those two.

On Friday, after twiddling her thumbs in the funeral home parking lot for over an hour and a half for the third morning that week, Holly had let some of her irritation show when Sheila finally arrived. She'd also suggested that perhaps she should start later in the day rather than waste her time and their money sitting in the parking lot waiting. Sheila had what she considered to be a better solution—she'd gone out and had a key made for her. Now Holly could get in on time.

She'd like to believe that it was her conscientiousness and responsible nature that had led Sheila to give her the key, but knew the truth was it was pure laziness and convenience. So long as Holly had a key and could open the office on time, Sheila could be as late as she liked. The other woman had proven that today, when she hadn't shown up until lunchtime, and then it was with lunch for them both that

Holly hadn't wanted but had paid her back for her half anyway.

Holly locked the door and turned to glance toward the crematorium, only to pause and frown when she couldn't see the building. It was the fog. It had made driving here something of a pain, but she'd forgotten about it while in the building. Now, she found herself staring into the misty darkness surrounding her and felt a little shiver of anxiety shimmy its way up her spine.

She was in a graveyard on a dark and foggy moonless night. This was way too much like a scene from a horror movie. Any minute decomposing corpses would begin to claw their way out of the ground and drag themselves toward her, lured by the scent of fresh flesh.

"Get a grip," Holly muttered to herself.

The sound of her own voice in the night was a bit bracing, but not enough to make her move in the direction of the crematorium.

Holly shuffled her slippered feet briefly, and then sighed and turned to unlock the door again. Perhaps there was an umbrella or something in the office that she could carry with her. Having a weapon, even a mostly useless one, might help boost her courage for the trek ahead.

When a quick search of the offices didn't turn up an umbrella, a cane, or a flame thrower to fend off those imagined zombie corpses, Holly resorted to grabbing a large pair of scissors she spotted sticking out of the pencil holder on the reception desk. She hefted them briefly, considered their size and then decided they would do. She probably wouldn't need anything anyway. She was just being a ninny, but felt better clutching the scissors as she headed back outside.

Sadly, there had been no helpful gust of wind to sweep away the fog during the few minutes she'd been inside. If anything, it seemed to her that the fog had thickened, but that might have simply been her own anxiety making it seem that way. It had probably been just as thick earlier as it was now, she reassured herself and wished she had a flashlight.

The thought made her glance toward the parking lot. She kept a flashlight in the glove compartment for emergencies. Holly hurried to her car, unlocked it and settled in the passenger seat to open the glove compartment and make a quick search. Not finding it, she sat back with a sigh, then grabbed the papers and the scissors and got out. She left her purse inside. It would eliminate the possibility of accidentally leaving it behind in the crematorium, she thought as she locked the door.

Trying not to think of movies like *The Fog* or *Night of the Living Dead*, Holly headed determinedly in the direction of the crematorium. She moved as quickly as she dared along the paved path, her ears straining for any sound that might indicate she wasn't alone. Now that she was resigned to the task, getting it over with and getting back home was all she cared about. It was always better to get unpleasant tasks done quickly.

Unfortunately, it did seem that the unpleasant tasks often took the most time. She knew it was probably just her fear and anxiety, but the walk to the crematorium seemed to be taking much longer than it should. Holly actually began to worry that she'd headed in the wrong direction in the fog and lost her way, that she could be wandering the graveyard in her pajamas until the sun rose to burn away the fog, so was relieved when she spotted the weak glow of a light ahead. Knowing it must be the wall sconce over the building entrance, Holly headed for it at a faster clip, relieved when she was able to see the door beneath it.

Holly released a little pent-up breath of relief once she slipped inside. She'd made it, alive and well and unmolested by rotting corpses.

"Awesome," she said, and grimaced at how weak her voice sounded in the dimly lit entryway. Giving herself a little shake, Holly started forward, moving quickly past the doors to both chapels and through the columbarium with its niche banks full of urns. Some were visible behind glass, some were hidden by brass plates with names and dates on them, and a lot had flowers and whatnot stuck in special holders on or beside them. Her gaze skated to the floral tributes and then determinedly away as she passed. Holly used to love flowers, but two weeks of working here had changed that. She now associated flowers with death.

She should have been more relaxed now that she was inside. After all, the urns held only the ashes of the dead, which couldn't spontaneously form into bodies to clamber after her in search of brains, but Holly found herself still anxious and jumpy. It didn't take much thought to figure out why. She was about to head into the crematorium itself, where coffins holding the newly departed waited to be burned.

During that tour on her first day working here, the process of cremation had been explained to her in fine detail. Definitely more than she'd wanted to know, but apparently, the fact that she was a temp in the office to work on the taxes and wasn't a sales associate didn't remove the possibility of her having to explain things to customers. Holly hoped to God that never happened, because she would not want to explain those details to the loved ones of the newly deceased. It had all seemed gruesome to her.

Holly had never really thought much about cremation, but if she had, she would have assumed that the coffin was rolled into the retort, flames shot out and poof, a nice urn of ashes came out the other end. Not so. First of all, it took much longer than she'd imagined. Despite reaching temperatures of 1600 or 1700 degrees, the actual cremation could take two to three hours. And no neat little urn of ashes came out at the end. The ashes, which weren't all ashes, remained in the retort to cool, and then a magnet was used to remove anything metal such as fillings and pins. Once cooled, the ashes were swept out onto a tray using a corn broom as if the remains were so much debris on the floor. They were then allowed to cool further before being placed into a cremulator, which looked much like a garbage disposal unit to Holly when she'd peered inside. There the remains, including some bone that didn't break down completely, were pulverized to make it all smooth and ash-like before it was placed in the urn if one was supplied. Otherwise it was bagged and boxed for the family to take away.

Gruesome, Holly thought as she pushed through another door into a short hall.

Here the dim lighting gave way to glaringly bright fluorescents overhead, and cinder-block walls painted a pale cream. It was almost sterile in its lack of color, and Holly paused and blinked, the buzz of the fluorescents loud in her ears as her attention shifted to the door ahead.

John Byron worked the 4:30-to-12:30 shift and should still be on duty, she thought, glancing at her wristwatch. She'd met him several times and while he was a bit of a cynic, with a sarcastic, self-deprecating sense of humor, he seemed a nice enough guy. She didn't think he'd give her too hard a time, although she'd no doubt have to explain why she was at the offices this late. Holly hoped he was alone though and Rick Mexler hadn't yet arrived. Rick was the man who took over the crematorium from 12:30 to 8:30. She didn't start work until 9:00 so hadn't yet met him, but had heard he was a grumpy S.O.B. who didn't like people. That really wasn't something she wanted to have to deal with, so she was a bit alarmed when she stepped through the door into the crematorium and heard two men's voices.

The crematorium was a large long rectangle, but the cooler took up a ten-by-ten space along the left on entering. The rest of the room was a large L shape, with the retorts against the wall that was around the corner of the cooler, out of sight. That was where the voices were coming from, so she didn't at first see the men. But Holly assumed it was John and Rick.

Her gaze slid to the front of the cooler as she started forward. The door was a metal roll-up almost as wide as a garage door. It was open at the moment, leaving the contents on view— a set of tall wide shelves with various coffins on it. Two were cardboard boxes, two were the less expensive blue coffins, and three were actual oak coffins. She noted that the mini forklift was positioned in front of the open door as if John had been about to retrieve a casket when he'd been interrupted by Rick's arrival.

Holly turned her gaze away from the cooler, trying not to think of the loved ones resting in the coffins . . . or their intended future. She'd nearly reached the corner when she realized that neither voice sounded like John Byron. Had he left already? And if so, who was Rick Mexler talking to? She slowed and then paused just out of sight around the corner to listen to the men's conversation.

Justin Bricker rolled the gurney stacked with dead rogues in front of the retort. After kicking the wheel locks to keep it in place, he then glanced to Anders, his partner in tonight's endeavor.

With his dark hair and skin and the black leather clothes he wore, Anders was like a shadow in the white room. He was presently looming over the crematorium technician who stood in the corner. The adult male mortal who had opened the back door at their knock now looked like little more than a naughty schoolboy put there for punishment by an irate teacher. Only the child's resentment was missing . . . the man's expression was blank as Anders worked to remove their arrival from his memory and keep him where he stood, safely out of the way.

When Anders relaxed and turned to walk toward him, Justin raised his eyebrows. "Are we good?"

Anders nodded. "But we have to be quick. His shift ends in fifteen minutes. A new guy will be showing up soon."

"No problem. We'll be out of here by then. As flammable as we are, these guys will be dust in minutes." Justin turned to open the door of the retort, and whistled at the wave of heat that blew out at him. He glanced to Anders as the other man reached his side. "So . . . What did you do to piss off Lucian?"

Rather than answer, Anders asked, "What makes you think I did anything to piss him off?"

Justin grinned. "Well, he gave me clean-up duty because I pissed him off. So I figure you must be in the same boat."

Anders merely grunted and pulled the top body off the stack to send it into the retort.

"Come on," Justin said as the flames shooting into the retort hit the body and it was set ablaze as if it were made of dry straw. "You must have done something."

Anders watched him pick up another body to send it into the retort. Finally, he said, "I might have made some joke or other about his missing so many meals at home since Leigh turned vegetarian."

Justin raised his eyebrows. "That wouldn't bother him . . . unless you said it in front of Leigh."

Anders grimaced, and then started to pick up the next body. "Unfortunately, Leigh came into the room behind me as I was saying it. I fear she overheard me."

"Ah." Justin winced, knowing Anders wouldn't have deliberately hurt the woman's feelings. None of the hunters would. Leigh was a good woman, they all liked her. "Yeah, I bet that—Look out! The head—"

Anders froze with this body half off the gurney, but it was too late. One of the heads had been dislodged and was rolling off the edge of the metal table. Justin made a grab for it, but wasn't in time and the decapitated head hit the floor with a wet splat.

Both men stood and grimaced at the mess, and then Anders nodded toward the crematorium technician and muttered, "I don't suppose we can make him clean this up?"

"You suppose right. It would be hard to erase that from his memory and ensure it stayed erased," Justin said with amusement as he watched Anders grab the head by the man's long hair and toss it into the retort. It rolled forward like a lopsided bowling ball wobbling into the flame jets where it exploded into immediate flames. Shaking his head, he murmured, "Like kindling."

"Yeah, we're pretty flammable," Anders commented.

"I guess that makes us hot stuff," Justin said and laughed at his own joke. It even brought a smile from Anders as he finished lifting the body he held and sent it into the retort after the head. Anders wasn't known for a sense of humor, so the smile was the equivalent of a belly laugh from anyone else, Justin thought.

A shuffling sound and a moan drew his attention around to a woman standing at the corner of the cooler. She was short and rounded with a wave of raven black hair pouring over her shoulders and down her back, a shiny black mass against the tan trench coat she wore. She also had one hand pressed against the cooler wall as if to hold herself up, and her complexion was positively green as she stared at the puddle on the floor where the head had been just seconds ago. Justin was pretty sure she'd witnessed the whole head-rolling-off-the-table–onto-the-floor bit. No doubt a gruesome sight for someone not used to dealing with the dead. Hell, he had to do it on a semi regular basis and it had been gruesome to him.

Her eyes lifted reluctantly to him and Anders now and Justin noted that they were a lovely pale blue. She had nice lips too, full and kissable, and the cutest little slightly turned up nose . . . and she was looking at him and Anders with a sort of mindless horror.

"I have the mess on the floor to clean up, so you get to deal with our tourist here," Anders announced grimly.

"Thanks," Justin said sarcastically, but didn't really mind. He loved women, always had, and this one was a cutie. The only shame was that he wouldn't get to play with more than her mind. Once he took control of her and wiped her memories, he'd have to avoid contact with her again to avoid those memories returning. Ah well, plenty more in the sea, he thought and concentrated his gaze on her forehead, trying to penetrate her thoughts.

"Well?" Anders asked after a moment. "What are you waiting for? Take control of her."

Justin blinked, confusion sliding through him and then said weakly, "I can't."

"What?" Anders asked with surprise.

"I can't read her," he clarified, hardly able to believe it himself. Her thoughts were a complete blank to him.

"Seriously?" Anders asked, eyes narrowing.

"Seriously," Justin assured him, aware that his voice sounded as dazed as he felt. Damn. He couldn't read her. That meant—

"Well, then I'd get after her if I were you," Anders suggested and when Bricker just stared at him in blank confusion, he gestured to where the woman had been just a moment before and pointed out, "She's running."

The closing of the door to the hall told him Anders was right before he could turn to see that she was no longer in the room. Cursing, Justin burst into a run. He'd be damned if he was going to let her get away . . . and not because of what she'd seen. He couldn't read her, and that might mean she could be a life mate for him. Finding a life mate this early in life was pretty damned rare. If he lost her, he wouldn't be likely to find another for centuries . . . maybe millennia, and Justin had no desire to wait millennia to experience what it was like to have a life mate.

She was quick, he noted with admiration on reaching the hall to see her disappearing through the door at the other end. But then panic could be one hell of a motivation and he had no doubt what she'd seen had raised panic in her.

The thought made Bricker frown as he went after her. He would have a lot of explaining to do once he caught up. He'd have to calm her, and then somehow explain that he wasn't some murderous bastard destroying evidence of his dastardly work . . . and all without the aid of mind control. That ought to be interesting, he thought unhappily, and his worrying over that made him move more slowly than he could have. He wanted to work out how to explain things before he caught up. He wanted to do it right the first time, calm her quickly, and gain her trust. He couldn't convince her to be his life mate if she was terrified or suspicious of him. The right words were needed here.

The problem was, Justin didn't have a clue what those right words were and he was running out of time. It did seem a good idea to stop her before she actually left the building, though, and at that moment she was racing through the last hall, flying past the chapels and columbaries, headed for the exit. Letting go of the worry about what to say, Justin picked up speed and caught her arm just as she reached the door. When he whirled her around, she immediately swung her free arm at him. Expecting paltry girly blows, Justin didn't react at first and only spotted the scissors she held a heartbeat before they sliced across his throat.

Justin sucked in his breath and released her as pain radiated through him. He saw the fine mist of blood that sprayed out and splashed across her tan coat and immediately covered his throat. The small amount of blood that had showered her told him it wasn't a deep wound. He was more surprised by the attack than anything else. Still, by the time he turned his attention back to the woman, she'd tugged the door open and was slipping away. Cursing, he ignored his stinging throat and quickly followed.

The woman—his woman—glanced over her shoulder at the sound of the door opening and Justin's mouth tightened at the sight of her wide terrified eyes. So much for winning her trust, he thought, and then cried out as she stumbled. She had been looking back rather than where she was going and that was her undoing. It left her unprepared for the sudden step down in the sidewalk and she lost her footing. She fell flat on her face. It wasn't much of a fall though and he fully expected her to pop back up fighting and with feet moving, but instead she lay prone until he reached her side.

Concerned by how still she was, Justin squatted and turned her over. He spotted the bloody gash on her forehead first. She'd obviously hit her head on the sidewalk as she fell. It was a good bump, but not that bad, he noted with a relief that turned to horror as he then spotted the scissors protruding from her chest in the small space where the loosely done up coat didn't meet. Even as Bricker saw that, her eyes opened and then widened with pain and fear of a different kind now. She no longer feared him, at least not as much as she feared for her life. The hell of it was, he was afraid for her life too. It looked bad.

"Didn't your mother ever tell you not to run with scissors?" he said shortly, ripping her coat open to reveal a pink pajama top with white bunnies. The sight startled him enough that he paused briefly, until he noted that those bunnies around the scissors were quickly growing red with the blood bubbling up from her wound. He was sure the presence of the shears in her body was the only thing keeping that blood from spraying out in a fountain. It looked like a mortal wound to him. He was going to lose his life mate before even learning her name.

"Screw that," Bricker muttered, and jerked his sleeve up to tear into his wrist with the fangs that slid forward in his mouth. He wasn't losing her.

Two

Holly smacked her lips together and ran her tongue around the inside of her mouth. She then grimaced at the serious case of morning breath she had. A truly serious case, she thought with disgust, and opened her eyes, expecting to see the canopy of her bed. Instead, she found herself staring at a somewhat clean white ceiling in a beige room. Her bedroom wasn't beige.

Pushing herself up on her elbows, Holly glanced around with confusion. There was a desk and chair, a wardrobe with a television in the upper inset, black-out curtains, two chairs set on either side of a small coffee table to the left of the bed she lay in, and a perfectly dreadful print on the wall. It all spoke of one thing . . .

"A hotel?" Holly breathed with surprise. "What the devil am I doing in a hotel?"

Sitting up, she started to swing her feet out of bed, but then froze and snatched up the sheet and blanket as they fell away to reveal that she was naked. Holly *never* slept naked. She held the bedclothes briefly to her chest, her gaze shifting around the room in search of her clothes, but didn't see them. That was distressing. Even more distressing though was the fact that she had no recollection of how she'd come to be in this state.

Her gaze slid to the clock on the bedside table, and Holly sucked in a startled gasp of dismay. Seven o'clock. Dear God, she'd been out all night. James would get home soon and wonder where the hell she was. He'd worry and want to know what had happened. Only she didn't have a clue what to tell him, because she didn't know herself.

Getting home before him seemed like a good idea, but getting dressed and getting out of this bed was an even better one, she decided, and got up, dragging the sheet with her. The blanket tried to come too, but eventually gave up the game and slid free to lie in a heap on the floor. Leaving it there, Holly moved to the closet and opened it to peer inside. Black filled the small space; black jeans, black leather pants, a black leather jacket and even black T-shirts hung neatly in the closet.

Someone was definitely fashion challenged, one part of her mind thought. The other part, however, was having a bit of a panic attack. These were not her clothes. They weren't even women's clothes. They were a man's clothes, and not a man she knew. Holly couldn't think of a single person she was acquainted with who would wear these items . . . and whose bed she should be naked in. At least, not that she could recall . . . although, for some reason, the sight of the clothes raised fear in her.

Suddenly desperate to get out of there, Holly

quickly turned to tug open the drawers in the dresser along the wall, hoping for other clothing options, but there was nothing but a bit of dust. Not even boxers or briefs. Apparently the mysterious man who liked black also liked to go commando. She tried not to think about that as she moved back to the closet and pulled out a pair of black jeans and a matching T-shirt.

The pants were big on her, but she fixed that by rolling up the bottoms and making use of a belt she found on another hanger. The T-shirt was large as well, blousing out over the puckered waistband and hanging down almost to her knees. Holly caught the hem and tied a knot in it at her side to make it more of a shirt and less a dress. She then pulled on the leather jacket to hide the mess she was wearing.

Holly headed for the door, only to pause when she caught a glimpse of herself in the mirror as she passed the open bathroom door along the way. Dear God, Holly thought with disgust, if she were to wring the grease out of her hair there would be enough to fry something. On top of that, it was a horrible mess, sticking out in the back in a forest of knots. It was the hair of a woman who had been thrashing her head around during crazy, hot, monkey sex.

Not that she'd ever experienced crazy, hot monkey sex . . . that she recalled, Holly tacked on grimly as she glanced toward the bed. But her roommate at college had always looked like this in the mornings after her boyfriend visited. She claimed it could be blamed on her boyfriend for being so good at "doing the nasty."

Holly tried to tame her usually sleek black mane with her fingers. When that didn't work, she quickly searched the bathroom for a brush. There wasn't one, of course. Why would anyone have a hair-brush when she needed it? Rolling her eyes, she gave up on that and instead began to search for something to wrap around her head to at least hide her bad hair. Holly was afraid if she went anywhere like this, she'd be locked up as a madwoman. Certainly, she'd draw attention to herself, and at that moment, she was thinking the less attention the better until she knew exactly what had happened and how she'd got here.

A hat or bandana would have done the trick, but apparently the mysterious man in black didn't have either of those. Blowing her breath out on a sigh, Holly shifted briefly from foot to foot, and then snatched another T-shirt off its hanger and began tearing at it until she had a nice, sleeveless square. After quickly wrapping that around her head and tying it, Holly once again headed for the door.

She needed to figure out where she was, how to get home from here, and then . . . well, once she was safely home she could sort out what had happened and what, if anything, she should do about it.

"Her name is Holly Bosley," Lucian announced.

"Yeah. Anders told me that the first night, when he got back with her purse," Justin said impatiently. He was only in Lucian's room because the man had insisted he had to speak to him. Lucian wasn't someone you refused. But Justin didn't want to be here; he wanted to be back in his own room across the hall with the woman presently in his bed. She'd been sleeping restlessly for two days and nights, something that had worried him. Every other turn he'd witnessed had gone more quickly, with the turnee thrashing and screaming their way through.

Justin had been very concerned at first by how silent and still Holly was . . . until Lucian had told him that Stephano Notte's turn had gone just as quietly and had taken several days. Oddly enough, Stephano's turn had been preceded by his being stabbed in the chest too. Lucian had speculated that it was possible the wound decided the tempo of the turn.

Justin didn't care. All he cared about was Holly surviving and waking up. He had no idea when that might happen, but he wanted to be there when it did.

Hoping to speed this conversation along, Justin now added, "There was a car in the cemetery parking lot with a purse in it. Anders broke the car window to get to her purse, searched it and found her driver's license. Holly Lynne Bosley. There were no car keys though, and she didn't have any keys on her, so Anders had to hotwire the car to get it back here to the hotel."

"He went back to the cemetery last night and found the keys near where she fell," Lucian announced. "I put them in her purse."

Justin glanced to the purse sitting on the table when Lucian gestured to it and found himself shaking his head. He still couldn't believe she hadn't been sleepwalking. He'd been sure that must have been the case when he'd spotted those pajamas of hers. The lack of anything like keys or a purse had just seemed to back that up. But it seemed she'd had both, just not on her. What the hell had she been doing at the cemetery at that hour of the night in pajamas?

"Holly is a temp, presently working in the office at the cemetery," Lucian said as if that might explain it.

To Justin it didn't and he pointed out dryly, "Yeah, well she wouldn't work in her pj's."

Lucian shrugged. "She must have recalled something she left behind and returned to collect it after already preparing for bed."

"That makes sense," Decker commented, drawing their attention his way. The dark-haired man dressed in Enforcer black was reclining on one of the two beds in the room.

"After midnight? In her pajamas?" Justin asked dubiously.

Lucian shrugged. "She probably didn't expect to encounter anyone at that hour."

"She was in the crematorium, the only place there *would* be anyone at that hour," he pointed out.

"So she was," Lucian agreed and then pointed out, "Only she can answer these questions."

"She might have been bringing down paperwork," Anders said, entering the room through the open connecting door.

When Lucian raised one questioning eyebrow it was Justin who explained, "The shuffle of papers and a moan are what drew our attention to her presence. Once I saw she was in pajamas though, I just assumed the papers had been lying on the floor and she'd kicked them or something as she walked."

"Or she could have been bringing them down for the guy working the ovens and dropped them when she saw us," Anders said now.

Lucian considered that and then nodded slowly. "That's possible."

"But she was in her *pajamas*," Bricker repeated, unable to get past that fact. The pajamas had been flannel, for God's sake, and she'd had on fluffy furry slippers too. He'd tossed the offensive items out once he'd got her back to the hotel and stripped her for the turn. No woman of his was wearing pink flannel pajamas and fluffy slippers.

Shaking his head over her apparel, he glanced to Lucian to note that he stood unnaturally still, his head cocked. "What is it?"

"She's awake," he announced with a frown.

Bricker was on his feet at once and headed for the door.

"Wait. Bricker! There's more you need to know," Lucian growled, but this time Justin didn't listen. His life mate was awake. He needed to get to her, and not even Lucian Argeneau was stopping him.

Holly opened the door and rushed out only to come to a startled halt when the door opposite opened and a man was suddenly before her in the hall. He appeared so quickly she almost wondered if she'd blanked out for a moment. No one could move that fast.

"Oh, hello. You're not just awake, you're up." The man's words brought her wide eyes to his face. He sounded surprised, but no more surprised than she was at his words. He acted like they knew each other, but she hadn't a clue who he was . . . Had she encountered him when she'd come to the hotel? If so, maybe he could tell her what condition she'd been in and who had brought her. That thought uppermost in her mind, she murmured, "I—Yes."

Holly then simply stared at him. He was definitely attractive, with dark hair and laughing eyes. He was dressed in black jeans and a black T-shirt. Copies of the clothes she was wearing, she realized as his eyes dropped down over her borrowed ensemble.

"My clothes don't quite fit you, do they?" he asked with amusement.

"*Your* clothes?" she asked with alarm. This was the owner of the room she was presently occupying? And apparently the one across from it too, since he'd just come from there, she reasoned.

"Yeah." He grinned. "Don't worry, though. I'll go out and pick up something more appropriate for you later, after we talk."

"Oh, no, no that's not necessary," Holly squeaked, hustling quickly backward when he began to move toward her. She realized her mistake at once. She had backed farther into the room she'd been trying to exit, allowing him to enter. Now he was between her and the exit. It only got worse when he closed the door. Somehow his presence in the room seemed to make it shrink.

Biting her lip, Holly continued to back up until she bumped into the desk chair. She promptly dropped to sit in it, her gaze skating nervously around the room before returning to him. He'd said he'd get her more appropriate clothes after they talked, but she was less interested in clothes than she was in talking, or at least in getting some answers. Holly had about a million questions floating around in her head right now. Little things like, who was he? How had she got here? Who had removed her clothes? Why had she been naked in the bed? Had she been alone in the bed the entire time she'd been in it? How long had she been in it? Where were her clothes?

They went on from there, but that pretty much

covered the main ones she'd like answers to. She peered at him warily, and asked, "Who are you?"

"Oh." He offered her a crooked smile. "I suppose I should have introduced myself. My name is Justin Bricker."

"Justin Bricker," she echoed in a murmur and didn't recognize the name at all. She was quite sure she'd never heard it before and he didn't look familiar either.

"How are you feeling?" he asked, stopping next to the desk and eyeing her with concern.

"Fine," she said automatically, only then pausing to pay attention to her body and see if that was true. It was mostly true. She felt like a dried-out sponge, but other than that, and a slight headache, she was fine. Was there a reason she shouldn't be? Like maybe some drugs that had been slipped to her and would explain her memory problem? That thought in mind, she asked warily, "How should I feel?"

For some reason the question made his lips quirk with wry amusement. "Well it's different for different people. Some wake up with a raging headache, probably from dehydration. Others just have a terrible case of dry mouth and otherwise feel better than they did before."

"Before what?" Holly asked sharply, suspicion rife within her. She did have a slight headache and definite dry mouth.

"Before the turn," he explained patiently.

"Before the turn?" she echoed with confusion. "Before my turn at what?"

Justin Bricker's eyes narrowed and he was silent for a minute and then asked, "What exactly do you remember?"

"Of what?" Holly countered, a wary sensation

creeping up the back of her neck. There was something about his sudden solemnity that was worrisome.

"What is the last thing you remember?" he asked instead of answering her question.

Holly briefly searched her mind for memories and came up with the same she'd had on first waking. She recalled brushing her teeth before bed, realizing she hadn't tested her blood yet, going out to the car to look for her purse and the tester in it, and then heading back to the office when she didn't find either in her car. She was obviously missing the memories between that and landing in a strange man's hotel room . . . naked in his bed.

"I was headed back to the office to get my purse," she said quietly.

His eyebrows rose and Holly suspected that meant she was missing a lot of memories, and probably important ones. She always missed the important stuff.

"Do you remember getting to the office?" he asked.

She performed a brief sweep of her memory and then shook her head before asking, "Did I get there?"

"Yes, you got to the office," Justin assured her and then pursed his lips and shifted before adding, "We think you had papers with you when you came down to the crematorium. Is it possible you found papers you felt needed to be delivered at that hour?"

Holly considered the question and then asked, "Was there a round metal disk attached to the corner?"

He hesitated and then turned and walked to the door, opened it, crossed the hall and leaned into the opposite room. She heard him ask, "Was there a metal disk on the papers on the floor in the crematorium?"

Holly didn't hear the answer, but he closed the door and came back, nodding. "Yes, there was."

"Then they were papers needed to cremate someone. If I found them and they should have gone down during the day but somehow didn't, then yes, I might have taken them down despite the hour," she said on a sigh.

"You were in your pajamas," he said and she raised an eyebrow at his tone of voice. He sounded bewildered. Or maybe disapproving. Or both. Before she could respond, Justin asked, "Has any of this sparked a memory? Do you remember heading for the crematorium to deliver the papers?"

Holly bit her lip and searched her memory again, but it was pretty spotty and nothing was coming.

"It was after midnight on a foggy night," he prompted. "You probably couldn't see two feet in front of you, but you traipsed down past the graves to the crematorium anyway . . . in pink flannel pajamas with white bunnies on them and fluffy slippers under a trench coat."

He described what she'd worn as if her fashion choice that night had alarmed him, and Holly supposed it had been somewhat unorthodox, but she hadn't expected to run into anyone. Apparently, she had. She didn't recall it though, so she shook her head again, but then cleared her throat and asked, "Where exactly are they? My pajamas?"

Justin hesitated, and then rather than answer, asked, "Do you remember the crematorium? Or leaving? Or falling?"

Holly's head came up slightly at that. She'd fallen?

Thinking it might explain a lot, she asked, "Did I hit my head or something?"

"Yes." Justin seemed relieved and she only understood why when he said, "So you do remember that?"

"No," she admitted almost apologetically. "I just figure that must be why my head hurts and why my memory is missing pieces."

"Ah. Yes, I see," he said on a sigh, and then grimaced and asked, "So none of this is ringing bells for you?"

Holly shook her head again, and admitted, "I don't even remember who you are. Your name doesn't sound familiar, or anything." She shrugged helplessly.

His lips twisted wryly, and he said gently, "There's no reason it should. We've never actually met."

"Oh," she murmured, and supposed that that explained that. So . . . he must have been the one to find her after her fall, Holly reasoned. She'd made it back to the office, found some papers she'd felt she should deliver to the crematorium, and had fallen and hit her head on the return journey. She must have taken quite a knock to lose not only consciousness, but some memory. Holly hadn't noticed a head wound earlier. She hadn't been looking for one, though.

"So you found me after I fell?" she asked, and when he hesitated, guessed, "Or saw me fall?"

"Yes," Justin said on a relieved hiss of air. "I saw you fall."

"And I didn't have my purse or any ID on me," she recalled ruefully and then narrowed her eyes and added, "But my purse *was* in my car and I did have my car keys."

"You didn't have your car keys when I got to you," Justin explained. "You must have dropped them when you fell." He paused briefly, and then added, "When I carried you inside and we realized you were wearing pajamas and had no purse, keys or anything else, we thought you must have been sleepwalking."

"Sleepwalking?" she asked with surprise, and then gave a slight laugh. "With a coat on? Do sleep-walkers usually put on coats?"

"I don't know," he said with a shrug. "I've never known anyone who sleepwalks."

"Oh." Holly nodded slowly and then tried to work it out, speaking her thoughts aloud. "So you brought me here because I didn't have my purse or ID." Before he could respond, she asked, "But why didn't you just take me to the hospital?" When he was silent again, she said thoughtfully, "Without a purse I wouldn't have my HMO card and I suppose a hospital would be reluctant to treat me without proof that I could pay."

Justin seemed to hesitate, and then he sighed and dropped to sit on the end of the bed. Peering at her solemnly, he said, "This situation is a little more complicated than you realize."

Holly tilted her head curiously, but simply asked, "Oh?"

"Yes, you see . . ." Justin paused, several expressions flickering across his face before he finally said cautiously, "I have to tell you some things that might sound . . . well, a bit crazy."

Holly merely raised her eyebrows.

"You see, it wasn't just your head you hit. I mean the head injury wasn't the only one. You were carrying scissors and—"

"Scissors?" she interrupted with surprise. "Why would I be carrying scissors down to the crematorium?"

"As I said, it was dark and foggy . . . a graveyard. Spooky." He shrugged. "Perhaps you were nervous."

Holly nodded slowly, supposing that would be enough to make her want a weapon of some sort. She wasn't usually a nervous Nelly, but then she'd never before even considered walking through a graveyard alone on a dark and foggy night.

"Anyway," Justin said when she remained silent. "You were running and fell and not only hit your head, but—"

"Why was I running?" Holly interrupted.

The question made him grimace. He also took a good deal of time to think before answering. "You saw something that you misunderstood."

"What did I see?"

"I'll get to that," he assured her. "But first I want you to understand that I would never harm you. In fact, when you fell on your scissors and stabbed yourself in the chest, I—"

"What?" Holly interrupted sharply. She hadn't noticed anything when she dressed. Holly tugged the T-shirt collar away from her skin to peer at herself, but there was nothing there. Scowling at him for scaring her like that, she said, "I'm not wounded."

"No. Well, I healed you," he explained.

Holly blinked several times at this claim and then asked slowly, "You *healed* me?"

Justin nodded.

"How?" she asked at once, unable to hide her doubt.

"Well, this is where it gets tricky," Justin said, looking uncomfortable.

"Oh?" she asked, eyes narrowing.

"Yes. You see . . ." He paused, rubbed one hand over his face, and then said determinedly under his breath, "I am not going to make a pickle of this like Bastien and the other guys did."

"That's good," Holly murmured, not sure what he was talking about.

"I mean seriously, how stupid is starting with, "Have you ever seen *An American Werewolf in London*?" he asked with disgust.

"Er . . ." Holly paused, growing confused.

"It was just stupid. I mean, we aren't werewolves, are we?"

"No?" Holly guessed. That seemed a pretty safe bet.

"Exactly," he said with satisfaction. "So why lead with that? It just confuses the matter further. Right?"

"Right?" she guessed.

He nodded. "Okay, so . . ." Justin paused and frowned and then repeated, "Remember, no matter how crazy this sounds, I'm not crazy. You are safe with me. I would never harm you. Ever. I promise you that."

"Okay," Holly murmured. But really, the more he said that, the more worried she got. It was the old, "The lady doth protest too much." But in this case it was a man doing the protesting. The more he assured her that he wouldn't harm her, the more anxious she got that he might.

"Right . . . so, you see . . ." He paused again and then warned, "I'm just going to tell you flat out."

"Okay," Holly said.

"Right." He nodded, and then added, "It's going to sound crazy."

"Okay," Holly repeated, not at all surprised. She

was already beginning to think there was something wrong with the man.

"So here goes," he said, and then blurted, "I'm a vampire."

Holly stared. She'd thought she'd been ready for anything from his weird prefacing, but " . . . Vampire?"

"Yes. But we're not really vampires," he assured her. "I mean, sure we have fangs and used to feed on mortals, and yes we're strong and all that stuff, but we aren't dead or soulless."

"Well that's . . . good?" She ended the comment on a question because, frankly, Holly wasn't sure what the right response was here. The poor man was obviously delusional. Vampire? Yeesh. She'd thought the craze for vampires had died out, but apparently Justin Bricker had been affected by its brief outbreak. The poor deluded soul thought he was one. It was sad, really. He was a good-looking man, personable and seemed smart enough, but he obviously had mental-health issues.

However, she kind of owed him one. He'd picked her up after she'd taken a tumble and knocked herself out. Holly suspected that part of his story was true. It made sense and explained her headache and memory loss.

The rest of his story, however, that she'd fallen on scissors and stabbed herself and that he'd healed her with his . . . well, she wasn't sure what he supposedly healed her with. Vampires bit and sucked blood, they didn't usually go around healing people. That was Jesus. Perhaps he was getting religion mixed up with his delusional fantasy, she speculated. She understood religion often played a role with crazy people.

"Yes, it *is* good," Justin assured her. "Life is much less complicated now that we don't feed off mortals."

"I can imagine," she said, keeping her voice soothing. At least he didn't take his fantasy to that level and go around trying to bite people. If he did, she'd be concerned. This seemed a mostly harmless fantasy though. He didn't bite, so didn't do anyone physical harm, which left sleeping in a coffin and avoiding sunlight and garlic as his M.O. and that was fine with her. Live and let live and all that stuff. Although Holly did wonder if she might not be doing him a disservice by not calling in some help, like maybe the police, and suggesting a seventy-two-hour evaluation in a psych ward.

"In fact, we're nothing like the television and movie versions of vampires," Justin assured her.

"Well, no, I guess not. None of them can heal," Holly murmured, her gaze sliding to the door as she wondered if she dared try to leave. Would he get physical in his effort to stop her leaving? She suspected he would unless she handled him right. She would have to remain calm and talk her way out of this room. She had to get home and . . . well, Holly wasn't sure what she should do after that. She had no idea what time it was. The bedside clock read 7:34 but was that morning or night? How long had she been here? She'd thought it was morning when she'd first woken, but now that she knew she'd been unconscious, she wasn't so sure. And the curtains were closed and thick enough to block out sunlight if there was any.

"We can't heal either as a rule," he explained, drawing her attention again. "I was only able to heal you by turning you."

Holly blinked at this and then tilted her head. "Into a vampire?"

"Yes. Well, we prefer the name *immortal*."

"Uh hmm." She hesitated and then stood. "Well, then I'd best get home and take care of things."

"You can't go. I have to explain everything," he said, straightening and positioning himself in her way.

"Can't you explain later?" Holly suggested, trying not to sound desperate, but wanting to leave. Hoping to use reason he might agree with, she pointed out, "If I'm a vampire now, there are loads of things to take care of. I mean I'll need to buy a coffin and maybe find some nice Igor type I can get to bring me . . ." She let her words trail away and simply waved a hand vaguely. She'd been going to say people to feed on, but recalled at the last moment that his delusion didn't include biting people.

"I think you mean Renfield," he said with a faint smile.

"Do I?" she asked, turning sideways as casually as she could in the hopes of maneuvering past him toward the door.

"Yes. I wasn't around when it first came out, but I read Stoker's work as a teenager. It's been a while but I have a good memory for names. I'm pretty sure it was Renfield who did Dracula's bidding."

Well at least he wasn't imagining he was hundreds of years old. So his delusions weren't completely out there, she assured herself and said with determined cheer, "Right. Sorry. Renfield then."

"You don't need a Renfield," he assured her. "Like I said, we don't bite mortals anymore. It's not allowed."

"Oh? Why is that?" Holly asked, with feigned interest, her gaze sliding sideways to the door and back.

"It was too risky," he explained. "There was too much chance of drawing attention to ourselves that way."

"Hmmm." Holly nodded as if she believed him and sidled toward the door an inch or two under the pretext of shifting her feet. "So how do we feed? Do we buy pig's blood from the slaughterhouse? If so, I guess I need to arrange for that instead. Lots to do. Must get to it."

"No, we get our blood delivered now."

That startled her enough to draw her full attention. "Delivered? Like pizza?"

"Pretty much," Justin admitted on a laugh. "We have our own blood banks and whatnot."

" 'We'?" she queried.

"There are a lot of us. Not like millions or anything," he added quickly. "We try to keep our numbers low. We wouldn't want to outgrow our food source."

" 'Food source'?" she queried carefully. "You mean people?"

"Mortals, yes. We even have laws and rules to ensure we don't turn too many."

"Laws?" she asked with feigned interest, managing another sliding sideways step. "What kind of laws?"

"Well, we're only allowed to have one child every hundred years, and we can turn only one mortal in a lifetime." His expression turned serious and he said, "Most save it to turn their life mate."

Holly frowned over the having-one-child-every-hundred-years bit, which seemed to suggest he believed he would live hundreds of years after all, but then the last bit stuck in her mind and she asked, "Life mate?"

"It's the one mortal or immortal we cannot read or control, and who cannot read or control us."

"You can read and control mortals?" she asked dubiously.

Justin nodded. "We all can. Immortals can control every mortal, except for the crazy or their life mates. It's how we recognize our life mate. That inability to read or control them is why they can be a proper life mate, the one we can live happily with for our very long life."

Holly shifted another step to the side, alarm beginning to creep up her spine as she absorbed what he was saying. Swallowing, she said, "And you used your turn on me."

He nodded solemnly. "You're the one, Holly. You are my life mate."

"Oh wow," she said weakly and thought, *You poor, crazy, deluded sap.* She'd started out thinking he was harmless enough and had helped her when she lay unconscious and helpless. She'd sort of convinced herself, if only subconsciously, that he wasn't a danger to anyone and not to bring the authorities down on him. But he'd built a whole vampire world in his mind, with blood deliveries and supposed other vampires wandering around. More important, he'd developed an unhealthy fixation on her as his "life mate" . . . and all without exchanging a word or even a smile with her. The guy was cuckoo for Cocoa Puffs and this was getting pretty creepy. She was starting to have visions of being locked in a cellar and forced to sleep in a coffin, maybe even raped in that coffin by this man who had decided she was "the one." He needed help. And she needed to get away from him as quickly as she could.

"I know it's a lot to take in," Justin said sympathetically. "But it's really all a good thing. Being a life mate is like . . ." He struggled briefly, obviously looking for something to compare it to and then finished with, "Well, it's like winning the lotto or something."

That made her jerk her head toward him with a start. "The lotto?"

"Yes," he assured her. "It's all good. You'll never age, never get sick, never have to go to a dentist again. You'll always be young and healthy." Grinning, he grasped her arms lightly and said, "Basically you *have* won a lotto of sorts. The Bricker lotto."

"Riiiight," she breathed and was about to knee him in the nuts when the hotel room door suddenly opened. Holly turned with surprise to stare at the man framed there. Tall, ice blond hair and even icier silver-blue eyes, the man was intimidation plus one. Seriously, her eyes went as wide as saucers and her jaw probably dropped at the sight of him. As for him, he barely spared her a glance, but pointed a finger at Justin and then crooked it toward himself saying, "Come here. Now."

"Umm." Justin frowned at the man and then turned to offer Holly a crooked smile. "I'll be right back." Urging her back into the chair she'd first sat in, he added, "Just sit down and relax. We can continue talking when I get back."

He then turned and followed the blond out of the room and closed the door. The moment it clicked shut, Holly was on her feet and following. If they actually went into the room across the hall, she was so out of there.

Three

"What now?" Justin asked with irritation, pulling his door closed and following Lucian into the room across the hall. His footsteps slowed as he noted that Anders and Decker were both now seated in the chairs on either side of a coffee table by the window, and both were grinning.

"Close the door," Lucian said grimly.

Mouth tightening, Justin drew his gaze from his colleagues and closed the door. He then ignored Anders and Decker and focused on Lucian, eyebrows raised in question, silently demanding some explanation for the interruption.

Lucian opened his mouth, presumably to give him that explanation, but before he could say anything, a stifled chuckle slipped from Decker's lips.

Justin scowled at the man. "What's so funny?"

Decker shook his head, but when Justin started to turn his gaze back to Lucian, the man blurted, " 'You've won the Bricker lotto'?"

Justin stiffened, aware and annoyed that the men had obviously read that from his memories.

"Seriously?" Decker asked with disbelief. "All that razzing you gave me, Lucian, and Mortimer about not knowing how to deal with women and you come out with that?"

"I was being charming," he said irritably.

"Oh, yeah, that was charming all right," Decker said on a laugh.

Justin scowled. "Well, she liked it. And my explanations were going great . . . until Lucian interrupted," he added resentfully. "We'd be in the middle of life mate sex by now if he hadn't."

"What?" Decker asked with patent disbelief.

"We would," Justin assured him. "I was about to plant a wet one on Holly's lips to prove to her that we are life mates. Wham! The life mate passion would have hit right away and—"

"And you'd have been writhing on the ground in agony," Lucian interrupted his bragging with the dry words. When Justin glanced sharply to him, he added, "My interruption saved you a physical assault."

"What?" Justin asked with disbelief.

"You heard me," Lucian said and then glanced to Decker. The other man was immediately on his feet and moving to the door. Once he'd cracked it open so that he could watch the hall, Lucian turned his attention back to Justin and continued, "You may have thought just being honest and telling her what was what would work far better than the 'sad, pathetic attempts' the rest of us made to explain matters to our life mates, but—"

"I did and still do. Certainly it's better than beating around the bush and—"

Lucian nodded solemnly. "It worked so well, she thinks you're 'cuckoo for Cocoa puffs' which I presume means crazy." He paused briefly, but when Justin just stared at him in disbelief, he assured him, "That comes directly from her mind. She thinks you need psychological help and was about to 'knee you in the nuts'—also her thought—when I opened the door,"

"You did not read her through the wall," Justin protested.

He shook his head. "I read it from her thoughts when I opened the door. It isn't the reason I intervened. You just got lucky I did."

"Right," Justin sighed wearily. "So why did you intervene?"

"Because there are some things you need to know that you didn't let me tell you before you rushed off the last time," Lucian said quietly and then added with a shrug, "Besides, you can't read or control her. It seemed smart to do a quick read and see how she was taking things."

Justin scowled and then asked reluctantly, "You're sure she . . ."

"Thought you are crazy?" Lucian finished when he hesitated. "Yes. I am sure."

Justin shook his head unhappily. "She seemed to be taking it so well."

"No doubt she thought it was best to humor you," Decker said from the door and Justin glanced to him with alarm.

"Relax. She can't hear us," Decker assured him, easing the door closed and leaning against the wall beside it, his pose relaxed.

Justin scowled. "Are you controlling her?"

"No need," he assured him, and then added, "She's gone."

"What?" Justin squawked and hurried to the door.

"No!" Lucian said, and this time his sharp tone brought Justin to an abrupt halt.

Turning reluctantly, he raised an eyebrow in question.

"There are some things you need to know before you go after her."

Justin waited impatiently.

"You have more obstacles than you think," he said quietly.

"You mean aside from the fact that she thinks I'm crazy?" Justin asked dryly. To his mind, it couldn't get much worse than that.

Lucian nodded. "I know you think you know modern women better than the rest of us."

"I do. I've been dating, wooing, and winning them since I was sixteen, while the rest of you hadn't even spoken to a mortal woman in centuries before meeting your life mate," he pointed out.

"Yes," Lucian agreed. "But you've been dating a certain kind of woman."

"What the hell does that mean?" Justin asked with affront. "I've dated all sorts of different women over the decades; blondes, brunettes, redheads, short, tall, skinny, not skinny . . . I've dated them all."

"Yes," Lucian agreed. "But they all have had one thing in common."

"And what's that?" Justin asked with a frown.

"They were all, every last one," he emphasized before finishing with, "single."

"Well, yeah, of course they were," Justin said with amusement. "I would hardly . . ." He paused abruptly as Lucian's meaning got through to him and then breathed, "Ah shit, no."

"Ah shit, yes," Lucian said. "Holly is married."

Justin suddenly found himself sitting down. He didn't plan it, wasn't sure how it happened, but his legs were no longer beneath him and he was sitting on the floor, his back against the closed door, and having trouble catching his breath.

"Head between your knees and breathe," Decker said sympathetically, pushing on his head even as he said it.

Justin didn't fight him, but let his head fall between his upraised knees, rested his wrists on his legs and took several deep breaths, then glanced up sharply and asked, "Are you sure?"

"It was in her thoughts, Bricker," Lucian said quietly. "Not on the surface, but under thoughts of how to handle you was the worry about what her husband must think with her not being home when he got in from work, that he must be worried and so on."

Justin merely dropped his head and took several more deep breaths. His life mate was married. He couldn't ignore that, couldn't interfere with it. He'd turned her and yet, even if she had been willing or proved willing now, he couldn't claim her. They had laws against that kind of thing. For a people to whom life mates were so important, it was almost sacrilegious to interfere in a marriage. It was also against one of their lesser laws, not a life losing offense, but an offense that could get you dragged in front of the council for sentencing and then punishment of an almost worse kind, one that threatened a man's genitalia.

Feeling hollow, he raised his head and peered at Lucian with confusion. "What do I do?"

"You turned her, you're responsible for her. You have to teach her to be one of us," Lucian said grimly.

"Sure, no problem," Justin said and then snorted.

"She doesn't even believe we exist or that she is one of us. How the hell am I supposed to train her?"

"She'll believe the minute she tries to bite her husband or someone else," Lucian said reasonably. "I suggest you stay close and ensure she doesn't succeed. Once she loses control and then regains it, she'll realize you are not crazy, that we do exist, that she is one of us and then she will allow you to train her."

Justin lowered his head and took several more deep breaths at the thought of having to train her. Being close enough to touch and kiss, but never able to actually do it. Knowing she was his life mate and that a mere caress or kiss would send them both up in flames, but never being able to ignite that fire . . . Dear God, it would be torture.

"Decker," he said abruptly, raising his head.

"Decker isn't doing this for you," Lucian announced, preventing his asking just that. "This is your responsibility. You turned her. She is your life mate."

"Who I can never claim," Justin said bitterly.

Lucian nodded solemnly in acknowledgment. "Perhaps not. Or you might be able to claim her some day and just have to wait to do so."

Justin peered at him in question. "What do you mean?"

"She could divorce, or be widowed," Lucian pointed out and shrugged. "You might have to wait ten, twenty, or forty years, but eventually she may be single."

"So long as she doesn't die before her husband does, or before they can divorce," Justin said grimly.

Lucian arched his eyebrows. "She isn't likely to die, Bricker. You turned her."

"Oh. Right," he muttered and realized he must truly be overset to have forgotten that for even a moment. Shaking his head, he met Lucian's gaze and asked, "What do I say about telling her husband? I mean, once she realizes it's true and she is immortal she'll want to explain it all to her husband. She'll have to explain her not aging and—"

"She cannot," he said simply. "Not until I have met with them both and say it is all right to do so."

"I see marriage to Leigh hasn't taught you a thing about modern women," Justin said with disgust. "She won't agree not to tell him just because you say so. She has no idea who you are."

"Then I suggest you ensure she knows who I am and why she should listen to me," Lucian said silkily. He allowed a moment for that to sink in and then added, "You should be on your way now. She wasn't feeling any hunger when she left, but who knows how long that will last? We don't want her biting anyone before you catch up to her."

"I don't know where—" Justin paused as Anders picked up the purse on the coffee table and walked over to hand it to him.

"Her license with her address is in it, as are her car keys," he reminded him. "And her car is down in the parking lot."

Justin took the purse and stared at it briefly. Married. He couldn't read her, had turned her, and she was married. He hadn't had a clue. There had been nothing to tell him that, no wedding ring, no . . . blinking, he glanced to Anders. "Was there a wedding ring in the purse?"

When the man shook his head, Justin let his breath out on a sigh and turned to the door. As he headed out into the hall, he wondered about that.

Why hadn't she been wearing a wedding ring? The question plagued him all the way down to her car. He forced it away though as he got in and quickly started it. Doing so didn't help much. He couldn't shut off his thoughts and as he drove toward the address on her license, he found his thoughts a confusion of . . . well, confusion.

He knew he was lucky he'd found his life mate while he was so young, even if he couldn't immediately claim her. Many immortals waited centuries, or even millennia, to find their mate and he was just over one century old. He was very fortunate in that way. Her being married, though, was a wrinkle he'd never considered. He still couldn't believe she was. What were the chances? Well, really, he supposed, pretty good for him.

Seriously, if there was anyone who was likely to meet their life mate only to find they were married, it was him. He had that kind of luck—really amazing, and really bad all at the same time. His life was full of such examples. Losing his wallet leading to meeting a really hot girl. A car accident leading to meeting a really hot girl. Being given a shit job, one no one would want on a hunt . . . leading to meeting a really hot girl.

Okay, so a lot of his examples included a hot girl. He couldn't help it. He was young, healthy, and basically horny. He liked girls, hot girls especially. But best of all was today's hot women. When he'd first reached the age of dating back some ninety years ago, wooing his way into a woman's bed had been a lot harder and more work. Good girls back then simply hadn't had sex unless they were married to the man they slept with. Nowadays though, women were much more sexually free. Good girls *did* have sex with men they weren't married to, and it didn't take months or even weeks of wooing to get them there anymore. Justin had taken full advantage of the benefits of this era . . . and he'd enjoyed it.

Now, however, it looked like his catting-around days were over. Maybe . . . or maybe not. He didn't know at this point. He had a life mate who was married, someone he couldn't claim. Technically, he could still cat around if he liked . . . but would he want to? Would other women hold any attraction now that he'd met his mate? Or was he now as good as a eunuch? Christ, Justin thought with horror, this had to be some cosmic joke.

"Here you are, lady. That'll be sixteen bucks even. Hmmph. That's a rarity. It's never an even buck, there's usually some change tacked on there too."

Holly forced a smile for the driver and peered out the window to her home. Much to her relief, James's car was in the driveway. She would have been in a real pickle if he weren't home. She still might be, she acknowledged grimly, and then cleared her throat and glanced to the driver. "I'll just run in and get the money for you."

"What? Oh, hey, no, no, no." The words were accompanied by a clicking sound as he used the automatic button to set the locks. "Your friend can come out and pay for you, but you aren't getting out of here and taking a runner on me."

Holly glanced toward the house and back. Forcing herself to remain calm, she said, "My husband, not my friend. And he isn't likely to come out. He isn't watching for me." She glanced toward the house

again and added, "This is my house. You know the
address. Doing a runner, as you call it, would hardly
do me any good with you knowing the address."

He eyed her thoughtfully in the rearview mirror,
and then said, "So show me some ID with this address on it and I'll unlock the doors."

Holly sighed unhappily. "I haven't got any ID, or
even my purse. That's why I had to take a taxi."

"Uh-huh," he muttered dubiously. "And you have
the house, but were staying at the hotel because . . . ?"

"I wasn't staying at the hotel, I was—" Holly cut
herself off, unsure how to describe what she'd been
doing at the hotel. Of course, the driver took it completely the wrong way.

"Right," he said, looking her over in her borrowed clothes. There was a touch of disgust in his
expression. "So maybe your husband won't want to
be paying for your return journey from your little
tryst."

"It wasn't a tryst," she said wearily. "I—"

"Okay. Go on in and bring me back the money."

Holly blinked at the driver's about-face. He was
smiling at her now, all signs of the disgust of just
moments ago gone. It was as if someone had taken
control of him and . . . She glanced to the door as the
locks were released with a click, and then quickly
opened her door and slid out, eager to escape before
he changed his mind. She was almost to the front
door before Holly recalled that she didn't have her
keys with her. It would mean knocking at her own
door.

She started to raise her hand to do so and then suddenly checked the door instead, both relieved and annoyed when it opened easily under her touch. James
was forever leaving the door unlocked. Pushing down

the irritation that tried to claim her, Holly turned to smile and wave at the taxi driver, then slid inside. She left the door open so he wouldn't get nervous that she was pulling a "runner."

"James?" she called, heading for the kitchen. She kept small bills and change in a jar there for emergencies, and automatically moved that way as she called his name again. Holly didn't wait for a response, but fetched the money she needed and then hurried back outside to pay the driver. He accepted the bills with a smile, wished her a good day and drove happily away.

Holly stared after him briefly, completely bewildered by his sudden change in attitude, but then hurried back inside, nearly running into James as he came off the stairs.

"Holly," he said with a smile, catching her arms to steady her. "I didn't think you'd get in before I left."

Holly blinked at his words, confusion rising within her. "What?"

"I already ate. Spaghetti," he said. "But I made enough for you too. It's in the fridge. Just nuke and enjoy." Leaning forward he kissed her forehead, then set her aside and started up the hall, headed for the kitchen.

Holly stared after him for a minute and then followed. "Wait. James?"

"Hmm?" he asked over his shoulder as he stopped in the kitchen to retrieve his lunch pail.

"I wasn't here this morning when you got home from work," she pointed out.

"Or yesterday morning or night either," he agreed easily and shrugged as he turned to cross to the door to the garage. "I wasn't surprised. You did say the mortuary's taxes were a mess. I figure you'll be

working a lot of overtime and starting early." He
paused with one hand on the door to the garage
and glanced to her with concern. "You won't have
to work on the weekend though, will you? We have
that dinner with Bill and Elaine Saturday night."

"I . . . no," she said with a frown.

"Oh, good." He smiled. "I'll see you in the morning then . . . well, if you haven't left early again,"
he added with a chuckle, and then slid out into the
garage and pulled the door closed.

Holly just stood there staring at the connecting
door to the garage as she listened to the whir of
the outer door rolling up and the engine of James's
pickup starting.

He'd said she hadn't been home that morning or
the one before. That meant she'd been unconscious
in that hotel room with Justin for two nights and
days . . . and her husband hadn't even noticed she'd
been missing other than to assume she was working
late and starting early. She'd been concerned that he
was sitting here worrying about her, and that was
when she'd thought she'd only been unconscious for
one night and day. She could have been dead from
the fall and he wouldn't have known. Had he even
texted her?

If he had, he'd apparently just assumed she was
too busy to answer. James hadn't even noticed that
she was wearing someone else's clothes, or that her
hair was wrapped up in a T-shirt.

The whir of the garage door closing sounded and
she heaved a sigh and leaned against the kitchen
counter, wondering when she and James had grown
so far apart. He worked nights—twelve-hour shifts,
7:30 P.M. to 7:30 A.M.—Monday through Thursday.
He left after dinner and arrived home between 8:00

and 8:30 in the morning, usually coming in just as she was leaving either for classes or for work herself. The weekends were the only time they had together, usually going out with friends Friday nights. He slept all day Saturdays and then played hockey with buddies Saturday night. Sundays they spent with their parents, his or hers on alternating weekends, visiting in the afternoons after he got up and then having Sunday dinner with them. Sunday night was the night they usually had sex.

Holly grimaced as she realized how regimented they were. Sex once a week, family once a week, friends once a week, work and school the rest of the time and precious little time alone together without friends or family around. Why was she surprised that he hadn't noticed she was missing?

She should be glad, Holly supposed. At least she didn't have to deal with the police and endless questions. The sound of a car pulling into the driveway drew her from her thoughts and she moved to peer out the window, eyes widening when she saw her own car parked there. No one was inside.

Pushing away from the counter, she hurried out of the kitchen and to the front door. There was no one in the driveway or on the sidewalk nearby when she rushed outside. Holly noted that as she rushed to the car; then her attention was taken up with the fact that the driver's-side window was missing, with just sharp bits of glass sticking out of the door frame. Groaning at how much it would cost to repair that, she opened the door and peered in, gasping when she saw her purse sitting on the passenger's seat with a folded piece of notepaper on top of it. Reaching in, she grabbed both items and quickly rifled through her purse until she found her wallet. Much to her relief all her credit and debit cards were still there.

Dropping the wallet back in her purse, Holly unfolded the notepaper and read the words scrawled on it.

Holly,

Sorry about the window. Anders didn't have keys and had to break it to get in. I'll call and arrange for the repairs.
  When you need me, I'll be here.

Justin

Holly crumpled the note and peered up, then down, the street. There was no sign of Justin. The note said he'd be here, not if she needed him, but *when* she needed him. And he'd be *here*? Here where? And who was Anders?

Swallowing, she backed up a couple feet, then turned and hurried back into the house. Slamming the door closed, Holly locked it, then stood there for a moment, unsure of what to do. Should she call the police?

And tell them what? That after picking her up when she fell and knocked herself out, and after apparently watching over her for two days and nights until she'd regained consciousness, he'd then had the audacity to return her car and purse?

That last thought made her frown, and Holly moved to the round mirror above a small hall table halfway up the pale yellow hall. She quickly unwound the T-shirt that covered her greasy hair and then leaned in to examine her scalp in search of the head wound that had knocked her out.

There was nothing. Not even a lump let alone a great gaping wound to explain such a long length of unconsciousness. Straightening, she stared at herself for a moment and then turned and walked upstairs. The main overriding emotion she was experiencing was bewilderment and confusion. She was home safe and sound, but had no idea what had happened. How could she have been unconscious for two days and nights and not have any kind of wound to show for it? Had she hit her head at all? And if not, what had happened? Had she been drugged? If so, how? When? For that matter, where?

These questions rolled around and around her mind as she walked into the upstairs bathroom, turned on the shower, stripped and stepped under the stream of steaming water. How and where could she have been drugged? She had been headed back to the office. She hardly would have changed direction and gone elsewhere dressed in her pajamas as she'd been. She would not have gone to a coffee shop or anywhere where she might have had a drink to be drugged. Heck, she wouldn't even have run into the corner store in her pajamas. The only reason she'd felt able to go to the office that way was because she'd known nobody would be there and—Holly froze in the process of shampooing her hair as it finally occurred to her that she had missed two days of work. Her husband may not have noticed that she was missing, but the office certainly would have.

Cursing under her breath, she quickly rinsed the shampoo out of her hair and turned off the water. In the next moment she'd pulled the shower door open, stepped out and snatched up a towel to wrap around herself as she hurried across the hall to the bedroom. There was a telephone on the nearest bedside table and Holly snatched up the receiver to quickly dial the cemetery office. It wasn't until the answering service picked up that she recalled that it was past office hours and it would now be closed.

Sighing, Holly set the phone back in its base without leaving a message and stood to return to the bathroom. She'd have to go into the office in the morning and try to clear everything up, she thought as she brushed her teeth. She was actually surprised that they hadn't called the house to ask why she wasn't showing up for work. Or maybe, like James, they hadn't noticed her absence, she thought, rinsing the foamy toothpaste out of her mouth. That didn't seem likely, but if someone had suggested that James wouldn't notice if she went missing for two days, she would have laughed at the very thought. Of course he would notice. He was her husband. They lived together. How could he not notice?

Very easily, apparently, because it had completely slipped his attention, she thought grimly as she set her toothbrush on the edge of the sink. That's when she spied her engagement and wedding rings. She didn't remember taking them off before showering. She must have taken them off the last time she showered, and forgot to collect them again. She had a habit of doing that. She really needed to get them sized. They were both a bit loose and she worried about losing them down the open tub drain when she showered so took them off before getting in. The problem was she kept forgetting to put them back on afterward, which meant she was ringless almost as often as she wore them.

Ah well, she knew she was married, so supposed it was fine. Holly moved back to the bedroom and dropped to sit on the side of the bed. She just couldn't believe James hadn't even noticed she had been missing. If the situation had been reversed, she certainly would have noticed his absence. Wouldn't she?

Suddenly terribly depressed . . . and exhausted, Holly glanced toward the open bedroom door and the bathroom beyond. She'd left her borrowed clothes on the floor and should really go collect them. She should dress and eat and check her blood too. But all of that seemed like too much effort. She'd just rest first, Holly decided and swung her feet up on the bed as she reclined. A little nap and she'd feel better.

Justin watched until Holly lay down and closed her eyes. He then settled to sit on the roof of the back porch. It was directly outside the bedroom window, resting about three feet below the window ledge. It had given him a perfect view into the room.

Lucian had said he was to watch over her. It would have been easier had Justin been able to read and control her. He could have waited inside then. This way he had to stay outside, on the roof, and hope none of her neighbors noticed. The thought made him glance around at the neighboring houses. Most of the upstairs lights weren't on yet. It was early enough that the inhabitants were relaxing after dinner, settling in front of the television or curled up with a good book. Most wouldn't be heading upstairs until bedtime. That was lucky for him. It was mid-spring. The days were getting longer and the nights starting later which meant that while the sun was setting, the night sky was still light. He would be noticed here if anyone looked.

Justin scanned the houses again, aware that he'd have to keep a sharp eye out until it grew dark, then he would disappear into the shadows. Until then, he probably stuck out like a sore thumb. Movement drew his gaze to the house directly behind Holly's and he spotted a wide-eyed teenage girl staring out at him from an upstairs window. He met her gaze, slipping into her thoughts just as she opened her mouth, probably to call out to her parents. A moment later the teenager turned away and went about her business. She wouldn't recall seeing him. Nor would she look out the window again. He'd seen to that.

Sighing, he scanned the other windows in the house and then glanced over the neighboring houses again. The next hour would be taken up with doing that over and over . . . unless Holly woke up and moved downstairs. If that happened, he'd have to move to a window on the lower floor.

Justin knew he didn't really have to watch this closely. There was no one in the house with her so no risk that she'd bite anyone, but he wanted to watch her. He enjoyed watching her. Besides, who knew when her hunger would kick in? They'd been giving her blood right up until about five minutes before she'd woken up. But she was a new turn. Hunger might claim her at any moment, or might not arrive for hours. The amount of blood a new turn needed was always more than a mature immortal, but it could vary widely depending on the physical well-being of the one turned. Justin had spotted an insulin pen and blood tester in her purse as he'd looked for her keys and knew Holly had been a diabetic before the turn. But he wasn't sure how much damage her body had incurred over the years from the ailment. That would affect her need for blood, though he wasn't sure by how much.

He supposed he'd just have to wait to see.

Four

"Holly? Holly! You slept through your alarm."

Moaning sleepily as someone shook her shoulder, Holly turned onto her back and peered blearily up at the fair-haired man bent over her. "James?"

"Yeah. Get up, girl. You'll be late for work," he warned and turned to walk out of the room.

Holly stared after him with confusion and then glanced at the clock on the bedside table. 8:11. She had slept through the night and—

"Crap!" she muttered and tossed the sheets aside to get up, realizing only then that it was actually the towel she'd fallen asleep in. Catching it up again, she stood and wrapped it around herself, then moved to the closet. She had to dress and—

Holly paused in front of the closet but rather than search for clothes, she merely shifted her feet as she thought. She wasn't even sure she had a job anymore. She'd missed two days and might be fired. She really needed to call and find out and . . . she was starved. Turning, Holly headed out of the room. She would eat first, and then call, and then dress. At least that way she would know what she was dressing for . . . work, or groveling at the temp agency for a new position.

A grimace claimed her lips at the very thought. Holly hate, hate, *hated* working for the temp agency, but appreciated the job at the same time because they were willing to work around her class schedule.

Holly had worked full-time to support them while James had got his applied sciences degree at the local college. He'd worked too, part-time, like she was doing now. The degree had got him a job with a low starting wage, but a lot of promise for the future. Now it was her turn. So, James had his full-time position and she had her part-time gig with the temp agency while finishing her degree. They were presently between spring and summer courses, so she had been working full-time the last week and was supposed to this week . . . but she'd missed two days. The temp agency may already have put someone else in her position.

Holly walked down to the kitchen and peered into the refrigerator, examining the contents. She'd gone shopping the night before her unfortunate trip to the cemetery and had bought loads of fruits and vegetables. Most of them were now gone and what remained didn't look very appealing.

Sighing, she closed the door and glanced to the cupboards. There should be cereal. James didn't eat cereal . . . and she had spotted a milk carton in the refrigerator. Whether there was any actual milk in it was another question. James had the annoying tendency to put empty cartons, or nearly empty cartons, back in the refrigerator. She started toward the cupboard where the cereal should be, but then changed her mind. Cereal just didn't seem appealing to her at the moment either.

Holly turned in a circle and then moved to the phone. She may as well get the call done. If she did have to go to work, she had to get moving and then she could grab something to eat on the way.

Holly knew the temp agency number by heart and quickly dialed it, then waited patiently for Gladys to answer. The woman took her business very seriously and showed up as early as 7:00 A.M. or even before that when things needed doing.

"Good morning, Temps for Hire."

Holly forced a smile into her voice and said, "Good morning, Gladys."

"Holly! Good morning, sweetie. I'm glad you called," Gladys said sounding happy. "I have to tell you, you're really making points for us at Sunnyside. They love you there."

Holly stilled, her eyebrows rising. Finally she asked in cautious tones, "They do?"

"Oh, my, yes. Every time I call they give me nothing but compliments on you and your work."

Holly hesitated, but then asked, "And when did you last talk to them?"

"Yesterday. I called for my weekly checkup," she answered promptly. "And they gave me an even more impressive report on you than last week. Keep up the great work, my girl. You're making the company look good."

Holly closed her eyes briefly and gave her head a small shake. This didn't make any sense at all. It seemed they hadn't tattled that she'd missed two days' work. That or they hadn't noticed, which didn't seem likely . . . unless neither the boss nor his daughter had bothered to show up themselves. But that couldn't be. Someone had to have been there to answer Gladys's call and give that stellar report.

"So, what did you call about, Holly?" Gladys asked when she remained silent.

Grimacing, she bit her lip briefly as she tried to come up with an excuse for calling, and then said, "I just wanted to remind you that I can only work part-time again after this week."

"Oh, yes, your classes start again," Gladys murmured, the sound of shuffling papers coming through the phone. "Well, that's okay. I'll put Nancy on the days you can't work," she assured her, and then asked, "You did schedule your classes so you have two days free each week again, didn't you?"

"Yes. I e-mailed my class hours to Beth on Monday," Holly assured her and glanced toward the ceiling when James called her name from upstairs.

"Oh, good, good," Gladys said. "I'll get them from her and work out how to handle the Sunnyside taxes. In the meantime, I should let you go. You need to leave for work soon, I'd guess."

"Yes. Thank you." Holly said good-bye and hung up, then headed upstairs to see what James wanted.

She found him in the bathroom, staring down at the clothes she'd stripped off earlier to take a shower. The black jeans, T-shirt, leather jacket and makeshift bandana all lay in a crumpled pile on the floor. Holly bit her lip, knowing he would want to know whose clothes they were. In his rush to get to work last night he hadn't seemed to notice the borrowed clothes she was wearing, but he wasn't in a rush now and there was no mistaking them for anything but a man's clothes. He would want to know whose they were and how she'd got them.

"Jeez, Holl, you give me hell all the time for leaving my socks laying around instead of putting them in the hamper, and then you go and just leave *all* of your clothes where you take them off?" he asked with a combination of amusement and irritation. "I saw them there when I came in, but then forgot they were there and tripped on them on the way out of the shower. I could have knocked myself out or something if I'd hit my head on the tub or toilet. As it is I think I wrenched my shoulder catching myself on the counter."

Holly let her breath out on a slow sigh. He hadn't noticed they were a man's clothes. She supposed it was hard to tell from a crumpled heap . . . maybe. Her gaze shifted to his shoulder as he rubbed at it with one hand, his expression pained. James was shirtless, wearing only his pajama bottoms. He had a nice chest, muscular enough to have some definition, but not overly so, and with just the slightest paunch. He was an attractive guy. Always had been. It had always made her wonder if she even would have caught his eye if they hadn't been thrown together by the lives their parents had led.

Holly's parents were archaeologists. She'd spent the first eighteen years of her life being dragged from one dig to another. Most of that time she'd lived in tents and had been homeschooled in camp . . . by James's mother. His father had also been an archaeologist and a lifelong friend to her father. They'd worked together. James's mother, a teacher before she'd married his father, had traveled with them to look after her and James and had schooled them both. Holly had grown up with James. They'd been each other's only friends. He'd been her first kiss, her first date, her first everything and she was the same for him. Marriage had been the natural next step and it was going beautifully. They never argued, never disagreed. In fact, this was the closest thing to a fight they'd ever had.

"I'm sorry," Holly murmured, stepping forward and urging him to turn his back to her. Once he did, she began to massage his shoulder. "How was work?"

"Oh, same old same old," he muttered as she pressed her thumbs into the knotted muscles. "That feels good. A little gentler though please."

Holly eased her grip, her eyes following the line of James's shoulder to the curve of his neck. He had his head turned away and her position behind and a little to the side gave her a perfect view of the muscle that ran down from his jaw to under his clavicle . . . and the external jugular vein that ran over it. She could almost see it throbbing under the skin. Holly found herself staring at it as she worked the muscles of his shoulder and had to fight the urge to touch and kiss him there. This wasn't the day they had sex. James was always exhausted after work and she was always in a rush to get out the door. It was no time to initiate something and she knew it, so just waited for the desire to recede.

But, instead of fading away as she'd expected, the hunger inside her seemed to grow stronger, and she couldn't seem to drag her gaze away from that pulsing vein. Holly had the oddest urge to run her tongue along it. Bizarre, but she blamed it on the smells coming off of him. James smelled . . . well, yummy. He'd just showered, so she expected it was a new cologne he was using or something. Whatever it was, it was heady with a deep rich scent, almost tinny but in a pleasant way.

"God woman, are you trying to dig a hole in my shoulder?" James said on a pained laugh. "Gentler, please."

Holly tore her gaze from his throat and glanced forward, freezing when she spotted herself in the mirror. Horror was rushing up within her when Holly noted movement behind her. In the next moment something snaked around her waist even as a palm slapped over her mouth. She was dragged away from James and out of the room so swiftly, it left her off balance and struggling to keep her feet under her as she was whisked down the stairs and through the house. It seemed like barely a blink later that she was being released in the garage and left to find her own balance as her captor stepped away.

Managing to keep her feet under her, Holly turned sharply on her attacker, not terribly surprised when she saw that it was Justin Bricker. The note he'd left in her car had said he'd be here when she needed him . . . and she needed him . . . or at least someone right now.

"I have fangs," Holly said faintly, hardly able to believe what she'd seen when she'd caught a glimpse of herself in the bathroom mirror upstairs.

Justin merely nodded and eyed her warily.

For some reason that infuriated her. At least, she was suddenly terribly furious, and demanded, "What have you done to me?"

"Saved you," he answered at once.

"For what?" she asked sharply. "Some sort of living death as a vampire?"

"You aren't dead," he assured her solemnly. "I turned you to save your life, not end it."

"Vampires are dead," she snapped.

"But you aren't a vampire. You're an immortal," he said firmly.

"Buddy, you can call it a retort, but it's still just an incinerator to burn bodies in," she said grimly.

He blinked in confusion at that. "What?"

"It's— Never mind," she said wearily. "The point is, you can call it immortal all you want, but if it has fangs and sucks blood it's a vampire."

"But if it has fangs, sucks blood and still has a beating heart and a soul, it's an immortal," he countered.

Holly merely stared at him as the last part of his comment repeated itself through her head. So she still had a beating heart and a soul?

"You should know you do . . . at least the heart. It's thundering up a storm right now. Surely you can feel it?"

Holly glanced to him sharply. "I thought you couldn't read me."

"I can't," he said with surprise.

"Then how did you know I was wondering about that?"

"Because you said it aloud," he explained, his words gentle.

Holly was silent for a moment, concentrating on paying attention to her body. After a moment, she became aware of the frantic thudding coming from her chest, as well as a pulsing in her head. Her heart was pumping, thundering up a storm as he'd said. She was alive. The news was such a relief that Holly nearly fell over. At least her knees went weak and she would have fallen had he not reached out to steady her. Once she was solid again though, he released her as if she were a hot potato. Holly found it oddly insulting.

Clearing his throat, he moved several steps away and then turned to say, "I'll need to train you."

"Train me for what?" she asked, wary now herself.

"For survival," he said grimly. "We have laws, rules, a certain conduct that is expected from us. Breaking the laws can see you punished and then beheaded."

"*Beheaded*? Are you kidding me?" she asked with amazement. When he shook his head, she protested, "But that's positively feudal."

"We're an old race," he said with a shrug and then shifted impatiently and moved toward the door. "You'll need to dress so we can go."

Holly blinked and glanced down at herself, becoming aware for the first time that she was still wrapped only in a towel. She supposed she'd been so shocked to see those fangs protruding from her mouth in the bathroom mirror that she'd forgotten everything else. She found it surprising, though, that she hadn't lost the towel when he'd grabbed her and dragged her down here. She was also rather surprised that James hadn't noticed and chased after them.

"My husband—"

"Is in bed sleeping," Justin assured her. "In his mind, he thanked you for the nice back massage and then crawled into bed."

"How do you know that?" Holly asked.

"Because that's the suggestion I put in his thoughts as I grabbed you when you were going to bite him."

"You controlled James?" she asked, outrage seeping out in her voice.

"He can't know about any of this," Justin said with a shrug.

"But . . . he's my husband. I shouldn't keep something like this from him."

"You'll have to," he said simply.

"But—"

"He'll just think you've had a nervous breakdown and are crazy. That's what you thought when I told you about us, isn't it?" he pointed out.

Holly felt herself flush guiltily. It was exactly what she'd thought. That he was a madman. It seemed he wasn't so mad after all. He had turned her. Did that mean she really had hit her head and fallen on scissors? She peered down, her hand moving slowly across the skin exposed above her towel as she wondered where the scissors had gone in.

"Is the turn why I can't remember anything that happened?" she asked finally.

"I don't know," Justin admitted. "It shouldn't be from the head wound since that's healed." His eyes narrowed thoughtfully, and then he added, "Or at least the visible part of it is healed. Marguerite did once say that the turn can continue long after the turnee is up and walking again. That it takes care of the big things first and then continues on to the smaller, more time-consuming repairs over time afterward." He shrugged as if that wasn't important. "If the nanos are still working on the inner repairs, you could yet regain those memories."

"What are nanos and who is Marguerite?" Holly asked at once.

Justin opened his mouth, closed it again, and then said, "Look I'll explain those two things and anything else you want to know, but not here, not now, and not with you standing there in nothing but a towel. Now let's go in and get you dressed. Then we can go somewhere and talk about anything and everything you want."

"Why can't we do it here?" she asked at once.

"Because your husband can't know about this,

and," he added firmly when she started to speak, "Because I don't have any blood here for you. And unless you want to do your first practice biting session on your husband, I suggest we go somewhere where I *do* have blood for you."

"Why would I practice biting at all?" she asked, alarm creeping into her voice. "Back at the hotel you said we don't feed on mortals anymore."

"I said it was against the law except in emergencies," he corrected. "The time may come when you're miles or hours away from bagged blood and may be in desperate need. Maybe you had an accident, or your supply was destroyed. If anything like that happens, you'll need to know how to feed off the hoof without killing the donor."

"Off the . . ." Holly peered at him with horror as she grasped what she thought he meant. "Seriously? You call it that?"

Justin sighed impatiently. "Off the hoof, takeout, two-footed fast food—call it whatever you want so long as you learn how to do it properly and without causing harm to the mortal you feed on."

"I would never—"

"Never say never," he interrupted solemnly. "Now, can you please get dressed?"

Holly would have liked more questions answered, but now that she was aware of her scantily clad state, she was self-conscious. Getting dressed seemed a good idea. Nodding, she moved past him and slid inside, aware that he was on her heels as she crossed the kitchen. That didn't surprise her, but she was a little surprised when he trailed her upstairs as well. When he then tried to follow her into the bedroom, she stopped dead and turned to hiss, "I can manage on my own from here."

"What if he wakes up?"

"So?" she asked with irritation. "He's my husband, he's seen me dress before." Well, not really, she acknowledged. Mostly she took her clothes with her into the bathroom and dressed there, or used the closet door as a shield. She wasn't comfortable being completely naked, even with her husband. He might notice the cellulite, or a stretch mark, or her muffin top. That was also why she insisted on the lights being out when they had sex.

Much to her relief, Justin backed off and let her enter the room alone. Tiptoeing now, Holly crossed to the closet and pulled out work clothes. She had agreed to talk to Justin mostly because of the promise of blood. She wasn't thrilled at the prospect of having to consume blood, but she didn't want to risk not having it and running around biting people willy-nilly. Sadly, Holly wasn't sure whether she would have bitten James or not, but certainly she'd had some strange thoughts going through her head as she'd eyed the pulsing vein in his neck. Kissing it had been her first thought, but that had been followed by the idea of licking it like it was a lollipop. Holly had never had the urge to lick his throat before or any other pulsing vein on the man. She couldn't say that she might not have licked and then bitten into the vein. All she'd been aware of was that she was terribly hungry and he'd smelled soooo good.

He still did, Holly thought, glancing to the sleeping man in the bed as she stopped at the closet. She could smell him from there, a distance of at least eight feet. That was new. Allergies had plagued her from childhood on and left her sniffling most of the time. She'd always been the last to smell anything, including skunk. Now she could smell her husband from across the room.

"Weird," she muttered, and firmly turned her back on him to consider what she should wear. In the end, it wasn't a hard choice. Holly didn't have an extensive wardrobe. She had a pair of black pants, a pair of navy blue pants, two pairs of jeans, half a dozen T-shirts in various colors and four blouses, one white, two cream, and one red that she had received from her mom for Christmas and hadn't yet had the courage to wear. Holly snatched up the red one now and her black pants, then walked over to the dresser beside the bed.

Laying the clothes on the foot of the bed, she opened the drawer and pulled out some standard white cotton panties. She tugged them on under the towel, noting that they fit a little loosely. Thinking she must have grabbed an older stretched-out pair, she shrugged and next grabbed a bra. It was also standard white, and Holly finally dropped the towel, surprised when she had to grab the panties to keep them from sliding right off with the towel. Jeez, they were really loose.

She'd probably lost some water weight while unconscious the last two days, she decided, but then glanced down at herself. As a rule, Holly avoided actually looking at herself. She didn't like seeing the lumps and bumps and the muffin top. It was depressing as hell and made her feel unattractive.

She didn't see any of those lumps and bumps now though, and her usual muffin top was missing. Her stomach had the slightest roundness to it and she definitely had hips and a waist. She would never make it on the runway where stick figures walked in high heels, but . . .

"Damn, I look good," Holly breathed as she actually braved appraising herself in the dresser mirror. She had the figure of a movie starlet of old, Marilyn Monroe and women of her ilk, who looked like women and not like flat-chested boys as seemed to be the rage now that thin was in.

This was not the loss of some water weight while unconscious for two days. This was a full body remodel. There wasn't a spot of cellulite or even a pimple. Her skin was like porcelain, and her figure perfection.

"Damn," she breathed again, hands rising to slide over her stomach and then down over her hips. This was . . . awesome! Grinning, Holly quickly tugged on the bra she'd retrieved, noting that it still mostly fit, though she had to do it up at the tightest fastenings rather than the loosest now.

Still smiling widely, Holly turned to the bed to collect the blouse and pants and then paused as James chose that moment to murmur in his sleep. He followed that up with turning onto his back, and tossing the sheets and blankets aside so that he lay sprawled on the bed in only a pair of boxers. It wasn't the sight of him in his drawers that made her halt, but the wave of James-smell that rolled over her. Not that he stunk: he *had* taken that shower just before lying down. That wasn't the smell that crashed over her like a wave. It was something else, a cocktail of strange scents she'd never smelled before yet seemed somehow familiar. Her senses were obviously a bit keener than before, and Holly suspected what she was smelling was pheromones, hormones, skin and that coppery something that had smelled so yummy earlier. Tinny and . . .

"Crap," she muttered. It was blood. She could

smell James's blood. How the hell could she scent it through his skin? And why was the aroma so damned delicious all of a sudden? She'd never even noticed the odor of blood before or that it was especially attractive. She certainly had never enjoyed the taste on the rare occasion when she'd stuck a cut finger in her mouth. Now . . . damn, but her mouth was watering at the scent of it and she was fighting the urge to crawl up the length of her husband on the bed. She could actually see herself sinking her teeth into several hot spots on his body along the way—behind his knee, his thigh, his groin, his wrists, inner elbow, his neck. They were all spots she was pretty sure housed major veins or arteries . . . and Holly had no idea how she knew that.

She'd like to think it was knowledge from some long forgotten anatomy class she'd taken, but the truth was that, like heat seeping through a part of the wall where the insulation was thinnest, those spots were where she could sense the smell was strongest and where most of his body heat seemed concentrated. It was where the veins were closest to the surface and easily accessible.

Realizing she was licking her lips, Holly forced her gaze away from James and picked up her blouse to quickly tug it on. It was as she buttoned the blouse that she became aware of a soft thudding sound coming from somewhere in the room. Pausing, she glanced around, trying to find the source, her perplexed gaze finally shifting to the bed. Tilting her head, she stared at it, listening. Yes, it was definitely coming from there.

What the devil was it? She wondered and knelt to peer under the bed, but there was nothing there that would make that slow, steady sound. Still on her knees, she raised her head and peered the length of the mattress and her husband's body on it. The sound seemed to be coming from somewhere by him. Without thinking, Holly found herself crawling onto the bed from the floor, and then moving up over her husband on her hands and knees, ears straining and nose working as the tinny smell cried out to her. The sound was loudest when her head was over his chest and she paused there, listening for a moment before she realized it was his heart. She could hear his heart beating . . . pumping all that lovely blood through his body, she thought. Vaguely aware of a shifting in her jaws, she lowered her head. That lovely slightly tinny smelling, rich red—

Holly squawked when she was suddenly grabbed around the waist and lifted off the bed. James murmured sleepily at the sound, but didn't wake up, she saw, before she was carried from the room. The moment the door closed behind them, she was unceremoniously dumped on the hall floor and cloth fell over her head.

"Dress," Justin Bricker ordered grimly.

Holly pulled the cloth off her head, recognizing the black pants she'd laid on the foot of the bed and never got around to donning. Raising her head, she scowled at Justin. "You could have just said something instead of acting like some barbarian and snatching me up. I wasn't doing anything."

"Your fangs were out. You were about to bite him," Bricker said grimly. "Now dress, or I just might let you bite him. Then you can explain why you did it to his corpse."

Holly scowled at him briefly, but then stuck her legs out on the hall floor and quickly tugged on her dress pants. She had to wiggle her butt on the floor to get them up over her hips. She stood then to do them up, tossing him the occasional scowl as she did and then stared at the pants themselves when she noted how they now hung on her. Like her panties, they were too big, of course. They would have to do, though. Everything she owned was the same size.

"Here."

She glanced up to see Justin holding out her belt. "Where did you—?"

"Your closet," he interrupted and when she opened her mouth to ask when, he said, "We're fast. I nipped in and back while you were gawking at your pants."

Holly just stared at him. She'd only looked down for a matter of seconds. Surely he hadn't "nipped" in and out that quickly?

"Put it on and we can go get you blood. Bagged blood," he added dryly.

"Bagged?" she asked with a grimace. The thought of bagged blood simply didn't hold much appeal, not like the smell of James had just now.

"Yes, bagged," he said dryly and then his lips quirked. "Save a man, bite a bag."

Holly shook her head at what she supposed was intended as a joke and turned her attention to threading the belt through her pant loops as her mind wandered. She hated to admit it, but she might have been going to bite James . . . and she should be very ashamed of that, she knew. Instead, she was disappointed that Justin had stopped her. How bad was that? Apparently, she wasn't handling this whole vampire/immortal thing well. She did need the training. At least she did if he could teach her to control herself. She also, apparently, needed the blood he said he would get for her. She didn't want to bite her husband. Well, part of her did, but the still human part knew it was wrong and didn't.

That thought made Holly sigh unhappily. She was thinking of herself as not quite human anymore. But Justin had said she was alive still and had a soul, so surely, she was still human . . . wasn't she?

"Let's go." Justin turned and started downstairs.

Holly stared after him briefly, and then heaved a resigned breath and followed. In truth, she didn't feel like she had much choice. It seemed obvious she couldn't stay here without risking feeding off her husband, possibly to death. That thought made her wonder how much blood was too much to take. Would she be able to tell when she should stop? And if so, would she be able to stop when she should?

Holly fretted over all of this as she followed Justin downstairs and out the front door. She expected him to have a vehicle of his own, so was surprised when he led the way to her own car.

"We're taking my car?" she asked, pausing in front of the old beater.

"It's how I got here from the hotel. I followed you," he announced and opened the passenger door for her.

Holly walked reluctantly to the open door, then paused and turned to peer at him with sudden understanding. "You made the taxi driver let me go into the house."

"You're welcome," he said for an answer and turned to walk around and get into the driver's side.

"Thank you," Holly mumbled and slid into the car to watch him dig her keys out of a side pocket of . . . her purse? She hadn't noticed him grabbing that on the way out. It must be when he'd done it, but she'd been so distracted with her own thoughts she'd apparently missed it.

Holly shrugged and simply waited for him to get in. She had no problem with his driving. If anything, she'd prefer it at that point. She was a bit shaken up by everything at the moment, a fine tremor running through her body, and was happy to leave the driving to him.

"Seat belt."

Holly glanced over with disbelief when Justin muttered that as he got behind the steering wheel. "Are you serious?"

He peered to her with surprise. "Well, yeah. It's safer."

"Safer how? I'm a vampire," she pointed out. "I can't die."

"You're an immortal, not a vampire. And of course you can die. Everyone can die. Even us," he assured her.

Holly goggled at him. "Do you even hear yourself? *Immortal* by definition means never dying."

"Yes, well, it's something of a misnomer then," he muttered, starting the engine. "You can die. You're just harder to kill . . . and you'll never age. Or get sick, and you'll heal from nearly every wound."

"Then how can we die?" she asked, curiosity getting the better of her.

"Beheading. Or burning. We're very flammable."

"Hot stuff," Holly murmured, unsure where the words came from. It was like a memory, but not . . . just the words echoing in her head. She glanced to Justin, surprised to find him staring at her with an odd expression on his face. "What?"

He hesitated, but then shook his head. "Nothing."

Holly peered at him silently for a moment, and then

leaned her head back. Her stomach was killing her. It had started with a mild gnawing sensation earlier, but now it was like someone had poured acid into her stomach. Or like a million little piranha were eating her alive from the inside out. And the shaky sensation she'd had earlier had turned into full-on tremors. In truth, she felt sick as a dog, but he'd said they didn't get sick, so Holly supposed this was something else . . . hunger maybe. Despite being away from James, she could still smell the tinny sweetness of blood in her nostrils . . . and she wanted it.

Closing her eyes, she inhaled deeply and repeatedly, trying to calm down and rid herself of the sensations attacking her. It didn't help though; the more she inhaled, the more that remembered tinny scent filled her head. It was like James had followed them into the car and was sitting right beside her.

Surely Justin couldn't be giving off that scent? Could he? She wondered suddenly. He had said they were still human, so she supposed they still had blood.

Holly felt something shifting in her mouth as she had that thought, and instinctively ran her tongue around her teeth, stiffening when she pricked her tongue on a needle sharp canine. One of the fangs she'd spotted in the bathroom mirror, she thought at once and then tasted the blood in her own mouth. It was a little bit of heaven. Holly found herself sucking at her own tongue, drawing it farther back from her teeth in an effort to draw more blood from it, but apparently the wound had already closed. There was no blood to be had.

She sat still and silent for a moment, but then couldn't resist deliberately running her tongue across one fang again, this time inflicting a good gash on the sensitive tip. It hurt like the devil, but tasted so good. If anyone had told Holly a month, a week, or even a day ago that she would enjoy and even begin to crave the taste of blood like a drug addict jonesing for heroin, she would have laughed in their face. But right at that moment, as the sweet juice slid over her taste buds and down her throat, it was nectar . . . and she wanted more . . . and if she was still human enough to have blood in her body, then so was Justin.

Justin glanced to Holly as he pulled into the hotel parking lot. He'd noticed her closing her eyes at the start of the drive and she now appeared to be sleeping. He turned his attention back to driving as he found a parking spot and steered into it. Then he turned off the engine, undid his seat belt and turned in his seat to peer at her. He'd stared at Holly a lot as she'd gone through the turn. Through most of that, though, her expression had been a rictus of agony, which was really unattractive. Not that he'd cared. He'd attended more than a couple of turnings over time and had known to expect that. Now however, while her mouth was stern and grim with what he suspected was pain, her expression was still more natural than he'd yet seen it.

Holly had lovely, long dark raven hair and . . . well, an average face, he supposed, but it was beautiful to him. Her face was almost an oval. At the beginning of the turn, it had been rounder. Her body had also been fuller with more curves to it. She'd been what people nowadays would have considered heavy. But he'd always liked larger women; they were soft and warm and . . .

Justin let those thoughts go. While Holly had carried the extra weight he liked on a woman, she no longer did . . . and he still liked her. Hell, she could be a bag of bones and he'd like her. The woman was his life mate . . . and completely untouchable, he reminded himself unhappily.

That thought firmly in mind, Justin leaned forward and gave her shoulder a shake to wake her. He barely touched her arm, though, before she moved. The woman struck like lightning, thrusting up out of her seat and launching at him, driving him back against the driver's door as she crawled into his lap like some nightmare creature. She was going for his throat, fangs bared when the driver's door suddenly opened behind him and they both spilled out onto the pavement. Justin was on the bottom, his head crashing into the black tar surface with enough impact to briefly stun him.

By the time the pain in his head receded enough to allow him to open his eyes, Lucian was standing over him with an unconscious Holly in his arms. There was a quickly fading red mark on her forehead. Scowling, he scrambled to his feet and reached for her at once. "What did you do?"

"Took control of the situation," Lucian said calmly. "Grab her purse and close the car door."

Justin hesitated, but then did as instructed, quickly snatching her purse off the car floor where it had fallen and then locking and closing the door. It was a waste of time though, since the front driver's window was broken.

"You hit her, didn't you?" Justin asked grimly as he

turned back toward Lucian. But Lucian wasn't there anymore. He was already halfway across the parking lot, heading swiftly for the hotel door. Cursing, Justin scrambled to catch up. He wanted to demand Lucian give her to him, but that didn't seem a good idea. Holding her close when he couldn't claim her was likely to be torture for him so instead he asked again, "You hit her, didn't you?"

"She was about to tear out your throat," Lucian said mildly. "I prevented that."

"By knocking her out with a blow to the head," Justin said grimly. "Why the hell didn't you just take control of her mind and stop her that way?"

"She was mad with blood lust and beyond controlling in that moment," Lucian answered and when Justin continued to glare, asked, "Would you rather I had let her tear out your throat and then executed her for doing it?"

Justin scowled, but then said, "I was raised that it isn't right to hit women."

"It isn't," Lucian agreed. "Unless they're new turns who don't know better than to rip out the throat of the first walking blood bag that comes along."

"I am not a walking blood bag," Justin said through clenched teeth as they entered the hotel.

"You were to her," Lucian said with a shrug.

Knowing he couldn't win the argument, Justin let it go and briefly fell silent as they crossed the lobby to the elevators. Other than a quick glance from one or two employees of the hotel, no one paid them any attention, and Justin knew Lucian was quickly taking control of minds and changing what was seen.

Justin let him concentrate on the task and didn't speak again until they entered the elevator, and then it was to ask, "What were you doing in the parking lot anyway?"

"Decker and Anders had just dropped me off when you pulled in."

"And where did they go after dropping you?" Justin asked.

Lucian shifted Holly over his shoulder to free up his hands. He then grabbed his phone out of his pocket, punched a button and lifted the phone to his ear, apparently completely oblivious to the fact that his arm rested under Holly's sweet derriere . . . and that Justin was growling deep in his throat with displeasure at that fact.

"He's here," Lucian barked into the phone and then added, "So is she, so finish your business quickly. Call when you're done and we'll meet at the airport."

"The airport?" Justin echoed.

Lucian stepped through the opening elevator doors and started up the hall.

"Why are we going to the airport?" Justin asked, scrambling after him.

"Because we're done here. We're going home," Lucian said as if that should be obvious."

"But—what about Holly?" Justin asked with concern.

"We're taking her with us."

"And her husband?" he asked with amazement.

"He can't come."

Justin stopped walking briefly and gaped after him. "Did you just make a joke?"

Lucian turned back to peer at him with one eyebrow raised. "When?"

"Never mind," Justin muttered, starting forward again. Of course, Lucian Argeneau hadn't made a joke. The man had absolutely no sense of humor.

"You have five minutes to pack your things," Lucian announced, stopping at the door across from Justin's and digging a keycard out of his pocket. "Then we have to leave."

"But—" Justin broke off. Lucian had already unlocked and entered the opposite room and was kicking the door closed behind him.

Mouth tightening, Justin turned to unlock his own door, muttering, "She's *my* damned life mate, or would be if she wasn't married. And first it was, 'She's your responsibility, you have to train and watch her.' Now it's, 'Go pack, Justin, I've got her in my caveman grip.'"

"Talking to yourself is the first sign of insanity."

Justin whirled around just in time to catch the bag of blood that Lucian tossed at him.

"For the road," Lucian announced and then closed the door again.

Heaving a sigh, Justin popped the bag to his fangs and went into his room. He didn't know what the hell was going on, but if Lucian said pack, it was probably best to do so.

Five

Holly turned sleepily onto her side and burrowed into the blankets with a little sigh. The bed was so warm and comfortable . . . too comfortable, she realized suddenly and pushed against the darkness trying to reclaim her, swimming for consciousness as her mind listed off what was wrong with this bed. The bed she shared with her husband was a cheap one she'd got on sale at eighteen. It had lumps and bumps and sagged in the middle. It was not this comfortable.

Managing to fight her way back to consciousness, she blinked her eyes open and simply stared at the pale blue wall before her, a sense of déjà vu creeping into her mind. Her bedroom was not pale blue. She was waking up in another strange place.

This definitely wasn't a hotel room though, Holly decided, as her gaze slid around what she could see. There was a closet door, an overstuffed royal blue chair, an attractive and antique oak dresser and not a single generic print on the wall. Instead, there was a lovely painting of a woman in white, curled up sleepily on a wicker chair in the sunlight streaming through a window. Not a hotel then.

"No. Not a hotel," someone agreed as if she'd spoken the thought aloud.

Holly turned on her back to peer wide-eyed at the woman seated in a second overstuffed royal blue chair on the side of the room she hadn't yet examined. The woman was petite, with bleached blond hair and twinkling eyes.

"Who are you?"

"Giacinta Notte. But you can call me Gia."

Holly raised her eyebrows. That told her absolutely nothing. This was a repeat of that morning in the hotel all over again, only with a woman there instead of a man. Feeling at a disadvantage on her back, Holly sat up abruptly in the bed. She pushed the sheets and blankets aside as she did, and was relieved to find that while she was waking up again in a strange bed, this time she was at least dressed.

"Were you not dressed the last time you woke up in a strange bed?" Gia asked curiously. "That sounds an interesting story."

"You have no idea," Holly muttered, swinging her feet over the side and grimacing as she noted that while she was still wearing the black dress pants and the red blouse she'd donned that morning, or what she presumed was that morning, they were a complete and utter wrinkled mess.

"I can help with that. Your clothes I mean," Gia announced.

Holly peered at the woman solemnly. Gia's eyes were twinkling as if Holly had just said something amusing. Since she hadn't, the expression was a bit unsettling.

Repressing her amusement, the woman offered an apologetic expression. "My apologies. When I said that sounds an interesting story, you reacted by—"

"By saying you have no idea," Holly interrupted. "I know. I *am* awake, I promise."

"Yes, you did, but you also thought of the last time you woke up in a strange bed," she explained. "That *was* an interesting story, by the way," she assured her with amusement and then mimicked in a deep voice, " 'You *have* won a lotto of sorts. The Bricker lotto.' Yeesh, *idiota*."

Holly's eyes narrowed. "Are you saying you can read my thoughts?"

"Oh yes," Gia assured her. "For instance, right now you're thinking, "Holy shit, Justin was telling the truth about immortals being able to read minds and stuff." She nodded solemnly and assured her, "Yes, he was. You haven't yet gained the ability and are new to our ways, but I assure you it's a skill necessary to our survival. Although," she added with a twinkle in her eyes, "I do understand your thinking me a rude bitch for reading you like this."

Holly slapped a dismayed hand over her own mouth. She never ever cursed. Well, okay, rarely ever. But she would definitely never call someone a bitch. Not out loud. She was constantly editing her thoughts when she spoke to avoid such things. Diplomacy and politeness had been drummed into her from the cradle. She couldn't edit her thoughts, however. They just came as they were and yes she *had* thought Gia was rude to read her mind like that. Although she would deny the bitch part to her grave and hadn't meant for her to hear that. "I'm really sorry, I didn't mean—"

Gia waved off her apology with a laugh. "I've heard worse . . . and so will you once you learn to read minds. Mortals never guard their thoughts. They don't realize anyone can hear them. They look at people and make snap judgments and have throwaway thoughts that could be terribly hurtful if you let them." Expression growing solemn, she warned, "You will hear many unpleasant things from mortals once you start to be able to read minds. When you do, you have to try not to take them personally, at least from the people who do not know you." She paused briefly and then added, "As for the ones who do know you . . ." Gia grimaced and then shrugged. "You will learn what they really think of you." Reaching out, she patted her arm. "Even the people who love us occasionally have unpleasant thoughts about us. It can be very painful . . . which may be good. It makes it easier for many turns to break away from their families."

Holly frowned. She had no intention of breaking away from her family, and she really didn't think they would have hurtful thoughts about her. She had very loving and supportive parents. They were tight-knit; they'd had to be. All they'd had was each other while she was growing up.

"So you have never had an unpleasant thought about anyone you love?" Gia asked, raising her eyebrows. "You've never thought your mother was a bit of a nag, or your father was anal and sometimes seemed to care more about a bunch of bones than he did the living breathing women in his life?"

Holly's eyes widened. "You read my mind," she realized and breathed out a little sigh before admitting, "Yes, I've thought both those things . . . and I guess they would be hurtful to my parents." She grimaced and added, "And I suppose they may have had the occasional unpleasant thought about me too."

Gia smiled faintly and shrugged. "No one's perfect. We all have moments when we're stubborn, or selfish, or act like a spoiled brat. People who truly love us know this, and love us despite it. The ones who ignore those tendencies and pretend we're perfect don't really see us at all, they see what they want us to be . . . and that's not really love. Anyway," she added, standing up and smiling now. "Enough of this serious business. We should see you changed and take you downstairs. Justin and the boys are waiting for you to wake up before deciding what to do about dinner."

"The boys?" Holly asked uncertainly.

"Anders and Decker are here too."

"Right," Holly breathed with a frown. She didn't recognize either name.

"They work with Justin," Gia explained. "Lucian dropped you all off before heading home to Leigh and the bambini."

Holly thought *bambini* might mean "baby." She had no idea who Lucian and Leigh were though. Frankly, she didn't much care either. She was too busy being relieved that Justin was there, and at the same time confused by that relief. He was mostly a stranger too.

"Bambini means babies," Gia explained, turning to head for the door as she continued, "Lucian and Leigh have twins. And of course Justin is here. You are his life mate. He turned you. It is his job to train you to survive as one of us."

"Right . . . as a vampire," Holly muttered. Standing to follow her, she asked. "So, you can read my mind because you're one?"

"Of course. So are the boys," Gia said on a laugh.

"So is this a . . . er . . . like a hive of vampires? You all live together and . . ." She let the question trail off because Gia had paused at the door and turned back, chuckling at the suggestion.

"No. This is not a hive, as you call it. This house belongs to Lucian's nephew, Vincent Argeneau. He and his wife, Jackie, are out of town and I offered to house-sit."

"Oh." Holly tilted her head. "So why are the rest of us here?"

"Ah." Gia wrinkled her nose. "Well, Lucian was going to take you back home to Canada for your training, but—"

"Canada!" Holly squawked with horror. She'd simply assumed she was still in California, but the mention of Canada made her wonder.

"You are still in California," Gia assured her.

"Oh," Holly murmured, wishing the woman would stop this mind-reading business. She let that thought go as she realized that Gia had said "back home to Canada." The words seemed to suggest that Justin and the others were just visiting California, that they hailed from Canada. Weather aside, it was hard to believe vampires came from there. Canadians were known for being so polite, so . . . nice. Heck, James liked to joke that if America ever invaded Canada, Canadians would probably apologize for being in their way. It seemed the unlikeliest place for vampires to come from.

When a burst of laughter slipped from Gia's lips,

Holly realized the woman must still be reading her thoughts, and flushed with embarrassment.

"Well," Gia said with amusement. "Vampires, or immortals as we prefer to be called, aren't exactly from Canada. I mean they didn't originate there, though that is where Lucian and some others now live. But you can find them all over. I am from Italy, for instance, and some live in the States as well. In fact, Justin is originally from here in California," she informed her.

"Is he?" Holly asked with surprise. Vampires from her home state . . . Who knew? It was often referred to as sunny California and for a reason . . . one that didn't seem to her to make it vampire friendly. She shook that thought away and asked, "Why was he going to take me to Canada for my training?"

"Because that is where Justin, Lucian, and the others now live. Actually, that's where I was staying too until I came to house-sit for Vincent and Jackie," she announced. "So, he thought it best to take you there, at least temporarily. But Justin argued against it."

Holly had been about to interrupt until she added that last part, but now blinked in surprise. "Justin did?"

"*Si.* He seemed to think you would be more comfortable getting your training here in California."

He was right, Holly thought. She would have been super stressed to wake up and find herself not only in a strange bed, but a strange country as well, with no passport or way home. At least this way she could get home under her own steam if Justin refused to take her there. She had agreed to talk to him, and to get blood, but she had no intention of spending any longer than she had to here. As soon as she had the thought, Holly tried to forget it. She didn't want Gia to get wind of that and try to stop her. Fortunately, the woman didn't seem to pick up on the thought, because she continued her explanations.

"And when Lucian heard that Dante and Tomasso were considering coming out to house-sit with me . . ." Gia shrugged. "Lucian knew they had helped Vincent train Jackie after her turning, and had done a fine job of it, so he said okay and brought you all here."

" 'All' being myself, Justin, Andrews, and Beckham," Holly said slowly, trying to recall the names.

"Anders and Decker," Gia corrected gently. "They are Rogue Hunters, like Justin, and offered to stay and help out until Dante and Tomasso get here."

"Anders and Decker. Rogue Hunters," Holly nodded, pretending she knew what that was. She hadn't a clue, but didn't care either.

"Mind you," Gia said, amusement back in her expression. "From what I can gather, Anders and Decker only offered to stay and help so they could give Justin a hard time."

"Right," Holly murmured. She didn't understand why or how the men planned to give Justin a hard time, but really had no desire or intention to get to know anyone or what was between them anyway. She hadn't agreed to this training business. And she hadn't thought talking to him would land her in another strange bed. How much time had passed since she'd got in the car with Justin? She wondered. The last time she'd woken up in a strange bed, two days had passed. How long had it been this time? And how had she got from her car to here? The last thing she remembered was riding in her car. No. She recalled him parking it and turning to her . . . Jeez, she'd attacked him like some wild animal, going mindlessly for his throat and the blood she could smell pumping through it, Holly recalled with dismay.

"You didn't hurt him," Gia said. "Lucian came upon you assaulting Justin and knocked you out."

"Oh," Holly said weakly, unsure how she should take that news. She was glad this Lucian had stopped her from hurting Justin, but knocking her out seemed a bit drastic. Couldn't he have just slapped her face or something to bring her back to her senses?

"Slapping you would not have brought you out of blood hunger," Gia said quietly. "You had been too long without feeding. New turns need more blood and more often than mature immortals. You needed to be fed. Knocking you out was the best thing he could do for you at that point."

"Oh," Holly repeated.

"Once he knocked you out, they took you up to the hotel room and Lucian administered sleeping sedatives to keep you quiet for the flight here."

That made her stiffen. They'd drugged her? And— "What do you mean flight? I thought I was still in California."

"You are," Gia assured her. "We're on the outskirts of LA here."

Holly groaned at this news. She was hours from home. "How long have I been out?"

Gia raised her eyebrows at the question, thought briefly and then shrugged. "I'm not sure. What day was it when you last remember being conscious?"

"What *day*?" Holly asked with disbelief.

"Yes."

Holly felt her jaw tighten with anger. She so knew she wasn't going to like the answer to her question when she got it, and her voice reflected that when she said, "It was early Thursday morning."

"Ah." Gia nodded. "Then you have been out about a day and a half. It's just after noon on Friday now."

"Friday?" Holly echoed, putting a hand out to lean against the wall as her legs went suddenly weak. Cripes, she'd missed another whole day. "Why have I been out so long? Surely it didn't take a day and a half to get here, especially if we flew?"

"No. But I gather one of the company planes is in the shop and the others are doing double time trying to keep up, so they had to wait a day at the hotel with you, which was unanticipated and apparently annoyed Lucian mightily when he got the news." She shrugged. "You only arrived this morning."

"And I'm only waking up *now*?" Holly asked, eyes narrowing. "That sedative must have been a strong one."

"Oh, well . . ." Gia nodded with a grimace. "Lucian put you on an IV drip with the sedative in it to keep you under until they got you here, got you settled in and could explain everything to me. And then, what with the problem they're having with flights, Lucian didn't want to make the plane wait here for a couple hours while he did that, so he let it go on another short run and waited for it to return to take him back to Toronto."

"And I had to remain unconscious for all of that?" Holly asked grimly.

"He said you would no doubt be difficult when you woke up. He thought you'd probably be angry, frightened and hysterical and he'd rather not be present," she said with amusement and then shrugged.

"We were to wait until he left to take the IV out . . . which happened half an hour ago."

Holly followed her gesture to peer back toward the bed and the IV stand beside it. There was a half-empty bag of clear liquid and an empty bag with traces of . . . blood?

"We gave you blood too so you wouldn't need to feed when you woke up," Gia explained.

Holly turned her gaze away from the IV. When she'd been in the car with Justin, her senses had been extremely keen. She'd been able to smell the blood as if he'd had an open gushing wound. It had been heady, intoxicating and had made her almost faint with hunger and need. Now, however, she felt no such hunger or need and it was simply blood. A bit off-putting really. To the point where she found it hard to believe she'd acted as she had in that car. But she had and wondered if Justin was upset with her.

"Justin understands," Gia said.

Holly heaved a deep sigh. He might understand, but she still owed him an apology. She'd tried to rip the man's throat out.

"At least it wasn't your husband or some other mortal," Gia said solemnly and opened the door to head out into a long cream-colored hall. "They wouldn't have been able to fight you off and chances are you would have killed them before Lucian could have got to you."

Holly stared after her with dismay and then hurried after her. "Would he have turned into a vampire too if I had?"

"Your husband?" Gia asked.

Holly nodded.

"No," she said. "That is not how you make an immortal."

"How—"

"You'll learn that . . . eventually. But first you'll learn to take care of your needs so that you don't attack anyone else," Gia said firmly, and then added, "I know you don't want to be here. I know you only agreed to talk to Justin and not to training, but you need it. Without training, you're a rabid dog." She stopped walking and turned to face her, expression empty of emotion as she added, "And rather than leave you to kill and maim mortals, we would have to treat you like a rabid dog and put you down if you refuse training."

Holly stared at her wide-eyed, her body going hot and then cold and then hot again. She didn't doubt for a minute that Gia was serious. The woman's expression and cold words convinced her of that. Swallowing, she said, "But my husband—"

"Has been handled," Gia assured her, turning to continue up the hall. "As have your employers and friends."

"How exactly have they been handled?" Holly asked worriedly as she followed again.

"They all think you had to go away on a special project for one of your courses. They believe you are at the top of your class, which you are, and were offered a once-in-a-lifetime temporary internship with one of the top four accounting firms in the world. As far as they know, you're presently at the head office in New York City. You'll be back in two weeks unless they keep you longer."

"One of the top four? With a head office in New York? Do you mean Deloitte?" she asked breathlessly.

"I am not sure if Lucian mentioned the name," Gia said with a frown and then shrugged. "It doesn't matter. It's not true anyway."

"Oh . . . right," Holly muttered, giving her head a shake.

"But I suppose we should find out so that you can keep up with the lie when you return home," Gia added thoughtfully as she paused at a door and opened it.

"Yes, that would probably be good," Holly agreed, trailing her into the new room. Her mind, though, was on the fact that she'd have been over the moon if she'd actually got such an internship. That would have been a dream come true. Instead she was a vampire who, when hungry, might well try to rip out a person's throat. *Lovely,* she thought unhappily.

"You will learn to recognize your hunger and feed to keep those around you safe," Gia assured her, walking across the rose-colored bedroom she'd led her into and to a set of closet doors. As she opened one, she added, "And how to read mortals, how to control them to protect your secret."

"What secret?" Holly asked distractedly, her eyes sliding over the clothes now revealed. Good Lord, how long was the woman going to be house-sitting? She had enough clothes in there for a year. And every single item appeared extremely short, or skimpy, Holly noted with a frown.

"What secret?" Gia echoed with disbelief.

Holly glanced to her distractedly and nodded.

Gia stared back for a moment, then shook her head and turned back to the closet's contents. She was muttering something in what Holly was sure must be Italian as she began shifting hangers along the rail, examining what she had available. Holly didn't understand most of what she said, but did catch a word here or there that sounded familiar. She was pretty sure she knew what *idiota* and *stu-*

pido translated to, for instance, but bit her lip and simply waited. At that point, her head was swimming with all the information she'd gained; all the names, the fact that she was now a vampire, that she could rip out a throat without compunction . . . That wasn't her. But it appeared to be her now. Her life had taken a definite turn, and she didn't know how to turn it back . . . or even if she could.

"I should be up there with her," Justin growled, pacing the kitchen for probably the hundredth time.

"You heard Lucian," Decker said, shaking his head. "No going anywhere near a bedroom with her. No being alone with her. No—"

"I wouldn't be alone with her. Gia would be there," Justin pointed out, pausing.

"*In a bedroom*," Anders tacked on firmly and repeated Decker's words, "No going anywhere *near* a bedroom with her."

Justin growled under his breath with frustration and returned to pacing, which made Decker chuckle with amusement. Spinning to scowl at the man, he snapped. "What's so damned funny?"

"Well, it was just a couple hours ago that you were begging Lucian to let you off the hook and have Dante and Tomasso do all the training so you could return to Canada," Decker pointed out. "Now you're pacing like a caged tiger and impatient to see her."

"She's my life mate," he said grimly, and then his mouth twisted and he paced away, adding, "And I can't claim her. She's married. It's against the law."

"That's tough," Anders said and actually did sound sympathetic. It was the first sign of sympathy he'd shown. Mostly he and Decker seemed to find this a big damn joke. Bricker getting payback for all the guff he'd given them while they were courting their life mates.

"Yeah, tough," he echoed bitterly.

"Not exactly," Decker argued.

Justin glanced to him with irritation. "Trust me, not being able to claim my life mate *is* tough. How would you like it if you couldn't have Dani?"

Decker winced at the suggestion, but argued, "No one says you can't have her. The rule is we aren't to use *undue influence to interfere in a marriage*," he pointed out. "Which means using our abilities like mind reading and mind control. They only instituted that law to prevent immortals from destroying otherwise happy and healthy marriages for a fling."

"Yeah," Justin agreed sharply. "And?"

"Ahhh," Anders murmured, nodding and then glanced to him and said, "You aren't a fling. You want her for your life mate."

"And while you can't use mind control or mind reading to win her, the law doesn't say anything about you not winning her on your own merits."

"On my own merits?" Justin asked uncertainly.

"He means using your dubious natural wit and charm," Anders said with dry amusement.

Justin's eyes widened and then he frowned. "I'm not sure . . ."

"Of what?" Decker asked mockingly. "The law? It can't be that you aren't sure you can woo her. Not Justin Bricker, the Casanova of the immortals. The man who has been telling the rest of us for years that he was such a ladies' man and we didn't have a clue."

"A clue about what?" Gia asked, entering the kitchen.

Justin's head swiveled to the woman. Ignoring her comment, he asked with alarm, "You left Holly alone? What if she wakes up and—?"

"She *is* awake," Gia interrupted. "She's changing. She'll be down in a minute."

"Oh." Justin relaxed with a sigh.

"So?" Gia asked. "Who doesn't have a clue about what?"

"We cavemen-type old fellas don't have a clue about women," Decker explained with amusement. "While Justin is the Casanova of the immortals."

Gia raised her eyebrows and glanced to Justin. After brief consideration, she shook her head. "No. He's nothing like Casanova."

"Did you know him?" Decker asked with interest.

"Of course," she said with a shrug. "Most of his reputation is due to his charm and skill at wooing rather than his abilities as a lover. He was only passable in that area."

"Back to the issue at hand," Justin said, scowling at the pair of them. "I can't read or control her, so I couldn't use those abilities to interfere with her marriage anyway, but life mate sex would probably be considered undue influence."

Gia shrugged. "Then woo her the old-fashioned way . . . no sex."

Justin frowned at the suggestion, not at all sure he could do that. He'd found it hard not to touch and caress her while he'd sat at her bedside, and she'd been unconscious then. Hell, when she'd attacked him in the car . . . Well, frankly, it hadn't been just her he'd been fighting. He'd liked the feel of her body on his enough that Justin had almost *wanted* her to bite him. His body had wanted to do a lot more. He'd had brief, hot visions of her doing the same thing naked, lowering herself onto his erection and riding him as she ripped into his throat with her teeth. Only the reality of their both being fully dressed had prevented his letting her have her way while he had his own . . . well . . . that and the fact that while she'd wanted to sink her teeth into him, Holly probably wouldn't have welcomed his sinking *anything* into her.

So, wooing her the old-fashioned way, without sex . . . not so appealing. Frankly, Justin didn't even know what that would entail. The realization was a lowering one. He'd wined and dined hundreds, maybe even thousands of women over the last hundred years, but every wooing had been with the strict aim of getting them into bed. Now he had to do it with no end game in mind except to win her. He couldn't even bloody kiss her. What was he supposed to do? Bring her flowers? Read her poetry? Throw his coat over puddles for her?

"Wow," Decker said on a laugh. "For the guy who's supposed to know so much about women, you don't seem to have a clue."

"What do you expect?" Gia asked with amusement. "He's a man. You men have never understood us women. Ever."

Justin glanced to her sharply. "You're a woman."

"Thank you for noticing," Gia said on a laugh.

"No, I mean . . . you can tell me what I should do. How can I win her?" he asked almost desperately.

Gia peered at him silently for a moment and then said, "I will think about it."

"About what?" he asked uncertainly. "About ways for me to woo her?"

"About whether you deserve my help," she corrected and then said heavily, "From your memories and thoughts it seems obvious to me that you think of women as little more than sheaths for your sword, and you've had many sheaths," she added dryly. "No doubt you've wined and dined them, charmed them with your wit and smile, and then discarded them with that same charming smile when you wearied of them, caring little how they felt about it all."

Justin opened his mouth, but then closed it again. He couldn't deny it. He hadn't thought about it the way she was describing it, but now realized he'd done just that.

"Oh, be fair, Gia," Decker said quietly. "None of them were his life mate. He would hardly treat Holly that way."

"So, because they were not his life mate, it is all right that he treated them like a commodity?" Gia asked, one eyebrow arched. "That he used them for his own pleasure, got what he could from them, and then tossed them aside like disposable tampons?"

All three men cringed at that analogy and Gia rolled her eyes. "Almost a millennia of experience between the three of you and you still act like mortal preteens when it comes to the mention of feminine hygiene," she said with disgust. "Honestly. It must be a North American thing. My cousins would not react with disgust to such a comment."

"No doubt they've learned better from their time with you," Anders said mildly.

Gia considered that and then nodded with a slow grin. "No doubt."

"Don't worry," Decker said now, slapping Justin on the shoulder. "Anders and I will help you out. We'll advise you on how to woo your Holly."

Justin gaped at the man with dismay, horrified at the very prospect. Decker and Anders giving him advice on women?

"Don't be a smartass," Anders growled. "Even in your head."

"Yeah," Decker agreed with a scowl. "We both have life mates; we've learned from them what women like. We can help."

"Dear God," Justin muttered. He then sank down in a seat and laid his head on the kitchen table with a miserable sigh.

Six

"Foot rubs?" Justin echoed with disbelief.

Decker nodded. "Dani likes it when I rub lotion into her feet while we watch television." He paused and pursed his lips briefly, and then added, "Mind you, that usually leads to rubbing her calves, and then her thighs and . . . On second thought, perhaps you should stay away from foot rubs," he decided.

Justin sagged back in his seat with disappointment and the men fell silent briefly.

"The bath," Anders suddenly said.

Justin raised his head with disbelief. "What?"

"If I know Valerie intends to bathe, I will slip into the bathroom ahead of her to start the water running and set out a clean towel and washcloth for her," he explained. "It takes but a moment, and she thinks I am the most considerate of men and gives me a grateful kiss." He paused, suddenly frowning. "Of course, that kiss usually leads to another, and then another and the next thing you know we are both naked in the bath, and—"

"I think it's probably better you don't run a bath for her either," Decker interrupted.

Anders paused, cleared his throat, and then tugged at the collar of his T-shirt and nodded. "Yes. Stay away from the bath business."

Justin hung his head in misery. The two men had been "helping" him for several minutes now, each coming up with a suggestion of something thoughtful and considerate that they did for their life mate. Unfortunately, each thoughtful endeavor had invariably led to sex and the suggestion that the action should be avoided rather than used. In other words, they weren't helping at all.

"You men," Gia said on a laugh. She shook her head and then said to Decker and Anders, "You are obviously good men and treat your women well, but—" She turned to Justin. "The simplest thing for you to do is to talk to her. Find out what she likes, what her interests are, and go from there."

"Gia?"

They all turned to glance toward the door at that uncertain call from the hall.

"In here, *piccola*," Gia responded.

"I'm not sure this outfit is quite me. I—Oh," Holly interrupted herself as she reached the doorway and noted the occupants of the room. Her gaze slid from Gia to Decker and Anders. She eyed them with a brief curiosity and then her gaze continued on to Justin, and he fancied there was a glimmer of relief in her eyes when they settled on him.

"The outfit is perfect, *piccola*," Gia pronounced, moving toward Holly to take her hand and hold it up. "Turn for me."

Holly flushed, but turned on the spot as instructed.

Once their eyes broke contact, Justin turned his attention to the outfit and now his eyes widened incredulously. Gia had given her another red top to wear, one that hung off one shoulder and reached down to her thighs, barely. It was belted at the waist over black tights.

"That's not a damned outfit, Gia. It's half of one at best. Where's the rest of it?" he asked with dismay. "Where are her pants?"

"Those *are* the pants," Gia said with amusement, brushing a bit of lint off Holly's lower thigh.

"They're panty hose," Justin protested.

"They're tights and are worn as pants in today's fashion," she lectured.

"I think they're cute," Decker complimented, grinning at Holly.

Justin scowled at him and then insisted, "At least give her one of those hankies you call skirts so she can feel half decently dressed."

Gia shrugged and waved Holly toward the door. "If you'd rather she wear a skirt than the tights, I guess I can—"

"With the tights, *with* the tights," he growled and thought, *Dammit, I need a skirt myself to hide the effects that Holly is having on me.*

"Yes, you do," Anders said. His expression was solemn, but Justin was sure there was amusement twinkling in his dark eyes.

Justin scowled at him, and then quickly moved to stand behind the table to hide the erection he'd sprouted as Holly started to follow everyone's amused glances to his groin.

"Skirt or tights, but not both," Gia said firmly. "Which will it be?"

Justin scowled at her, and then dropped to sit in the chair Decker caught with one ankle and shifted toward him.

"Just . . . Fine, whatever," he muttered in defeat and lowered his head to try to concentrate on making his erection go away. Damn. It was going to make things difficult if this problem kept popping up.

Decker suddenly laughed. "Good one."

Justin peered at him blankly, not understanding, and it was Anders who said, "Popping up? Either a perfect, or unfortunate, turn of phrase, I think."

Justin closed his eyes and shook his head, wondering when he had become the grown-up. Usually he was the one cracking jokes and—

"Gia says I have to stay here for training."

Justin raised his head to find that Holly had crossed the room to stand beside him. He hesitated and then nodded solemnly. "It's for the best."

She pursed her lips, obviously displeased. "How long will it take?"

He shrugged helplessly. "It's different for different people."

"Right," she said grimly and he could see that she was gritting her teeth. "Gia said something about two weeks."

"Well, yes, your family and acquaintances have been given a cover story to allow for two weeks. But we can extend it if necessary," he assured her.

"Extend it?" Holly squawked and then snapped her mouth closed. She seemed to be building up a good head of steam with her thoughts and he was just wishing he could read them and know what to expect, when she suddenly relaxed and dropped to sit in the chair next to him with a little sigh. Shaking her head, she muttered, "We were supposed to go out with Elaine and Bill tomorrow night. I guess I'm not going to make it."

"No," Justin agreed.

"And I'll be out two weeks' pay and two weeks of classes," she added unhappily and shifted in her chair.

"Yes," Justin agreed, guilt plucking at him.

"But at least you're alive to miss it," Gia pointed out. "If Justin hadn't turned you, you wouldn't be."

"Right," Holly muttered and offered him an apologetic, "Sorry. I do appreciate that, I guess." She didn't sound overly certain on that point and seeming to realize it herself, smiled at him crookedly and said, "I'm sorry, but I'm a little unclear on exactly what happened to make you turn me. I mean, I know you explained this to me in the hotel. At least I think you did, but I'm afraid I—"

"Thought I was a lunatic so wasn't paying attention?" Justin suggested wryly.

"Basically," she acknowledged apologetically, blew out a breath and then said, "If I recall, I think you said I was running with scissors and fell?"

Justin nodded.

"Why was I running?" she asked. "You said I misunderstood something. What was it?"

Justin grimaced and glanced from Anders and Decker to Gia, but there was no help there. Sighing, he said, "Anders and I were in the crematorium. It scared you."

"Why?" she asked with a frown. "Your just being there wouldn't scare me. So, you must have been doing something that scared me," she reasoned, and then tilted her head. "What was it?"

Justin shifted uncomfortably. It was pretty early

on for him to have to explain this. She would be horrified, he was sure. "I'm an Enforcer."

"What is that?" she asked at once.

"It's basically an immortal police officer. We go after rogues, which are immortals who break our laws," he explained.

"Rogue Hunter," she murmured and he thought Gia must have mentioned the term to her.

"Yes, we're sometimes called Rogue Hunters because that is the most important part of our job, hunting down rogues, or immortals who have broken our laws."

"Okay," she said slowly. "And what were you doing at the crematorium? Is John Byron an immortal? Were you after him?"

"No. John Byron is mortal," he assured her. "Actually, we had already caught our rogues."

"More than one?" she asked curiously.

Justin nodded. "This time it was a group. Sometimes it's just one rogue. Other times . . ." He shrugged. "We've had to go into nests of twenty and thirty rogues on occasion. This time there were only a dozen or so in the nest, but they were bad ones. Their leader was old and quite mad, but his turns were all mortals of a criminal nature. He apparently made a practice of turning sadistic, conscienceless men who were angry, nasty fellows happy to torment and rip out the throats of mortals . . . and for pleasure, not to feed on."

Holly frowned at his description and shook her head. "I haven't heard anything on the news about people getting their throats ripped out in town."

"They lived in the foothills," Justin explained. "A small town about an hour away from your own and there were no bodies found, no murders reported, just a couple of locals going missing. The majority of their kills were tourists driving through with no way to be sure where they had actually gone missing from." He paused briefly and then continued, "We went into the nest, tried to take them peaceably to present them to the council for judgment, but they weren't interested. They fought, we won, and we were disposing of their bodies when you came upon us in the crematorium."

"Disposing of their bodies?" she asked with dismay.

"They were immortals. We can't allow our dead to land in the hands of mortals. If they autopsied them . . ." He shrugged. "All our dead are cremated quickly to prevent that risk."

"Cremated," Holly murmured as a memory of a head lying in a pool of blood on the floor came to mind. In that memory, she saw Justin, she also saw—her gaze slid to Anders, and she recalled his picking up the head by the hair and tossing it into the retort like a bowling ball. She clearly recalled it wobbling its way into the flames.

"She's remembering," Anders warned in a low tone.

"I think I'm going to be sick." Holly heard the words, but was so disassociated at that moment that it took a count of ten before she realized that they'd come from her.

"Okay," Gia was suddenly there beside her, lifting her to her feet with a hand under her arm. It didn't seem like more than a heartbeat later that she found herself in a bathroom, on her knees in front of a porcelain bowl. How the hell had they got there so quickly?

"We're fast," Gia answered the unspoken question as she brushed the hair back from her face. "Take deep breaths. It will help."

Holly took deep breaths.

"You remember everything now," Gia murmured.

Holly nodded and took another deep breath. Yep, she remembered it all. The stacked-up bodies, the head, the headless body they threw in after it. That one made her stomach roll over again and she leaned her head on the cold porcelain, trying to breathe slowly. But she was wondering why they had all been beheaded.

"It's one of the few ways to kill our kind—decapitation or fire," Gia said quietly, rubbing her back. "Lucian, Anders, Decker and Bricker were up against three times their number. They couldn't afford to merely maim or wound. The rogues would have simply healed quickly and continued to battle. Besides, they weren't sure there weren't others there in hiding. Quick, efficient death blows were necessary."

"Right," Holly breathed, her mind already moving on to her reaction to the sight of those bodies. Her terror, running . . .

"I stabbed Justin in the throat," she realized with dismay. Jeez, and she'd thought just trying to rip his throat out had been bad.

"Slashed, I'd say from the memory I read," Gia said conversationally. "And he healed."

"Right," Holly breathed. Because he was a vampire.

"Immortal," Gia corrected gently.

"Right," Holly repeated, not really caring what they wanted to call it. But then her brows drew together on her forehead and she said, "I remember him leaning over me in the dark. The ground was cold beneath me. The night sky a hazy starless mist behind him."

"And you had those scissors buried in your chest," Gia nodded, apparently still picking up her thoughts.

"I was dying. I knew it," she whispered. "And I was so scared."

"But instead, he turned you," Gia said soothingly.

"Yes." Holly breathed, recalling how fangs had suddenly appeared in his mouth and he'd used them to tear into his own wrist. He'd then pressed the gushing wound to her open, gasping mouth. She'd tried not to swallow, tried to turn her head away, but she was too weak and then he'd plugged her nose, like she was a child he was trying to get medicine down, and she'd had no choice. She'd swallowed in an effort to clear her throat and breathe, and then she'd swallowed again, and then . . . the memory ended.

"You probably passed out, *piccola*," Gia said sympathetically. "And that is good. You do not need memories of the turn. It is supposed to be terribly painful."

"Is it?" she asked, glancing to her with surprise.

"I was born immortal so cannot say for sure, but yes, I understand it is very bad."

"I guess I'm glad I wasn't awake for it then," Holly muttered. She had never been a fan of pain. Toothaches, earaches and headaches could all reduce her to a sniveling mass. She wasn't much better at being sick either; pathetic really, and whiny.

"Then it is good you will suffer none of those things again," Gia said with amusement.

"Yeah," Holly agreed and realized it was true.

Well, if what they were telling her was true, it was. She'd never be down and miserable with illness again. It was a pleasant prospect.

Gia smiled and pointed out, "Your nausea has passed."

Holly lowered her head briefly to concentrate on the sensations in her body and realized she was right. The nausea had passed.

"Can you stand?"

"I think so," she murmured and did with Gia's help. Once upright, she took several deep breaths and then grimaced and said, "Sorry. I don't usually have such a weak stomach, but those memories were just . . ."

"Gruesome?" Gia suggested.

Holly wrinkled her nose and nodded and so did Gia.

"I have seen a lot in my eight hundred years, but I would have to agree, they were among the worst."

"Eight hundred?" Holly asked with amazement.

Gia nodded and grinned. "I don't look a day over seven hundred, hmmm?"

Holly snorted. "More like seventeen . . . years not hundred."

"You are good for my ego," Gia said with a chuckle. "I think we should be friends."

Holly smiled faintly at the comment. She was pretty sure she'd like that. She didn't really have girlfriends. The only friends she had were Bill and Elaine, and they were "couple friends." Bill worked with James and they went out as couples, doing couple things; dinner and a movie, dinner and a play, dinner and a concert and so on. Bill and James had become good friends, but she and Elaine hadn't really bonded. Holly blamed that on herself.

Her less than normal childhood had hampered her somewhat socially and she was often awkward or silent in such situations. It made it difficult to gain friends. It would be nice to have one, especially one who understood her new and special needs. Cripes, she was a vampire. The words echoed in her head, sounding as inconceivable now as they had the first time she'd acknowledged it. She was a vampire. Nosferatu. Satan spawn. A bloodsucker.

"Please, Holly. You have to start thinking of us as immortals. I do not think I can take much more of this vampire and Nosferatu nonsense," Gia said, her voice pained as she urged her out of the bathroom and back along the hall toward the kitchens. "We are not cursed and soulless. You are alive. Deal with it."

"Sorry," she muttered. "It's just . . . I mean we suck blood."

"We need extra blood to survive," Gia agreed. "So does a hemophiliac. Would you call them Nosferatu?"

"That's different," Holly protested.

"Is it?" Gia asked quietly.

"Yes, we have fangs . . . and they have a disease," Holly pointed out. "While you—I mean we," she corrected herself quickly and then frowned. "What exactly *does* make us vampires? Is it a disease for us too? It must be, Justin passed it to me in his blood." She stopped walking as she recalled, "He said something about nanos at my house. How do they tie into it?"

"I think I'll leave that up to Justin to explain to you," Gia said as she urged her to continue on into the kitchen.

Justin was on his feet, watching for their return, Holly noted, and wondered if he'd just been standing there the whole time they'd been gone. Not that it had been that long, just a few minutes, still . . .

"How are you feeling?" he asked with concern, doing a strange sort of shuffle. He started to move forward as if to approach her, his hands rising, but then caught himself back and dropped his hands to his sides again as if he didn't dare get too close.

"Don't worry, I don't have puke breath. I didn't get sick in the end," she assured him, thinking that must be the reason he avoided getting too near.

"Good," he muttered and then glanced around briefly before returning his gaze to hers and asking, "Are you hungry? I mean for food," he added quickly. "I'm hungry."

"So am I," Decker said.

"And me," Anders added.

"You boys have eaten three times already today," Gia said with a shake of the head. "I swear, you three are as bad as my uncle and cousins. They are always hungry too."

"Wait until you meet your life mate, Gia. You'll understand then," Anders said with a shrug.

When that brought a snort from the woman, Decker assured her, "You will. Besides, it's breakfast time."

"You mean dinnertime," Holly said quietly.

Gia laughed and moved toward the refrigerator. "No, he means breakfast, *piccola*. We sleep during the day as a rule. If Lucian hadn't arrived this morning and kept the three of us up all day until he left, we'd all be sleeping, or just waking up."

"So you can't go out in sunlight?" Holly asked.

"We can," Gia assured her, frowning at the contents of the refrigerator. "But it means we need more blood so we avoid it." Closing the refrigerator door, she turned to say apologetically. "There is noth-ing left to eat. Vincent knows I do not eat, so did not leave much and what he did leave is now gone thanks to you three."

"We can go out for something to eat," Justin said quietly.

"That is best, and you perhaps should stop and get groceries on your way back," Gia said, turning to head for the door. "Have fun, *piccola*. I'm to bed for a nap. Wake me when you get back if you want to talk."

"Why does she keep calling me *piccola*?" Holly asked the moment the other woman was out of ear-shot. "What does it mean?"

" 'Little one,' " Justin answered.

"It can mean that," Decker agreed, "But it also means 'young one.' It's a term of affection. Gia must like you."

"She hardly knows me," Holly said dryly.

"She can read your mind," Anders pointed out quietly. "She probably knows you better than people who have been in your life for years. We all do."

"Except me," Justin said with a scowl. "I can't read her."

"Except Bricker," Anders allowed.

"Oh," Holly murmured and immediately began to worry about what might be in her thoughts. Just how well could they all read her? Did she have to con-sciously think of something for them to read it? Or could they pluck out thoughts and memories from her mind like a harpist picked strings, all of them visible and available and there for the plucking?

"Between being a new turn and—" Decker's gaze slid to Justin. "Other things, you will be very readable to most immortals. Younger immortals will only be able to read your surface thoughts. Anyone over three or four hundred years old, though, should be able to read some of the thoughts not on the surface unless you use tricks to block them."

"There are tricks to stop you from reading me?" Holly asked with interest and when all three men nodded, she asked, "What are they?"

"That is part of your training," Decker said.

"You have other more important things to learn first, though," Anders added firmly.

"Right," Holly muttered with resentment. To her, preventing their reading her was the most important thing. Of course, they wouldn't think so. No doubt being able to read her came in handy. For instance, she could hardly plan an escape with them able to read her every thought.

"True," Decker said with amusement, obviously having read the thought she'd had. Standing, he crossed toward her adding, "Come on. I need food before I faint . . . and Justin can explain about nanos on the way to the restaurant," he added coaxingly.

Holly wasn't hungry, but supposed if she wanted answers she'd best go with them, so didn't protest when Decker took her arm and turned her toward the door. At least they weren't going to keep her locked up in the house like a prisoner.

"You are not a prisoner," Decker assured her.

"Unless you try to escape," Anders added, stepping up to her other side.

"She won't try to escape," Justin said, sounding annoyed and Holly glanced over her shoulder to see that his expression matched his tone of voice as he followed them.

"You can't read her, Bricker," Anders said solemnly, which made Justin turn a worried gaze her way, his eyebrows raised in question.

Holly just turned her head forward. What did he expect? She didn't know any of them. She'd been knocked out and transported to some house outside Los Angeles and was being kept there for training with four strangers. Of course she had thoughts of escaping. That was just common sense, she assured herself. So why had his expression made her feel guilty?

Seven

"So . . . nanos?" Holly prompted. They were in an expensive black sedan with tinted windows, one that belonged to her absent hosts, Vincent and Jackie, would be her guess. Anders was driving, with Decker in the front passenger seat and Justin in the back next to her. But she couldn't help noticing he was scrunched up against his window, as far away as he could get. Holly tried not to be insulted by that. Was he afraid she'd try to bite him again? Shrugging the question away, she said, "Justin? Nanos?"

For one moment Justin continued to peer out the window and she thought perhaps he hadn't heard her, but then he turned and said, "That's what I gave you with my blood. Nanos. Right now there are millions of bio-engineered nanos racing through your blood stream, traveling to any parts of your body that need repair, or where viruses or germs have gathered."

"Millions?" Holly asked with disbelief. "Surely you didn't give me millions when you—"

"No," he assured her. "But they multiply quickly when necessary, using our blood to clone themselves. That would have been the first thing they started doing after I gave them to you. Well, one of the first things. Some would have been busily doing that while others were sent to stop the bleeding and begin repairs on your chest wound. They act like white blood cells and surround and remove germs, parasites, fungus, poisons, and whatnot from our systems, but they also repair anything that needs repairing in us: organs, cells, skin—"

"Is that why Gia looks so young when she's eight hundred years old?" Holly asked.

"Yes. The nanos are programmed to keep us at our peak condition, so we never age past a certain stage."

"You all look about my age," Holly murmured, glancing to the two men in the front seat. "How old are you three?"

When Justin hesitated, Decker announced, "Anders is over six hundred and I'm over two hundred and sixty."

Holly's eyebrows rose, though she wasn't sure why. Gia was much older. She turned to Justin curiously. "And you?"

"Over a hundred," he said evasively.

"Okaaay," she said slowly. She was riding in a car with three octogenarians, she thought and then frowned. No, that was someone in their eighties, wasn't it? Not over a hundred. So was she riding with centurions?

"We're centenarians," Anders corrected. "A centurion was a commander of a century, a hundred soldiers."

"Oh," Holly murmured and thought, *you really do learn something new every day. Well, some days anyway.* Shaking her head, she glanced to Justin. "So these nanos keep you young and healthy. Why the need for blood?"

"They use blood to do their work as well as to clone and propel themselves," Justin explained. "It takes a lot of blood, more than we can produce ourselves."

She considered that. "So, if you stopped taking in the extra blood, would the nanos just die off and leave you mortal again?"

"No," he assured her solemnly. "They would devour the blood in your veins and then go after the blood in your organs, causing excruciating pain and eventually madness, so that you became a ravening beast who would attack and destroy anything to get blood."

"Riiiight," Holly said weakly. "So taking blood regularly is good."

"Definitely," he said dryly. "I'm sorry. There is no cure, no way to rid yourself of the nanos. Not yet anyway."

Holly sighed. "Well, I guess it's better than dead."

"Yes," he agreed.

Holly nodded, "So, you gave it to me through blood. Can it be passed via other bodily liquids? Say kissing or sex?"

He shook his head. "Blood only."

"So a blood transfusion or . . ." She didn't bother finishing because he was already shaking his head.

"Too many nanos are needed to start a turn. A blood transfusion wouldn't work."

"Why?" she asked with surprise. "If they're in the blood, then—"

"Think of it like fish in a dammed-up river. You stick a net in to try to catch one and the fish will all scram. Knock a small hole in the dam and maybe one or two fish who happen to be close by come out with the water, but the rest will instinctively swim away as quickly as possible from that small hole, maybe out of that tributary altogether and to another part of the system. But if you open the floodgates, or blow up a section of the dam, loads of them come flowing out before they can get away from it."

"So you're saying the nanos would flee from the needle like fish would flee a net or a hole in a dam?" Holly asked slowly. When he nodded, she said, "And opening the floodgates is like biting into your wrist?"

He nodded again.

"What about slicing your wrist open?"

"That would work, but only if the wound is deep and severs the vein entirely. Otherwise the nanos would repair and stop the bleeding too quickly."

"We're here."

Holly glanced forward at that announcement and noted that they were at a California Pizza Kitchen. That was when her stomach gave a loud rumble. It seemed she was hungry after all, Holly acknowledged with a grimace and reached for the door handle.

She was halfway across the parking lot, Decker and Anders on either side of her, and Justin behind when she suddenly came to an abrupt halt. "Wait a minute!"

All three men stopped, concern on their faces. At least they all three looked concerned for all of a heartbeat and then Decker and Anders relaxed. She guessed they'd read her thoughts. Of course,

Justin couldn't and it was him she turned to, to say, "Gia said she was eight hundred, and you guys are over one hundred, two hundred and six hundred. Right?"

"Yeah," Justin nodded with confusion, unsure where this was leading.

"Well, there is no way this kind of technology was around eight hundred or even one hundred years ago. Just no way," Holly said with certainty.

Justin relaxed and smiled faintly as he agreed, "No, it definitely wasn't around eight hundred or even one hundred years ago."

"Then . . . oh, hell," she breathed suddenly, taking a step back from them before accusing, "You're aliens, aren't you?"

Justin blinked. "What?"

"That's the only explanation," she said with certainty. "You're aliens from another planet."

"No, we're not from another planet," Justin assured her, and then glanced nervously around at the passing people coming and going from the restaurant. Holly hadn't been whispering. If anything, she was speaking in a louder than normal voice.

"Yes, you are," she exclaimed, sure she was right.

Justin winced. "Holly, honey, you maybe want to keep your voice down. We're in public and—"

"You're from a more advanced planet," she accused. "And you crash-landed here or came here to study us and— Cripes, we're like cows to you!"

"Honey," he began, and then glanced to Decker and Anders. "A little help here guys?"

"Nah," Decker said with amusement. "This is too interesting."

Anders nodded. "I want to hear more of her theories."

"I want to see how he explains away her theories," Decker countered.

"You're going to farm us," Holly accused. "You're going to get the extra blood you need for your people by using us as cows and milking us by the millions. You'll lock us up on farms and bleed us daily."

Justin cringed. Her voice was getting louder with every word and they were definitely garnering attention. "Holly, honey. You need to calm down. We aren't aliens. Our ancestors come from Atlantis, not space."

"Atlantis?" She stared at him as if he was crazy.

"Yes. Surely you've heard of it?" He barely waited for her to nod before rushing on, "Well, it did exist, and as the myths claim, it was much more evolved scientifically than the rest of the planet and that is where the nanos were developed. They were created as a medical aid, to help cure the sick or seriously injured. And when Atlantis fell, the only survivors were those who had been treated with nanos."

He paused briefly to see how she was taking this. Noting the frown on her face and uncertainty, he added, "We aren't going to hurt you, Holly. I made you one of us, remember, honey? I saved your life. I'm the good guy."

She frowned harder at those words, which was at least better than the screeching she'd been doing a minute ago, he thought, and then Holly asked, "Why *did* you save my life?"

"What?" Justin asked, caught by surprise.

"In the hotel you said something about turning me because I was your life mate or something. What is that?"

Justin hesitated, his gaze sliding to Decker and Anders. There was no help there, of course, the two men were watching the entire exchange with amused interest and offering little assistance. Scowling at them for it, he turned back to Holly. "Do you think we could take this conversation inside? I really would rather not hold it in a parking lot."

Holly looked like she was about to say no, but then nodded abruptly and turned to stride inside. Decker and Anders immediately chased after her, trying to maintain their positions at her side, but Justin watched her go with a frown. He had absolutely no idea how he was going to explain the life mate business to her. He didn't even know if he could. Would it be interfering to tell her that she was his? He didn't know. The council might consider that undue influence, or tantamount to bribery. After all, he could promise her the best sex of her life: mind-blowing, lose-your-head—not to mention consciousness— sex. Who wouldn't jump at that?

Maybe he should just call Lucian and ask if he could explain it or not, Justin thought, and reached a hand into his jacket pocket for his cell phone.

"Hey!"

He glanced around to see that Holly was standing in the open door of the restaurant, scowling at him. Decker and Anders were behind her, amusement on their faces. It was an expression that they couldn't seem to get rid of, Justin noted grimly. The bastards were enjoying this.

"Are you coming, or what?" Holly called impatiently.

Cursing under his breath, Justin released his phone and headed for the door. He just wouldn't tell her, he decided. He'd say, "I'm sorry, I can't explain that at this time. Perhaps later though," and then change the subject. It would be easier that way anyway, he thought grimly. He really didn't want to even think about how hot the sex with her could be, let alone put it into words. Just sitting beside her in the car had been a trial. He'd been trapped in the backseat with her scent, feeling the heat coming off her body and washing over him in a heady wave of *Hollyness*. Justin had actually considered sitting on his hands to keep from touching her. Fortunately, he'd managed to make it all the way here without doing either.

"Really? And what does he do?" Decker was asking when Justin caught up to them at the table where they'd been seated. At first, Justin didn't know who they were talking about, but Holly's answer quickly got him up to speed.

"He works for a company that designs and manufactures photonic-integrated circuit-based components," Holly explained, and then smiled at their blank expressions and admitted, "Yeah, I don't really know what the heck that means either."

Decker and Anders chuckled, but all Justin could work up was a forced smile. He really didn't want to even think of her husband, let alone discuss how brilliant she thought he was.

"Basically, James is really smart," Holly said. "He has a degree in applied science and he works in the company's repair department. He does warranty work as well as repairing the components the manufacturing department messes up."

"I see," Anders murmured and Justin glanced to him sharply. There was something fishy about his tone of voice. It was distracted, and Justin understood why the minute he looked at him. The other man was staring at Holly's forehead as she talked, concentrating on it.

Anders was reading Holly's thoughts about her husband, Justin realized. The inner, subconscious thoughts that she was unknowingly exposing in thinking of him. Thoughts Justin would have liked to read, but couldn't. It was damned annoying that the other two men could . . . and were, he thought, noting that Decker had the same expression on his face.

"It's a starting position," Holly went on. "But if he proves himself, they've promised him a promotion, and I have no doubt James will prove himself. He's brilliant and he loves what he does." She smiled at the thought and then suddenly turned to Justin and said, "Anyway, you were going to explain this life mate business to me."

Justin froze, holding his breath briefly as he fought the terrible temptation to just tell her. How could he not be tempted? The minute he explained about life mate sex, she'd probably jump his bones on the spot. However, Justin still wasn't sure that wouldn't get him into trouble. If the council considered it unfair or tampering, they might wipe her memory and insist he stay away from her until she was either divorced or widowed. Justin couldn't bear the thought of that, so he let his breath out slowly and then forced himself to say, "I'm sorry. I'm afraid I cannot explain about life mates to you until I've spoken to Lucian and found out if it is all right to explain. It might be considered undue influence or something."

"Undue influence how? And to do what?" she asked with obvious confusion and then narrowed her eyes. "Is this just your way of avoiding explaining?"

"No. Justin is right to refuse. He could be punished for telling you about life mates," Decker said solemnly.

Holly scowled at this news, but then heaved a sigh, glanced around and then stood. "I'm going to the ladies' room. If the waitress comes before I get back, could you please order me a California club sandwich?"

"Of course," Decker agreed.

Justin was still watching her walk away when Decker turned to him and said, "You were smart to refuse to tell her. It could be seen as interfering."

Justin nodded unhappily and then glanced sharply to Anders when he added, "But our telling her would not be."

Decker raised his eyebrows. "Do you think we should?"

"Definitely," Anders said solemnly. "We should really help Justin with this."

"Seriously? You'll explain for me?" he asked with disbelief.

"If Anders is willing, so am I," Decker said with a smile. "We did say we'd help after all."

"Damn," Justin breathed, hardly able to believe his luck. The minute they explained, Holly would be all over him. They really were trying to help him. It made him kind of feel bad for giving them such a hard time when they'd met their life mates. Yeah, they'd been pathetic, but they'd done their best and he could have been a little more sympathetic. Really, this wasn't as easy as he'd thought. Even for him.

"Why don't you go take a little walk around the parking lot," Anders suggested.

When Justin glanced to him with surprise, it was Decker who pointed out, "That way you can't be accused of being at all involved in the explanations."

"Oh, right. Good thinking." Justin stood at once, nodded in thanks to them, and said, "Tell Holly

I'll be waiting for her outside when you're done, so we can have a private little talk of our own." Grinning happily, he started away and then paused to add, "And order me the carnitas tacos when the girl comes to take orders, will you?"

He didn't wait for them to agree, but hurried away whistling a snappy tune. This was going to change everything, he thought as he headed back out to the parking lot. His life was about to change.

Justin started out pacing in the parking lot. However, after twenty minutes of that he was bored and impatient enough to get in the car to wait there. He started the engine, put some tunes on loud, and watched the entrance of the restaurant, waiting for someone to come tell him they were done. Probably Holly, and then she'd kiss him and whisper that she wanted to experience the incredible, mind-blowing life mate sex, and they'd do it right there in the car like a couple of animals, uncaring who heard or saw.

That was the first fantasy. More lurid ones followed. Sex on the car rather than in it, right on the hood while Decker and Anders had to control the minds of anyone passing to prevent their remembering seeing it. Then they passed out and Decker and Anders had to pile them in the car. But they regained consciousness halfway back to Jackie and Vincent's and did it in the backseat, screaming their heads off down the freeway until they collapsed again.

Justin then began imagining all the places they could do it at Jackie and Vincent's house. His room, her room, the kitchen, the living room, the office, the pool . . . The options were endless and the positions more and more impossible, well for mortals they would be, not for them. But eventually even that began to bore him, and he began to wonder what the hell was taking so long?

"So Justin is the only one of you who can't read or control me and that is usually the sign of a life mate?" Holly said slowly, frowning at this news. She was a married woman and she loved James. Had grown up loving him. She wasn't interested in being anyone's life mate, she was already a wife.

"It is one sign of a possible life mate, yes," Anders said calmly. "It does not always work that way though."

"Sometimes it is just a symptom of someone who has spent a great deal of time around immortals," Decker put in. "The mortal may have built up a natural resistance to being read and younger immortals can have trouble overcoming that subconscious barrier."

"Yes, well, you guys are the first immortals I've met so that doesn't—"

"You may not have known they were immortal," Anders interrupted quietly. "We do not go about announcing ourselves to others. Had Justin not turned you to save your life, we would never have admitted what we are to you."

"Oh, of course," Holly murmured.

"The inability to be read can also be a result of madness or damage done to the mortal's brain by injuries," Decker added, filling the silence that had fallen. He then added pointedly, "Such as the blow you took to the head."

Holly reached instinctively toward her head despite not having a clue where it had even been injured. Had she hit the front, the back, the side . . . ? She didn't know, and there wasn't even a faded bruise to tell her.

"There may have been some damage done that the nanos have yet to repair," Decker said gently. "I understand you have some memory issues about the incident that led to your turning."

"I did," Holly agreed. "But I remember now."

"However, you didn't at first," he pointed out.

"No, I didn't," Holly agreed with a frown and supposed if Justin had tried to read her then that she might have been harder to read and he might have thought he couldn't read her and then not tried again.

"It's sad really," Decker said on a small sigh.

"What is?" Holly asked with uncertainty.

"Well, Bricker is desperate to find a life mate," Decker told her with a little moue.

Anders nodded. "He's seen so many of us find our life mates recently he's suffering terrible envy."

"We've pointed out that the rest of us have waited more than two hundred years for our mates. Some as many as two thousand or more and that he's still young, but I imagine it's hard to watch everyone else finding their life mate while he is alone."

"So he's desperate to believe you are his life mate," Anders said with another sad shake of the head.

"But I'm married," Holly pointed out. It was the only response she had to their suggestion that Justin might be crushing on her because he hoped she was his life mate. To her, it said everything. Life mate or not—which she highly doubted—she was married and therefore unavailable.

"Yes," Decker nodded. "Still, he's positive that you are his life mate, and that you won't be able to resist him."

"Is that why he keeps calling me honey and babe and stuff like that?" she asked with a scowl. She'd noted it, but had mostly ignored it because the circumstances were all so bizarre. Also because she'd assumed he was seeing her as a protégé to his mentor and the terms were meant with a sort of avuncular affection. Apparently not.

"Exactly," he assured her. "He's fixated on you, and he's quite sure that you will . . ."

"Will what?" Holly asked when he hesitated.

"Basically, that you will respond to his amorous attentions," Anders finished with an apologetic expression.

"But I'm married," Holly repeated. Justin was a good-looking man, and yes she had noticed that amongst the madness that had taken over her life, but she had a husband, a man she had loved since she was a child. She would never break her vows, and she would never hurt James.

"Yes, well, we didn't say that his thinking was clear or sensible," Decker pointed out solemnly. "In fact, that's why we wanted to talk to you instead of letting him explain."

"You probably would have thought he was mad," Anders pointed out.

"And he's not really," Decker assured her. "He's just a tad confused . . . and desperate. Think of him like a puppy at the pound, eagerly licking the hand of anyone who stops to pet them."

"Why would I have thought he was mad?" Holly asked with uncertainty. "I mean if he just explained as you have . . ."

"Well, you have to understand, as far as he's concerned it's a fait accompli," Decker said solemnly. "To his mind, you are just seconds away from throwing yourself at him and dragging him off to bed."

"I would never!" Holly gasped with amazement. She'd never thrown herself at a man in her life . . . ever. Heck, the only experience she had in that area was James and even now, after almost four years of marriage, she had yet to initiate any sort of intimacy herself. He was always the aggressor. Of course, she kissed and hugged him, but not in the take-me-to-bed way. She just wouldn't know how. But even if she did, she was married. She cared too much for James to hurt him that way.

"Right, well there you go," Anders said with a nod. "That's why we wanted to tell you. We wanted to explain it in such a way that you would understand without his accidentally insulting you."

"Hmmm." Decker nodded. "We wanted to give him back the . . . er . . . support he gave to us when we each met our life mates."

"Oh," Holly murmured, but her attention was on Anders. He'd made a choking sound and turned away to hack violently into his hand as Decker had said that.

"Anyway, we'll do our best to help keep Bricker in line. But, it would probably also be best if you avoided being alone with him as much as possible. You might very well be saving his life if you do."

"Saving his life?" she asked with confusion.

"Oh, yes. You see we have a law against interfering with a married couple," Anders explained solemnly. "If he's even suspected of trying to seduce you away from your husband, he could be . . . punished."

Holly's eyes widened. She'd already heard what their idea of punishment was—execution Bricker had said. Good Lord! She wouldn't want to see the poor man executed when he was just confused and desperate enough for a life mate that he was mistaking her for his.

"Yes," she said solemnly. "I will be sure to avoid being alone with him."

"Well, that's grand then," Decker said cheerily and then glanced up with a smile as the waitress stopped at their table. "And here is our meal."

Holly smiled at the girl as well, but once she'd set their plates down and both men dug in, she glanced to the tacos they'd ordered for Justin and said uncertainly, "Where *is* Justin?"

"Oh, he's fine," Decker assured her. "He went for a walk,"

"A walk?" she asked blankly, and when neither man responded, added, "But his food will get cold."

"We'll have it packaged and take it out to him if he doesn't return by the time we're done eating," Decker assured her.

"Or maybe split it ourselves," Anders commented, eyeing the tacos. "They look pretty good and I'm hungry enough to eat my meal and his too."

"Me too," Decker said cheerfully and glanced at the plate. "We'll split it."

"Good idea," Anders decided with a grin.

Holly just shook her head at the pair of them and turned her attention to her sandwich. Still, she did wonder where Bricker had gone off to. A walk? Why? She wondered, but in the next moment bit into her sandwich and forgot all about Justin Bricker.

"So, Holly," Decker said a moment later. "Do you like flowers?"

"I used to," she said, lowering the sandwich she'd been about to bite into again. "But after working at the cemetery for a couple weeks I'm kind of off flowers. They represent death to me now rather than happiness and cheer."

"Yes, I can imagine," Anders said sympathetically. "What about picnics?"

She burst out laughing and shook her head. "I grew up being dragged from one archaeological dig to another. Every meal was basically a picnic. Can't stand them, or camping or anything that has to do with the great outdoors anymore." She sighed. "One thing that lifestyle did was turn me into a definite city girl. Give me restaurants any day."

"So, no camping for you, huh?" Decker asked with amusement as she started to raise her sandwich again.

Holly shook her head. "Definitely not."

"Dogs or cats?" Anders asked.

"Neither. Allergic, but also I was mauled by a dog as a child. They terrify me now," she said with a shudder.

"Favorite and least favorite foods?" Decker asked.

Holly paused, lowering her sandwich once more without taking a bite, and glanced from man to man. "Why all the questions?"

"Just trying to get to know you better," Anders said mildly, and repeated, "So favorite and least favorite foods?"

Justin glanced toward the restaurant door, an irritated frown claiming his lips as he wondered for the umpteenth time what the hell was taking them so long. Surely they'd finished explaining about life mates to Holly by now? Someone should have come to get him . . . preferably Holly.

How long had it been since they'd got to the restaurant? He glanced at his watch to note the time, but he hadn't bothered to check before this so couldn't be sure how long he'd been waiting, and it could just seem like a long time because he *was* waiting. It always seemed to take forever for something to happen when you were waiting.

Sighing, he leaned his head back and closed his eyes briefly. If no one came to get him in the next fifteen minutes, he'd go take a look inside and see if they were still talking or whatnot. If they were, he could at least grab his meal and eat it out here. He was starving. Rubbing his aching stomach, he opened his eyes and glanced toward the restaurant, and then stilled when he saw Holly heading across the parking lot with Decker and Anders on either side.

"What—?" he began, sitting up abruptly and frowning as they reached the car. His words died though when Anders slid into the front passenger seat and tossed a white styrofoam take-out container into his lap.

"We brought your meal," Anders announced.

Justin peered down at the container and lifted it with confusion. "It feels pretty light."

"Yeah. Sorry, but talking is a hungry business and Decker and I kind of picked at your tacos."

Picked at them? Justin thought with dismay at he opened it to see that not only had they eaten the tacos, they'd pretty much demolished the nachos that came as a side. All the container held was a couple of nachos and a smattering of salsa.

"We were going to order you something else to go, but then figured you wouldn't want to wait, and we *are* going shopping now anyway, so you can pick up whatever you want there," Decker put in.

"Thanks," Justin said sarcastically and popped a nacho into his mouth. He wasn't too upset though. Anders's comment about talking being a hungry business had reassured him that they had talked to Holly, and he supposed he owed them for doing that favor. That thought in mind, he popped the second nacho into his mouth, closed the box and then turned to peer at Holly. Unfortunately, she was peering silently out her window, her face turned away from him. He wasn't at all sure what that meant. Was she embarrassed and shy to be around him now that she knew she was his life mate?

It was more likely that she was anxious about the whole thing now, he decided as his gaze landed on her finger and the ring there. She would have to end her marriage, or at least tell her husband it was over before she would say or do anything with him, he realized. She was just that kind of woman. At least he suspected she was. The truth was, he didn't know much about Holly except that she was his life mate. Perhaps he should find out more about her while they had the chance. Once she explained things to her husband and was free to be with him, they would no doubt be spending all their free time in bed, and talking would be the last thing on their minds.

"So," he said brightly, turning a bit in his seat to smile at her. "What made you want to work at a cemetery?"

Holly turned to peer at him with surprise, and then smiled wryly. "Money. Although I don't really work at the cemetery. At least, not as a permanent position. I actually work for a temp agency and they placed me there for the cemetery's tax season."

"Oh. Right," he murmured and thought that was

good to know. Not that there was anything wrong with working at a cemetery but . . . Well, okay, he would be a little worried about anyone who picked it as their first choice in job options. Of course, now-adays, people took jobs where they could get them and he understood that.

"So . . ." He hesitated, unsure what to ask next. Did he dare ask how long she'd been married? That seemed an insensitive question to ask a woman you were stealing away from her husband.

"Here we are," Decker announced, turning into the grocery store parking lot.

Justin let his breath out on a slow sigh and let go of the debate on what to ask next. He could think about it while they shopped and ask more questions later, he decided.

"Bricker."

Justin closed his door and glanced to Anders in question as the man urged Holly around the SUV with a hand on her arm. Rather than walk her up to him though, he led her toward Decker as they reached the front of the vehicle and said, "You two go ahead. We'll be right behind you."

"What's up?" Bricker asked when the man then turned to him, blocking him from following.

"We learned a bit about Holly in the restaurant," Anders announced.

"Like what?" Justin asked curiously.

"Well, first off, she doesn't like questions," he said with wry amusement. "I suspect it's because of her upbringing, but she's a very private person."

Justin merely nodded at this news and supposed it was good that he hadn't asked too much then.

"Also, she loves fish, flowers, wine, puppies, kit-ties, picnics, documentaries, nature shows and anything to do with nature," Anders added, and then slapped him on the shoulder. "We thought that information might help you out in the wooing department."

"Yeah. Thanks," Justin said with a grin. "Thanks a lot."

"Just helping out a fellow Enforcer," Anders said with a shrug, and then turned to follow Holly and Decker. Justin hurried after him.

Eight

Holly surveyed the three carts the men were pushing. Each had insisted on grabbing one on the way in. She'd had no idea why at the time, but was beginning to understand. Dear Lord, they were in the last section, produce, and each cart was stacked to overflowing. It was like they were feeding an army instead of three men and two women. *They must have half the store in those carts between them*, Holly thought. She followed the men, slowing as she realized that they were heading for the checkout after doing nothing more than picking up a bag of potatoes each from produce. No lettuce, no broccoli, nothing at all healthy.

"I don't know if you guys know this, but a while ago they invented these things called fruits and vegetables," she said conversationally. When the men all stopped walking and turned to stare at her blankly, she added, "I gather some guy named God came up with them at the beginning of time. You might like to give them a try."

"Oh," Justin said finally when the other two remained silent, their gazes shifting over the groceries in their carts. "Well . . . er . . . we're kind of meat and potato type guys. Potatoes are vegetables," he added brightly and gestured to his cart as if to show that he'd collected all the vegetables they needed.

"So are broccoli, cauliflower and lettuce," Holly pointed with amusement.

This time Justin and the other two men exchanged grimaces and glances, before Justin spoke for all three of them again, saying, "Yeah, not so much. I mean sure they *are* vegetables, but they aren't *real* vegetables if you know what I mean."

"You mean they aren't manly type vegetables?" she asked, one eyebrow arching and her expression stern.

"Exactly," he said seeming relieved that she understood. "Potatoes and jalapenos are manly type vegetables. Lettuce and that stuff . . . well . . . they're more rabbit food . . . don't you think?"

"No, I don't think," she assured him and then added, "My James loves all the vegetables and fruits . . . and he seems pretty manly to me."

For some reason Justin scowled at that and then muttered, "I bet he eats quiche too, huh?"

"Sure," Holly answered as she snatched up a shopping basket from the end of the nearest checkout.

"Of course he does," Justin said.

Noting the almost snide tone to his voice, she turned to peer at him curiously. "Is there something wrong with that?"

"Not a thing," Anders assured her, turning his

cart to head back toward the vegetables. "There's no need for the basket. There is still room in my cart."

"Yeah, not much though, huh?" Holly said, eyeing his cart dubiously. If she fit more than a tomato onto that stack she'd be surprised. "I think I'll just hold on to the basket."

"As you wish," Anders said mildly, following when she headed back through produce.

"You do realize, Justin, that Holly didn't understand your reference to real men not eating quiche," Decker said as he watched Justin turn his cart around. "She's too young to get it . . . or perhaps it is fairer to say that the reference, like yourself, is too old."

"I'm not old," Justin squawked, shocked at the very suggestion. He was the baby of the Enforcers. The young hip one to their grumpy old codgers. He was *not* old.

"You may not be old in comparison to us, but you're ancient in comparison to mortals. Old enough to be her great-great grandfather, in fact," Decker said with obvious enjoyment. "There is a definite generation gap between you two, sonny boy."

Justin fell into step with Decker as he headed after Holly and Anders, but his mind was now racing as he absorbed the man's suggestion. Old? Him? He was the young hip one, the one who knew the ways of the world and the women in it. He wasn't old. Was he? Certainly there was no way he was old enough to be her great-great grandfather, he assured himself and then frowned. Well, okay he was over a hundred while she was maybe twenty-five. So maybe he was a good eighty years older, but . . .

"Damn, I'm an old man compared to her," he muttered with dismay.

"A dirty old man too," Decker informed him, and when Justin glanced to him with surprise, pointed out, "You can't look at her without imagining her naked and in some sexual position or other." He shook his head. "It's a good thing she can't read your thoughts or she'd be slapping that smiling face of yours."

Justin merely shook his head, feeling dazed. "I'm an old man."

"Yes, you are," Decker said cheerfully, then glanced at him sideways and said, "Ah, don't worry about it, Bricker. We all get there eventually. Well, unless we die," he added dryly and then shrugged. "Better to be old than dead, huh?"

"But I've always been the young one." Justin heard the whine in his voice, but too late to stop it.

"Yeah, well them's the breaks my friend. Get over it," Decker said with a distinct lack of sympathy.

"What did you do? Buy out the store?" Gia asked as she held the door open between the garage and kitchen and watched them cart in the first load of groceries.

"Don't look at me," Holly said on a laugh as she stepped inside and set her bags down. "Most of this is down to the guys. Each of them filled a whole cart to overflowing on their own. It was almost embarrassing when we went to the checkout."

Gia shook her head and glanced from Anders to Decker. "You won't even be here to eat any of it."

"We were thinking of Dante and Tomasso," Anders said with a shrug as he turned to head back out.

"Ah." Gia nodded her head, and then arched an eyebrow at Justin. "And what's your excuse?"

"I was thinking of your cousins too," Justin assured her. "Those two could put away an entire cow at one sitting . . . each. I'm lucky to get anything at all to eat when they're around. It seemed a good idea to pack in the food. That way Holly and I might at least get a sandwich or something here or there."

"Si." Gia grinned and then confided to Holly, "My cousins are big boys who like their food."

"We can get the rest, Holly," Justin said, stopping her when she started back out to the garage. "Why don't you start unpacking while we lug the bags in?"

Nodding, Holly turned to move back to the bags she'd set down and began to pull out and sort items. Gia immediately moved to help her. Neither of them knew the kitchen layout though, so it was slow going.

"You will like my cousins Tomasso and Dante," Gia announced suddenly as they worked.

"Why is that?" Straightening from sticking half a dozen frozen pizzas in the freezer, Holly turned in time to see Justin scowling as he dumped a bunch of grocery bags on the counter.

Gia waited until he'd stomped out, then grinned and said, "I mostly said that to annoy Bricker. He is sometimes acting too big for his bitches."

Holly blinked once and then gave her head a shake. "I think you mean he is growing too big for his britches."

"Britches?" Gia stopped with a box of pasta in hand and eyed her uncertainly. "What is britches?"

"They're pants or slacks," Holly explained.

"Why would he grow too big for his pants? We are immortal. We never gain weight," she pointed out with a frown.

"No, well, it's just a saying. When someone gets conceited or puts on airs, they say they are getting too big for their britches."

"Not bitches?" Gia asked with surprise.

"No," Holly said gently, biting her lip to keep from laughing. She didn't want to make the woman feel bad.

"Oh." Gia shrugged. "Okay then, yes, that is what I meant. These britches." She pursed her lips. "It makes more sense than bitches anyway."

"Yes," Holly murmured as she moved back to the bags.

"But you really will like my cousins," Gia announced. "They are both big, beautiful bad boys."

"Bad boys? And you think I'll like them?" Holly asked with confusion.

"They are not really bad boys," Gia assured her. "They just look like bad boys with their long hair and leather. Inside though, they are *dolce*."

"*Dolce*?"

"Sweet," Anders announced, carrying in more bags. "*Dolce* means 'sweet.'"

"*Si*, and Dante and Tomasso look big and *pauroso*—scary, but inside they are as sweet as gelato."

"Sure they are, big as bears and sweet as ice cream," Decker said with a smile as he entered now as well. "Speaking of which, I just got the call, they will be landing in an hour. Anders and I won't be able to help put this stuff away after all. We have to head to the airport if we want a ride home." He grimaced and added apologetically, "Otherwise we'll be waiting for at least a couple hours for the plane to come back for us."

Holly nodded with understanding, recalling Gia explaining that the planes they used were apparently behind on pickups.

Decker glanced back out to the garage, where Bricker was loading himself up with more bags, and then turned back to Holly and murmured, "Remember what we said."

"I will," she assured him solemnly. She was to avoid being alone with Justin. That shouldn't be too hard with Gia and her cousins around, should it?

Justin stifled a yawn and shifted his gaze from the television screen to Holly. They were watching a nature show on lions. So far they'd watched them hunt, sleep, and have sex. It seemed to be all they did and while it was more interesting than his own life right then—at least the sex part was—it was boring as hell to watch. But Anders had said Holly liked nature shows so when they'd sat down with Gia to wait for Dante and Tomasso in front of the television, he'd spotted the show on the guide and put it on.

Gia had fallen asleep in her chair within the first three minutes of its starting and he was desperately struggling to stay awake himself. He hoped to hell that Holly was enjoying it at least, but it was hard to tell. She was lying on her side in front of the coffee table, her head pillowed on her arm, while he was sitting on the couch behind it. He couldn't see her expression.

Sighing, he picked up his glass, noticed that it was empty, and then picked up both it and the empty plate he'd set on the table and stood, but then paused to peer at the woman on the floor.

"Holly? Would you like a drink or anything while

I'm in the kitchen?" Justin asked softly, not wanting to wake up Gia. Too softly, apparently: Holly didn't appear to hear him. Moving around the coffee table to get closer, he asked a little louder, "Would you like a coffee or something? I'm heading to the kitchen."

Still no answer.

Frowning, Justin shifted around in front of her and then stilled. The woman was sound asleep. He'd been suffering the nature show for nothing. Cripes.

Shaking his head, he straightened and headed to the kitchen with his dirty dishes. Even hungrier when they'd finished unpacking the groceries than he had been at the restaurant, Justin had made himself four sandwiches to eat while they watched TV. He'd then pretty much inhaled the food and had considered going back for a couple more, but had decided against it. He didn't want to spoil his dinner and no doubt they'd be having that shortly after Dante and Tomasso arrived.

Justin rinsed the crumbs off of his plate and put it in the dishwasher. He then grabbed a glass, got some ice from the icemaker on the refrigerator door and grabbed a pop. He took the time to pour it slowly over the ice, to prevent too much foam, and then headed out of the kitchen and back up the hall to the living room, but froze in the doorway when he spotted the duffel bags on the floor inside the front door. Dante and Tomasso were here. But where?

His gaze slid to the empty stairs and he started forward again, only to pause once more when Dante came out of the living room with a sleeping Gia looking like a child against his massive chest. The tall, wide-shouldered Italian nodded at him solemnly as he started upstairs with Gia, no doubt intending to carry her up and put her in her bed.

Justin nodded back, and then started forward again, only to freeze when Tomasso came out of the living room carrying Holly in his arms. She was asleep, curled against his chest and nuzzling her head sleepily into the crook of his neck as if looking for somewhere soft on the massive man's hard body. Justin stared, noted the man's nod, and scowled in return, showing teeth.

"Which room?" the man asked, his voice a soft growl.

"End of the hall on the left," Justin hissed, battling an incredibly strong urge to jump the huge bastard and beat him silly. He wanted to smash his stupid face and—

The glass Justin held suddenly shattered in his hand, sending ice and soda splashing him in the face and chest. Tearing his gaze from a now-amused Tomasso, Justin glanced down to see the liquid dribbling down his legs to the floor. Sighing, he turned to head back into the kitchen in search of something to clean up the mess he'd made.

He'd just finished cleaning up the hall and was putting away the Swiffer in the broom closet when the kitchen door opened behind him and Dante and Tomasso entered. Closing the closet door, he turned reluctantly to face the duo.

"Food?" Tomasso grunted. He was a one word kind of guy, while Dante was more likely to string three or four words into a sentence.

"We just went shopping this afternoon. There's lots in the fridge, freezer, and cupboards. Help yourself," he suggested and headed for the door. Now that the floor in the hall was clean, there was still himself to consider. He needed a quick shower to remove the sticky liquid that had seeped through his clothes to his skin, and a change of clothes would be good.

"Both girls were dead to the world," Dante commented. "Neither even stirred when we picked them up."

Justin paused at the door. "Gia's had no more than a short nap since yesterday and Holly is a new turn. They'll probably both sleep for a while."

Both men nodded and then Tomasso asked, "Life mate?"

"Yes," he said grimly.

"She's married," Dante put in solemnly.

"I'm aware of that," Justin growled, feeling his jaw tighten with tension.

"Tough break," they said together.

"No shit," Justin muttered and pushed out of the room. He was halfway up the hall when a knock sounded at the door. Moving a little more quickly, he opened it and peered out at the man in a black jacket with a rental agency name on the pocket.

"Justin Bricker?" the man asked.

"Yes." He accepted the pen and clipboard the man offered and glanced over the rental agreement on it. Lucian had rented an SUV for them to use while here. What he held was acknowledgment of having received the vehicle. Justin glanced out at the SUV now parked in the driveway, then to a white car with the rental logo on the side and a man behind the wheel. He quickly signed the bottom and handed pen and clipboard back.

"Thanks." He took the pen and clipboard in one hand and held out a set of keys with the other. "Have a good day."

Justin muttered a thank-you as he took the keys, and then closed the door and returned to the stairs. He considered looking in on Holly, but Gia wasn't the only one who had been up for quite a while and he was exhausted. Too exhausted to even want to think about the situation he found himself in for now. A life mate with a mortal husband. *Tough break indeed*, he thought grimly as he dragged himself upstairs to his room.

Holly opened her eyes and found herself peering into darkness. Biting her lip, she sat up and reached out blindly to her side until her arm bumped into something. A quick exploration proved it to be a lamp and after a bit of fumbling she found the switch and turned it on. She peered around then, releasing a little relieved sigh. It was the same room she'd woken in when Gia had been there. The last thing she recalled was watching that horrid, boring nature show in the living room and for a minute she'd feared she'd find herself in yet another strange room.

She didn't recall coming up to bed again. So either she'd staggered up here half asleep, or Justin had carried her up and put her in bed. That thought had her glancing down and quickly shifting the blankets and sheet off herself. Much to her relief, she was fully dressed, only her shoes missing. Sliding off the bed, she paused to stretch her back and arms, then moved to the bathroom to relieve herself, run a brush through her hair, splash some water on her face and then quickly brush her teeth before heading through her room to the hall door.

The sound of squealing wheels and explosions

met her ears as she stepped into the hall. The television, Holly guessed as she made her way to the stairs and down. She moved to the door to the living room, expecting to find Justin and Gia there, but instead there were two of the largest men she'd ever seen inside. One was draped over the chair Gia had previously sat in, turned sideways, his legs over one chair arm and his back up against the other. His eyes were fixed on the television screen, where a car chase was in progress. A second man lay on the couch, his feet overshooting the end of it by a good foot. They were the only thing she could see of him from where she stood.

Holly couldn't see the face of the man on the couch, but the other man sat in profile to her, revealing a hard face and roman nose. Gia's cousins, she guessed, and recalled that they were twins. Gia certainly hadn't been kidding when she'd said big, and yes the black leather they wore made them appear bad. The long hair just added to that image.

Shy about meeting them, Holly eased back from the door to avoid drawing their attention, and then turned and made her way into the kitchen. She'd expected to find Gia and Justin there, so was surprised to find it empty. Gia had been complaining that she was exhausted when they'd sat down to watch that horrid wildlife show, so Holly supposed she was probably in bed.

Wondering where Justin was, Holly moved to the refrigerator. She was starving, her stomach aching with it. Thanks to their shopping trip there was plenty of food, but unsure what the plans were for supper, she didn't want anything too heavy. Just something to ease the ache would be enough, she thought, and grabbed an apple. After polishing it on her borrowed top, she took a bite and moved to peer out the glass doors at the backyard. While it was dark, there were lights on in the yard, enough for her to see a large pool.

Wondering how deep it was, Holly eased the door open and stepped outside, then moved to sit cross-legged at the edge of the pool. She leaned forward to dip her fingers into the water, surprised at just how warm it was. The water still retained the day's heat.

A swim would have been nice, Holly thought, taking another bite of her apple. Unfortunately, she didn't have a swimsuit. She wouldn't use the pool without permission anyway, so stood up and walked around it instead. A row of hedges made the pool seem secluded, but there was a gate in the center of the hedgerow and Holly moved to it now to peer out over a large lawn with something rippling beyond it.

The ocean, she realized after examining it for a minute. This house was on the beach . . . and yet they had a pool.

"Yeesh, talk about extravagance," she muttered and opened the gate. A nice walk on the beach while she ate her apple sounded appealing. It might help clear her mind, and Holly could definitely use that. So much had happened, and all of it taking place so quickly . . .

It was hard to believe that only a couple of days had passed since she'd headed back to the office to get her forgotten purse, she thought, as she crossed the lawn to the beach.

Actually, it had been more than a couple days, she supposed. It was just that she'd only been conscious for parts of two of them. Or was it three?

She went over her memories as she reached the

beach and started along it. She'd woken naked in that hotel and gone home, where she'd slept and rose the next day. She'd then gone to the hotel, where she'd been knocked out, and then woken up here today. All told, it had been three days for her, or parts of three days. At least that's how much time she'd been conscious. But it felt like a lifetime had passed. Although not really. It felt all at once like a long time and no time at all.

Weird. She thought, raising her apple to take another bite, only to find that she had finished it. She'd eaten the damned thing down to the core, but her stomach felt no better. It was still aching something horrible.

Holly turned and started back to the house, cutting across the lawn rather than walking back along the beach to where she'd started. Her mind was on what they'd bought today and what she might eat to satisfy her hunger, so she didn't notice Justin until she nearly ran him over.

"Whoa," he said on a deep laugh as he caught her arms to steady her.

"Sorry." Holly tipped her head back to peer at him and managed a smile. "I wasn't watching where I was going."

"That's all right," he responded. His voice deepened a bit as he said that, but she barely noticed. She was too distracted by the scent filling her nostrils.

She'd noticed before that Justin smelled delicious, and now she inhaled deeply, holding the aroma in her lungs. God! It was incredible, irresistible, soooo . . . yummy, she could just eat him all up.

Holly rose up on her tiptoes and leaned toward him on that thought, her hands knotting in the front of his shirt to pull him to her as she did.

Justin went willingly when Holly tugged at him, his heart racing, and mind awhirl. Finally! *Finally*, he thought. She was experiencing the life mate attraction and ready to give up her old life for her new one with him. He'd known she would. Nothing could beat life mate sex and she was hungry for it. He could see that in her eyes and he couldn't even be accused of influencing her in any way. In fact, he decided to let her do all the work and seduce him so that if his memories were read, it would be known she was the aggressor . . . and she was definitely the aggressor here. The woman was lusting after him like a cat in heat and he was more than happy to fulfill her needs, he thought, and closed his eyes, then started to let his hands slide down her arms but she was suddenly gone.

Blinking his eyes open, he found himself staring out at the sea. Confusion rising within him, he whirled to see Dante walking back toward the house, holding Holly by the waist, well out in front of him as if she were a baby with a dirty diaper.

"She wasn't lusting after *you* so much as your blood," the other man announced over his shoulder and it was only then that Justin realized why the man was holding her as he was. Her fangs were out and she was clawing at his hands and twisting her head this way and that, blindly seeking something, or someone to bite into. She was in the throes of blood lust again . . . and a bit mad with it, he noted with a frown. The realization made him quickly work out how long it had been since she'd fed. They'd given her blood along with the sedative while she was sleeping after they'd first got here. That was hours ago now though, he realized, glancing at his wristwatch. Nearly twelve hours ago in fact.

No, it had been longer than that, Justin thought as he followed Dante and Holly back to the house. While they'd hooked up Holly to both the sedative and blood when they'd first got her here, they hadn't replaced that bag of blood when it had run out. As a new turn she needed to feed more than that.

"She needs to feed a lot more than that," Dante announced, pausing at the door to wait for Justin to open it for him. "She was diabetic while mortal. No doubt there was a lot of damage to different systems over the years for the nanos to repair. She'll probably need a lot of blood for quite a while to mend everything."

"Of course," Justin said with a sigh, as he pulled the door open for him to enter. Holly had calmed down somewhat now. At least she wasn't twisting her head about anymore.

"I'll get her a bag of blood," Justin said as he followed him inside and pulled the door closed.

"You better grab several of them," Dante advised as he set Holly in a chair at the kitchen table and held her there with his hands on her shoulders.

Justin nodded and moved to the fridge. He retrieved six bags of blood, set four on the counter and took the other two with him to the table. One glance showed him that her fangs had retreated during the walk inside and he expected to have to cut his finger or something to bring them back out. New turns usually had to have their fangs coaxed out in such a way, but he had barely raised his hand in front of her face with the intent to do so when she inhaled deeply and her mouth dropped open, her fangs suddenly sliding out.

Eyebrows rising, he immediately popped one of the bags to her upper fangs and prevented her attempt to push it away. It was just an instinctual reaction. After a moment, she calmed and let her hands drop. When the first bag was empty and he replaced it, she raised her hands again, but this time to hold it herself.

Nodding, Justin offered her a half smile and returned to the counter for the rest of the bags. When he saw that Dante was no longer having to hold Holly in the chair, he offered him a bag, then popped one to his own mouth.

"I'm sorry," Holly murmured, avoiding Justin's gaze as she pulled the now empty bag from her mouth a moment later. "I don't know what I was thinking."

"You were not thinking. You were in the throes of blood lust," Dante said after removing his own bag. "It is difficult to think at that stage."

Holly shook her head unhappily. "I was hungry when I got up, but I thought it was just for food, so I grabbed an apple and . . ." She shrugged helplessly.

"Then that will be our first lesson," Dante announced. "Teaching you to recognize the difference between hunger for food and blood hunger."

Holly nodded solemnly, and accepted the third bag of blood Justin offered. This time, she popped it to her own mouth. He smiled encouragingly at her, and watched her feed, his mind now considering ways to woo her. It seemed Decker and Anders explaining about life mates hadn't made much difference in her reaction to him. At least she hadn't broached the subject with him and wasn't treating him any differently. Which meant he would have to woo the woman. The next time she grabbed him and rose up on her toes, he wanted it to be because she was hungry for him, not his blood.

Anders had said she liked fish, flowers, wine, puppies, kittens, picnics, documentaries, nature shows and anything to do with nature, he recalled and ran through the list slowly in his head. Well, it was too late to get her flowers, take a picnic, or find a pet store, but there was plenty of wine here at Jackie and Vincent's. They'd got it in for Tiny while he was still mortal, but then he'd turned and so it sat languishing in a rack. He could make dinner and serve her wine to start and impress her with the knowledge that he knew how to cook. That was a newer skill. He'd always been more of an eater than a cook, but after trying to help Cale Argeneau claim his mate, Alex, who owned a pair of fine dining restaurants in Toronto, Justin had found he was interested in cooking. He'd been terrible at it at first, but between watching the Food Network and helping Sam at the house, he'd picked up some skills and was sure he could manage to cook Holly a meal that would impress her.

Justin was smiling widely at the thought, when he noted that Dante was looking at him with one eyebrow raised dubiously.

"What?" he asked.

"Nothing," the other man said and took a fourth bag of blood from him to replace the one Holly was tearing away. "Nothing at all."

Justin frowned at him, then set the remaining bag on the table and turned to start searching the kitchen. They hadn't bought any fish when they'd been shopping, but with any luck, Jackie and Vincent might have some in the freezer or something. They were newly mated and both ate and he'd been here before and knew they had a huge freezer. Surely they'd have at least one fish in it, he hoped. He needed a cookbook too, though, or a computer so that he could find a recipe. Something gourmet, he thought, his mind planning feverishly.

Nine

A loud crash came muffled from the back of the house and Holly tore her gaze from the action movie Dante and Tomasso had put on the television to glance toward the door to the hall. Her instinct was to go see if Justin was all right or needed any help, but he'd turned her away the last three times she'd checked on him after such sounds, so she remained where she was seated and forced her gaze back to the television. The man was determined to cook a meal for them and had refused all offers of assistance. But the crashes and bangs coming from the room were a bit alarming. It sounded like he was pitching pots across the kitchen or something. The curses that had occasionally sounded were no more encouraging and she suspected the meal was going to be a complete mess.

Biting her lip, Holly glanced toward the door to the hall again. It had been just after ten P.M. when she'd woken up, well past dinnertime . . . and Justin had been working in the kitchen for what seemed like hours now. It had to be after midnight. She'd been absolutely starved when she'd woken, but enough time had passed that her hunger had turned to nausea now. As a diabetic she had always had to eat on a strict regimen. Skipping meals had not been allowed, so she was not used to it. That thought made her glance to Gia who was seated on the couch next to her.

As if sensing her attention, the woman turned to her in question.

Holly hesitated and then said, "I haven't tested my blood since . . ."

"You are no longer a diabetic," Gia assured her solemnly. "The nanos will have repaired your system, removing all illnesses or lack in your system. You will no longer need to test your blood or take insulin anymore."

Holly stared at her as those words drifted around inside her head. No more shots of insulin, or poking her fingers to test her blood sugars. No more watching every little thing she ate, or strict regimens for mealtimes. She was normal.

Normal, she thought faintly, and the concept was sweet. Like other people, she could now eat what and when she wanted. She savored that thought for a moment, until it occurred to her that she wasn't really normal at all. She had to have blood now instead of insulin, she reminded herself and frowned.

In truth, Holly supposed she'd traded in one ailment for another. Instead of not producing enough insulin, her body now could not produce enough blood to support the nanos that had invaded it. Instead of taking insulin shots, she had to take in blood, either intravenously or through her teeth.

While teaching her how to recognize the difference between a hunger for food and the hunger for blood, Dante and Tomasso had said she could even drink blood if necessary and that immortals without fangs did that. The thought of drinking it, though, was terribly unappealing. Holly wasn't sure why that was, when she'd nearly attacked her husband and then Justin both twice in search of the tinny substance. It certainly hadn't seemed unappealing then. Well, to be fair, it wasn't like she'd been imagining biting their throats and allowing their warm blood to flow over her tongue and down her throat, she thought now. Actually, she wasn't even sure that would have happened if she'd bitten them. Certainly, she didn't get any blood in her mouth when she bit the bags. Her new fangs seemed to suck it up like straws without her ever having to taste it.

So . . . she was no longer diabetic, but still not normal.

"I have lived a long time, Holly," Gia said suddenly, her voice soft so as not to prevent Dante and Tomasso from being able to hear the television. "And if there is one thing I have learned in all that time, it is that no one is this supposed normal you are thinking of. Everyone is a different creature with different flukes or tics whether they are physical or mental." She paused briefly, and then grinned and added, "Besides, this normal thing is like sanity, it's vastly overrated. Embrace your differences, they make you who you are and I like you."

Holly smiled faintly, and then glanced to the door at the sound of someone clearing their throat.

"Dinner is ready," Justin announced when her gaze found him in the doorway.

Her eyes widened as she peered at the man. His

face was flushed, his hair disheveled as if he'd been running his hands repeatedly through it, and his clothes were splattered with various foodstuffs. But he also had an air of banked excitement about him. He was obviously eager for them to see the results of his hard work.

"Well, great," Holly said with a smile as she got up. "I'm beyond starved."

There were rumbles of agreement from Dante and Tomasso as they turned off the television and stood as well, though she couldn't help noticing that they were a little less enthusiastic than her. Still, they were playing along and even Gia got up to follow Justin to the kitchen, though Holly knew the woman was old enough that she no longer bothered much with food.

A heavy curry scent hit her as Justin opened the kitchen door and Holly's stomach, already nauseous, rebelled somewhat. Swallowing, she assured herself that her stomach would settle once she had something in it, and moved to the table to peer over it curiously. Justin had gone all out, using what she guessed was their hosts' good china and even folding napkins into fancy little figures she suspected might be birds. There were candles and covered warming plates and it looked amazing.

"Sit, sit," Justin said, releasing the door once Gia and the boys followed her in. He rushed forward to pull out a chair for her.

Holly settled in the chair, murmuring a thank-you as he eased it forward, but she was mostly concentrating on breathing slowly in and out through her mouth rather than her nose in the hopes of easing the nausea roiling through her stomach. It wasn't that the food smelled bad, it was just that she was so nauseous with hunger she wasn't handling the spicy smells assaulting her.

She really should have had another apple or something while they'd waited for Justin to finish cooking, Holly thought unhappily. He had gone to so much effort and was obviously excited, acting like a kid who had made something for his mother in art class and was presenting it, eager for her reaction.

"It all looks beautiful," she praised, and that was certainly true. Crystal wineglasses sparkled in the candlelight, and the silver covers on the serving dishes in the center of the table gleamed.

"Wine," Justin announced, picking up an already open bottle with a flourish and pouring some into her glass.

Holly bit her lip to keep from refusing the offering. She didn't care for wine. The taste had never appealed to her, which was a good thing since she always seemed to get a shooting pain at the base of her skull with the first sip or two when she drank it. Still, she smiled her thanks to Justin and picked up the glass as if to drink from it, but then merely held it until he moved on to pour wine for Dante and Tomasso as well. Setting the glass back then, she swallowed and continued to breathe slowly in and out to manage her nausea as her gaze moved curiously to the covered serving plates.

Justin had refused to say what he planned to make for dinner, insisting that it was to be a surprise, but there were three covered dishes on the table, a basket with buns, and a large bowl of a mixed salad. The sight of that cheered her. If nothing else, she could eat the buns and salad to get something in her stomach and ease her nausea before moving on to trying whatever it was he'd cooked for them.

"There we are," Justin said drawing her attention back to him as he finished off by pouring wine into his own glass and then set the bottle aside. "Now, for the pièce de résistance."

Like a magician performing an amazing trick, Justin grasped the silver cover on the largest serving dish, which was right in front of Holly, and whisked it off with a grandiose gesture bursting with pride and expectation.

Holly stared . . . and their dinner stared back. What he had uncovered was some sort of very large fish, roasted and covered with lemons and what appeared to be julienned green onions. There was even what might have been a clove of garlic or something similar protruding from its gaping mouth. Its still present mouth in its still present head. It also still had its skin and fins. Holly's already roiling stomach rebelled and she jumped up from the table, heaving as she rushed out of the room, desperate to find a bathroom before she tossed up whatever she did have in her stomach. Mostly bile, with a couple of chunks of apple, she was sure.

"I don't think she likes fish," Dante said into the silence.

Justin tore his gaze from the door Holly had just disappeared through and peered at the man with blank dismay. "But she does. She likes fish. Anders said so."

"Hmmm," Dante said, and exchanged a glance with his twin that made Justin frown.

Gia distracted him from wondering about that look by suggesting gently, "Perhaps she is not used to it being served with the head and tail still attached. It was quite common a couple hundred years ago, but is less so now."

Justin sagged at that observation; all the excitement and eagerness he'd been swimming in as he'd set the table and laid out his offerings were now dust in his mouth. He'd made the woman sick, for God's sake. They could all hear her retching in the bathroom up the hall.

He dropped the cover back on the fish, then turned and headed out of the kitchen. The guest bathroom was halfway up the hall. Justin paused outside of it, listened briefly and when the retching paused, asked, "Holly? Are you all right?"

"Fine." There was a good cheer in her tone that he was quite sure was forced.

Justin sighed and leaned his head against the doorjamb. "I'm sorry. I guess I should have made something else."

"No, no," she said quickly through the door. "I just . . . er . . . have a tummy bug or something. It looked . . . er . . . lovely. Really."

Yeah, and if he bought that, she had a bridge in the swamps of Florida that she could sell him too. The woman was a terrible liar, he thought and then stepped quickly back when the door opened.

Holly stepped out, face pale and hair disheveled, but a stiff smile pinned to her face. "You go back and enjoy your meal. I think I'll just go lie down until my tummy settles."

Justin remained silent and simply watched her walk away up the hall until she disappeared upstairs. Then he turned and moved slowly back to the kitchen.

"It's good," Tomasso announced when he entered the room.

Justin glanced to the table to see that the twins had split the fish down the middle, each taking half. They'd also piled their plates with the curried rice and brussels sprouts he'd made as well and were demolishing it all.

"It *is* good," Dante assured him. "We left the head for you."

Justin peered at the head still on the platter and then just turned around and walked out again. All that work and the twins would have it gone in seconds . . . and Holly hadn't touched a bite of it.

"Bricker?"

Pausing halfway up the hall, he glanced over his shoulder to see Gia walking toward him.

"It all looked very impressive," the woman said quietly, patting his arm as she reached him. "And you obviously worked hard. I'm sure she appreciated that."

"Yeah, I wasn't sensing a lot of appreciation as she hung over the toilet," he said wearily.

She smiled sympathetically and shrugged. "I suspect she just is not used to her food looking back at her."

Justin shook his head and ran a hand through his hair. "I suppose I should go back in and start cleaning up. I made a hell of a mess in the kitchen and—"

"I'll do that," Gia interrupted. "Why don't you go pick up some subs or something and take one up to Holly? I'm sure she'd like that. She was so hungry she was nauseous while we were waiting for you to finish."

"Was she?" he asked with surprise.

Gia nodded and then pointed out, "That probably did not help."

"No," he agreed, a little relieved that it might not have been all down to the meal he'd made. "Subs, huh?"

Gia nodded. "Or something else if you like. I just said subs because the boys like those second only to pizza, and if you got pizza they might—"

"Eat it all on us," Justin suggested with wry amusement when she hesitated.

Grinning, she nodded and then said with a shrug, "They are big boys."

"Yeah," he agreed dryly. "I'll have to keep that in mind the next time I cook."

"Good thinking," she commented.

Nodding, he started away, then paused and turned back to hug her, offering a soft, "Thanks."

"For what?" she asked with surprise.

"The suggestion," Justin said as he straightened. "And the encouragement. I appreciate it. This life mate business is a little trickier than I expected, what with Holly being married and everything. I'm sure it would have been a breeze for me otherwise, but this was an unexpected complication."

"Oh yes, I'm sure it would have been a breeze were she not married," Gia agreed.

Justin peered at her closely. Despite being straight-faced, he got the feeling she was mocking him, but after a moment he shrugged that concern aside and checked his pocket for the keys to the SUV that had been delivered earlier. Satisfied that he had them, he thanked her again and headed out of the house.

Holly turned restlessly onto her side and sighed unhappily. Despite her charming bout of hanging over the porcelain throne, she was still starved. Unfortunately, she simply couldn't go downstairs in search of food without having to hurt Justin's feelings by refusing the fish.

That thought made her remember the fishy eyes staring dully at her from the platter and Holly shuddered and closed her own eyes on a grimace. She was not a fish eater to begin with. She didn't mind fish-and-chip-type fish, but she had never cared for the fishy flavor some fish had and that fish down on the table in the kitchen had looked pretty fishy to her. Disgusting even. What had Justin been thinking? Good Lord, it was like serving a cow with its head on instead of a roast. Nothing like reminding the eater that their meal had been alive and kicking before it hit the table. Gad!

Rolling onto her back, she tried to sleep, but her thoughts returned to Justin. Despite the debacle it had turned out to be, it had been terribly sweet of him to go to all that trouble. And the man could cook more than spaghetti, which was impressive, she thought. While she didn't care for fish, it had been obvious that what Justin had provided was a gourmet meal. It made her wonder what else he could cook.

Justin also had impeccable manners, she thought as she recalled his holding the door and then seating her at the table like she was a lady of old. It wasn't something she was used to and it had made her feel . . . fussed over, she supposed. Delicate, maybe. Like a lady.

A knock sounded at the door and Holly's eyes popped open.

"Yes?" she said uncertainly after the briefest of hesitations, and then quickly sat up when the door opened to reveal the man she'd been thinking of.

"Hi," Justin said, hesitating in the doorway. "How are you feeling?"

"Better." Holly got quickly to her feet and offered a stiff smile. "What—?"

"I thought if the nausea had passed, you might be hungry," Justin said quickly and held up a take-out bag she hadn't noticed until then. "So I picked up a couple of subs."

"Oh," Holly breathed and was hard put not to launch herself at the man, or at least at the bag he carried as he now closed the door and carried his offerings to a table and chairs positioned in the corner of the room.

"I wasn't sure what you like so I just ordered you an assorted," he said as he set the bag on the table and opened it to begin retrieving items. "I hope that's okay?"

"Fine," Holly assured him, hurrying to join him at the table. She normally ordered a veggie one, or chicken, but right now assorted sounded like heaven. Her eyes widened though when he pulled out a second sandwich, and then a third. Good Lord, he must think she ate like a horse if he thought she—

"I got myself a couple too and thought I'd join you," Justin announced as he began to remove bags of chips and bottles of pop from the bag. "I hope that's okay?"

"Of course," Holly said politely. What else could she do? Say, "No, give me my food and get out"? But she did ask, "What about that . . . er . . . lovely fish you made?"

"By the time I got back to the kitchen Dante and Tomasso had staked their claim to all of it but the head. I'm not big on fish head."

Holly felt her stomach roll alarmingly at just the mention of the fish head and almost groaned aloud.

"I should have grabbed glasses," Justin muttered as he set the bottles of pop on the table. "Again I didn't know what you like so just got Coke."

"Coke is fine," she assured him, and then as she noted the variety of chips he'd chosen, added, "And I love salt and vinegar chips with my sandwiches."

"Me too," he said with a grin, then set the now empty take-out bag aside and headed for the door. "Sit down and start. I'm just going to grab a couple of glasses. Do you want ice too?"

"Sure," Holly murmured, settling at the table and reaching for the nearest bag of chips. She wouldn't even open the sandwich until he got back, but couldn't resist the chips while she waited. Dear God, she was hungry enough to eat a horse . . . as long as its head wasn't still attached, she thought wryly as she opened the chip bag. The astringent scent of vinegar hit her nose as the bag opened. Much to her relief the smell did not make her nauseous like the spicy, curry scent had earlier, so Holly popped a chip in her mouth and moaned as the sharp flavor hit her tongue. Salt and vinegar had never tasted so good as they did in that moment. She really had been hungry. Still was, she acknowledged, her gaze moving idly around the room until it stopped on the bed.

Her eyes widened then as she realized that she was entertaining a man in her bedroom . . . who wasn't her husband. There was nothing sexual about it, but . . . well, Anders and Decker had warned against it.

Biting her lip, she glanced toward the balcony doors and then stood and walked over to peer out at the balcony off her room. It was small and quaint, but it also held a table and chairs . . . and didn't have a bed.

Holly quickly opened the doors and stepped out to examine the table. It looked clean enough, but as she'd expected, there was a fine dusting of dirt or dust across the surface from being outside all the time. Hurrying back into the room, she crossed to the bathroom, found a fresh washcloth, dampened it, grabbed a hand towel and rushed back out to the balcony to give the table and chairs a quick cleaning. She then returned the now dirty items to the bathroom and then gathered up the sandwiches and chips and rushed out to the balcony with them. She'd just set them on the table when she heard Justin call her name.

Stepping back into the room, she noted that he stood in the open door, confusion on his face as he stared at the table in her room that now held only the bottles of pop. Smiling brightly, she hurried over to collect them, as well as the empty take-out bag, announcing, "I thought it would be nice to eat on the balcony.

"Oh." Justin relaxed and closed the door, then followed her outside with the glasses of ice he'd gone to collect.

"See, isn't this nice?" Holly asked cheerfully as she set the pops down and settled in one of the chairs.

"Yes, it is," he said with a smile, peering out over the landscape. "A nice ocean breeze, beautiful views and moonlight. What could be more romantic?"

In the process of unwrapping her sandwich, Holly stilled, alarm coursing through her. Cripes, it *was* romantic when you put it that way. What had she been thinking? Well, she knew what she'd been thinking, that it was better to eat on the balcony than in her bedroom with a big old bed there to give poor love-lorn Justin ideas. Cripes. This was no better.

"Maybe I should get some candles," Justin said now.

"No!" Holly squawked with dismay. The last thing they needed was to make the setting more romantic. Noting that she'd startled him, she forced herself to pitch her voice to a less panicked level, and added, "I'm so hungry, Justin. I can't wait. Let's just eat. Hmmm?"

Fortunately, he nodded agreeably and started to open one of his own sandwiches, rather than go in search of candles.

"I'm sorry about dinner," Justin said after they'd eaten in silence for a few moments. "It didn't occur to me that you might be disturbed by it being served with the head on."

"That's all right," Holly murmured, more interested in her food than the subject at the moment. "It was kind of you to cook for all of us . . . and at least Dante and Tomasso apparently enjoyed your efforts."

"Yeah. They did," he said with a wry smile, and told her, "They ate every last bite of it. They even split the head in the end."

Holly didn't comment, she was too busy trying to swallow the food in her mouth, which had suddenly transformed into a dry nasty ball at the reminder of that damned fish. Deciding a change of topic was necessary if she wanted to enjoy her meal, Holly asked, "So, you were born here in California but live in Canada now?"

In the midst of biting into his sandwich, Justin merely nodded. Once he'd chewed and swallowed though, he added, "My family still lives here, though."

"Oh," she said with surprise, and then tilted her head and asked, "Family?"

"Yeah, you know, mother, father, brothers and sisters. Family." He grinned and teased, "We do have 'em you know. We aren't hatched."

"Yes, of course, I just—are they all vampires too?" she asked, and then tsked with exasperation at herself and said, "Of course they are. If you're over a hundred, you'd hardly still have parents and siblings alive if they weren't."

Justin nodded at her deduction. "My parents are old. Not as old as Lucian or anything, but old enough. Dad was born around the time of William the Conqueror. He fought alongside him in battle, in fact. Mom, though, wasn't born until the late fourteenth century, during the peasants' revolt in England, about 1381 I think, he added, to give her a reference point.

"Oh," Holly breathed, sitting back slightly. Cripes, his parents were ancient.

"I have three brothers and three sisters," he added. "Each the dutiful century apart. I'm the second youngest. The oldest is my brother Cam. He was born shortly after my parents mated and is over six hundred years old. My younger sister is six, no seven, this year."

"Wow," she murmured. "That's . . . wow."

Justin chuckled softly and shrugged. "I suppose it would be to a mortal. To me, it's just my family."

"Right." Holly shook her head, finding it hard to imagine that seeming normal to anyone. But then she'd grown up in the mortal world, where older siblings were usually one to ten years and sometimes even as much as twenty years older, but never five or six centuries.

"Do you have any brothers or sisters?" Justin asked.

She watched him pick up the last of his first sandwich and pop it in his mouth, marveling that he had finished a whole foot-long sub while she was only halfway through one half of hers. It seemed Dante and Tomasso weren't the only ones who ate a lot. Her mother would have said it was because he was eating too fast, and if he'd just slow down he'd realize one sandwich would more than fill him up. Thoughts of her mom reminded her of his question, and Holly cleared her throat.

"No. I was an only child," she said, and then smiled wryly and added. "Apparently, I was pretty much an accident."

His eyebrows rose. "Why would you say that?"

"Because my parents told me so," Holly said with a shrug and added, "Mom and Dad are archaeologists. They love what they do and are pretty much obsessed with it to the exclusion of everything else. If they aren't on a dig, they're planning and finding the funding for one. It doesn't leave a lot of time for kids."

He nodded slowly, his brows drawing together with what appeared to be concern. "Where did you stay when they went on these digs?"

"Oh, they took me with them," she said lightly, and noting his surprise, nodded. "They did. I grew up in tents around the world, a couple months or a year in one place, and then on to the next."

"You never went to school?" he asked with a frown.

"James's mom taught us," she explained and when he looked blank, added, "My husband, James. His father was an archaeologist on my father's team too.

His mother was a schoolteacher, but she gave up her job to join his dad on the digs and homeschooled us both. It was really very handy all the way around."

"Yes, I guess so," he murmured thoughtfully, and then commented, "So you've known James a long time."

"All of my life," she said with a small smile. "We were playmates as tiny tots, best friends during the preteens, boyfriend and girlfriend as teens and then . . ." She shrugged. "When I turned eighteen, we went off to college together. Well, actually, university," she said with a smile. "We both went to the university of British Columbia."

"British Columbia, Canada?" he clarified, and when she nodded, asked curiously, "Why?"

"It's where James's mom is from and where she went to university."

"So she steered you toward it," Justin guessed.

Holly nodded. "But both our families live down here in California. Well, our families' families I guess," she corrected. "Grandparents, aunts and uncles and such. James's dad was from California. He met James's mom while lecturing at her university. Anyway, after growing up in places like Egypt and such, BC seemed a bit chilly to us, and we both wanted to be closer to family, so once James graduated last year, we moved down here to look for work."

"And then you married," he guessed.

Holly shook her head. "Actually, we married almost four years ago. We had both finished our bachelors in our fields. We were living in different dorms on campus and finding it a bit difficult to handle after the life we'd led, so we decided to marry and move off campus together. I worked while he got his MBA in applied science, and now he's working while I finish my courses to become an accountant."

"But you've always been together," he said slowly, a frown plucking at his face.

"Always," she said solemnly. "He was my first kiss, my first date, and my first love."

"I see," Justin whispered, then grabbed his second sandwich and rather than open it, slid it back into the take-out bag, grabbed it, his empty chip bag and his pop and glass and headed inside. "I have to talk to Gia."

Holly stared after him silently. She wasn't terribly surprised by his reaction. That might even be part of the reason she'd said what she had. He had to understand that she was married, and happily, and that she loved her husband. She was not open to being his life mate. Still, she hated to hurt his feelings.

Sighing, Holly glanced down to the remainder of her sandwich and then began wrapping it up. She'd finish it later, maybe. For now, she'd lost her appetite.

"I shouldn't have turned her," Justin muttered, pacing the length of Gia's bedroom. "I should have waited for Marguerite to find me a mate. She never messes up like this."

"You did what you thought was right at the time," Gia said solemnly.

"Well, it was a mistake," Justin said harshly. "She's married."

"Yes, she is," Gia agreed.

"But I mean *really* married. She's known this guy since she was a kid. She grew up with him. He was her first kiss and her first love, for God's sake. She'll never leave him. Not even for me," he said with dismay.

"Maybe not," Gia agreed. "Or maybe she will."

"I threw my one turn away for nothing," Justin realized with horror.

"Would you really rather she had died?" Gia asked patiently.

"Of course not," he snapped. "I would rather she hadn't fallen on the damned scissors at all. What kind of an idiot runs with scissors?" he asked with sudden fury.

Gia bit her lip, he suspected to keep from laughing, and shook her head. "Well, sadly, she did run with scissors, did fall on them, and you did turn her to save her life when you realized she was your life mate. Now, I suggest you deal with it."

Justin scowled at her grimly and then snatched up the take-out bag and his drink from her dresser, where he'd set them on entering and whirled to storm out of her room.

"Deal with it," he muttered to himself as he stomped downstairs. "Just deal with the fact that you turned a woman you can't have. Nice. Thanks for that, Gia. Very helpful advice."

"Talking to yourself, Bricker?"

Pausing at the foot of the stairs, he scowled at Dante as the man passed with several jumbo bags of chips and a six-pack of cola in hand. Scowling, Justin said, "It's more useful than talking to members of the fairer sex."

"Don't let Gia hear you say that. She'll kick your ass," Dante warned before disappearing into the living room.

"Too late," Justin muttered, turning toward the

kitchen. "Life has already kicked my ass, and has left precious little for her to have at."

"Trouble?" Tomasso asked as Justin pushed into the kitchen.

Justin glanced to the big guy, noting that he was folding a dish towel and setting it on the counter. The twins had helped Gia clean, obviously, or perhaps even done it all themselves. He wouldn't have been surprised. It wasn't like she had eaten anything. The pair probably would have felt bad to make her do the cleaning up when they'd eaten every last scrap of food he'd made.

"I gather you overheard what I said to your brother?" Justin asked finally, carrying his sandwich over to put it in the refrigerator for later . . . when he'd regained his appetite.

Tomasso grunted in the affirmative and Justin closed the fridge door with a sigh. "Holly has known her husband all her life. They were childhood friends and sweethearts. She isn't likely to throw him over for me. She hardly knows me."

"Then maybe she needs to," Tomasso said mildly as he moved to open the cupboard and began to retrieve the rest of the jumbo-sized bags of chips inside.

Justin watched him, but his mind was on what he'd said. "You think I should continue to woo her? Let her get to know me? You think she might choose me then?"

"Only one way to find out," Tomasso said with a shrug. Chips stacked in one beefy arm, he reached into the refrigerator with his free hand and retrieved a six-pack of soda. "What have you got to lose?"

"Right," Justin murmured thoughtfully, and then noted what the man had in his arms and said, "Dante already took out chips and pop."

"Those were for him." Tomasso moved to the door to the hall. As he pushed through, he added, "These are for me."

"Oh," Justin said as he watched the door swing closed. Shaking his head, he turned back toward the table, muttering, "We're going to need to go shopping again."

He started to sit down at the table, but then paused and moved to the drawer beside the refrigerator to retrieve one of the notepads and pens Jackie kept there. She kept them there for making grocery lists. He wanted it for another list entirely. He was going to make up a list of ways to woo Holly.

Dropping to sit at the kitchen table, he opened the notebook to the first page and wrote, "Battle Strategy." He then sat back and smiled at what he'd written . . . because this was war. He was fighting for his life mate, and perhaps even his very life . . . and in the battle of the sexes, he was king. There wasn't a woman he had wanted that he hadn't been able to win, and he wanted Holly.

Ten

"Think sex."

"What?" Holly gaped at the trio in front of her. It was Saturday morning after the fish debacle. After Justin had left her room, Holly had laid down to rest rather than risk running into him again for a bit, and she'd slept through what little had been left of the night. Now it was morning, they'd all had breakfast and Justin, Dante, and Tomasso had all decided it was time to move ahead with her lessons on how to be an immortal. Apparently, it wasn't a natural thing. One didn't become immortal and simply automatically know how to do everything they needed to know how to do. She'd thought they were ridiculous when they'd said that, until they'd asked her to "get" her fangs out.

She'd laughed at the comment. The way they said it made it sound as if she had them in her pocket. But she'd stopped laughing when they'd insisted and she'd tried, only to realize she hadn't a clue how to "get" them out. Thinking, "Come on, fangs. Pop out of my mouth . . . please . . . pretty please." Hadn't worked at all. Now they were giving her suggestions.

"Think sex," Tomasso repeated completely straight-faced.

"Like the smell of blood when you're hungry, sexual excitement can bring on your fangs," Justin explained quietly.

"Oh," she said weakly.

"It's all right," Dante said quietly. "Just close your eyes and imagine you and your husband in bed."

Holly blushed furiously at the suggestion, and then shook her head. "I'm not sitting here thinking of sex with the three of you all standing there grinning at me like a bunch of perverts."

Actually, Justin wasn't grinning at the suggestion, she noticed. If anything, he looked strained, but she didn't take back her words.

Dante nodded as if he'd expected as much and then turned to Bricker. "Kiss her."

"What?" They both squawked that word together.

"Kiss her," Dante insisted. "She has to learn to control her fangs. Especially how to put them away."

"Dante is right," Gia said from the kitchen door. She'd been up most of the night after the fish incident and apparently was just now rising. Letting the kitchen door close, she moved to join them at the table and pointed out, "Bringing out her fangs is important, but being able to make them recede again is more important. She has to know how to put them away in case they come out of their own volition while she is among mortals. You wouldn't want her standing in a grocery store or a restaurant with her fangs out and not be able to force them away."

"Exactly," Dante said with satisfaction. "Kiss her."

Holly frowned, but then so did Justin. He also glanced to her uncertainly and seeing her expression, shook his head unhappily. "I don't think—"

"Then I will," Dante announced and stepped forward.

"The hell you will!" Justin protested, grabbing his arm and hauling him back.

"Then kiss her," Dante growled. "Bring on her passion and her fangs."

"Oh, I'm sure that's not really necessary," Holly began to babble at once when Justin turned grimly toward her. Beginning to back away, she added quickly, "I mean, no offense, but I'm sure he can't bring on my passion. I'm married, and I love my husband, and mummph mmmm mummph—" The end of her protest was muffled by his mouth when it closed over hers. But it stopped entirely when he took advantage of her attempt at continued denial and sucked one of her flapping lips between his own.

Good Lord, what the hell was he doing? She wondered faintly as his arms slid around her, his hands moving down to cup her behind and urge her up against him. That wasn't kissing. That was . . . oh dear, she thought weakly as his tongue thrust into her mouth and she felt not just a flutter of passion, but an entire damned tsunami of it washing through her body. Dear God, the man was devouring her. He was . . . he was . . .

Not caring what the hell he was, she gave up her thoughts and reached up to wrap her arms around his neck as her mouth opened wider in welcome. Holly had never been kissed like this. James had never kissed her as if his very life depended on it, as if he was desperate to explore every nook and cranny of her lips, teeth and tongue. As if she held the secret to the universe somewhere in her mouth and he was determined to find it with his own. His body was giving off so much heat she felt singed, and there was a hardness growing between them that she was quite sure was not expanding foam someone had shot between their groins—although she would have understood if they had, and the insulation would have been appreciated. Holly was quite sure she was about to burst into flames down there and the hardness growing between his legs was hot enough to curl her hair.

Tasting blood on her tongue was enough to shock these ridiculous thoughts right out of her head. She'd bitten him, Holly realized and pulled her head back with alarm.

"I'm thorry," she lisped around the fangs protruding from her jaw, feeling horrible about biting the man in the tongue.

"Good job," Dante said gruffly and slapped Justin on the shoulder.

He'd still been holding her in his arms, a pained expression on his face, but now eased away from her. He didn't just let her go, though, but turned and walked out of the kitchen.

"Ith he o'ay?" she asked, the words garbled around her fangs. God, it was hard to talk with these darned things out.

"He's fine," Gia said reassuringly. "He's probably going to rinse his mouth."

"And take a cold shower," Dante added with amusement.

"Definitely," Tomasso agreed, grinning from ear to ear.

Gia gave her cousins a look and then stepped up next to Holly. "Now, let's concentrate on getting your fangs back where they belong. Shall we?"

"Idiot, idiot, idiot," Justin chanted, banging his head repeatedly against the ceramic tile of the shower wall as cold water poured down over the back of his black T-shirt and jeans.

Getting undressed before the cold shower he was suffering would have taken too long for him to bother with. Especially since he'd been battling mightily against the insane urge to march right back to the kitchen, pick up Holly, carry her up here to his room, rip off her clothes and ravish her.

He banged his head against the wall again to remove the images that thought brought to mind. What had he been thinking? How had he let those two big buffoons goad him into kissing her? That had been the worst possible thing he could have done at this stage. Now he'd had a taste of what he would lose if he didn't win her over, and . . . dear God, nothing he'd experienced before had prepared him for the way his body had reacted when he'd kissed Holly.

Justin was no virgin. Nor was he an ancient immortal who had given up women ages ago and couldn't remember sex. He'd had more women in the last century than he'd care to admit. And he'd had some damned fine sex too. Hot, sweaty, knock your socks off, unforgettable sex.

And every one of those experiences faded to nothing next to a simple kiss from Holly.

"Holy, fuck a duck," he muttered, banging his head again. If he'd known . . .

Hell, if he'd known what the others had been experiencing with this wave of immortals finding their life mates . . . well, he might just have kidnapped Marguerite at sword point and demanded she find him his mate. That or blow his own head off with envy.

"Christ on a cracker," he muttered, slamming his head again. His entire body was still vibrating with his response to their kiss. It was as if the millions of nanos in his body had turned into sparklers and were doing little "Whoopee" dances from his head to his toes.

"Whoop-dee-fucking-doo!" Justin growled, hitting the wall again. How was he supposed to act natural around her after this? How was he supposed to keep his hands off of her? And why the heck wasn't she up here, crawling all over him like flies on shit?

That thought had him growling under his breath with frustration. Holly hadn't seemed as affected by the kiss as him. Sure, she'd kissed him back almost desperately, but the moment she'd tasted a little blood, she'd jumped back with a sort of horror, as if she'd mortally wounded him.

"Screw the blood," he muttered, banging his head again. She could have bitten his tongue clean off and he wouldn't have stopped kissing her. Who cared? It would grow back, for cripes sake and kissing her was worth losing a lot of body parts over and having to grow them back. Sex with her, though . . . he thought he might risk his life for that. How could they not have told him what he was missing?

"Bastards," Justin growled, but instead of banging his head again, he turned in the shower and let the cold water hit his front. It certainly hadn't been doing much good on his back. He was still hard as a damned flagpole . . . for all the good that did him. He was a flagpole without a flag, a tent pole without a tent to cover him, a fishing pole without a—okay not a fishing pole. They were bendy and—

"And why the hell am I having this conversation in my poor muddled head?" he asked himself with disgust. But the answer was obvious enough. Because he *was* muddled. He was a muddled, horny dog who presently couldn't think of anything but getting Holly naked and planting his flagpole in her sweet wet ground.

"All right, Bricker, old boy. You've lost your everloving mind," Justin told himself grimly as he took note of his own thoughts. Fortunately, he'd also lost his erection with the shame of spouting such nonsense. Sighing his relief, he turned off the shower and stepped out to drip all over the bathroom floor. A mess he'd have to clean up later, Justin realized. Man, he really was an idiot.

He began to strip off his soaking clothes, removing his T-shirt first and tossing it back into the shower before setting to work on his jeans. That was a mammoth task. Wet jeans did not come off easily and he struggled with it, banging against the wall repeatedly as he nearly toppled over. Once off, those joined the T-shirt on the shower floor, then Justin grabbed a towel and quickly dried himself off.

He was in his bedroom, standing in front of the closet, donning a fresh pair of black jeans when a knock sounded at the door.

Snapping the snap, and doing up the zipper, he called, "Yeah?" and wasn't surprised when the door opened.

Gia stuck her head in, glanced around until she

spotted him and then seeing him, smiled and stepped into the room. "How are you feeling?"

"Fine," Justin growled, snatching a fresh T-shirt off a hanger, and tugging it over his head. "What's going on downstairs?"

"Holly has mastered bringing on and retracting her fangs," Gia told him with a smile.

"What?" he squawked, stilling with his shirt half on. "Already?"

Gia nodded. "She's a very fast learner, and your kisses helped. All she has to do now is think of you kissing her to make them come out."

Justin grunted and finished pulling the shirt on, not sure how to take that. Was it good that thoughts of his kisses brought her teeth out? It meant just thinking of or remembering their kiss turned her on. That had to be good, right?

"You even helped her with retracting them," she added and the amusement in her voice made him suspicious until she added, "She just thinks of your fish dinner and they go away—Poof!" she said and laughed at his expression. Moving forward, Gia gave him a motherly hug, cooing, "Oh, do not be sad. She appreciated the effort. And you definitely got her attention with that kiss."

"Did I?" he asked dubiously.

"Of course, you did," she assured him.

"Well, she sure pulled away in a hurry," Justin complained.

"She thought she'd hurt you," Gia said solemnly. She hesitated, and then added, "Of course, now she feels just horrible and her guilt is twofold."

"Twofold?" he asked with a frown.

Gia nodded. "She feels bad because she fears she hurt you, and she is experiencing a great deal of guilt. One, because she feels that she was unfaithful to her husband by responding to your kisses."

Justin ran a weary hand through his hair and shook his head. He didn't like the idea that she was feeling guilty about the kiss. She hadn't chosen it. They'd pretty much forced it on her. Actually, it had been pretty much forced on both of them since there was no way in hell he would have stood by and allowed Dante to try to build that kind of fire in Holly, and Dante had known it.

"Yes, Dante was very naughty," Gia murmured, apparently reading his mind. "He wanted you both to have a little taste of what you could have together. Holly so that she knows what she is missing, and you so that you understand just what you are fighting for here and take it seriously."

"He told you that?" Justin asked with surprise.

"No. I read his mind," she said with amusement. "Dante and Tomasso are easy for me to read."

"Right, well Holly won't think about what she could have with me so long as she's suffering guilt over what she considers being unfaithful to her husband," Justin said grimly and was quite sure it was true . . . although he couldn't say how he knew that about her. "And I could be in trouble for it. Kissing her and rousing the life mate passion could be considered undue influence."

"Dante forced you. It wasn't your idea," Gia argued.

"I could have let him kiss her."

"Few immortals could stand by and allow another immortal to kiss their life mate. Nor would they expect you to."

"I hope you're right. Otherwise, my favorite body part might be in peril."

"I thought you had decided her kiss was worth losing body parts and growing them back?" she said with amusement. "I'm pretty sure I read that from your mind when she stopped the kiss."

"Stay out of my head," he snapped and then, sorry for snapping at her when she was just trying to help, ran a weary hand through his hair and admitted, "Yeah. I thought that, and still do. But having to grow back a body part once is a different story than having your dick shredded over a hundred times. With the healing time in between, it would mean agony for—Hell I don't even know how long," he muttered, fighting the urge to cross his legs and cover his groin protectively with his hands. "Besides, I don't want to lose my job."

"Why would you lose your job?" she asked with surprise.

"The council tends to frown on having Enforcers who break our own laws," he said dryly.

"Oh." She bit her lip briefly and then said, "There is another reason Holly feels guilty, you know."

Justin's eyebrows rose slightly. The comment was so out of the blue . . . and he'd thought they were done with that part of the conversation. It seemed not, he thought and asked, "What reason is that?"

"Because thoughts of your one kiss bring on her fangs, while memories of all of her husband's kisses do not," she said quietly.

Justin's head jerked up at these words, his mind whirling. This was good, wasn't it? Not the guilt, of course, but that his kisses did what her husband's couldn't. At least the memories of them. Of course, as her life mate he'd known his kisses would have more affect than her mortal husband's, but it surprised him that her husband's kisses didn't stir enough passion to bring on her fangs. That was rather interesting, actually, and telling.

"Well," Gia headed for the door. "I came to tell you that we are ending lessons for the day and taking Holly shopping." Pausing at the door, she glanced back and added, "And to see if you want to join us. The boys want more food and Holly needs clothes."

Justin considered the matter briefly and then shook his head. He wasn't going to get to woo Holly with Gia and the twins along. But their absence would give him the chance to move his wooing campaign ahead in other ways.

"You go on," he said now, a smile pulling at his lips. "I have things to do around here."

Gia peered at him curiously. Reading his mind, no doubt, he thought when concentration filled her face. After a moment, she smiled faintly, and nodded. *"Buona fortuna amico mio."*

Justin merely grunted as she closed the door to his room. "Good luck, my friend," she'd said, but he didn't need luck. He had a plan.

"Why don't you go upstairs and change into your new clothes?" Gia suggested as she followed Holly into the house from the garage.

"I was going to help bring in the groceries," Holly said uncertainly, glancing back toward the loaded SUV. Dante and Tomasso were bigger shoppers than Decker, Anders, and Justin put together. But then they were also bigger eaters. In the two short days since they'd arrived, the twins had gone through nearly half the groceries the other men had bought.

"The boys can handle it," Gia assured her. "And

you aren't terribly comfortable in those clothes of mine."

Holly grimaced at the comment and glanced down at herself. She had got up this morning, re-donned the sweater and tights Gia had given her the day before and then opened her bedroom door to find another outfit neatly folded and set on the hall floor. Relieved that she wouldn't have to wear the same clothes twice, Holly had scooped them up and backed into the room to change. But the moment she'd realized how short the skirt was, and how see-through the top, she'd nearly changed back. Gia's style was definitely edgy/sexy, while Holly's style was . . . well, just not. She was more the jeans and T-shirt kind of gal when she wasn't dressed up for work. And yes, she had been terribly uncomfortable in the other woman's clothes.

Mind you, she hadn't been any more comfortable at allowing the woman to pay for the clothes she was now wearing. Even when Gia had explained that she wasn't buying them, the Enforcers were. Apparently, since Justin had turned her while on an Enforcer job, they were footing the bill for everything from the food they were eating to the clothes on her back.

"You're right," Holly said finally. "I guess I'm just not brave enough for your clothes. But they are beautiful and I do appreciate your letting me borrow them."

"Bah." Gia waved away her words. "I knew that. I can read your mind," she reminded her and then urged her forward. "Come, let's get these up to your room."

Nodding, Holly turned and led the way upstairs. She had to do some juggling once they got to her door to open it, but then she stumbled in, headed for the bed, only to pause after just a couple of steps.

"What the—?" She turned slowly, her gaze moving over the flowers on every surface in the room. Flower arrangements sat on the bedside tables, crowded the dresser and covered every inch of the sitting table in the corner of the room. There were even flowers strewn on the bed and petals on the floor.

"Ah," Gia said, and that was it. Just "ah."

Holly shook her head with bewilderment. "Did someone die?"

Gia choked on a laugh and moved past her to the bed. She started to set the bags down, then paused to brush some of the flowers out of the way first. Setting the bags down then, she turned to survey the room and said, "I think maybe this is Justin's idea of the *romanticismo*."

"*Romanticismo*?" Holly echoed blankly. "What the devil is that?"

Gia frowned briefly and then offered, "The romance?"

Holly groaned at the suggestion. Decker and Anders had warned her that he might go a bit over the top in his desperation, but this was . . .

Well, it was kind of sweet, really, she supposed. Or would be if she hadn't developed such an aversion to flowers since working at the funeral home. Prior to that she would have welcomed such a gesture. From James, she added quickly to the thought. She would have welcomed flowers from James before working at the funeral home, but they had both been as poor as church mice since getting married and hadn't been able to afford the extravagance of even a vase of flowers let alone a whole bloody store's stock, and that's what it looked like to her. There were so many she was quite sure Justin must have left the store he'd bought them from completely barren of flowers. They'd probably closed shop the moment he left.

Shaking her head, she carried her bags over to the bed and set them next to the ones Gia had put down. She then glanced worriedly at the pale blue carpeting, concerned that the crushed petals might be staining the carpet.

"I don't suppose you noticed if there was a rake in the garage, did you?" Holly asked, surveying the floor with a frown. For some reason that made Gia burst out laughing.

"I will go see," Gia said, heading for the door.

"Oh, no," Holly protested at once, turning to move after her. "I didn't mean for you to—"

"I know, I know," Gia said, waving her to a stop. "I can read your mind, remember? You change. I shall get the rake."

"Thank you," Holly breathed sincerely and watched her go before returning to the bags that held the clothes she'd bought that day. She quickly dug through them in search of underwear, a bra, jeans and a T-shirt, and then paused, unsure what to do. Gia had told her to change, but the woman had also left the door open. She wasn't changing right there when any passing person might see. On the other hand, she didn't really want to risk crushing any more color into the carpet by walking anywhere again.

Clucking her tongue with exasperation, she toed a couple petals aside in front of her until she'd made a spot large enough to place her foot. She then stepped forward and did that again and again until she'd made her way to the bathroom. She opened that door, only to find it also full of flowers and crushed petals.

"Honestly," Holly muttered, using her foot to sweep several petals aside. "What the heck was he thinking?"

As soon as the exasperated words left her mouth, a smile followed. The gesture was just so over the top and romantic. Much like the gourmet meal, she acknowledged. She would have been happy with salad, Shake 'N Bake pork chops, and macaroni and cheese for dinner. Instead, he'd spent hours making a fancy meal and gone to all the effort of setting that beautiful table. And a simple bouquet of flowers would have been much less bother than this sea of blooms. The man was trying. It was just a shame his efforts kept missing the mark.

Holly blinked and gave her head a shake as she realized what she was thinking. It wasn't a shame at all, she assured herself firmly if silently. She was a married woman. He shouldn't even be making these gestures. And she certainly shouldn't be enjoying them and feeling all warm and fuzzy inside because of them.

Satisfied that she'd set herself straight, Holly slipped into the bathroom, closed the door, and quickly began ripping her clothes off. She was determined to be changed and ready to rake up this mess when Gia returned. There was no way she was letting the other woman do it. This was her mess and—well, really it was Justin's mess, she corrected herself. But after experiencing that morning's kiss, she wasn't ever letting him in her bedroom again. Ever. Like never ever.

Holly's parents hadn't raised an idiot. They had taught her that life was full of temptation. And her mother had sat down on her wedding day and flat out told her that while she knew Holly loved James, there may come a day when a good-looking, sweet, funny, charming man like Justin might come along and tempt her to break the vows she'd made when she married James. Well, okay, so she hadn't mentioned Justin's name, and she hadn't used all those descriptors either. Holly had inserted those herself because they fit. But her mother had said a man might one day come along to tempt her to break her vows. She'd also said that while it was her choice what to do about that, she should be aware that James had known and loved her, her whole life. That he would never do anything to hurt her, and that there was always another man who might come along to tempt her from that one. Life was full of temptation and she could either spend her life chasing after the next merry-go-round, or ride the one she was on until the end, knowing it was a comfortable fit.

James was the merry-go-round she planned to stick with to the end. She'd known him all her life, loved him all her life, and knew that he loved her the same way. And while Justin was sweet and kind and had saved her life by turning her into an immortal when she fell on her scissors . . . well, what if she broke her marriage vows for him and then encountered another Justin, and then another?

Holly didn't want to be one of those women with countless lovers and six marriages under their belt, who seemed always to be dissatisfied and searching for something special. She would be satisfied with what she had and continue to build the life that she'd started with James. She'd finish her classes, get the on-the-job experience necessary and gain her license as a CPA. Then they'd both work for a couple of years to save up money to buy a house, have children, raise them, see them married and have grandchildren. She would have the normal life she'd always longed for while she'd been dragged around the world as a child. Both she and James wanted that.

And they would have it, Holly thought grimly, as she finished changing and opened the door, only to pause with surprise. Not only had Gia returned with the rake, she'd already raked up the petals. The carpet was completely petal free. It was also rake and Gia free. The other woman had apparently returned, raked up the petals, and left in the time it had taken her to change. Holly had been told that immortals were fast, but this was crazy.

The thought made her pause and tilt her head. She was an immortal. That meant she was supposed to be incredibly fast now too, and strong. She hadn't seen any evidence of that yet, but then she hadn't done anything to test it either. Stepping into the bedroom, Holly glanced around until her gaze settled on the dresser. She crossed to it, took a corner in hand, and nearly tossed the damned thing across the room when she tried to lift the end. Seriously, she put the effort into it that she would have had to prior to being turned, when she might have managed to lift the solid oak dresser an inch or so. But instead of that, it flew up, onto its side and then crashed down onto its top.

"Oh crap," she muttered, scrambling to quickly straighten the dresser. Once she had it upright and in position again, Holly spent a minute looking it over to be sure she hadn't damaged it and then stepped back with relief and simply peered at the dresser.

"Wow," she said finally. She was definitely stronger. A slow smile curved her lips. Now she just had to test speed. Turning abruptly, she headed out of the room and jogged downstairs.

Dante and Tomasso were at the kitchen table, eating again. Each had a double chocolate cake before them, a whole cake each. Really, those two had appetites that were scary. There was no sign of the groceries they'd bought, so either they'd tossed the bags straight into the pantry without unpacking them, or they'd used that super speed she was about to test.

"Have you seen Justin?" she asked, slowing as she crossed to the terrace doors.

"I think he's in the garage looking for a basket," Dante answered, and then frowned. "Or upstairs fetching a blanket."

Holly bit her lip, but didn't stop. She needed to thank him for the flowers, and explain that he should never do that again. But she didn't really want to wait for him. Besides, she wouldn't be long.

"Well, I'll find him when I get back then," she said aloud and added, "I'm just going for a jog on the beach. Be back soon."

Both men grunted, their mouths full of cake.

Shaking her head, Holly stepped outside and pulled the door closed, then headed around the pool to the gate in the hedges. A moment later, she was crossing the lawn to the beach. Once there, she looked first one way and then the other up the beach, chose right and burst into a run.

Increased speed they'd said? Dear God, she thought as the world whizzed by. This was almost superman speed. Okay, the world wasn't a complete blur, but it was blurring. She was definitely moving faster than mortally possible. Scary fast, in fact, she thought and put the brakes on. That's when she figured out just how fast she was going. Instead of coming to a graceful stop, she skidded briefly and then went ass over teakettle, landing flat on her back with a thud.

Lying still for a moment, Holly quickly took inventory to see if she'd hurt anything. The answer was no. Nothing hurt but her pride, and even that wasn't suffering much. It wasn't like anyone was around to see. Besides, she was too busy being amazed at just how fast she could move now to worry about anything else.

"Wow," she breathed, staring up at the darkening sky, and then she smiled. "I rock."

The words made her laugh slightly, which made her realize that she wasn't even out of breath, which just impressed her more. Gym had not been a part of the homeschooling James's mom had given them. Not that Holly had minded. She'd never been the athletic sort. She was more the bookish type, but then she hadn't had access to television in those tents they'd lived in while she was growing up. Now she loved movies, action adventures especially, with horrors and comedies tying as second favorites.

Realizing she was lying in the sand, something she wasn't too keen on, Holly got quickly to her feet, brushed herself down and then turned to head back the way she'd come. She'd run a lot farther than she'd realized, but while she could have run back just as quickly as she'd run out, she didn't bother. Walking back would give her the chance to think about what she was going to say to Justin. Manners had been drummed into her as she'd grown up, and those manners suggested she should thank him for the flowers. On the other hand, she was married. He shouldn't be giving her flowers. And she shouldn't be accepting them.

Sighing, Holly brushed the hair back from her face and tried to think what she should say to him. "Thank you for the thought, Justin. But I really can't accept your flowers. I'm married."

That was nice and simple and to the point. She also wouldn't be thanking him for the actual flowers themselves, which, honestly, she didn't really appreciate at all. She had definitely gained a serious aversion to them, it seemed. She hadn't been joking when she'd asked if someone had died on seeing them. That had been her first thought . . . which was kind of sad, Holly acknowledged. She was only going to work at the cemetery for another . . . well, actually, she wasn't even sure if she'd be going back once she had finished her training. It seemed a shame to let less than two weeks working at the place affect her view of flowers for the rest of her life.

Perhaps she just needed to think of them differently, she considered and then raised her eyebrows when she noted that someone was on the beach in front of Jackie and Vincent's house.

Justin, she realized. Why was he laying out a blanket? The sun was setting. Besides, she didn't think vampires were likely to be sun worshippers so he couldn't be interested in sunbathing. Although, she wouldn't mind seeing that; Justin in a bathing suit, his chest bare, his muscular legs—

Holly slowed as her wandering thoughts brought guilt crashing down over her. Married, she reminded herself. No lusting after other men . . . even if they were handsome, built, sweet as pie and amazing kissers. That last thought caused a sigh to slip between her lips. Justin *was* an amazing kisser.

Parts of her started tingling just at the memory, parts that had no business tingling for anyone but her husband.

As distressing as it was for Holly to admit, James had never made her tingle like that. James's kisses were more . . . well, she hated to say it, but the best description she could come up with was almost avuncular. They were affectionate and . . . tepid? She winced even as she admitted that.

But marriage wasn't all about hot, sweaty sex, she assured herself. She and James had more than that. They had a common past, friendship, and affection. They had history . . . and the same dream for the future. That was more likely to last, she was sure. Justin was like a shooting star, burning bright before fizzing out as all such heated passion must . . . while James was like the moon, always there, giving off a soft, steady glow. She just had to keep that in the forefront of her mind while she was here, Holly determined. It would help keep her head straight and prevent her giving in to the temptation Justin was quickly becoming. Avoiding him, or at least avoiding being alone with him would help too, she decided.

"Hi."

Holly stopped walking with surprise as that word drew her from her thoughts. While she'd been thinking, her feet had carried her across the distance between them and brought her to the edge of the blanket he sat on in the sand. So much for avoiding him, she thought with mild self-disgust. Sucking in a deep breath, she raised her shoulders determinedly, and opened her mouth, intending to respond to his greeting and then continue on to the house.

"Sit," Justin said before she could do anything. He

patted the blanket next to a covered basket that sat in front of him. "I thought it would be nice to have a picnic."

"Oh . . . er . . ." Holly shifted and glanced from Justin to the basket and finally toward the house, her head moving slowly back and forth, before she said, "I don't think—"

"I need to tell you our laws and rules as part of your training," Justin interrupted.

Holly stilled briefly, feeling somewhat trapped, but then said, "Can't we do that in the house?"

"It's just a picnic, Holly," he said solemnly. "What are you afraid of?"

She suspected it wouldn't be a good thing to tell him that she was afraid of herself and her response to him, so avoided answering the question by using truth as a shield. "After spending the first eighteen years of my life digging sand out of crevices and spots it should never be, including my food, I'm not really keen on picnics on the beach."

Oh." He looked stunned at this news, and then glanced at the blanket he sat on. After a moment, he grabbed the basket and stood. "Right. I should have thought."

He looked so disappointed that Holly felt another wave of guilt roll over her. As with the flowers and last night's meal, he'd probably gone to a lot of trouble preparing this picnic. The problem was she didn't want him to expend effort on her. Still, she didn't like hurting anyone's feelings and he looked hurt just then. Mouth tightening, Holly bent and grabbed a corner of the blanket as he stepped off.

"There's no reason you should have thought of that," she said with a shrug as she straightened, lifting the blanket off the ground as she did.

Justin didn't comment, merely murmuring thank you as she quickly folded the blanket and laid it over her arm. But as they started to walk back up the lawn toward the gate in the hedges, he said pensively, "It sounds like you didn't really enjoy following your parents around on their digs."

"There were some good points, I guess," she said slowly.

"But?" he prompted when she fell silent.

Holly shrugged and admitted, "Well, there were a lot of things I didn't have growing up that it would have been nice to have."

"Like?" he asked, sounding sincerely interested.

Holly smiled crookedly and quickly listed off, "Television, wifi, cell phones, the mall . . . friends. Female friends," she added quickly. "I mean, of course, James was my friend."

"Of course," he said tightly.

Sighing, she stopped walking and when he did as well, turned to face him. "The flowers were a nice thought, but—"

"You're married," Justin said quietly for her.

She nodded. "I know you think I'm a possible life mate, Justin. But I *am* married, and I take my vows seriously. I'd appreciate it if you just got on with my training so that I can go home and continue my life with my husband."

Rather than respond, he turned and continued walking again. After a moment, Holly followed, trailing him back to the house and into the kitchen. It was empty now. Apparently Dante and Tomasso had finished their cake and, judging by the muffled sounds coming from the front of the house, were back in the living room watching another action movie. That or they were having a very quiet shoot out. She doubted real explosions and gunfire would sound so muted.

"There's fried chicken and potato salad in the basket," Justin said, setting it on the table as she closed the door. "Help yourself."

"Aren't you having any?" she asked with surprise when he started out of the kitchen.

"No," was all he said.

Holly frowned after him as he slipped out of the room, letting the door swing closed behind him. Then she set the blanket over a chair, opened the basket and began transferring the food it held to the refrigerator. She wasn't really hungry. She should be, it had been hours since she'd eaten, but she just wasn't.

Eleven

"She doesn't like picnics on the beach," Justin muttered to himself with disgust as he paced the room he was using while here.

He should have realized. Justin briefly berated himself for not knowing, and then more fairly thought, well, okay, how could he know that? But, really, once she'd said that bit about picking sand out of everything for the first part of her life it had made perfect sense. He didn't care for picnics on the beach himself for that very reason and he hadn't spent years doing it. He should have arranged the picnic on the lawn instead. No sand there.

And she didn't like fish with the head and tails on. That one, he definitely should have thought of. He knew she liked fish, Anders and Decker had found that out for him, but he was sure a lot of people who liked fish would probably be turned off by the head and tails and skin being left on. He

should have considered that possibility and prepared trout almondine or something.

As for the flowers, of course it hadn't been appropriate to give them to a married woman. And, of
course, he'd gone over the top with them.

Justin peered out the window, mentally kicking
himself. He should have been more subtle and avoided
such an overt gesture. He should have bought flowers
and put them in the kitchen, maybe in the hallway
and living room too, as if for the whole house to enjoy
rather than filling her room with them and sprinkling
petals on the floor.

The thought made him flush with embarrassment.
He'd been waiting in the kitchen with anticipation
when Gia had returned from Holly's room. Like
a fool, he'd fully expected Holly herself to come
running down. He'd hoped she'd throw her arms
around him, kissing him excitedly as she thanked
him for the flowers. Instead, Gia was the one to
come down, and when he'd asked how she'd reacted
to the flowers, Gia had hesitated and then admitted,
"She asked if someone died."

While he'd stood gaping in dismay at this news,
Gia had gone out to the garage. Justin's upset had
only increased when the woman had come back
inside seconds later with a rake. At first bewildered,
he'd then been mortified when she'd explained they
were for the petals. The women were concerned
about stepping on them and staining the carpet.

Flushing, Justin had taken the rake from her and
hurried upstairs. It had been his brilliant idea to
strew the petals around, he would clean it up. Determined as he'd been to clean up the mess himself, he'd
also been extremely relieved to not run into Holly
as he did. He'd heard rustling from her bathroom

and known she was in there, so had worked at top speed to remove the petals before she came out. He'd just gathered the last of them and stepped out of the room when he'd heard the bathroom door open.

Justin knew he should have taken the failure of his first two attempts at wooing her as a sign, and given up there and then. Instead he'd plowed determinedly forward with the second part of the plans he'd made that day while she was out with the others. The minute they'd left, he'd called in an order for the flowers that had filled her room, paying the exorbitant fee for express delivery. He'd then called a local gourmet restaurant to order the meal for their picnic. After cleaning up the mess in her room, he'd rushed out to the garage to fetch the picnic basket and blanket. He'd found both of them earlier and stowed them out there so that she wouldn't see them until he was ready. When he'd come back in the house, Dante had mentioned that Holly had just gone out to take a jog up the beach, and Justin had thought it a sign that this attempt at wooing her would definitely work. He wouldn't have to find an excuse to get her down to the beach and surprise her with the picnic, she was already there. He would set the scene and she would come back from her jog, see what he'd done, and blush with pleasure and embrace him.

"Yeah, right," Justin muttered to himself on a sigh. He followed that up with shaking his head with bewilderment. Why were his efforts going so wrong? Hell, he had harassed the other men horribly about their stumbling about while trying to claim their own life mates, and here was he, with actual inside information about what she liked and didn't like and everything he did backfired on him.

Groaning, he scrubbed his fingers through his

hair and then massaged his temples miserably. Justin wanted to give up. He wanted to just pack his bag, head to the airport and fly back to Canada. But he couldn't. First off, Lucian had ordered him to train her. But more important, she was his *life mate* . . . and unless he wanted to spend the next several centuries or even millennia alone, he had to make this work. He had to convince her that they were life mates . . . the old-fashioned way.

Damn, it would be so much easier if he could just take her to bed. One round of life mate sex and she would forget she even had a husband. Unfortunately, that was not allowed. It would be considered undue influence if he deliberately seduced her knowing how the nanos would send them up in flame. So if he wanted to avoid the pain, and keep his position as an Enforcer, sex was out.

But what about dream sex?

Justin blinked as that question ran through his mind. The fabled dream sex that life mates were supposed to enjoy even if they were unacknowledged life mates. Let them sleep in the same vicinity and they experienced apparently incredibly realistic sex dreams about, or perhaps with, each other. He wasn't sure which it was since he'd never experienced them.

And why was that? He suddenly wondered with concern. They should be experiencing sex dreams if they truly were life mates. Biting his lip, he considered the matter briefly, then headed out of his room in search of Gia.

He checked the living room first, but while Dante and Tomasso were there watching television, there was no sign of Gia so he continued on to the kitchen. Much to his relief the woman was there and alone.

She was seated at the table with a nearly empty bag of blood at her mouth and a book open on the table.

Justin eased into the room, allowing the kitchen door to close behind him, then moved to stand by the table, waiting patiently as Gia finished feeding. It only took a moment.

"Holly went to bed," Gia announced after tearing the now empty blood bag from her fangs. "Her hours are all screwed up after the last couple of days and she said she was more tired than hungry."

"Oh," Justin nodded, but then asked with concern, "She didn't eat?"

"No. But she did have blood. Three bags," Gia assured him, and then smiled and added, "She brought her teeth out on her own and went to it like a pro."

"Good, good," he murmured, and glanced to the fridge, considering having some of the chicken and salad he'd packed in their picnic. But he wasn't really hungry at the moment, which was unusual. Justin was always hungry.

"What's going on in that little head of yours?" Gia asked suddenly, drawing his gaze back to her to see that she was staring at his head with a concentration that told him she was reading his thoughts. After a moment, she arched an eyebrow. "Dream sex?"

Justin sagged and then pulled out the chair across from hers and sat down before blurting, "I haven't had any dream sex with Holly. That's something that happens with life mates, but it hasn't happened with us. Maybe she's not my life mate. Maybe this has all been a terrible mistake. Maybe I turned the wrong woman. We—"

"Justin," Gia interrupted. When he paused and peered at her uncertainly, she said, "I do not think you have even slept at the same time yet. How can you have shared dream sex if only one of you is sleeping?

He blinked, and then quickly ran back through the time they'd spent together since that night at the funeral home. "I did sleep while she was in the turn. Not much, mostly nodding off now and then in a chair beside the bed, but—"

"I hardly think it likely that she would have any kind of dreams while going through the turn," Gia said dryly. "Nightmares perhaps, thanks to the pain, but not dreams, sexual or otherwise."

"You're probably right," Justin said with a grimace.

Gia nodded. "Anders mentioned that you watched over her the night she returned home. Did you both sleep then?"

"No. I sat on the roof outside her window and watched her sleep," he admitted quietly and when her eyebrows rose, he shrugged. "Lucian said watch her, so I watched her. Besides, it was a steep roof. I was afraid I'd fall off if I fell asleep. And I did have to watch for anyone spotting me."

"I see," Gia murmured and then pointed out, "Well, I'm quite sure you haven't slept at the same time as Holly since arriving here."

Justin shook his head. "I went to bed after the boys carried you two sleeping beauties to your rooms."

"You didn't sleep though. Not unless you sleep pace." When Justin blinked, she said, "I woke up when Dante laid me in my bed, and then I couldn't get back to sleep so I got up, bathed, painted my toenails . . ." She shrugged. "I heard you pacing through most of the night."

Justin bowed his head, not denying it. Worried and fretting over how close Holly and her husband must be after actually growing up together, and how diffi-cult that was going to make it for him to woo her, he'd found it impossible to lie down and relax enough for sleep to claim him. He'd spent most of the night, pacing his room like a caged tiger. The rest of it he'd spent lying in the bed, staring at the ceiling, his brain running around in circles until he'd given up and got up. Skipping sleep like that had meant that he'd had to take more blood than usual to get through the day without feeling like yesterday's lunch, but . . .

"You must be exhausted. You should really go to bed now," Gia said with a grin. "You will probably have those shared dreams everyone goes on about."

Justin started to smile in response, but the smile died before fully formed and he didn't move from his chair. Instead, he dropped his head on his arms on the tabletop and moaned, "I can't. They might consider dream sex as undue influence."

"What?" Gia squawked at the suggestion, and shook her head, waving the idea away like a cat bat-ting away a pesky mouse. "Do not be ridiculous. They can hardly punish you for your dreams. You have no control over those."

"Yes, but I do have control over whether I sleep at the same time as Holly," he pointed out sadly.

She snorted at the words. "Did Lucian not insist that you are to train Holly yourself?"

"Yes," he agreed miserably.

"How can you do that if you are sleeping when she is awake and awake only when she is sleeping?" she asked pointedly.

He sat up slowly, hope rising within him.

"You have to sleep, Justin," she said firmly. "And you cannot be punished for dreams you have no real control over."

"You're sure of that?" he asked dubiously. In his experience, Lucian could blame you for whatever he chose.

Gia clucked her tongue and pulled a cell phone out of her pocket. She quickly punched buttons then placed the phone to her ear and waited. It took a couple of moments before her call was answered and she said, "*Buonasera*, Lucian. Did I wake you?"

Justin grimaced. Lucian was a grumpy bastard at the best of times. Tired, he would be completely miserable, he was sure.

"*Mi scusi*. I will make this quick, *si*?" Gia said. "Tell Justin to sleep, *per favore*."

Blinking, Justin raised his head, eyes widening.

"*Si*. He has not slept since you left. He is exhausted and going through more blood than he should to make up for his lack of—*Si. Un momento*." She held the phone out to Justin.

Eyebrows rising, he took the phone and pressed it cautiously to his ear. "Yeah?"

"Go to bed," Lucian growled. The order was followed by a click as he hung up.

Short and sweet, that was Lucian, Justin thought as he handed the phone back to Gia.

"You heard him, *mio caro*," Gia said, a slow smile spreading her lips. Winking at him, she added, "You cannot be punished now if you go to bed and have the shared dreams. You were ordered there."

"Yeah, but it probably didn't occur to him about the shared dreams," Justin pointed out. "Especially if you woke him up and—"

"That is not our problem," Gia said, unconcerned. "He ordered you to bed, so go to bed."

After a hesitation, Justin muttered, "right," and stood to head for the door.

"Sweet dreams," Gia called out on a laugh.

He merely nodded in response as he pushed through the door. Justin wasn't sure Gia was right and he would avoid being blamed for any shared dream sex that might occur once he slept, but Lucian *had* ordered him to bed. Surely that would at least mitigate any punishment? He didn't know, but was desperate enough to take the risk. He needed to know for sure that Holly was his life mate, and that he hadn't given his one turn to a woman who would never be his.

Of course, her being his life mate didn't guarantee he would ever gain her agreement to be his mate. There was still the problem of her being married. But at least if she was his life mate he might be able to claim her eventually . . . in twenty or thirty years maybe, when her mortal husband died. Maybe even ten or so, if the fact that her husband was aging while she was not became a problem. It at least gave him hope he'd briefly lost when he'd realized they hadn't experienced the shared dream sex that plagued life mates.

Justin picked up his pace as he started upstairs, his mind now thoroughly entrenched in what might be coming. From what he'd heard, even dream sex with a life mate was better than the real thing with a non life mate. He had no idea if that was true, but had every intention of finding out.

Holly shifted restlessly onto her back and opened her eyes. She had been tired when she'd come up here to her room, but was now finding it impossible to go to sleep. Maybe she should have had some of the chicken and potato salad Bricker had prepared for their picnic after all. Or maybe having the blood before bed had perked her up and washed away the weariness. Whichever the case, she wasn't sleeping now and that fried chicken and potato salad she'd put into the refrigerator was practically calling out to her like a siren's song.

Clucking under her tongue, she tossed aside the sheet and blankets covering her and got out of bed, switching on the bedside lamp as she did. Pausing as she took note of the pajamas she'd bought that day and now wore, she briefly considered changing into clothes or grabbing a housecoat, but really, was there any reason to? They were flannel after all, with dancing bears in pink tutus on them. She'd thought they were charming when she'd bought them, and they were cute as could be, but they were hardly skimpy or seductive. No one would accuse of her of trying to seduce anyone if she were caught out in them.

Smiling faintly to herself, Holly headed out of her room only to pause again as she stepped into the hall and found it in darkness. Everyone else had obviously gone to bed too, which was rather surprising to her. She'd thought vampires were night people and that she would naturally fall into that pattern too once she'd got more regulated. But it seemed she was wrong. The house was as silent as a tomb, and as dark as the cemetery had been the other night.

Not wanting to turn on the hall light and wake everyone, Holly reached for the wall and began to ease carefully toward the end of the hall, feeling her way when she got close to where she thought the steps were. Once she reached the top of the stairs, she grasped the railing to make her way cautiously down those as well. It was a relief when she reached the main floor without breaking her neck, and she moved a little more quickly along the hall to the kitchen, where she turned the light on the moment she pushed the door open.

Bright light immediately poured down over her and she slid into the room with a little sigh. The idea of returning upstairs without light was not a pleasant one and Holly decided that after she'd eaten she'd search the drawers for a flashlight or one of the candles Justin had used at dinner the other night, so that she'd have light for the return journey. With that problem solved, if only in her mind, she headed for the refrigerator and the fried chicken waiting inside.

She had removed the food, set it on the counter and was just reaching into the refrigerator for the potato salad when her gaze caught on the can of spray whip cream. Grinning, she grabbed that instead, the idea of the sweet, creamy foam doing more for her appetite at the moment than either the chicken or the potato salad. Probably because it was one of those things she'd had to avoid in the past. When she was mortal and diabetic, she'd had to be very careful of what she ate in an effort to keep her sugars balanced. But now . . .

Not even thinking first, she popped the plastic lid, tipped her head, aimed the spout into her mouth and shot a wad of lovely whipped cream onto her tongue. She'd just lowered her head and closed her mouth on the sweet treat with a moan of pleasure when the kitchen door opened.

Lowering the can to her side, Holly spun guiltily in the open refrigerator door to see Justin entering the kitchen. He wore a pair of low slung, red plaid pajama bottoms and nothing else. His feet were bare, but more important, so was his chest, and she found herself gaping at the sight. Holly had thought the man was good-looking from the start, and the tight T-shirts he wore showed off that he had a nice figure, but not nearly as much as nakedness did. Dear God, the man was all sculpted pecs and rippling abs as he entered the room.

Realizing that her mouth had dropped open and the wad of rapidly dissolving whipped cream was in danger of drooling out, Holly closed her mouth and swallowed guiltily just as he took note of her presence.

"Hi," he said, his voice husky from sleep.

"Hi," she responded weakly.

"I see I wasn't the only one who was hungry," he added wryly, moving toward her.

Holly muttered something that even she found unintelligible and instinctively backed up a step as he neared. But she came up short when she bumped into the open refrigerator door. Fortunately, her action made Justin pause a couple of steps away. Or maybe he'd planned to stop there, she acknowledged as he surveyed the chicken on the counter.

"There's potato salad too," he announced, turning his attention to her again.

"I know," Holly said and then just stood there . . . staring at his chest. It was obvious the man did not sunbathe. His skin was pale enough she doubted it had ever been exposed to the sun's rays, but that didn't take away from the beauty of it. Justin could have posed for Michelangelo or one of those other artists who sculpted the male form. He was perfect, with large, hard-looking pecs above a stomach that bragged an eight-pack rather than six and rippled down to the start of a V that disappeared under the waist of his pajama bottoms. In that moment, Holly thought that she would have given a lot to see what those plaid pants hid, but then she remembered that she was married and closed her eyes to try to banish the temptation along with her vision of him.

"Are you all right?"

Holly blinked her eyes open at that question, and sucked in a breath as she realized that he'd closed the small space between them and was reaching to touch her face. Obviously, he'd completely misconstrued why she'd closed her eyes, she thought and opened her mouth to assure him that she was fine, only to pause again with surprise when his fingers lightly grazed her cheeks and her stomach seemed to jump in response.

"I . . ." Holly breathed the single word and that was it. Nothing followed it into the silence in the room. Whatever she'd meant to say had flown from her mind, leaving her simply standing there, a brainless twit.

"You are so beautiful and sexy," Justin said solemnly and her eyes widened incredulously at the claim. She was without makeup, her hair no doubt a ruffled mess from her tossing and turning, and she was wearing flannel pajamas with dancing bears on them, for cripes sake. And they had tutus on no less. She couldn't imagine anything less sexy than dancing bears.

He moved another step closer, removing the last inch of space that had separated them and Holly bit her lip on a gasp as his chest brushed lightly against the flannel that covered the tips of her nipples. The resulting riot that caused in her body had her eyes widening and her hand clenching around the can of whipped cream she still held.

"I—" she repeated, and this time stopped there because his mouth was suddenly covering hers. The heat that poured over Holly then was a familiar one from that morning, but this time it seemed to catch fire even faster than it had then. There was no questing, or nibbling at her lips to gain entry. Her mouth was already open and Justin took full advantage, plunging his tongue in to explore her depths. Holly stood completely still, her conscience battling with her body's response, and then Justin broke the kiss and shifted to nibble at her ear before whispering. "It's okay. It's a dream."

"It is?" she asked with confusion.

"Look. It's a dream," he assured her, and she forced her eyes open to look around.

They had magically moved from the refrigerator to the kitchen table. Instead of standing, she was now seated on the table and he stood between her spread legs while his hands busily worked at the buttons of her flannel top. And while she still clutched the whipped cream in her hand, the chicken was no longer on the counter and the refrigerator door was closed as if she had never opened it.

"A dream," she realized with bewilderment. It had to be. He couldn't have got her over here and set her on the table without her noticing—

She was distracted from that thought when he suddenly tugged her pajama top open, revealing her bare chest.

"How did you do that so quickly?" she gasped with amazement, automatically reaching to grab the edges of her flannel top to pull them closed again.

"A dream, remember?" he chuckled. Letting her hold her top closed like the ninny she was, he clasped her face instead and kissed her again.

Holly didn't fight him, but she didn't respond either. While passion poured over her in waves, she was struggling to sort out if it would be cheating if it was a dream, or if it even was one. It was possible he'd just used immortal speed.

When she felt his hand clasp her breast through the flannel of her top and lightly pinch her nipple, she moaned and broke their kiss to gasp, "But I'm married."

"This is a dream," he repeated gruffly by her ear, and then ran his tongue around the rim of her ear before dropping his lips to nibble at her neck between whispers.

"It's okay. It's a dream."

Holly frowned, her hand releasing her top to grasp his shoulders to keep her balance on the table as his hands slid under her bottom to ease her forward to press against him. Maybe it was, she thought. Maybe she was imagining that it was Justin kissing and touching her . . .

Holly gasped as their groins rubbed together through their pajamas sending liquid fire shooting through her. This time when his mouth covered hers, she kissed back even as she wondered why she was imagining Justin here touching and kissing her instead of her husband.

If this was a dream, shouldn't she be imagining her husband? She wondered and with her eyes closed tried to do that, but it wasn't her husband's cologne filling her nose, it was the spicy woodsy scent she'd noticed that Justin wore. Shaking her head, she broke their kiss and said, "This is wrong."

"It's just a dream," he repeated, licking his way down her throat and Holly glanced around wildly as she realized they'd moved again. They were no longer in the kitchen. Now they were in a bedroom, though it wasn't one she recognized. This one was decorated in dark brown and beige. A man's room, obviously, with heavy oak furniture and a massive king-sized bed covered with dark chocolate satin sheets. She was now lying on her back on those sheets, the satin slippery beneath her skin as he crawled down her body.

"How . . . ?" Holly began with bewilderment, and then nearly bit her tongue off as she realized that the satin was slippery beneath her skin because her flannel pajamas were gone. She was completely naked on that bed. No more dancing bears to protect her.

Definitely a dream, she realized, and that thought made her raise her head slightly to peer down his body in the hopes of seeing what his plaid pajama pants hid, but those were still in place. Only she was starkers. So unfair, she thought and then stared in surprise when he suddenly had the whipped cream can in his hand that she'd held earlier.

Where the devil had that come from? Apparently it had followed them from the first part of the dream, her mind reasoned and she bit her lip, simply watching as he shifted the can above one nipple and sprayed a circle over it. It was surprisingly warm for having just come out of the refrigerator, and stupidly, she said as much. "It should be cold. Why isn't it cold?"

"It's a dream," he reminded her on a chuckle and then swooped down to close his mouth over the cream and her nipple both. Holly gasped, her back arching violently off the bed as his hot mouth suckled then licked her breast clean.

"Oh God," she moaned, and shook her head in

denial, then blurted, "It's not cheating if it's a dream, right?"

"No," he agreed, and then swiped her breast again, removing the last of the whipped cream.

"No," Holly decided and grabbed him by the ears to drag him back up her body.

Dream Justin came willingly. His pajama-clad groin pressed against the center of her as she claimed his mouth. Holly immediately spread her legs, and then wrapped them around his hips, urging him tighter against her as she thrust her tongue out.

With that one action she seemed to open the floodgates to an erotic world of pleasure. His body was hot and hard against her, his smell enveloped her, and his hands were everywhere, bringing every inch of her body to singing life as they caressed her side, her back, her ass, and then moved between them to clasp her breasts and squeeze firmly.

Holly broke their kiss and threw her head back on a gasp when he did that, and Justin immediately eased back enough to claim one nipple with his mouth again. This time she didn't pull him away from what he was doing, but knotted her hands in his hair and gasped and moaned and then murmured encouragingly as he laved first one breast and then the other. When he reached up with one hand to caress her cheek as he worked on her breasts, she turned her head to nip and then suckle at one of his fingers, and then gasped around the digit when his other hand slid between her legs.

At first he merely cupped her, pressing firmly against the heated skin, but then he eased a finger between her lips to find the nub at the center of her excitement and began to run teasing circles around it that had her hips gyrating in response. Panting and moaning by turn, Holly tried to reach down to touch him, but he was positioned so that his erection was out of her reach. Growling in her throat with frustration, she scraped her nails up his back instead, then caught him under the arms and tugged upward.

Again, Dream Justin responded to her silent demand. A soft chuckle slipping from his lips, he released the nipple he'd been teasing and moved up her body, positioning himself between her legs. He didn't thrust into her right away as she wanted, though, but stared down into her face, smiling softly.

"You're a wild one," he accused gently, rubbing himself teasingly against her opening. "You act all prim and proper, but underneath it all, you're a wildcat with claws."

Holly merely dug those claws into his shoulder and shifted her hips, trying to pull him into her.

Justin chuckled at the attempt, but shifted his hips backward, then bent to nuzzle her ear and whispered, "Tell me you want me."

"I want you," Holly panted, wrapping her legs around his hips and trying to lift herself onto the erection taunting her.

"Say my name," he whispered, nipping at her ear.

Cursing, Holly let her legs drop, and then shifted quickly, catching him by surprise and throwing him onto his back. She followed, coming to rest on top of him, then pushed at his chest to sit up, shifted slightly and reached down to grasp his penis and lowered herself onto it.

"Oh," she moaned and closed her eyes as he filled her. He felt so damned good. All of it felt so damned good. Holly was never the aggressor with James, and couldn't imagine ever doing so, but here in her dream with Justin, she could be, and she liked it.

Opening her eyes, she peered down at his face, smiling when she saw that his eyes were closed, his face squinched up with what she guessed was ecstasy though it looked perilously close to pain. Pursing her lips, she slowly raised herself slightly and then lowered herself again, feeling incredibly powerful when he moaned, his face tightening even further. She did that three more times very slowly before he opened his eyes and caught her watching him.

Justin met her gaze briefly, and then took one of the hands that had been clasping her hips and moved it between them to begin teasing her again, rubbing against the nub of her excitement as she raised herself once more.

Holly bit her lip, struggling to remain in control. But the passion that had temporarily been banked rushed back now, stealing her self-control from her and she began to move more swiftly. When his other hand moved up to clasp one breast, she covered it with both of her own hands, nails digging into his skin as she rode him. She watched Justin's face tighten, was aware that his caresses were becoming faster and firmer even as his hips pumped up to meet hers, and just as he thrust up into her one last time and stiffened on a shout, something snapped inside of Holly. Some small thread that had been holding back an ocean of pleasure broke and she threw her head back and screamed his name as her orgasm washed over her.

Holly sat up in bed with a cry and found herself staring into darkness. For one moment she listened to the silence in the room, and peered into the dark room with confusion, then she reached for the lamp on the table and turned it on. She was in bed, in her flannel dancing bear pajamas, alone.

She closed her eyes briefly and then pushed the blankets and sheets aside and moved to the bathroom, slowly becoming aware of the dampness between her legs. A lot of dampness, she acknowledged.

Cripes, she'd had her first wet dream, Holly realized with a shake of her head as she stepped into the bathroom and felt for the light switch. She had to blink rapidly against the brightness when the light came on, but once her eyes adjusted, she peered at herself in the mirror and wrinkled her nose. Her face was flush, her hair all knotted in the back and standing up. She'd obviously been thrashing her head in her sleep.

"A wet dream," she muttered, turning on the tap to splash her face. It probably wasn't her first wet dream, but it was the first she recalled . . . and it had been incredibly . . . well . . . incredible. It had also been about Justin Bricker, she thought grimly. There was something wrong with that. She even felt briefly guilty about it. But it was just a dream, she told herself. Her subconscious was obviously working through something, although she didn't know what the heck it was working through. Maybe she was a lot more attracted to him than she'd realized. Or maybe rather than having to do with her own feelings, it was about his fixating on her. Whatever the case, it was just a dream. It wasn't like she'd cheated on her husband.

Sighing, Holly turned off the water and dried her face on a hand towel, meeting her guilty gaze in the mirror as she did.

"Really," she said suddenly, lowering the towel.

"Having sex with another man in a dream is not cheating on your husband. It was a dream. You aren't in control of your dreams. Besides, James doesn't know you had it, and Justin doesn't know. It's all good. Just relax and go back to sleep."

Folding the hand towel once, she set it back on its holder, turned out the bathroom light and headed back to bed. She would have liked to claim that she was hoping that was the last of her dreams for the night, but suspected that wouldn't be true. It had been incredible, the best orgasm she'd ever had. How pathetic was it that the best orgasm of her life was one she'd had in a dream?

"Sex with him probably wouldn't have been as good in real life," Holly assured herself as she crossed the dark bedroom back to bed. "It's just that you're less inhibited in your dreams. Wilder."

That was definitely true, she acknowledged. Holly always refused to be on top with James. She was afraid she wouldn't do it right, wouldn't be able to keep the rhythm or something. And he never pushed the issue.

"You love James," Holly reassured herself as she climbed onto the bed and pulled the covers up. "Orgasms aren't the be-all and end-all of life."

Turning onto her side, she slid a hand under her pillow and closed her eyes, telling herself, "Everything is fine."

Twelve

Justin finished cleaning up, started out of the bathroom and then paused to grab a towel to take with him. Better to be safe than sorry, he thought, as he crossed back to the bed. It was only a little after midnight and he doubted that would be the last of the shared sex dreams they'd have that night. Certainly, he was eager for more after that first one. Even waking up to find he'd had an orgasm in his sleep and made a mess of his boxers wasn't enough to dampen his enthusiasm.

Holly had been a revelation. Honestly, she was so straitlaced in reality that he'd expected her to be the same in bed, at least at first. Instead, she'd taken control, tossed him on his back and ridden him like a pro . . . after scratching the hell out of his back. He actually felt tender there even awake, as if she'd really scratched him, though there had been no welts or redness when he'd checked in the bathroom mirror. But then his whole body had been quivering and shaky as he'd made his way to the bathroom a couple minutes ago, as if they'd really had sex and it hadn't just been a shared dream. Justin supposed his muscles must have been clenching in real life in response to the dream.

And what a dream! It had been pretty short and sweet compared to the marathon bang-a-thons he'd been into of late in reality. While he'd been an eager beaver when he was young, getting to the main course of the meal as quickly as he could, he'd found after a while that that was boring and begun trying other things. Just lately his deal had been to prolong it as long as possible, drawing out the foreplay and extending the pleasure for himself and his partner for as long as he could. That hadn't been possible with Holly. He couldn't take control of her and keep her from touching him. And she was strong too, much stronger than a mortal. Justin was stronger still, but she'd taken him by surprise with her moves and he hadn't known what hit him when he suddenly found himself on his back with her on top. After that it was Game. Set. Match. And he was toast. All he'd been able to do was ride the wave with her to Nirvana. And it hadn't even been true life mate sex, where the pleasure, instead of the dream, was shared, multiplying their mutual pleasure to unbearable levels. That was enough to knock immortals out cold. He couldn't wait to experience it, but in the meantime, this would do . . . especially since, dream or not, it was his name Holly had screamed as she'd found her pleasure.

That was the last thing Justin had heard before waking up, his name on her lips . . . and it had been sweet. He wanted to hear it again. He wanted to hear her begging for him to enter her, wanted her to sob his name with need, and now that he'd experienced his first shared dream with her, Justin was pretty sure he could have it. He was going right back to sleep to find her again, and this time, he was going to take control. He was going to strip her, lay her out, feast on her and when he had her trembling and weeping with need, he would pound into her, giving them both the release they wanted.

That thought firmly in mind, Justin closed his eyes to go to sleep. It seemed like he'd barely done so when he found himself in a dark crowded room with blinking lights and loud music thundering all around him.

"What the hell," he muttered, turning slowly and surveying the strangers bumping and grinding on every side.

It was a nightclub, he realized. He'd been in enough of them to recognize that. Justin loved nightclubs. He loved dancing and he loved watching women dance. It was also a great place to pick up chicks. But there was only one chick he was interested in anymore and he began searching the sea of faces for her, sure this was her dream and he'd find her somewhere here.

It didn't take him long to spot her. Holly was in the middle of the dance floor, twirling and grinding like a pro. Damn, the girl could move. He suspected she would never dance so freely in reality, but here in her dreams, she was fluid, every move screaming of sexuality and animal grace.

Smiling, Justin wove his way through the undulating bodies until he stood behind her, and then he slid his arms around her from behind, urging her back against his front.

"Justin," she said with surprise, peering over her shoulder at him.

"Hi," he murmured, shifting his hands to her rotating hips and following her moves with his own as he ground against her bottom.

Despite the loud music, she appeared to hear him.

"Hi yourself," she laughed before turning swiftly in his arms and grinding up against him front to front. "I didn't know you like to dance," she said on a chuckle, slipping her hands up around his neck. The move pressed her chest against his and he reveled in the feel of her firm breasts rubbing against him as they moved.

"There's a lot you don't know about me," he murmured, clasping her ass with both hands as they ground to the sultry beat.

She had been wearing jeans and a blouse when he'd first spotted her on the dance floor, but now suddenly had on the short black leather skirt, black leather vest and thigh-high black leather boots Gia had worn that day. Since he hadn't made that happen, she must have, and Justin thought that was probably a good sign. Holly wanted to look sexy for him. She also wasn't the least bit reticent in this dream, he noticed as she raised one booted leg and wrapped it around him so that she could press her core against the growing hardness between his legs.

Justin bit back a groan and lifted her by the clasp he had on her ass, rubbing her against himself more fully, then dropped his head to growl, "Let's get out of here."

Chuckling deep in her throat, she was suddenly out of his arms and moving away through the crowd of people. Justin was just starting to frown when she glanced back, raised her hand, and then crooked her finger, inviting him to follow.

Curious to see how this played out, Justin did just

that rather than imagine another setting as he had in their earlier dream. While he had joined her in the kitchen in what had obviously been her dream then too, he was the one who had first moved it to the table and then to his own bedroom back in Canada. This time he followed her deeper into her dream, moving through the crowd and following her off the dance floor to a hallway that led to the bathrooms. Holly paused there and turned to lean back against the wall and smile at him wickedly as she waited for him to reach her.

When he stopped in front of her, she reached out to run her hands up his chest over his black T-shirt, then caught her fingers in it and drew him roughly forward so that she could lean up and press her lips to his. Justin smiled against her mouth and then braced his hands on the wall on either side of her head and kissed her back, allowing his tongue to slide out and explore her mouth in a fashion that he'd intended to be leisurely, but that quickly turned hot and wild.

"What are we doing?" he growled against her lips when she reached between their bodies to rub his burgeoning erection.

"I want you," she growled right back and the next thing he knew his pants were undone and she had him in hand, right there in the bloody hallway where anyone might see. Though a quick glance around proved that no one was there with them at the moment.

Turning back to peer down at her, he bit the inside of his cheek to try to damp down his excitement as she caressed him, and growled with amazement, "You like to take risks."

Her response was to catch his hand and pull it

down under her skirt as she claimed his mouth once more. Justin wasn't strong enough to refuse that invitation. He rubbed her lightly through the silk of the panties she wore, capturing her groan in his mouth as he did, then eased the cloth aside to touch her warm, damp skin. This time he was the one who groaned as he felt how hot and wet she was for him. The woman was seriously turned on and he knew right then that taking control, going slowly and driving her out of her mind with need was out the window. Somehow, this woman had turned the tables on him. He was the one suddenly out of his mind with need and completely lacking control.

Tearing his mouth from hers with a curse, he tore her panties off with one quick jerk then clasped her by the waist to lift her up and press her back against the wall. He then lowered her onto his erection. Her skirt caught between them, riding up the few inches necessary to be out of the way.

They both hissed, "Yes," with pleasure as he entered her. It was the last word either of them spoke, the next few moments were filled with moans and gasps and grunts as he pounded into her. Jason felt her nails digging into his shoulders through his T-shirt and that just spurred him on. When she broke their kiss to bite into his neck with excitement, he growled and buried his own in her shoulder. That's when she suddenly pushed him back.

Startled, Justin fell back against what he saw with some confusion was the backseat of an open convertible. Blinking, he turned to peer at Holly. She was sitting up in his lap and smiling, her hands clasping each side of the top of Gia's black vest. As he watched blankly, she suddenly tore the vest open, baring herself just inches from his face.

She'd changed the dream, he realized. He'd been about to have an orgasm and she'd changed the damned dream. She gave a little shimmy as her nipples pebbled in the cool night air and Justin responded automatically, his hands coming up to clasp her sides as he leaned forward to close his mouth around one sweet bud.

"Oh, yeah," Holly breathed, grinding against him. He was no longer inside of her, but back in his pants, he noted absently as he suckled and nipped at her nipple. And she had her panties on again, he found, when he slid a hand under her skirt to touch her again. Holly gasped as he caressed her, her hips moving with his touch, then gave a small cry of pleasure when he tugged the panties aside so that he could caress her with his thumb while sliding a finger inside of her. She let him do that for a minute, her body shuddering and dancing for him, and then suddenly she was sliding off of him to crouch between his legs. A real car wouldn't have been large enough for her to do that, but this dream car was and before he quite realized what she was up to, she had his pants open and had taken him, not into her hand this time, but her mouth.

"Ai-yee!" Justin shouted, bucking on the leather seat.

Holly removed her mouth long enough to say, "Drive the car," then claimed him again and Justin blinked his eyes open to find they were shooting down the freeway and he was behind the wheel with her now crouched in the passenger seat and her head in his lap. She'd changed the dream again midstream. Christ, the woman was going to kill him, he thought faintly and despite knowing it was a dream, instinctively grabbed the steering wheel.

For a moment, Justin actually tried to drive while she drove him crazy. Her warm wet mouth rode his length, her tongue swirling around the tip as she raised her head, then sliding his length again as she lowered it. Justin groaned and then growled with irritation as someone shook his shoulder, determined to get his attention.

"Bricker?'

"Bricker!"

His arm was shaken again and Justin snapped his eyes open and turned to glower at the intruder. He then blinked in surprise when he saw Dante straightening away from him in the light spilling through his bedroom door.

"What the . . . ?" Justin sat up and glanced around with confusion. He was in his bed, alone. Holly was gone. Instead, Dante and Tomasso stood at his bedside, concern on their expressions.

"You screamed in your sleep," Dante explained when Justin turned his bewildered gaze back to him.

Justin's confusion faded and dismay replaced it as he realized— "You woke me up!"

"We were concerned," Dante said with a shrug.

"You screamed," Tomasso reminded him.

"With passion!" he snapped furiously. "We were—shared dreams," he finished meaningfully, and when both men merely raised an eyebrow, Justin growled with frustration. "Oh, for the love of—" Grabbing a pillow, he tossed it at the pair of them. "Get out, get out, get out! Christ, Holly was— And you're ruining it. Get out!"

"Ah," Dante murmured and turned to exchange a glance with his twin. The two men then shrugged and walked out, pulling the door closed behind them.

Justin fell back on the bed with a weary sigh, and

closed his eyes determinedly. He had to get back to sleep and back to Holly.

Holly gasped with surprise when Justin suddenly caught her arm and turned her away from the fridge. One minute she'd been in the car with him and the next he'd been gone. She wasn't sure how she'd got back here in the kitchen, except that she'd been hungry.

Justin stepped forward, and Holly took a step back, glancing around with surprise when her back hit something solid. She stared blankly at the kitchen table with some confusion, wondering how the hell they'd got over by the table.

The feel of his lips moving up her thigh drew her attention from her thoughts and she peered down the length of her body to see that she was on her back on the kitchen table, her legs dangling over the end and that Justin was—

"Holy crap!" she gasped, and tried to sit up as his tongue found and suddenly rasped over the center of her. Justin prevented that with a hand at her chest, urging her to lie back again as he continued to lave her with his tongue. He was stronger than her, which she thought was completely unfair considering it was *her* dream. But there was little she could do about it and after struggling against his hold for a minute, she fell back weakly and grabbed at the sides of the table, clutching at the wood desperately as he licked and suckled and thrust his tongue in and out, driving her wild until she screamed her pleasure.

Unlike the first dream, this one didn't end there, however. Instead, Justin rose up to stand between her legs like some victorious warrior, pulled her to sit upright on the edge of the table, then clasped her to his chest and kissed her as he thrust into her. Holly cried out into his mouth with that first hard thrust, and then wrapped her legs around his hips to urge him on as her excitement came screaming back to full-blown life.

She let him pound into her half a dozen times, then unwrapped her legs and pushed him back. Smiling at his startled expression as he stumbled back a couple of steps, she slid off the table and turned to bend over it, then glanced over her shoulder at once.

"Witch," Justin breathed as he stepped up behind her. Straightening, she ground her butt against him and tilted her head back in a silent demand for a kiss. The moment his mouth covered hers, she grabbed his hands and pulled them around to cover her breasts. He began squeezing and kneading them at once as he thrust his tongue into her mouth. When she broke the kiss and bent forward to brace herself on the table, he released her breasts to clasp her hips and thrust into her from behind. Then he bent to reach around and began caressing her as he continued to thrust into her, first fondling her breasts as he nibbled at her neck, and then as he picked up the pace of his thrusts, sliding one hand down between her legs to find the center of her excitement again.

Holly gasped and then cried out and slammed back into him hard as he pushed her over the edge into orgasm. Justin's hand clenched on her hip and he thrust into her one last time, and then froze, crying out his release as well.

Holly stepped out of the shower and grabbed a towel to dry herself, avoiding her own reflection in the mirror. She knew what she would see if she looked . . . accusation. She'd spent the entire night having one dream after another where she did things to Justin, and let him do things to her that no married woman should even think about doing with a man who wasn't her husband. The worst part was, she hadn't a clue why.

Sure, she thought the guy was good-looking, and yes he was sweet with his flowers and his attempt to cook for her and such. But she didn't even know the guy, not really. Besides, James was good-looking and sweet too and not only did she know him, she had known him all her life . . . and they were married.

She really had no idea what had brought on the round of crazy monkey sex dreams. Outside the bathrooms of a nightclub? Where anyone might see them? In an open convertible in a parking lot, again where anyone might see them? Driving down the highway where any passing semi driver could glance down and see them? And on the kitchen table right here in this house where Dante, Tomasso, and Gia could have seen them? Sure, they had all been dreams, but still . . . who knew she had this streak of exhibitionism? She hadn't known. She was pretty pedestrian when it came to sex. At least she had always been pretty pedestrian when it came to sex with James. It was usually in bed, lights out, and missionary position. She had never stopped him partway through, turned over and had him take her doggy style like she had with Justin. She'd never gone down on him in a moving vehicle either, or in a car at all, really.

But in her dreams she'd . . . well, she'd felt powerful and sexy and adventurous. She'd taken control instead of lying passively back, waiting for him to handle things. What did that mean?

Perhaps the sex in the dream hadn't really represented sex at all, Holly thought suddenly as she finished drying herself and began to dress. Maybe the dreams had more to do with Justin's efforts to woo her in front of the others. Anders and Decker knew about his determination that they were life mates. Gia had seen the flowers in her room, and Holly was sure Gia and the twins all knew about the aborted picnic attempt.

Perhaps the dreams were saying that Justin's attempts at wooing her made her feel attractive and powerful. Perhaps her rebuffing him made her feel in control and even sexy. That kind of made a sort of sense, Holly supposed.

It also made it so that she didn't have to admit that she was subconsciously lusting after Justin Bricker.

Holly grimaced at that thought and knew it was true. She'd thought the man was attractive from the start, but ever since he'd kissed her . . . She let her breath out slowly. Yes, she was lusting after Justin Bricker like a bitch in heat. She wanted to experience more of his kisses and enjoy his caresses for real, see if they felt as good in reality as they had in her dreams.

"Which is just too darned bad," she told her reflection grimly. "You are a married woman, and a couple of hours of pleasure aren't worth risking your marriage over. So get over it, concentrate on what you need to learn and get the heck out of here and home to your husband."

Nodding in response to her own lecture, Holly did up the jeans she'd pulled on, then quickly tugged on a T-shirt over her bra and smoothed it into place.

She hadn't gone wild on the clothes shopping. Gia had said to buy as much as she wanted, but she'd restricted herself to two pairs of jeans, a couple T-shirts, a pair of black dress pants, a pair of blue dress pants, and a couple of blouses. Basically, she'd pretty much replaced the small wardrobe she'd owned prior to turning and becoming too small for her own clothes. It would do. Once she'd graduated and was working full-time, she could buy more clothes, but she didn't want to have to explain to James how she had come by a sudden wealth of clothes now.

After running a brush through her hair, Holly left her room and headed downstairs. She made it all the way to the hallway outside the kitchen door before her courage failed her. Pausing there, she bit her lip and told herself not to be a ninny. Justin would not be able to tell, just by looking at her, that she'd been dreaming of doing the nasty with his naked self all night.

"Dear God," she muttered under her breath and pushed the door open to enter the room. At first, she thought it was empty, but then a rattle drew her attention to the refrigerator. Justin was standing in the open door, surveying the contents. He glanced over now and smiled at her.

"Good morning."

Holly felt a shiver run down her back at his husky tone. It was the same pitch his voice had dropped into last night when he'd growled, "Say my name."

Giving her head a shake, she managed a smile and moved nervously to the table. "Good morning."

Good Lord, she sounded like a Victorian chick with the vapors, Holly thought with disgust as she heard her weak voice. Really? That was the best she could do? She couldn't—

Her self-flagellation ended abruptly as Justin suddenly grabbed a can of whipped cream out of the refrigerator, tipped his head, aimed the spout into his mouth and shot some of the creamy foam onto his tongue just as she had done in her first dream last night. That had been just before he'd entered the room, and kissed her and then begun to—

Holly cut that thought off quickly and forced her gaze away from him. "So, training," she said in strained tones.

"Right."

She braved a glance in his direction to see him returning the can to the refrigerator and felt herself relax a little. Good, the last thing she needed was to be thinking about what else he'd done with that whipped cream in her dreams . . . which she was doing now, she realized with dismay as her nipples began to tingle. She could vividly recall the feel of his tongue rasping across her nipples as he laved away every last drop of whipped cream and then—

The refrigerator door slammed closed with a jingle of bottles and Holly jumped guiltily, then instinctively caught the bag of blood he tossed her.

Justin headed for the door to the garage, saying, "Actually, we're going out today."

"What?" Holly asked blankly. "Where?"

"To my parents' place," he responded, opening the door and then turning sideways for her to precede him out to the garage. "It's Sunday. They'd never forgive me if I didn't go see them while I'm in town."

Holly remained by the table, biting her lip.

"Come on," he insisted, waving toward the open door.

Holly shifted uncertainly and then said, "Maybe I should just stay here. Dante and Tomasso could teach me to . . . well . . . do whatever," she finished lamely, and then rushed on, "And you can visit your parents in peace."

"Nope." He shook his head firmly. "Gia and the twins are just backup. Lucian made it plain that you are my responsibility. You're with me. Besides," he added with a smile. "I have a surprise for you."

Holly grimaced and blew her breath out on a sigh. Another surprise. Great. Probably more fish, or flowers, or something to do with nature that she would absolutely hate. Jeez.

Shaking her head with mild disgust, she slapped the blood bag to her teeth and trudged across the kitchen to slip past him through the door.

"Buck up," he said cheerfully as he opened the door of the SUV for her. "You'll like this one."

"Uh-huh," she mumbled around the bag in her mouth as she climbed into the vehicle. She did up her seat belt as he closed the door. The bag was empty by the time he'd walked around and got into the driver's seat. Holly pulled it from her mouth and asked, "Where are Gia and the twins this morning?"

"This afternoon," he corrected, taking the empty bag from her and tossing it in a small garbage bag hanging from the dash. As he started the engine, she glanced to the clock on the dash, amazed to see that it was indeed afternoon. It was just after two o'clock in the afternoon, in fact. Good Lord, it had only been seven when she'd gone to bed. She'd slept more than seventeen hours.

"Gia and the boys went to bed at dawn and are still sleeping," Justin said, answering her original question as he pressed the button to open the garage door. Reaching for his seat belt then, he added, "Mostly we're night owls. Our hours just got messed around a bit after the flight here and everything."

"Right," Holly breathed, wondering why the hell she'd slept so long. She wasn't fighting an illness or something, was she? No, of course not. She was a vampire now. They didn't get sick, according to Justin. But Dante had said something about her needing a lot of blood for a while, and still being in the turn. Perhaps that was the reason for her long sleep. Perhaps the nanos had been finishing the repairs to her brain.

Or perhaps banging Justin all night in her dreams had been exhausting, a naughty part of her mind taunted. Holly choked that little voice in her head and tried to think about something to talk about that wouldn't lead her to thoughts of her dreams. She continued to try to think of something until they were on the freeway, and finally said, "So, tell me about your parents."

Holly had considered it from every angle and was quite satisfied that it was a safe question to ask. Certainly, thoughts of her own parents never led anywhere near sex. As far as she was concerned, her parents did not have sex anymore. At least, she didn't want to think they did, and even the possibility that they might was a complete turnoff.

"What do you want to know?" he asked after a hesitation.

"I don't know," Holly murmured. She'd really only asked the question to get her mind off of sex, but now found herself curious and asked, "Were they both born immortal?"

"My father was born immortal," he said. "He's an offshoot of the Verdis."

"What's that?" she asked curiously.

"The Verdi family, one of the original ancestors who came out of Atlantis," he explained. "My father's mother was a daughter of Maximus Verdi, one of the few who survived the fall of Atlantis. She met my grandfather, Niall Brice, a mortal Irishman around nine fifty A.D. He was taken by the Vikings in a raid as a boy. My grandmother bought him, found she couldn't read him, realized that he was her life mate, set him free, educated him, and when he was old enough, turned and married him. I gather they switched back and forth between the name Verdi and Brice after that. Spending ten years as Verdis and then ten as Brices."

"Why?" Holly asked at once. "Why switch names at all?"

"We don't age," he pointed out solemnly. "To hide that fact, our people have traditionally had to move every ten years or so. They usually change at least their last names as well. Trading back and forth between Verdi and Brice honored both my grandmother's family and my grandfather's."

"Oh," Holly murmured and wondered if she and James would have to switch between his last name of Bosley and her maiden name of McCord.

"Anyway," Justin continued, "My father, Aidan Verdi Brice, was born fifty years later." He was silent for a moment as he negotiated his way off the freeway and then continued. "My mother wasn't born until the late thirteen hundreds though, as I mentioned. Like my grandfather, she was mortal. Matild Blount. She was the daughter of a shopkeeper," he added with a smile. "When Father turned and married her, they switched between the names Brice and Blount."

"No Verdi?" she asked.

Justin shook his head. "I gather my father didn't like his grandfather, Maximus Verdi. From what he's said, the man was a bit of an arrogant ass."

"Ah," Holly said, and then asked, "And where does the Bricker come in?"

"Brice is Irish for Brick," he said with a wry smile. "And when my parents moved to America they thought it would be nice to use a more American name, so Brice . . . Brick . . ."

"Bricker," she said with him, and then smiled. "What are they like?"

She was a little more than curious about that. He was talking about people who were older than America, for heaven's sake. She didn't expect them to be like normal people. Well, normal mortal people, anyway.

Justin was silent for a minute and then shrugged helplessly. "They're a nice, happy couple who love each other and their children and do their best to be good people."

"Hmmm." Holly pursed her lips at that. The description sounded like an average everyday couple to her, and it just didn't seem to her that people who had lived as long as Justin's parents had could be nice and normal.

"Here we are," Justin announced suddenly, and Holly glanced out the window to see that they were turning into a driveway that wound through what appeared to be a forest of trees. She eyed the woods they drove through curiously, amazed to find they went on for more than a couple hundred feet before giving way to a large front lawn. But a quick glance showed her that the same woods appeared to surround the clearing where the house and manicured lawn sat.

"So are the woods to keep people out or in?" she asked dryly.

"Out," he assured her. "Mom and Dad haven't had

to move for decades thanks to those woods. Neighbors can't see who lives here and don't notice they aren't aging. They can just stay here, changing the land title every fifty years or so to be sure that some government worker doesn't notice anything that might seem fishy to a mortal."

"Clever," she decided, shifting her attention to the house itself. It was a very large one-story stucco building painted a sand color. Elegant arches gave way to what appeared to be a shady terrace that ran along the front of the house, giving glimpses of darkened windows in the late afternoon as the sun made its downward journey.

"There was another house here when I was born," Justin said as he parked the car to the side of the driveway. "They tore it down and built this one about ten years ago."

Holly nodded at that, and opened her door to get out. She had just straightened in the V between the car and the door when a bark made her glance toward the house. Spotting the large bear of a dog barreling toward them, she released a startled squeal and threw herself back inside the car, pulling the door closed firmly as she went.

Thirteen

Justin peered from the dog galloping toward him to where Holly had been standing a moment ago, and then bent to look into the front seat to see her staring out, wide-eyed with terror.

"Holly, what—?" he began with bewilderment. Then he heard his mother's shout of warning and instinctively turned just as Samson reached him. Unprepared for 120 pounds of dog hitting him in the chest, Justin went down like a pin under a bowling ball, his back hitting the ground hard to the sound of Holly's hysterical shrieks.

"Samson! Cut it out! Dammit Samson!" Worried by the alien, high ululating sounds now coming from Holly, Justin tried to push the amorous dog off of him to get up, but Samson was determined to lick his face. He'd pushed the big black beast away and started to sit up, only to be knocked back as the dog crawled onto his chest to try to get in another lick.

"Yes, hello," Justin muttered, pushing the dog's

head away again. "What the devil's wrong with you? You have better manners than this."

"Octavius! Heel," his mother barked, and the dog immediately leapt off of Justin and moved to sit beside Matild Bricker.

"Octavius?" Justin asked with surprise, sitting up in the dirt to eye the dog with amazement. The last time he'd seen Octavius was six or seven months ago. The dog had been a fluffy little ball of black fur then. Born half the weight of his littermates, he hadn't been expected to live, but Justin had been visiting when Octavius's mother had given birth and he'd nursed the little guy, bottle-feeding him several times a day. By the time he'd left, the dog had doubled in weight and been as happy and exuberant as his brothers and sisters.

"He's grown a bit," his mother said dryly, bending to pet the dog, who sat quivering excitedly beside her, his adoring gaze firmly on Justin. "And he's usually very well behaved for a puppy, but it looks like he remembers you."

"This is really Octavius?" Justin asked with disbelief as he got to his feet and brushed himself down.

"It is," his mother assured him with a faint smile. "Eight months old and he weighs more than his father, Samson, now."

Shaking his head, Justin moved forward to pet the big fellow, smiling with pride at how well the puppy had turned out. It had been worth every bottle-feeding, he decided now.

"Perhaps you should look after your friend," his mother said solemnly. "I'll take Octavius to the kennels while she's here."

"Oh, but I wanted her to meet the dogs," Justin protested, glancing back to the car and frowning when he saw Holly's clenched expression through the car window. Honest to God, she had the same expression Lucian and Leigh's babies got when they were dropping a particularly hard dirty in their diaper. He wouldn't have been surprised to hear she was taking a dump on the front seat.

"She's not taking a dump on your front seat," his mother assured him on a laugh, and then in more solemn tones said, "But she *is* terrified, Justin. Why on earth didn't you call ahead and tell me that she was terrified of dogs? I would have made sure they were all in the kennel before you got here."

"She's not terrified of dogs," he said, turning to his mother with surprise. "She loves them."

Matild Bricker looked dubious at this claim and then turned back to peer at Holly. After a moment, she shook her head. "I don't know who told you that girl loves dogs, but they were wrong. She was mauled by a pack of wild dogs at three and has been terrified of them ever since."

"What?" he squawked with dismay.

His mother nodded, and then turned away, patting her leg. Octavius immediately obeyed the silent order and stood to follow her. But he also glanced back forlornly at Justin as he went, obviously unhappy about leaving him behind.

Mind racing, Justin watched until his mother and Octavius had walked out of sight around the house, and then turned slowly to the car to peer at Holly. Now that Octavius was gone, she looked a touch calmer. Not more than a touch though. She was as white as a sheet and even from where he stood, he could see that she was shaking.

Holly so did not love dogs, he acknowledged grimly. Anders had definitely got that wrong.

Sighing, he opened the driver's door and slid back behind the steering wheel.

"Close the door. The dog might come back," Holly said at once.

Justin dutifully closed the door, then turned sideways in his seat to take her hands. "It's okay, Holly. Octavius would never hurt you. I promise."

"But he attacked you," she protested. "He—"

"No, honey, he was just excited to see me," he assured her. "And I wasn't ready for all of his weight coming at me at once."

"But—"

"Look," he interrupted, holding out his hands and arms and turning them over. "No bite marks or scratches. He just wanted to lick me in greeting, honey." As she looked him over, he added, "I bottle-fed Octavius as a pup. He apparently recognized me and was happy to see me, that's all."

"Oh," Holly whispered.

Justin remained silent as she obviously tried to gather herself.

After a moment, she seemed almost her normal self again. At least, she stopped shaking and some color had come back to her cheeks when she offered him an embarrassed smile and muttered, "Sorry, I must have sounded like a crazy person."

"No," Justin lied. She really had been screaming like a loon. And he didn't know what the hell that one alien noise she'd been making had been, it had sounded to his ears like half shriek and half mindless twitter. Yeah, she'd definitely sounded crazy. Pushing that thought aside, he cleared his throat and said, "My mother says you were mauled by dogs as a little girl."

She nodded her head jerkily, concentrating on taking deep breaths now.

"But Anders told me you love dogs."

That startled her and she turned to him with surprise. "Why would he say that? I told him about being mauled as a kid."

Justin's head went back slightly at this news. There was no way the man could have mistaken "I was mauled by dogs as a child," for "Gosh I love dogs." His brain ticked that over briefly and then he asked, "What about picnics?"

"What?" she asked with confusion.

"Do you like picnics, but just not on the beach? Or—"

"Actually, I'm not keen on anything to do with nature," she admitted apologetically. "Eighteen years in a tent made me a definite city girl. I like four walls and a bathroom . . . and tables and chairs and a bed," she added firmly.

"Right." Justin nodded slowly. "And flowers?"

"No," she said with a grimace. "They make me think of death ever since starting at the cemetery."

"I can see how that could be," he said grimly. "What about wine? Do you like wine?"

She wrinkled her nose. "Wine is just vinegar with a fancy name."

"Fish?" he queried.

"Can't stand it, head on or off," she admitted, and then added, "Well, unless it's battered and deep fried. I do like fish-and-chips-type fish. Just can't stand the rest of it."

"Right," Justin said wearily, lifting his hands to massage his temples.

Holly eyed him curiously, and then suddenly asked, "Did Anders say I liked all those things?"

He nodded grimly.

"Wow," she said with a frown. "I wonder why. I

mean I told them all of this stuff that day in the restaurant while you were off on your walk."

"I know why," Justin said grimly. He was also
pretty sure Decker had been in on the deal as well.
The two had been messing with him. Paying him
back for the hard time he'd given each of them when
they'd met their life mates. The bastards were probably sitting in Canada right now laughing their
asses off as they imagined him trying to woo Holly
with everything she hated. Payback was indeed a
bitch, he thought grimly.

"Why?" Holly asked when he didn't explain himself.

Rather than answer, Justin opened his door and
got out. "Come on. They've put the dog in the
kennel. It's safe."

Holly didn't exactly rush to follow him, but after
a hesitation, she did open her car door and get out.
After braving a couple of steps though, she paused
and said, "I feel terrible that they had to put the dog
away. Maybe I should just wait here in the car while
you visit with your parents."

Translation, she couldn't see the dogs but knew
they were here somewhere and was terrified enough
that she'd rather sit in the car and wait then come
inside. Feeling terrible about the dog having to be
put away was just an excuse, he knew.

Pausing, he turned and moved back to take her
arm.

"It's okay," Justin assured her quietly, urging her
forward. "I won't let anyone or anything hurt you.
Besides, Holly, you're not a helpless three-year-old
child anymore. You're an immortal. You could have
snapped Octavius's neck, or ripped his jaw in half
had he attacked you," he pointed out, and then

added quickly, "Not that he would. He only jumped on me to try to lick my face. My parents' dogs aren't vicious."

"Dogs?" she asked worriedly. "Like more than one?"

"It's all right, dear."

Justin glanced forward to see that his mother had returned and was waiting in the shade of the terrace.

"Leave her with me and go greet your father," she suggested. "I'll take care of her."

Justin smiled his relief at his mother. "Thank you. Mom, this is Holly. Holly, this is my mother."

"Hello," Holly said politely, holding out her hand as they joined her.

His mother grinned at the politely offered hand and then took it to pull Holly into her arms for a hug. "Welcome to the family, dear."

Justin's eyes widened in horror and he shook his head quickly while running his hand across his throat in a slicing action. His mother arched an eyebrow in question at the gesture and then glanced down with surprise when Holly pulled quickly back.

"What?" she squawked, wide eyes flying between Justin and his mother.

"Holly is a friend, mother," Justin said quickly. "A very *married* friend."

Now it was his mother's turn to peer from Holly to him wide-eyed as she squawked, "What?"

Justin heaved a sigh, and then simply said, "Mother, read my mind."

His mother arched a surprised eyebrow at the request. He supposed it had something to do with the fact that he was usually complaining when she read his mind. But then she shrugged and concentrated on his forehead. A moment passed, then another, and then she let her hands drop and stepped to the side.

"Your father is in his study," she said quietly. "You go ahead. I'll take Holly to the kitchen for some coffee and cookies."

"Thank you," Justin said quietly and then turned to Holly. "Will you be all right?"

"Of course, she will," his mother assured him, slipping her arm around Holly and turning toward the house. "Go on and see your father," she suggested. "We'll be waiting in the kitchen.

Justin watched his mother lead Holly inside and toward the back of the house and then followed them in and headed for the study.

"So you breed dogs for a living, Mrs. Bricker?" Holly asked, staring out the kitchen window at a large kennel with half a dozen huge-looking, bear-like black dogs either resting or playing inside.

"Call me Mattie," Justin's mother instructed. "Mrs. Bricker makes me feel so old. Which I am, of course, but no one wants to feel that way."

Holly turned to peer at the other woman curiously. Matild Bricker was a tall, statuesque blonde who looked no more than twenty-two or -three with her ponytail, jeans, and T-shirt. Despite knowing that immortals all looked in their mid-twenties, it was still difficult to believe that Justin was her son. Actually, it was difficult to believe what her eyes were seeing when she looked at her. The woman talked like a much older woman than her looks suggested and the contrast was continually confusing to the mind. Holly watched the other woman carry a tray of coffee and cookies to the table beside her.

"As for the dogs, they're more a passion than a

living." Matild Bricker set down her tray and then straightened and glanced out the window at the kenneled animals. "Dogs are wonderful creatures. They never judge, don't care what you look like, how smart you are, or how much money you have. They just love you and want you to love them."

Holly turned to peer out at the dogs again.

"The only sad thing is that they have such short life spans," Matild added on a sigh. "Much shorter than humans, whom I don't like nearly as much."

The words surprised a laugh from Holly and she turned to glance at Justin's mother with amusement. "Is that a little anti-mortal sentiment I detect?"

Matild Bricker shook her head and pointed out, "I did say humans, not mortals. Both mortals and immortals can be complete shites at times."

Holly chuckled at that and moved to sit at the table as Justin's mother did. She then grimaced and admitted, "That's kind of depressing. I was rather hoping immortals might be a little more impressive than mortals. I'd think after living so long, they'd . . ."

"Be better versions of themselves?" Matild suggested when she hesitated.

Holly nodded.

"Sadly, age doesn't always mean wisdom," Matild said solemnly. "Some do improve with age, shedding the rough edges of youth and growing into good people. But others . . ." She shrugged. "Depending on their experiences, immortals can get twisted up by time and events and go rogue. That's why we need men like Justin out there." Patting her hand gently, she added, "Immortals are no better than mortals as people, Holly. They just have longer to make mistakes. Fortunately, they often also have the time to fix those mistakes."

Holly was silent for a moment as she doctored the coffee Mrs. Bricker set before her and then she glanced at her and said, "You're being very kind to me, considering."

"Considering what?" Matild asked.

"Considering your son used his one turn on me and may now never get to claim his true life mate," she said solemnly.

Matild smiled faintly. "But you *are* his true life mate, dear."

Holly shook her head firmly. "I'm not. I'm married. And I don't intend to break my vows."

"Then Justin may have to wait until your husband passes," Matild said with a shrug. "Fortunately, he is young. Very young for finding his life mate. Few are that lucky. If he has to wait fifty years or so for you, he can do it. We'll help him through it."

Holly sat back, a confusion of thoughts running through her head at those words. The reference to James's someday passing actually hurt her heart. He had always been a part of her life. She couldn't imagine a life without him in it. But aside from that, she didn't understand why this woman was so certain she was Justin's life mate. Decker and Anders hadn't seemed to think so. They'd seemed to think he was deluded.

"Would this be the same Decker and Anders who told my son that you love dogs, cats, wine, fish, flowers, picnics, nature shows, and everything to do with nature?" Matild asked mildly as she fixed her own coffee.

Holly stared at her with surprise, and then realized that the woman had read her mind. It was a bit disconcerting when these immortals did that and she couldn't wait to learn to block them from doing it.

"Yes," she said finally.

"Then is it not possible that they were lying about your being his life mate as well?" Matild asked.

"Why would they do that?" Holly asked. "And why are you so sure that I'm a possible life mate to Justin?"

Matild hesitated, her head turned toward the door as if she were listening to something from another room that Holly couldn't hear, and then a frown flickered briefly on her face as she said with distraction, "Because I've read both your minds and you're perfect for him, dear."

Holly's mouth tightened at the claim. It made her wonder what the woman had found in her mind that made her think she was perfect for her son.

"Oh." Mattie clucked under her tongue and stood up to move back to the coffeepot. Pouring two more cups, she carried them toward the door saying, "I'm just going to take the boys some coffee and check on them. Have a cookie. I baked them myself."

"It is the most ridiculous situation," Justin growled, pacing his father's study like a caged tiger. "She is my life mate. I've turned her. But I can't claim her. And I'm not even allowed to tell her what I can offer her as her life mate. How great it will be. About the life mate sex, and the shared pleasure, and the shared sexual dreams and the—"

"Justin, life mates share a good deal more than sex."

Justin whirled toward the door at those short words from his mother, and watched with resentment as she entered carrying coffee.

"I was talking to Dad, Mom," he growled with irritation.

"Actually, you were talking to both of us," she announced dryly, pushing a coffee at him before moving on to deliver the other to his father as she continued, "You were complaining so loudly it was impossible for me not to hear, and your voice was growing in volume. I thought I'd better come inform you of that before Holly overheard your whining."

"I wasn't whining," Justin muttered and then grimaced because he knew he had been and said, "Well, if I was, I deserve to, don't you think? This situation is some kind of hell."

Sighing, Matild turned from giving his father his coffee and eyed him sympathetically. "I know it must seem so to you right now. But the situation isn't as dire as you've convinced yourself."

"The hell it isn't," he argued with amazement. "My life mate is *married*. I can't claim her."

"You are forgetting one thing," his mother said solemnly.

"What's that?" he asked shortly.

"That you only can't claim her *yet*," she said, and then pointed out, "You do have one very large advantage over her husband, son, and that is time. You are immortal. He is not. All you have to do is be patient and wait for him to die of old age or whatever end Death deals him and she will be yours."

Justin stared at her blankly for a moment and then exploded. "Are you insane?"

Matild blinked in surprise and then gave a short laugh. "No, I don't think so. But then they do say if you think you're crazy you're not, so perhaps if you think you're sane you're really crazy." When he didn't even smile at her words, she sighed and asked, "What is wrong with my reasoning?"

"You must be joking," he said grimly. "There is no damned way I can just sit by and wait fifty or sixty years for that bastard husband of hers to die."

"Why not?" she asked reasonably.

"She sleeps with him," he snapped, furious at the thought of having to stand idly by imagining Holly sharing a bed with her husband for fifty years or so. He couldn't do it. She was his.

"He has a point, Mattie," his father said solemnly.

"Oh . . . yes . . . I see," she said with a frown, and then brightened suddenly. "But darling, you are forgetting something else."

"What's that?" he asked dubiously. Certainly the last thing she'd claimed he'd forgotten had not been terribly helpful.

"She is immortal now. He is not. She will be able to read his mind and you know how impossible it is to live with someone when their every thought is open to you."

That one had possibilities, he admitted. But . . . "She can't read minds yet."

"Then I suggest that is the very next thing you teach her," his mother said firmly.

Justin hesitated and then asked, "But what if I teach her to read minds and she can't read him? What if he's a possible life mate for her too?"

Her expression turned somber at that question and then she simply asked, "Do you not think it is better to find that out as quickly as you can, so that you can move on if it is the case?"

"The chances that her husband is a possible life mate to her too are pretty slim," his father said reassuringly.

"Are they?" Justin asked. "They grew up together. Have all the same experiences, and have loved each other all their lives." He paced across the room restlessly and then whirled back to ask, "Just how the hell do nanos decide who would be your perfect mate?"

"I don't know," his father admitted quietly.

Sadly, Justin didn't know either . . . and that worried him.

"Your parents are . . ."

Justin shifted his gaze from the road to Holly when she hesitated and suggested dryly, "Weird?"

Chuckling, she shook her head. "No, not weird," she assured him and then added, "If anything, my parents get that crown. They dig up dead people for a living . . . and they like it."

Justin smiled faintly, his concentration returning to the road until she said, "I was kind of impressed, actually."

That drew his attention again and he arched an eyebrow. "Why? Because my father was as handsome and charming as myself?"

Holly laughed outright at his words, but then admitted, "Yes, your father is handsome, and yes, he looks almost exactly like you . . . and yes, he was charming."

"Where do you think I got it?" he asked lightly.

She shook her head at that, but said, "Actually, what impressed me was how your parents *are* together. They seem still to love each other after so very long together," she said with obvious admiration, and then grinned and added, "That or they put on a good show for visitors."

"That wasn't a show," Justin assured her. "They really do love each other that deeply after all this time."

"Pretty impressive," Holly murmured.

"Not so impressive," he assured her, as he turned onto the street where Jackie and Vincent lived. "They're life mates. All life mates are like that. The nanos are good at pairing up couples."

When Holly didn't respond, Justin glanced over at her, but her face was turned toward the window. He couldn't tell how she was reacting to what he'd said, but his guess would have been that she was reacting with resistance. She was so damned determined to stay married to her mortal . . .

"Anders and Decker said you probably couldn't read me because of the head trauma I'd taken," Holly blurted suddenly. "That there was damage that still needed repairing, and obviously there was. I couldn't remember everything that led up to my fall at first."

Justin was silent as he turned into the driveway to the house. But once he'd pulled into the garage and shifted into park, he turned to peer at her solemnly. "I couldn't read or control you before you fell, Holly," he said quietly. "Why do you think I had to chase after you? If I'd been able to control you I would have just made you stop before you ever left the crematorium."

She blinked in surprise at that. "You couldn't read or control me then?"

"No," he assured her, having to fight himself to keep from reaching for her.

Holly stared at him briefly, a struggle taking place in her eyes, and then she turned and reached for her door handle, saying, "It doesn't matter. I'm married."

Justin watched her get out of the car and hurry

into the house. Then leaned back in the driver's seat with a sigh. She was going to fight this to the bitter end. Which meant his only option was to get them to that end as quickly as possible. His parents were right. His best bet was to teach her to read and control mortals and then reunite her with her husband . . . and hope like hell that Holly could read and control him. Because there was just no way she could live with the thousands and perhaps even millions of cuts that knowing every little thing another person thought or felt about you would bring. She just hadn't experienced the pain of people's thoughts yet.

Slipping out of the car, he entered the house. Much to his surprise Dante and Tomasso were not eating at the kitchen table . . . nor were they eating in the living room. The dynamic duo were actually taking a moonlight dip in the pool.

"We need to teach Holly to read and control minds," Justin announced grimly as he stepped outside.

Dante slicked his damp hair back from his face and turned to peer at him. "Sounds good," he said, then slammed an open palm in the water bringing Tomasso's swimming to an abrupt halt. When his twin swam to the edge of the pool and surfaced to peer around, Dante announced, "Justin wants to start teaching Holly to read and control minds."

"About time," the giant growled, running a hand down his face to brush away the water.

"Right. Now, how the hell do we do that?" Justin asked. He'd never actually been a part of training a new turn in reading minds, and didn't really see how it would be done. It was hard to explain the concept of searching out a person's thoughts to someone who had never done it. It wasn't like hunting Easter eggs or anything as concrete as that.

Noting the glance the twins were exchanging, Justin frowned and raised his eyebrows. He then waited patiently as the two men pulled themselves out of the pool and retrieved their towels.

Running the towel over his large chest and then up his arms, Dante said, "We do what we did with Jackie."

"Which was?" Justin asked curiously when the other man paused to concentrate on drying his hair, throwing the towel over his head and rubbing it roughly with both hands over every part of his head.

Justin had to bite back a smile when Dante pulled the towel off of his head. The man looked like one of the Bouviers after his mother had bathed and towel-dried them. His long hair now stood up every which way.

Running his fingers through the knotted mess, Dante pointed out, "Even young immortals can hear the thoughts of other immortals because they project their thoughts. Right?"

"Right," Justin agreed.

Dante shrugged. "So, we start by projecting our thoughts to her as loud as we can. When she begins picking that up easily, we project them with a little less power, then less and less until we are merely leaving our minds open and she is searching out our thoughts. Then we take her to mortals to try."

Justin stared at the man for a moment and then said slowly, "That's brilliant."

"Why do you think Lucian wanted us to help you?" Dante asked with amusement. "We might be pretty boys, but we're not stupid."

"No, you're not," Justin agreed on a chuckle.

"We'll start first thing tomorrow," Dante announced.

"Why not now?" Justin asked, fighting disappointment.

"Because you've had her out all evening," Dante said patiently.

"She'll be tired," Tomasso added. "She needs to be fresh."

"We also need no distractions and no interruptions," Dante added. "So you aren't invited."

Justin stiffened at this news. "But I'm the one who is supposed to be training her. Lucian said I was responsible for—"

"You can take her out to the mall when we get to the point where she can read with some competency and needs to practice reading and controlling mortals," Dante said with a shrug. "But until then, leave her to us."

Justin scowled, reluctant to leave her to these two men. Actually, it wasn't so much that he was reluctant to leave her with them. He trusted Dante and Tomasso. He just didn't want to be away from her. She was his life mate, which meant he was naturally drawn to her and wanted to spend time with her. Shifting unhappily, he asked, "How long do you think it will take to get her to the point where she needs to practice reading mortals?"

Dante and Tomasso exchanged another look, and then both shrugged.

"Couple days," Tomasso said when they turned back to Justin.

"Maybe as many as three," Dante added. "But no more than that."

"Three days!" Justin complained with dismay. Three days of staying away from Holly? That was like asking him not to eat for three days, he thought, and then recalled that it wouldn't really be three days until he saw her again. He would still have their shared dreams while they were sleeping. That thought made him smile. He supposed he could survive three days of avoiding her in person as long as he had the dreams to look forward to. In their dreams was where he could hold and kiss and lick her wet, eager body and—

Justin's thoughts ended on a squawk as Dante gave him a shove in passing that sent him flying into the pool. He surfaced quickly, spitting out water and cursing, but even so, heard Tomasso laugh and say, "Nice one, brother."

"He needed to cool off," was Dante's response as the two men went inside.

Justin swam to the edge of the pool and leaned his face against the cold tiles with a sigh. He had needed to cool off. His thoughts had brought on an erection. But then thoughts of Holly often did that. The woman was like a drug in his blood. At first it had just been the idea that she was his life mate that brought on his interest in her, but after that kiss in the kitchen to bring on her fangs, and especially after the shared dreams . . .

Damn, she was addictive and he just couldn't get enough. Aside from that, the more he got to know her, the more he actually liked her.

After dispensing what advice they could, his parents and he had joined Holly at the table in the kitchen to visit. Justin had mostly watched and listened as his parents had drawn Holly out, and he'd liked what he saw and heard. She was smart and sweet, with a good sense of humor, and she'd been kind and respectful to his parents. He even admired her determination to stick to her marital vows. He didn't like it, but it showed she had honor.

On top of that, while she'd screamed like a crazy person when Octavius had come charging out of the house, later she'd asked to go out to the kennels to see the dogs his mother obviously loved so much. Justin was pretty sure she hadn't done it because she had any great desire to see them, herself. He knew she'd caught him looking out toward the kennels several times during the visit. He'd wanted to see Octavius again before he left. She'd sensed that and braved her fears so that he could see the dog he'd nursed as a puppy. She'd even slipped one hand through the gate to allow the dogs to smell and lick her fingers. She'd trembled as she'd done it, but she'd done it. It gave Justin hope that someday she might actually get over her fear of the beasts.

Yeah, he had it bad for Holly. She was quickly becoming the focus of his life, the only thing he could see clearly. He just worried she would never allow herself to feel the same for him. That she would stick doggedly to her marriage vows and sacrifice all that they could be together.

Sighing, Justin pulled himself out of the water and sat on the edge of the pool to dry.

Fourteen

Holly set her toothbrush on the side of the sink and quickly rinsed her mouth, then stepped out into the bedroom, only to pause and eye the bed warily. If this was the Garden of Eden, that bed was her snake. Well, okay, not the bed, but the dreams she might have in it. They were temptation incarnate . . . and as she'd feared, they had made her look at Justin differently today. Recalling the feel of Dream Justin's hands and lips on her body and the excitement and passion she'd felt with him, she'd found herself staring at his hands and mouth that day, and wondering if they could give the same pleasure to her waking body. She'd also found herself paying undue attention to his physique in his tight clothes. Dream Justin had nothing on the real Justin's body.

Where James was wiry with the slightest paunch, Justin was built like a man who lifted weights. Not with big brawny muscles like Dante and Tomasso, but with muscle and definition.

Holly grimaced guiltily at comparing her husband to Justin in her head. It wasn't fair. Aside from that, she'd never seen Justin even near a weight. She suspected his perfect form was thanks to the nanos. James didn't have that advantage.

Sighing, she walked over to the bed and sat on the edge of it. But she didn't lie down right away . . . mostly because she wanted to. She wanted to throw herself under the covers, close her eyes, and sink into sleep in the hopes that she had more of those amazing erotic dreams about Justin. And there lay the problem. Her enjoyment of and desire to have those dreams made her feel as guilty as hell.

Shaking her head, Holly peered around the room. She had no idea where these dreams were coming from. She hadn't thought she was that attracted to the man before them. Well, okay, not before the kiss, really. That kiss in the kitchen had been the first temptation she'd encountered with the man. He really knew his business in that area. But that wasn't the point, the point was Holly didn't want to be attracted to Justin, and if she went to sleep and had more dreams, would her attraction to him grow? Because she didn't want that either. Although she had enjoyed the dreams themselves, which was making her crazy with guilt.

Realizing she'd gone full circle, Holly cursed and picked up the bedside phone to dial the one person she had always gone to for advice . . . James's mother.

"Hello?"

"Mom?" Holly breathed with confusion, sure she'd dialed James's parents' number.

"Holly," her mother said happily. "James told us all about your internship in New York."

"Oh, God," Holly muttered, and then grimaced. "I'm sorry. I should have called and—"

"Don't be silly. James told us it was all very sudden. I'm sure it was all a whirlwind affair. We're very proud of you, darling."

"Thanks," Holly muttered, wishing she hadn't used the term *affair*, and wondering what her mother would think if she knew the truth of things. "What are you doing at the Bosleys?"

"Well, right now I'm helping Joyce pack. You know how useless she is at it," she said with a laugh. "We're staying here tonight because it's closer to the airport. We're all flying out on our own little adventure tomorrow."

"Are you? What's up?" Holly asked.

"They've dug up some seven-hundred-year-old latrines in Denmark. The poop still stinks apparently!" she said with delight. "Your father wants to . . ."

Holly stared at the wall, listening to what sounded like *blah, blah, blah* to her. She'd sort of cut out after the first part. Really, only her parents could get excited about seven-hundred-year-old poop.

"Anyway, you don't want to hear about this," her mother said suddenly. "And I'm really a bit crushed here, so if you called for a reason, darling . . ."

"Get to it?" Holly suggested wryly, quite used to getting the bum's rush. She suspected if she hadn't been "accidentally" conceived, her parents wouldn't have had any children at all. It wasn't that they were horrible people, it was just that their careers filled up so much of their thoughts and time, there really wasn't room for anything else.

"Yes, dear," her mother said unapologetically.

"Actually, I was calling Mrs. Bosley," Holly said

after a hesitation. "I wanted her opinion on something."

"And you called Joyce instead of your own mother?"

Holly grimaced, thinking, here comes the guilt trip. While her parents didn't have a lot of time for her, they did want to think they were good parents.

"Mom, it's kind of an ethical question type thing, so I didn't think you'd be interested," she said soothingly.

"Well, I am," her mother said firmly. "Spill, and do it quickly. I really am busy."

Holly sighed, but then decided maybe she didn't want to ask this particular question of James's mother anyway and just went with it. "Fine. Is having wet dreams about a man other than your husband like cheating on him?"

"What?" she asked with amazement and then burst out laughing. "Of course not, darling. It's not like you actually did the dirty, it's just a dream. Saying it's wrong or bad is . . . well, really, they can't arrest you for dreaming about robbing a bank, can they? They can't even arrest you for thinking about it. Heck, I've had loads of wet dreams about men who weren't your father. It's normal," she assured her. "Besides, dreams are just your subconscious mind's way of working out issues you have. Perhaps you find this man attractive. Or, perhaps you just wish James was more like him. Whatever the case, just relax and enjoy them. I know I do." She gave a chuckle that sounded decidedly dirty and Holly closed her eyes. She really could have done without knowing her mother ever had wet dreams, let alone loads of them about other men. Really.

"Now," her mother said sounding businesslike.

"If we've handled your little situation, I really need to get back to helping Joyce. Bye, darling."

Holly heard the click and listened to the dial tone for a moment, then slowly hung up on her end. She then sat for a moment, trying not to resent the fact that her mother hadn't even waited to see if they had indeed handled her "little situation." The woman was . . . well, she was who she was, and whining about it and wishing she'd had a mother more like Joyce or Matild really wasn't going to get her anywhere.

Shaking her head, Holly slid under the covers and reached out to turn off the lamp. It seemed she could go gently into sleep and enjoy her dreams without guilt. It was just her subconscious working out her issues.

At least they weren't slasher nightmares, she thought and smiled faintly as she closed her eyes.

"Her."

Holly shifted in her seat to peer across the food court at the woman Justin had gestured to, a middle-aged woman pushing a baby carriage. She was to be her first read. Well, her first mortal one. She'd been working with Dante and Tomasso for the past two days to learn to read. Now Justin had brought her out to the mall to see if she could translate what she'd learned to real situations.

Swallowing nervously, she concentrated on the woman. For a moment, she was afraid that all her work had been for nothing, she wasn't picking up a single thing. But then suddenly it was as if a door opened. "Her name is Melanie Jones. The baby is her granddaughter."

"Good," Justin said. "Now him."

He was pointing at an elderly man with a cane just sitting down at a table on the other side of the food court. Holly turned her concentration to him, a slow smile blooming on her face. "He's a retired bus driver. His wife died recently. He comes here to avoid feeling lonely."

"Her," Justin shot out and she turned her gaze to a harried looking woman, rushing into a yogurt store.

"A businesswoman on her lunch. Linda Jenk—"

"Her."

Holly blinked and shifted her attention to the teenager he was now pointing to. Her eyes widened incredulously. The kid looked like she was twelve, but . . . "She's a drug dealer," she said with amazement. "She's here to meet a kid from her science class to—"

"Him," Justin said and Holly automatically shifted her attention again, and again, and again. Justin shot out "him" or "her" like bullets, one after the other for the rest of the afternoon. By the time he called it quits and led her back out to the SUV, Holly was exhausted, and her head was pounding. She was sure she would also be proud of herself, except that she was too busy feeling extremely confused. It was the way Justin was acting.

Actually, it was the way Justin had been acting for the past couple of days, she acknowledged. This was the first time she'd seen him since they'd gone to visit his parents. That in itself had seemed strange to her. What had seemed stranger was that she had not only noticed, but she'd kind of missed him. Holly blamed it on the dreams. After that first night, the dreams were no longer all about sex. Yes, there was sex, but there was so much more . . . In a way, the dreams had turned into something like dating. They'd gone bowling, laughing and joking as they'd competed against each other, although neither of them had won in the end; they'd gotten distracted halfway through the game and ended up making love against the ball return. In another dream he'd taken her to an amusement park. They'd ridden the rides, he'd won her a stuffed animal, and then they'd finished off the evening by having sex on the roller coaster. In last night's dreams they'd gone to a water park, a zoo, and then Paris, where they'd made love under the Arc de Triomphe.

Okay, it always ended in sex, Holly acknowledged, but Dream Justin was charming and funny and sweet and an amazing lover, and Holly very much feared she was starting to confuse him with the real Justin. And that made her wonder why he was never around anymore when she was awake. It was unexpected, especially since he had said he was supposed to oversee her training. Instead of Justin being there, Dante and Tomasso had taken over her training the last couple of days . . . and she'd found herself missing Justin, wondering where he was, what he was doing, and why he wasn't training her as he was supposed to be doing.

Holly was trying to figure out how to ask him that, when Justin pulled into the driveway of Jackie and Vincent's house.

"You must be exhausted," he commented as they pulled into the garage. Putting the car in park, he shut down the engine and opened his door, saying, "Go get some rest. Tonight we hit the nightclubs so you can practice controlling minds and feeding."

With that he got out of the car and disappeared into the house. Holly stared at the door he closed behind him and then blew her breath out on a sigh as she got out as well. The man had just walked away. It was like he was avoiding her . . . and for some reason, that really bothered her.

"You are an idiot, Holly Bosley," she muttered to herself as she entered the house. "A big stupid dummy of an idiot."

"No, you're not, *piccola*," Gia's voice drew her attention to where the woman sat at the kitchen table, a book in hand. "Why would you even say that?"

"No reason," Holly said quickly as she closed the door to the garage. Noticing the way Gia was now focusing on her and recognizing that it meant the woman was reading her, she tried to distract her. "We're going to the nightclub tonight to practice feeding. Are you coming?"

Gia hesitated, but then raised her eyebrows. "Have you even tried yet to control anyone?"

"No," Holly admitted worriedly. "Isn't it like reading minds?"

Gia clucked her tongue and stood to move to the phone.

"Who are you calling?" Holly asked curiously as she watched Gia run her finger down a list of numbers stuck to the side of the refrigerator and then begin punching numbers into the phone.

"I'm ordering pizza to be delivered," Gia announced, placing the receiver to her ear. Grinning, she added, "The boys can eat the pizzas and you can eat the driver."

"Er . . . I think you mean feed on the driver," Holly said on a little laugh.

"Feed . . . eat . . ." Gia shrugged. "Is the same thing."

Holly didn't argue with her, but moved to the table

to sit down while she waited. In the next moment the woman was giving her order to someone on the other end of the line.

"So . . ." she asked nervously as Gia hung up. "Is controlling someone like reading their mind? I mean, do I just slip into their thoughts and take control?"

"*Si*. Is easy," Gia assured her moving to join her at the table. "Find the thoughts and then put yours in."

Holly nodded, but was now biting her lips nervously.

"With the first delivery, we will just have you control them I think," Gia announced, eyeing her consideringly. "Maybe make them do something they would not normally do, like clap their hands. You are too nervous for more than that."

"The first delivery?" Holly asked uncertainly.

"Hmm." She nodded. "We will order Chinese next and you can make that delivery person do something else."

"Oh," Holly said faintly.

"Relax, *piccola*," Gia said, reaching out to squeeze her hand. "You will do fine. And I am here to make sure all is well, *si*?"

"*Si*," Holly breathed, but it didn't ease her nervousness much.

Justin opened his eyes and stared at the sunlight coming through his windows with confusion. The sun had been setting when he'd lain down to sleep after getting back from the mall. He'd set his alarm clock for nine that night, intending to get up and take Holly to a nightclub so she could practice controlling and feeding on mortals. Sunlight should not be coming through his windows.

Turning his head, he peered at the bedside clock and frowned. It read 6:30 A.M. Cursing, he tossed the sheets and blankets aside and leapt out of bed. He was wide awake now, completely rested for the first time in days, at least since he'd started having shared dreams with Holly. While the shared dreams were amazing and awesome, they weren't exactly restful and he'd been waking up most days almost as tired as when he went to bed. Now, though, he wasn't . . . because he'd slept a deep, dreamless sleep and for a good twelve hours, apparently.

"What the hell?" he muttered, crossing to the bedroom door and rushing out into the hall, nearly crashing into Gia.

"Whoa," the petite woman said on a laugh, catching at his arms, either to steady herself or him. "Slow down. You will tumble down the stairs racing around like that."

"Where's Holly?" Justin asked as she released him and stepped back.

"She just went to her room to get ready for bed," Gia told him, and then arched an eyebrow and pointed out, "It's dawn."

"Yes, I know," he said with irritation.

"Holly said you were going to take her to a nightclub to test her ability to control and feed. She waited all night, but you never came down," Gia said accusingly.

"I was napping," he muttered, and then sighed and ran a hand through his sleep-ruffled hair. It was probably standing on end, he thought distractedly, and then noting Gia's arched eyebrows, said quickly, "I set the alarm on my bedside table before

I laid down, but my alarm didn't go off." Scowling now, he asked, "Why didn't someone wake me up?"

"At first we were busy," Gia said mildly. "And when we realized what time it was, it was too late to go to the clubs anyway, so . . ." She shrugged, apparently the Italian's answer to everything. Moving around him, she added, "We can go to the clubs tonight so you can test her. Is busier on Fridays anyway."

Justin turned to watch her walk to her door. Once there, she paused and glanced back with a smile. "She will do well. We were practicing most of the night."

"Practicing?" he asked uncertainly.

"*Si*. At least until the pizza places closed," she added, and then merely smiled at his confused expression, and said, "*Buona notte, bello*."

"It's morning now, not night," Justin muttered, but she'd already slipped into her room and was closing the door.

Shaking his head, Justin turned and continued downstairs. He needed a drink. His mouth was as dry as a desert. Then he'd go back to bed and sleep and have those shared dreams with Holly that he'd expected to have when he'd lain down to nap. It was why he'd told her to rest. After an entire afternoon at the mall with her, feeling the heat of her body next to his, her delicate vanilla scent filling his head, but being unable to touch her or behave as he wanted to around her, all Justin had been able to think of was getting her back to the house. He'd planned for both of them to lie down for a nap so that they could have shared dreams. There at least, he could do all the things he'd been imagining as he'd sat across from her at the mall pointing out people for her to read.

Instead, she'd apparently stayed up with Gia

while he'd actually slept. Some people might have been happy to get such a long and deep sleep after a week of exhausting dreams. He wasn't. He'd looked forward to those dreams. They were the only thing that had kept him sane during the three days of not seeing her while she worked with Dante and To-masso.

Now she was going to sleep and he was up. But not for long, Justin decided as he reached the bottom of the stairs and started up the hall toward the kitchen. He'd grab a drink and then head right back upstairs to bed and force himself to go to sleep. He'd kept imagining making love to her in the middle of the food court on the table, and he could do that in their dreams . . . and Justin fully intended to—

His thoughts died abruptly as he stepped into the kitchen and took in the state of it. There were pizza boxes and take-out bags on every surface in the room. Some of them were actually open, their contents wholly or half eaten, but most were not.

"What the hell?" Justin muttered with bewilder-ment, and then gave his head a shake and hurried to the refrigerator to grab and slap a bag of blood to his fangs as he fetched himself a glass of water. He could ask about the fast food-a-thon later, when everyone was up. Right now his main interest was getting back to sleep and ravishing Holly.

That thought made him hesitate and then move to the refrigerator again. This time to retrieve the last IV of sedative mixed with saline that sat on the top shelf. It was a leftover from what Lucian had had brought in to keep Holly under until he could leave on the day they'd brought her here.

Grabbing the bag, he started to let the refrigerator door close, then the bottled water inside caught his eye. Justin eyed it briefly, then set down his glass of water and turned to move to the garbage as he ripped the now empty blood bag from his mouth. Once he'd disposed of the bag, he then returned to the fridge to grab the bottled water.

"Easier to carry," he muttered to himself as he turned away, and that was important since his next stop was the broom closet to grab the IV stand they'd stored there. After sleeping more than twelve hours, Justin was quite sure he wasn't going to be able to get back to sleep without a little aid, but he was also desperate to sleep now that he knew Holly would be sleeping as well.

"Man, what I'll do to get laid," Justin muttered to himself with a shake of the head as he tucked the IV bag under his arm, leaving his hands free for the bottled water and the IV stand.

He headed back to his room then, hands full of his bootie. Much to his relief, Justin didn't encounter anyone on the return journey. He really didn't want to have to explain himself. Fortunately, everyone was apparently abed and sleeping. Once in his room with the door safely closed, he set the bottled water on the bedside table, then quickly set up the IV stand next to the bed and hung the saline bag from it. After that, he nipped into the bathroom to take care of personal matters.

Once back in the room, he approached the IV, only to realize that he hadn't thought to grab the IV needle, tape and tubing. Clucking under his tongue with irritation, Justin jogged back downstairs for the items, then returned to attach the tubing and primed the chamber, then sat down on the side of the bed.

He had just finished inserting the IV needle in the

crook of his elbow and taping it in place when his cell phone began to chirp. One look told him it was Mortimer. While Lucian was the big boss, Mortimer was now the head of the Enforcers, basically his supervisor. It was a call he had to take.

Muttering to himself, he snatched up his phone with the hand not hooked up to the IV and pressed the button to answer the call as he placed the phone at his ear.

"Lucian wants a report on how Holly's training is going," was the greeting.

"And good morning to you too," Justin growled, silently calculating the time difference in his head. It was just after 10 A.M. back in Toronto. Mortimer would normally be sleeping at this hour. "What are you doing up?"

"Working," was the grim answer, and then he added pointedly, "We're really shorthanded here, Bricker."

"I know," Justin said on a sigh. "Sorry about that."

"Don't be sorry," Mortimer said. "It's not like it's your fault. But I'll be glad when you're back. You are coming back, aren't you?"

Justin considered the question. He really didn't know the answer. If he managed to convince Holly to be his life mate . . . well, he didn't know if he would be able to convince her to move to Canada. She was from here, as were both their families. But if he failed at claiming Holly as his life mate, he supposed going back to Canada to work was better than hanging around here in the hopes of catching a glimpse of her.

Running a hand through his hair he admitted, "I don't know, Mortimer."

"I was afraid you'd say that." The other man

sighed down the line, cleared his throat and then said, "So a progress report for Lucian?"

"Good," Justin said quietly. "She's pretty much learned everything she needs to. I've taught her all the important laws and she can bring on and retract her fangs. She can also read minds and tonight we're going to a club to teach her to control minds and feed."

"So you're nearly done," Mortimer said thoughtfully. "And the wooing?"

Justin's mouth tightened, but he wasn't surprised at the question. Mortimer wasn't just his supervisor, he'd been a Rogue Hunter before being promoted and had been his partner on patrol. They were also friends. Finally, he simply said, "She's married."

"Yeah, but surely now that she can read minds it will cause trouble with the marriage," Mortimer said quietly. "Do you think—?"

"I don't know," Justin interrupted unhappily. "I just don't know, Mortimer. She's receptive in the shared dreams, but the woman is as stubborn as hell. She's definitely determined to stay married when she's awake."

"She's responsive in the dreams though?" Mortimer asked, and Justin could hear the frown in his voice.

"Yeah. Very," he assured him. "A wildcat."

There was silence for a minute and then Mortimer asked, "Does she know the dreams are shared?"

"What?" he asked with surprise.

"Have you explained about shared dreams? Or does she just think she's having them herself?" Mortimer explained. "Because it doesn't make sense that she'd be so receptive, as you put it, in the dreams but so determined when awake. I mean I'd think she'd be a little resistant in the dreams too if she knew she was sharing them with you."

Justin stilled, trying to recall if he'd explained about shared dreams to her. He was pretty sure he hadn't. In fact, the thought now of doing so was rather alarming. If he explained about them to her and she did become resistant . . . he'd lose the only part of her he had.

"No, I don't think she knows that," Justin admitted quietly.

"It might help if you told her they were shared, Bricker," Mortimer said quietly.

"Or she might start resisting me in the dreams too," he pointed out.

"She might," he acknowledged. "But she will also have to reexamine herself and her feelings and acknowledge that she's attracted to you at least. Then, when the marriage fails . . ."

"*If* the marriage fails," Justin said grimly.

"Just think about it," Mortimer suggested.

"Yeah," he muttered.

They talked for a few more minutes, with Mortimer updating him on what was going on back in Canada, and then ended the call. Justin stared at his phone for several minutes before setting it down. He then grabbed the bottle of water, opened it, and quickly drank half. If the next couple hours went as it usually did when he shared dreams with Holly, he was going to need the liquid.

Smiling faintly at the thought, Justin reached up to remove the clamp from the IV bag to allow the liquid to start to flow. He then got carefully back under the covers, already thinking about where he should take Holly in their shared dream this time.

Fifteen

"God, it's loud in here," Holly complained, her gaze sliding over the dance floor. It hadn't seemed this loud in her dream . . . or maybe it had been and she just didn't recall because she'd had so many other dreams since that first night.

A tap on her arm drew her attention and she glanced around to see Justin gesturing for her to follow as he led the way to an open table. She fell into step behind him, glancing over her shoulder to be sure the others were following as well and smiled faintly at the size difference between the petite Gia and the two mammoth men behind her. She didn't think she'd ever get used to how big Dante and Tomasso were. Honestly, she'd never met anyone as big as the twins, but then not many archaeologists were into body building.

"Drink?" Justin asked, leaning his mouth to her ear as she sat down.

Holly nodded, and then turned to say, "Just a Coke."

There seemed little use to drinking alcohol. Apparently she couldn't get a buzz anymore. Not that she'd drank to that point much while she was mortal anyway. She'd had a few memorable nights while attending the University of British Columbia, but not more than a handful. She wasn't much of a drinker.

She watched Justin wave a waitress to their table, then turned to peer at the dance floor.

"Want to dance?" Gia asked, and Holly turned to her with surprise, not because of the suggestion, but because she'd heard her so clearly. She understood why when Gia said, "I'll dance with you," without moving her lips at all. She hadn't spoken the question, trying to be heard over the loud crowd, she'd thought her question at her. Justin probably hadn't done it because he couldn't read her mind nor she his.

Holly nodded in response to Gia's suggestion and stood when the other woman did, then followed her out to the dance floor. She didn't know if Gia made some signal or simply sent the thought to Justin to let him know where they were going, but she must have done so because Justin didn't stop her to ask where they were headed.

Dancing was something Holly loved to do. There was just something about moving her body to the primal beat that made her feel free, and sexy. It was also one of the things she'd missed most about the way she'd grown up. There had been no high school dances or nights out clubbing with a fake ID while growing up.

"Make that guy come and dance with us."

Holly heard Gia's words in her head and followed the woman's gesture to a blond guy in a white dress shirt and jeans. He was good looking, and was dancing with a young pretty brunette in a skimpy dress.

Hoping she wasn't going to cause problems in a relationship, Holly slipped into the man's thoughts.

They weren't in a relationship, she read as she took control and made the guy think he wanted to come dance with her and Gia. She could have just made him walk over to them without adding the thought that he wanted to, but his movements would have been wooden and possibly noticeable to the others dancing around them. This way, he sort of danced his way over to offer them both a wide, interested smile, looking for all the world as if it had been his idea.

The moment he reached them, Gia turned and concentrated on the DJ in his glass box and within seconds the loud, fast music that had been playing faded away to be replaced by a slow, sexy beat.

"Dance with him." Gia's voice sounded in her head and Holly concentrated on making the blond take her in his arms. It wasn't that hard. She barely had to put the thought in. She could read that he was attracted to her and the knowledge made her feel sexy and powerful as she slid her arms around his neck and pressed against him.

"Feed," Gia encouraged, and Holly glanced to her with alarm over the man's shoulder. While she had controlled several delivery men last night, making them clap their hands, jump up and down, and even do little dances, she hadn't fed off of any of them.

Despite saying she would practice that skill with the delivery men, in the end, Gia hadn't suggested she try it and Holly certainly hadn't volunteered. In truth, she was afraid to feed off of anyone. What if she lost control of their minds and they became aware of what she was doing mid bite? Or what if she took too much blood and harmed or even killed someone? Those same worries were in her mind now, along with the concern that they were in the middle of the dance floor where anyone might see.

"It's dark and no one is paying attention," Gia assured her. "Remember to stay in his thoughts. Find his vein with your lips and tongue. It's hard to explain, but you'll know when you find it. Then count out slowly to thirty as you feed. Stop after thirty and he should be fine," Gia instructed. "You can always feed off of more than one person if the need arises."

Holly bit her lip and glanced to the blond man's neck. He was holding her terribly close, his head bowed next to hers, leaving his neck exposed at a level she could reach. She peered at the unmarred skin for a moment and then leaned her face toward him and merely rested her lips against his throat, trying to find the vein before letting her teeth out.

"Mmmm," her dance partner murmured by her ear in reaction. His hands then dropped to slide over her behind to squeeze her cheeks and lift her slightly, urging her snugly against him.

Ignoring that, Holly concentrated on trying to find the vein, allowing her tongue to lightly trace the skin of his neck.

"You don't want him to feel pain and you'll experience pleasure when you bite him. Let him feel your pleasure to cover the pain. But give him the thought that you're just kissing his neck or giving him a hickey or something as you do," Gia's words came into her head unimpeded just as Holly found the vein. As Gia had said, it was hard to describe how she knew it was the right spot, but she did. Still she hesitated another moment, afraid to mess this up and have the guy start screaming his head off and shoving her away.

"I'm right here," Gia reassured her. "I'll control him if anything goes wrong."

Right, Holly thought, then took a deep breath and let her fangs slide out to pierce his skin. She gasped in surprise as pleasure slid through her, tingling along her tongue and through her body. But then she felt the man holding her stiffen and she quickly tried to transfer her pleasure to him as well. When he shifted so that one of his legs was between both of hers and he ground himself against her hip while rubbing his thigh against her core to the slow beat, she knew she'd succeeded and turned her attention to counting to thirty. It was amazing how long it could take to count to thirty slowly. But the amount of pleasure she felt at feeding off a mortal was even more amazing. Holly had never felt this reaction to bagged blood being popped to her teeth. With that there was just a sort of relief and she could only think the nanos caused this response to make feeding off of mortals more appealing than it otherwise would be. And it *was* appealing. She could have gone on for hours sucking at his neck while he held her in his warm embrace, their bodies moving together, but Holly was worried enough about hurting him that she stopped the minute she reached thirty.

"Oh, baby, don't stop," her dance partner moaned, turning his head to try to claim her lips.

"Send him away," Gia said with amusement when Holly twisted her head away and began to struggle in an effort to get out of his hold.

She'd forgotten she could control him, that she was, in fact, still inside his thoughts, Holly realized.

Feeling stupid, she quickly put the suggestion in his thoughts that he wanted a drink. Something with orange juice, she added, just in case, and sent him on the way to the bar.

"Remove yourself from his thoughts and put in an explanation for the marks on his neck," Gia instructed, and Holly followed the man with her eyes as she slid back into his thoughts to remove herself from his memory. She paused there though and glanced to Gia wondering just what kind of explanation she could put in his mind for the puncture wounds on his neck.

"An accident with a barbecue fork?" Gia suggested with a laugh.

Holly shook her head, but couldn't come up with anything better, so quickly slipped the idea into the man's mind and then withdrew from his thoughts.

"*Splendido, piccola!*" Gia congratulated, grabbing her by the arms and pulling her into a hug. "Very good. *Superbo*! I'm so proud!"

Holly laughed with relief and hugged her back, but then pulled back and said, "It was much nicer than bagged blood."

"*Si*," Gia agreed with a smile, but then her expression turned serious and she added somberly, "But remember, we feed like this only in emergencies."

"And in training," Holly put in.

"*Si*," Gia agreed. "But if you do it at any other time you will be punished."

"What's the punishment?" Holly asked curiously.

"Death," Gia answered. "Feeding off mortals is risky. It raises the likelihood of our existence being discovered. It is not allowed except in emergencies . . . and training."

"Right," Holly breathed. Blood bags were suddenly looking more attractive.

"Again," Gia said now. "We must find you another to practice on."

"**Y**our fangs are showing."

Justin glanced to Dante with a start, and then became aware that he was snarling, and his fangs were indeed out. Forcing them back in, he snapped his mouth closed and took a deep breath as his gaze shifted back to the dance floor where Holly seemed to be dry humping every mortal in the place as she fed on them. That was an exaggeration, he acknowledged. She'd only fed on four so far, and on a sensible level, he knew a certain amount of contact happened when you fed, but that didn't make it any easier to watch.

She was dancing with a girl now, her face buried in the woman's throat while the woman moaned and ran her hands up and down her back. Gia was an equal opportunity picker it seemed, since he was quite sure the other woman was the one who had pointed out each of Holly's targets. Justin had wanted to tear into the two men, and even the women Holly had fed on. He would have thought he'd enjoy seeing her with another girl at least. He'd certainly enjoyed threesomes in the past, but not with Holly. She was his. He didn't want anyone touching her that way.

"More than a couple of the donor hosts Gia picked were a little the worse for wear, it seems," Dante said suddenly and Justin narrowed his eyes as he noted the way Holly stumbled as she stepped back from her latest donor. Drinking from a drunk donor resulted in a drunk immortal, if only temporarily. The nanos would clean it out of her system quicker than the mortal would sober up. Even so, it was as dangerous for her to be feeding in this shape as it would be to drive.

He'd barely had the thought when a mammoth of a man almost as big as Dante and Tomasso approached the girls. Justin expected Gia to send the fellow on his way, so was surprised when Holly turned wide-eyed to the woman and then back to the man, her mouth making a round O. She then slid into the man's arms, looking like a sylph stepping into King Kong's embrace. When she slid her arms around his neck and tugged him down and still couldn't reach even the vicinity of his neck, Justin almost smiled. But he immediately lost that urge when she slid from his arms and started away, crooking her finger at him to follow.

Justin recognized that gesture from the first night they'd shared dreams . . . and she was heading for the bathrooms, or at least the hallway to the bathrooms. Amusement turning into the green dragon that was jealousy, Justin lunged out of his seat and hurried after them.

Holly led her latest donor off the dance floor, down the hallway with the bathrooms and past both doors to one marked employees only. She expected it to be an office or a broom closet, but it was a third bathroom she found when she pushed through the door. She'd expected to have to use her new skills to control whatever employee was inside and send them out, but the room was empty. Smiling at that fact, she paused and turned to face her donor.

"Pick me up." Holly hadn't meant to say the words aloud. She'd intended to slip them into his brain, but she did both. That or the man was just happy to do as she requested. Moving forward, he clasped her by the waist and lifted her until she was at face level.

"Closer," she mumbled, unable to reach his neck from where he held her. She put the image of what she wanted into his head and then sighed with relief when he pulled her close, one arm under her behind and the other around her back, cradling her against his huge body so that she could reach his neck.

"Thank you," she muttered, and then took a moment to concentrate on his thoughts, sinking herself into them as she bent her head forward to run her mouth over his neck. She'd barely started when her eyes popped open in surprise as her back suddenly slammed into the tile bathroom wall. A quick check of his thoughts told her he was just a little unsteady on his feet and was using the wall to help him stay upright.

Relaxing, she wrapped her legs around his waist—well, more like his chest, God the guy was huge—and turned her attention back to his neck until she found the vein. She'd just sunk her fangs in when the door to the room opened.

Opening her eyes, she spotted Justin and hesitated. He looked pretty grim, like she was doing something wrong. She frowned around King Kong's throat as she tried to recall where she'd been with her thirty count, and then sighed with exasperation and retracted her fangs from King Kong's neck and made him put her down.

Once she was back on her feet, Holly sent King Kong out of the bathroom and on his way with no memory of what had happened.

The silence that fell in the room once the door had closed was rife with tension and Holly peered uncertainly at Justin. "Is something wrong?"

Justin smiled suddenly, the tension sliding out of his body. "Yes, actually," he murmured, moving closer and reaching toward her head. "You looked better in that outfit with your hair down."

Holly glanced down at the black leather vest and mini skirt she'd borrowed from Gia. It's what she'd worn that first night in the dream at the nightclub. Only then she'd had on Gia's thigh-high black leather boots too. Holly had foregone those for flat sandals tonight only because she liked to dance and her feet would have been aching like crazy in five minutes of trying to dance in them.

"And with the boots," Justin added. "Those boots were sexy as hell."

Holly's head came up just as he released the banana clip Gia had used to put her hair up for tonight when they were getting ready. She stared at him blankly as her hair fell around her shoulders. "What boots?"

"The thigh-high ones you wore to the nightclub the first night we had our shared—" Justin stopped abruptly, something flickering in his eyes. She would have called it a silent "oh shit."

"Our shared what?" she asked grimly. The only time she'd ever worn this outfit was in a dream. Gia had worn it that day and she'd admired it and wished she had the courage to wear something like that even just once . . . and then she had, in her dream. The dream and what had happened in it were what had given her the courage to wear it tonight when Gia had suggested it. Although she suspected Gia may have given her courage a little nudge too to help her along, because she'd been about to say a definite no when she'd suddenly found herself saying yes.

That didn't matter right now, though, of course. What did was that Justin was claiming to have seen her in it before, and since the only place she'd worn it was her dreams, she suspected— "You can read me."

"What?" Justin said with surprise.

"You've been lying all this time," she accused. "You can read me and you read that memory from my mind."

"No, Holly, I didn't," he assured her quickly.

"Then how could you know about the dream I had?

Justin hesitated and then ran a hand through his hair with a deep sigh. Turning, he paced a couple steps away and then turned back. "Another symptom of life mates is shared dreams."

Holly stiffened. "What are shared dreams?"

"They're just what they sound like, dreams the life mates share," he said simply, and then seeing her bemused expression, explained, "If life mates sleep within a certain distance of each other, their minds sort of merge in sleep and share their dreams. It's the only time, aside from sex, when life mates' minds open to each other."

Holly sucked in a breath at this news, her mind whirling. Shared dreams? Her wet dreams? Like the one where he'd screwed her up against the wall of a nightclub? Or in a car? Or—dear God, did he actually know what she had dreamt? Was he dreaming that stuff too? Or, she wondered suddenly, was he making her have them?

"You put those dreams in my head," she accused, suddenly furious.

"No," he assured her. "It doesn't work like that. Our minds merge; one doesn't dominate the other. I couldn't make you do anything you don't want to do in the dreams. We are both contributing to them subconsciously."

Holly stepped back with dismay, her mind racing. Oh God, oh God, oh God. That had to be cheating. It was certainly more cheating than just having those dreams by herself. And he'd known all along what was happening. Dear God, he'd actually been a party to it when she'd invited him to screw her up against the wall in the nightclub, and then in a car, and then—Oh God, he'd laid her out on the table like a feast and then gone at her like he was eating a quarter slice of watermelon. And that was after she'd acted like he was her own personal pogo stick and then tried to swallow his sausage whole on the freeway.

It was one thing when she'd thought they were just her own mind trying to work through what might be a subconscious attraction, but if they were both there, doing those things, even if it was in dreams . . .

They might not be able to arrest you for dreaming about a robbery as a rule, but what if you woke up with the bags of money in your bed? Because she'd woken up drenched from orgasm after orgasm, and she knew from the dreams that he'd reached completion too. They might not have physically touched each other, but they'd had orgasms together and that had to be cheating. Where did one draw the line?

"I'm going to be sick," Holly muttered, pushing past him to stumble out of the bathroom.

"Holly." Justin followed, concern in his voice. "Honey, shared dreams are a normal part of being a life mate. They're natural."

Suddenly furious, Holly turned and slapped his face. "Get this through your thick goddamned skull, Justin. I'm a married woman. I have a husband I made vows to that I plan to keep. We can never be life mates."

Whirling away then, she rushed into the ladies' room to escape him and slammed into the first open stall. In the next moment she had the door locked and was perched on the edge of the toilet seat, sobbing into her hands.

She'd cheated on her husband. She hadn't thought she was cheating, and her mother had assured her that the dreams she was having weren't cheating, but they were. They weren't normal dreams. Justin had been right there with her, in mind if not body. She was a cheater. A slut. A two-timing ho-bag.

"Holly?"

Stifling her sobs, Holly tried to regain control of herself at the sound of Gia's voice and after a moment managed to sound relatively normal when she said, "Yes?"

"Can you come out here, *piccola*?"

"No," Holly moaned, and then had to fight to keep from bursting into sobs again.

"Please don't force me to make you, piccola," Gia said gently.

"You can't," she sniffled. "You have to see the person to control them." At least she'd learned something useful the last two weeks. Well, besides the fact that she was the whore of Babylon.

"I can see you through the crack, Holly. I can take control. Please don't make me," Gia said grimly.

Her gaze immediately shot to the space between the door and the stall wall, and Holly saw that Gia could indeed see in. Certainly, she could see a sliver of Gia through it. Cursing under her breath, she pulled a wad of toilet paper off the roll on the wall next to her, blew her nose and stood up to unlock the stall door.

"What?" Holly muttered resentfully as she stepped out.

"Are you okay?" Gia asked.

"What do you think?" Holly said bitterly, throwing the tissue in the garbage and moving to the sink to turn on the tap. "I just found out I've been having an affair on my husband and didn't even realize it." Whirling suddenly, she glared at her. "Why didn't you tell me about shared dreams?"

"It wasn't my place to tell you. Justin—"

"Oh, like he'd tell me," she snapped, and whirled back to the sink. "Thanks for nothing."

Gia hesitated, and then straightened her shoulders and added, "And because I thought you might try to put an end to them and—"

"Of course I'd have put an end to them," Holly growled, splashing cold water on her face.

"And," Gia repeated, "I thought it would be better for you to have them."

Face dripping, Holly whirled. "What?"

Gia sighed and shook her head. "Holly, whether you like it or not, you are Justin's life mate."

"Possible life mate," Holly snapped. "Possible, but since I'm married it's not possible."

"It is when your marriage fails," Gia said quietly.

Holly gaped at her. "You want my marriage to fail?"

"No, *piccola*, of course not," Gia said gently and

stepped forward to hug her. Rubbing her back, she added, "But I fear it will."

Holly stiffened and tried to pull out of her arms, but Gia tightened them grimly and continued, "I have lived a long time, *piccola*. You are not the first married mortal who has been turned for one reason or another."

"You mean because they were a possible life mate to an immortal," she muttered into her shoulder.

"No. There are other reasons. There have been mortals in the past who have saved the life of an immortal, or even many immortals, and who have been turned for their selfless act."

"Really?" Holly asked with surprise, pulling back slightly. This time Gia let her so that she could see her nod.

"*Si*. It is very rare, but it has happened," she assured her. "And in the two cases I know of, the mortals were married to other mortals. Those unions did not go well after the one was turned. The new immortal could read their partner, and even control them once trained. For one of the two new immortals, they could not bear what their mortal mate truly thought of them. It was too hurtful to hear their thoughts all the time." She paused briefly to let her absorb that and then added, "The second new immortal could not resist controlling her mortal husband and making him do what she wished. He became little more than her puppet, and she hated herself for doing that to him. In both cases, the unions ended badly, and the new immortal had to go on alone."

Hugging her again, she patted her back and said, "Fortunately, for you it can be different. You are Justin's life mate, and he gave up his one turn for you.

The fact that you have had shared dreams with him proves that you are life mates, and the fact that you enjoyed them so thoroughly—"

"How would you know I enjoyed—You read it in my mind," Holly asked, and answered, her own question.

"Yes," she said unapologetically. "And you *did* enjoy your shared dreams with Justin. You are attracted to him."

"But I'm—"

"Married," Gia finished for her dryly. "Yes, I know. And I know you will not just accept my suggestion that your marriage may not now work. You need to go home and see for yourself." Releasing her completely, she stepped back. "I suggest you do that now."

Holly blinked. "What? Now, now? Like this minute?"

Gia shrugged. "Your training is over. You have learned all that you need to survive as an immortal without risking harm to mortals. I will see that Justin arranges for regular deliveries of blood. And," she added solemnly, "If you sleep at the house tonight, you will not be able to prevent yourself from having shared dreams with Justin again."

Holly's eyes widened at that and Gia nodded.

"I hope you may be able to forgive yourself for the dreams you've had, because you did not know they were shared. But I know you will never forgive yourself if you return to the house tonight and knowingly have them again." Meeting Holly's gaze she added, "Trust me when I say that if you sleep in the same house as Justin, you will have them again, *piccola*."

While Holly absorbed that, Gia reached down the front of her top and retrieved a wad of money that she had apparently tucked in her bra. Taking Holly's hand, she pressed the money into her palm and closed her fingers over it. "Take a taxi to the bus station. One leaves at 1:45 in the morning which is in a little under an hour."

"You know the bus schedules?" Holly asked with disbelief.

"I looked into it a couple days ago. I knew you would not take it well when you learned that you were not having your dreams alone. I thought it best to be prepared," she said gently, and then offered a crooked smile and added, "Fortunately, you did not find out until your training was done. I feared you would find out sooner and be forced to stay, in which case . . ."

"I'd have still had the dreams and have to deal with my feelings about that," Holly guessed.

Gia nodded, and then hugged her quickly. "There is a slip of paper in amongst the money with the number to my cell phone on it. Call me if you need to, or even if you just want to." Straightening, she smiled and added, "I like you, *piccola*. And I think we could be good friends if your marriage does not work out and you accept Justin as your mate."

Releasing her then, she turned to move to the door. "Wait here for a couple of minutes. I will get Justin to accompany me back to the table so that you can slip out."

"You won't get in trouble for this, will you?" Holly asked with concern.

Gia shook her head. "You are done with your training, there is nothing to be in trouble for." Turning back, she offered a crooked smile and added, "Justin will be very angry at me at first, but he is not the type to hold a grudge. Safe journey, *piccola*."

"Thank you," Holly murmured and watched her walk out. She then paced the bathroom, silently counting slowly to 120 before moving to the door and easing it open. The hall was empty. Holly slipped out and let the door close silently behind her.

Justin tore his gaze from the hallway leading to the bathrooms, and glanced worriedly at Gia on the dance floor. She'd urged him away from the ladies' room and back to their table some time ago, at least half an hour by his watch, and told him that Holly would be fine, she just needed some time alone. The woman had then gone out onto the dance floor and hadn't returned to their table since . . . and neither had Holly.

He was about to go check on Holly himself when Gia suddenly waved at where he and the twins sat at the table and then headed for the hall to the washrooms.

She was checking on Holly, he thought and relaxed back in his seat. She'd bring her back, he assured himself. Hopefully, after smoothing everything over with Holly and reassuring her that shared dreams were perfectly natural between life mates and she had nothing to feel guilty—or angry at him—for.

That thought made him sigh unhappily. He'd known Holly would be angry when she discovered the dreams she was enjoying were shared. He'd just hoped . . . he didn't know what he'd hoped. Justin supposed he'd simply not wanted to think about her being angry because the shared dreams were the only real connection he had to her and he hadn't wanted to give them up. There had been no doubt in his mind that if she knew that he was sharing in the dreams she was having, she was stubborn enough to try to stop them from happening. She probably would have taken to sleeping out on the lawn or something ridiculous like that to try to prevent them. When that didn't work, she no doubt would have demanded he sleep in a hotel on the other side of Los Angeles to avoid it happening again.

Justin peered at his watch and saw that another fifteen minutes had passed since Gia had gone in the washroom. What the hell were the women doing? And what was this proclivity women had to spend so much damned time in the bathroom together? Did they play poker in there? Have tea parties? Book club meetings at the sinks? Napkin-folding practice with the paper hand towels? What?

Just when Justin was about to lose all patience and storm after them himself, Dante poked his arm and pointed out, "Here comes Gia."

Yes, here came Gia . . . alone, he noted grimly and stood up.

"Okay, let's go," the woman said brightly, breezing past the table, headed for the exit.

"Wait!" Justin barked, hurrying to catch her arm and stop her. "Where is Holly?"

Gia eyed him solemnly, and then said in a gentle voice, "She's gone home, Justin."

"What?" he snapped, his fingers tightening unintentionally.

Gia reached up and wrenched his hand from her arm, but her voice was still gentle when she said, "Her training is done. She has learned all she needs to know to survive as one of us and she has now gone home to her husband."

Justin stared at her with bewilderment and then shook his head faintly. "But . . . how?"

"I gave her money. She took a taxi to the bus station. Her bus leaves in five minutes. She is on the way home."

Justin's mouth snapped closed and he rushed past her, his only thought to get to that bus station and stop Holly.

"You'll never make it to the station in time," Gia said patiently, following him out of the nightclub. "I deliberately waited to tell you until it would be too late for you to stop her."

"Why?" He whirled to scowl at her furiously. "What the hell have I ever done to you that would make you do this to me?"

Gia shook her head sadly and walked forward to rub his arm. "I didn't do this to hurt you, Justin. I did this to help you. She is drenched in guilt over your shared dreams and too angry right now to be reasonable. The sooner she goes home, the sooner she will realize that there is no way she can make her marriage work now that she is immortal. And that means the sooner she will return to you. This way she left before she or you could say something that you both might later regret."

Justin turned his head away and then asked, "Do you really think her marriage won't work out now?"

"Of course. She can read his mind and control him. A relationship that is so unbalanced cannot work."

"What if he is a possible life mate to her too?" he asked, naming his biggest fear.

"I don't think so," Gia said with slow certainty.

Justin immediately turned back to look at her. "Why?"

"Because in her thoughts her upset is that she cheated, even that she cheated on her husband, but never once did she think she had cheated on James."

"But James *is* her husband," Justin pointed out with confusion.

"Yes, but she thinks of him as her husband, not as James, the man she loves," she tried to explain, and then waved that away and said, "Never mind, only a girl would understand. The point is I do not think it will take long for her to realize the marriage cannot work. So the sooner she gets home the better. And you have to let her go so that she can see that and return to you free of all doubts and reservations."

Justin narrowed his eyes. "This is sounding like that stupid 'if you love her let her go' bit."

"I suppose it is," Gia said with a crooked smile. "In this instance it is true."

Sighing miserably, Justin glanced to Dante and Tomasso who had been silent throughout.

"She's a woman," Dante said with a shrug. "Women always seem to understand this nonsense better than us poor men."

"Women know women," Tomasso added.

Shaking his head, Justin turned to continue on to the car, saying, "Come on. Let's get back to Jackie and Vincent's. I could use something to eat. Maybe ice cream."

"Ice cream is good for drowning sorrows," Dante said approvingly.

"Spoken like a woman," Justin muttered as he pushed the button on the key fob to unlock the SUV. Christ, Holly was gone and he was left with two eating machines and a sprightly little Italian female who . . . who had his best interests at heart, Justin told himself wearily as he got behind the steering wheel.

Sixteen

Holly paid the taxi driver the fare for the ride home from the bus station and slid quickly out of the car, wincing as bright sunlight struck her face. It had been a long exhausting ten hours and three transfers since she'd got on the bus in Los Angeles and she hadn't slept a wink the whole way. Instead, she'd spent the entire journey mentally beating herself for everything from dream cheating on her husband to running with scissors.

Two weeks ago her life had been settled. She was married to a man she'd grown up with, had always loved, and could never imagine cheating on. She was working on the last year of her degree with the promise of a good career before her . . . and she was mortal. Now she had a marriage everyone seemed to think would quickly crumble to pieces, she had cheated on her husband, in her mind if not physically, and she was immortal.

She did still have her career though, Holly thought

wryly. That, at least, hadn't been affected by the events of that night at the cemetery. She still had her marriage too, though, and it was up to her to keep it. Holly was determined that she would.

She mounted the steps to the front porch and raised her hand to knock, then paused and tried the door knob instead. Her mouth immediately twisted with irritation when it opened. Honest to God, sometimes she could just smack James, she thought with irritation. Both her parents and his had co-signed on the mortgage. Both sets of parents had also gifted them with the down payment. This house was the best they could afford, but it wasn't exactly in a good neighborhood . . . and she didn't mind that. What she did mind was that her husband kept forgetting to lock the damned door in this less than sterling neighborhood. She understood that he had been raised in various tents where there was no such thing as a lock, but so had she and she didn't forget to lock the door. Besides, they'd stopped living in tents seven years ago. Just how long was it going to take for him to start remembering to lock it?

Realizing that she was standing in the open door mentally ranting to herself, Holly shook off her anger and slid inside. Instead of being upset that he hadn't locked it, she should be grateful that he had forgotten and she could enter, she told herself, because James was no doubt sleeping right now and the man slept like the dead. She could have been knocking a heck of a long time.

They would work on ways to help him remember to lock the door, Holly told herself as she closed and locked it herself. She headed up the hall and turned into the kitchen, heading first to the refrigerator. She hadn't had anything but a coffee and donut since getting on the bus last night and was starved. Unfortunately, she opened the refrigerator to find it completely barren. It looked like James hadn't shopped at all since she'd left. He'd probably hit the drive-thru on the way home and then on the way to work every day. The man wasn't much of a cook. He could manage macaroni and cheese, or spaghetti, but that was it. It wasn't like he was Justin, who could—

Holly cut that thought off abruptly. Having been raised in tents, neither of them had known much about proper cooking when they'd left their parents to start out on their own. Besides, Justin was over a hundred years old. He'd had a lot more time to learn to cook. It wasn't fair to compare the two men, she told herself.

The doorbell rang and Holly quickly closed the refrigerator door and then rushed out of the kitchen and back up the hall to answer it before the bell rang again and woke up her sleeping husband. She pulled the door open, a polite smile of inquiry on her face, and then raised her eyebrows at the courier standing there.

"Delivery for Mrs. Holly Bosley."

"Who from?" Holly asked curiously as she took the clipboard he held out.

"Argeneau Blood Bank."

"Oh." Holly flushed, a combination of embarrassment and alarm assailing her as she worried what the man might think she needed blood for. Did hemophiliacs keep blood in their homes?

"You'll need a separate refrigerator for the blood," the fellow announced as he took back his clipboard. "I gather someone will be out today to deliver one."

"A separate refrigerator?" she asked uncertainly, stepping back as he picked up the cooler and stepped forward.

"Yes. In case of nosy visitors," he explained. "You

don't want them opening the kitchen refrigerator in search of milk for their coffee and seeing stacks of blood lying around."

"No," Holly said faintly as she closed the door and led the way to the kitchen. That wasn't something she'd even considered. Perhaps she hadn't learned everything she needed to know about being an immortal after all.

"Don't worry, you'll get the hang of it," the young man said, setting the cooler on the kitchen floor in front of the refrigerator. Pausing then, he offered a hand. "I'm Mac, by the way. I'll be delivering all your blood."

"Oh." Holly managed a smiled and shook his hand. "Thank you."

"Just doing my job," he said lightly, and then turned to open the refrigerator door and suggested, "I'd recommend your bedroom closet for the mini fridge they're delivering. Even the nosiest visitor won't poke far in there. Unless of course your husband is mortal and doesn't know . . . as is apparently the case," he added dryly as he quickly transferred the blood into the fridge.

"How did you know—" she began uncertainly.

"Newbies are easy to read," he said apologetically. "Sorry."

"You're an immortal?" Holly asked with amazement.

Pausing, he glanced up and smiled, allowing his fangs to drop as he did.

"Oh . . . wow," she said weakly and for some reason that made him chuckle.

"Don't worry. You'll start to recognize when an immortal is in your vicinity quick enough," Mac assured her, going back to work.

"How?" Holly asked at once.

"You'll feel a very faint sort of buzzing through your body," he explained. "It's probably happening right now, but because you're still adjusting to being more sensitive to so many things at once, that one won't get noticed at first."

"I suppose you mean the hearing, smelling and seeing better?" Holly asked, and while she had noticed being able to see farther and hear conversations she wouldn't have been able to before, it wasn't like she suddenly had X-ray vision or anything.

"Your brain is overwhelmed right now with all the new levels of information. It's not used to taking in so much data. You'll notice the difference over time though," Mac assured her as he finished transferring the blood, closed the refrigerator, and straightened with the cooler in hand.

"Oh," Holly murmured as she followed him out of the kitchen. When they reached the front door, she asked, "Are you a newbie too?"

"Yeah. Two years tomorrow," he announced with a grin as he opened the door. "It's great, huh?"

"Great," Holly said and his eyebrows rose at her lack of enthusiasm.

Reaching out, Mac patted her shoulder. "It'll get better. Change can be hard, but once you adjust, you'll enjoy it. I promise."

"Thank you," Holly whispered, and then watched silently as he walked out to the van parked in her driveway.

Closing the door, she let her forehead rest against it and closed her eyes. *I'll adjust*, she assured herself. But right now, she had to sort out where to put the mini fridge that was apparently coming. Not her bedroom. She needed it somewhere James wouldn't notice. Holly knew she had to tell him about the change in her at some point, but she wasn't ready for that conversation right now. She needed a little time to adjust to the changes herself before she tried to help him adjust.

The laundry room downstairs, Holly decided suddenly. James hated laundry. She'd put the refrigerator in there and then take over the chore of doing laundry from now on, until she explained everything. Yes, that would do, she decided and then gave a start when the doorbell rang again.

Whirling, she opened the door. The refrigerator had arrived.

"Honey?"

Holly shifted sleepily on the couch and blinked her eyes open. When she recognized the man leaning over her, she sat up abruptly, the blanket she'd pulled over herself dropping to her waist. "James."

"What are you doing sleeping on the couch, honey? When did you get home?"

"Around noon," she answered running a hand through her hair to be sure it wasn't standing on end. "I laid down on the couch because I didn't want to wake you."

"Well, you're home now. How about a hug for the poor husband who had to do without you for so long?"

"Oh." Flushing, Holly stood, allowing the blanket to slip to the floor, but rather than hug her, James stepped back, eyes widening.

"Whoa, wow, what are you wearing?"

Holly glanced down, blushing brightly as she stared at Gia's leather outfit. She wasn't surprised by his reaction. She didn't even own a skirt in her meager wardrobe. Jeans and dress pants were all she usually wore, and this skirt was a little short . . . okay a lot short, she acknowledged, tugging at the hem to make it look a little longer.

"Oh, I borrowed this from a friend and didn't have time to change before the bus left," she lied.

"Plane."

Holly glanced at him blankly. "What?"

"You mean before your plane left," James explained. "You surely didn't take a bus all the way home from New York," he added with a laugh.

"Yes, plane," she said weakly, giving her head a shake. She had always been a horrible liar, but how could she have forgotten she was supposed to have been in New York on an internship rather than in Los Angeles playing Bela Lugosi?

"Well, good. I'm glad the outfit's borrowed," James said on a laugh. "For a minute I thought you were—" Cutting himself off abruptly, he shook his head. "It doesn't matter. You look great. You've lost weight, haven't you?"

"I—a little," she murmured.

"Good." Smiling, he turned to head for the kitchen. "I'm starved. Let's have some breakfast."

Holly stared after him, unmoving. He might not have said what he was thinking, but she'd read his mind. That was something she'd promised herself she wouldn't do on the bus ride home, but she hadn't been able to resist. The thought he'd cut off was that he'd thought she was going slutty on him, and his

comment about her losing weight had been followed
by the unspoken thought that he was relieved. He'd
feared she was going to "chunk out" now that they
were married, and had found her extra pounds unattractive before this weight loss.

The worst thing about it was that she couldn't
confront him about his thoughts because she
shouldn't know them. And Holly couldn't even be
mad because they were his thoughts. He had every
right to think her outfit was slutty, and it wasn't his
fault if he'd found her less attractive with the extra
twenty pounds she'd been carrying before the
turn. He hadn't said that. He'd kept his thoughts
to himself, no doubt, to avoid hurting her. She was
the one who had intruded into his mind and read
them.

Holly let her breath out slowly. Gia was right. It
was going to be hard to keep this marriage together
now that she could read his thoughts. She really
needed to refrain from using her new skills with
him. And she would, Holly promised herself grimly.
She would never read his thoughts again.

"Hey, honey. We don't have anything in the refrigerator. Do you want to go out to supper?"

Holly glanced toward the kitchen at that shout and
bit her lip. All her old clothes would be too big, and
she hadn't packed and brought any of the new ones
she'd bought with Gia. Clearing her throat, she said,
"I don't know. Why don't we order—" She paused
when the doorbell rang, and then hurried to answer
it. It was another deliveryman. Holly accepted the
envelope and the clipboard he handed her, and then
watched with surprise as he turned to hurry back to
his truck. Noting that *Gia Notte* was in the slot as the

sender, Holly quickly opened the envelope and read
the short letter inside.

I thought you might need your new clothes.
Hope everything is going well.
You have my number.

Giacinta

Sighing with relief, Holly stuffed the letter and envelope into her pocket and quickly signed the docu-
ment on the clipboard in the spot marked with an
X. She then offered the clipboard and a smile to the
deliveryman as he returned with a box.

"Thank you," she murmured, taking it from him.

"My pleasure. Have a good day," the man said
turning to head back to his truck.

"Holly? Did you want to go out to dinner or not?
We can invite Bill and Elaine to make up for having
to cancel last time." James stuck his head out of the
kitchen, then raised his eyebrows as he noted the
box she was carrying. "What's that?

"My clothes," Holly said, moving toward the
stairs. Now that she knew what James thought of
her outfit, she wanted to change. She'd have to ship
the skirt and vest back to Gia, of course.

"Airport misplaced it?" he guessed and when Holly
glanced at him blankly, James clucked his tongue impatiently and explained, "Your suitcase. I gather the
airport lost it briefly?" He paused, one eyebrow rising
as he noticed the box she was holding. "Although it
looks more like they wrecked your suitcase or something. I doubt you took your clothes out there in a box."

"No," Holly agreed vaguely, and then hurried upstairs to avoid further questions.

"**I**'m surprised you aren't coming back with us."

Justin shifted his gaze from the small plane that had just taxied to a halt twenty feet in front of them to glance at Dante, and then shook his head. "I need to stay close."

He didn't explain why, but then he didn't have to. They all knew he was waiting there in the desperate hope that Holly would realize her marriage couldn't work and would give him a chance.

"Well, I'm surprised Mortimer is okay with you hanging around here when he's so shorthanded," Dante said.

"I left a message and he didn't call back so he must be," Justin said mildly. He didn't admit though that he'd shut off his phone after making the call.

"Hmmm," Tomasso grunted. "I wonder."

Justin raised his eyebrows and then followed the man's gaze to the plane. The door was open, the stairs down and—Justin straightened abruptly when he saw who was coming down the steps out of it.

"Crap," he muttered, fighting the sudden instinct to jump in the SUV and drive off.

"*Si*. It could mean *merda*," Dante said thoughtfully.

"For you," Tomasso added.

They all fell silent as Lucian approached. Stopping in front of them, he skimmed them with a gaze before focusing on Dante and Tomasso. "Go ahead. And I'm sure Justin thanks you for your assistance," he added as the two giants headed toward the plane.

"I thanked them before we left the house," Justin said tensely.

Lucian gave an abrupt nod and then raised an eyebrow. "Where is your bag?"

Crap, Justin thought, but said, "At the house. I'm staying."

Lucian nodded and then asked. "Where?"

He blinked in surprise. "Well, at—"

"Jackie and Vincent gave us permission to use their home for Holly's training. That's done. Did you call and ask them if you could stay longer?" he asked mildly. "Or do you plan to stay at your parents' for the next year or so? You and Mortimer did sell your condo, did you not?"

Justin cursed under his breath. He'd planned to stay at Jackie and Vincent's, but . . . "The next year or so?" he asked, his frown deepening.

Lucian shrugged. "I am just guessing how long this could take. Holly could change her mind and come around in a couple weeks or months, or she might never. I'm guessing you won't give up for a good year though."

Justin scowled at the thought of her not coming around at all. She had to. She was his life mate.

"So how do you plan to fill your time while you're waiting?" Lucian asked. "Helping out your parents with the dogs?"

He so wasn't living at his parents'. He loved them, they were great and everything, but they would drive him mad in no time.

"And did you write up a resignation for me to give to Mortimer?" Lucian added pleasantly.

Justin gave a start at that. "A resignation? I'm not resigning."

Lucian raised his eyebrows, nodded, and then barked, "Then get your ass on the plane."

"But—" But how would Holly find him if she did change her mind? he wanted to ask. He couldn't get the words out though.

"Gia gave Holly both her number and yours. If she comes around, she will undoubtedly call one of you.

In the meantime, you do nobody any good pacing around Vincent's house, or your mother's, eating cheese puffs and refusing to bathe."

"How do you—"

"You smell," Lucian interrupted succinctly. "And you have orange powder on your cheek and—" He reached out and plucked something from his hair above his right ear and then held it up in front of Justin's face. It was the broken end of a cheese puff. Justin had been eating them in bed last night. One must have rolled down his cheek into his hair, he realized. Lucian turned to flick away the remnant of food, then turned back and eyed him solemnly. "It is hard. I know. You are hurting. I know. But if she does change her mind and come for you, do you really want her to find you sitting around here feeling sorry for yourself?" He let that sink in and then added, "You would do better to get back to work, take out your frustration on some rogues, and hold on to your self-respect. Mortimer needs you."

Justin stared at him blankly for a minute and then shook his head, murmuring, "Wow."

Lucian narrowed his eyes. "Wow, what?"

"It's like Leigh is making you almost human," Justin said, a crooked smile twisting his lips. "You even speak in whole sentences now and everything."

Lucian scowled. "Get your ass on the plane."

Justin shoved his hands in his pockets and started walking toward the plane, a little cockiness in his walk. "You need me. You said so."

"I said Mortimer needs you," Lucian growled, following.

"Yeah, but you missed me. I can tell," he said, his smile becoming more natural.

"I missed you like a pain in the ass," Lucian snapped.

"That's still missing me," Justin said on a laugh as he jogged up the plane steps. He was still smiling as he entered the plane and threw himself into one of the four empty seats Dante and Tomasso had left. He watched silently as Lucian pulled the plane door closed and the engine fired up. When the plane began to taxi, Justin turned to peer out the window at the sun-splashed tarmac, his smile fading. He was leaving Holly behind in sunny California, and didn't know if or when he'd see her again . . . It felt like a part of him was dying.

"Are we supposed to go in, or are Bill and Elaine meeting us out here?" Holly asked James as he steered her car into the restaurant parking lot.

"Inside," James answered, parking. "Whoever gets here first gets a booth." *Undoubtedly that'll be them since we're late as usual.*

Holly bit her lip and tried to ignore that thought when it hit her. It hadn't been directed at her, and hadn't even been a complaint about her really. It was just a generally unhappy thought, and it was true. They *were* usually late. Between work and classes, Holly always seemed to be scrambling.

James was always ready on time; he only had work to contend with and after sleeping all day, he'd got up, showered, dressed, and was ready to go when she'd got home. It was she who had rushed in the door after spending all morning in classes and all afternoon at work and then had to rush to get ready. It hadn't helped that her boss at the present temp job she was working had stopped her on the way out to ask a question. Holly had spent fifteen minutes explaining something she'd already explained to him earlier that day before she could get away. It had put her behind the gun before she'd even walked in the door. They would have had to leave right then to get here on time, but she'd needed to change.

Sighing, she undid her seat belt as James turned off the engine, then slid out of the car when he did and walked around to meet him in front of the vehicle. When he held his hand out, she automatically slid hers into it, and they crossed the parking lot hand in hand. It was the first affectionate gesture she'd felt comfortable with in the two weeks since she'd been home.

Things had been weird since her return, Holly acknowledged, but knew it was all her fault. She was the one who kept reading his thoughts. She'd promised herself she wouldn't, but had broken that promise repeatedly. She just couldn't help it, and it was making her crazy.

"There they are."

Holly tore herself from her thoughts and peered around the restaurant, smiling when she spotted Bill standing up to wave at them. James started forward at once, pulling her along with him and they made their way quickly to the table.

"Oh, baby! Someone's turned into hot sauce," Bill said on a surprised laugh as he took Holly into his arms for a bear hug and bussed both her cheeks. He stepped back then, but kept his hold on her arms to look her over, adding, "What the hell have you done to yourself? I mean I can see you've lost weight, but it's like you've taken a sexy drug or something."

Holly blushed furiously at the compliment. It was

the weirdest damned thing. Ever since getting home, people were acting like she'd turned into Angelina Jolie while she was gone. Not just the men, but the women. It was like the nanos were some sort of chick magnet that attracted members of both sexes. It was bizarre, and discomfiting for Holly, who wasn't at all comfortable in social situations to begin with. Although, she'd never felt anxious around Justin, Gia, Dante, and Tomasso, she recalled.

"You do look good," Elaine agreed, nudging her husband out of the way to hug Holly as well. She then looked her over as she released her and shook her head. "What is it? Some amazing and weird New York diet?"

Holly shook her head on a strained laugh and quickly slid into the booth to hide behind the table as she said, "Just lots of fresh air I guess."

"Yeah, right, fresh air. In New York?" Bill snorted as they all settled in the booth, he and Elaine taking the opposite bench seat and James sliding in beside her. "That would be the pollution diet then?"

"If that's what pollution does for you, I'm in," Elaine said with a grin.

Holly smiled faintly and picked up the menu lying on the table in front of her, hoping they'd change the subject.

"You must be happy to see her, James my boy," Bill said and then teased, "I bet the house hasn't stopped rocking for the last two weeks."

James gave a weak laugh and muttered, "You know it."

Holly bit her lip and glanced sideways at her husband behind the protection of the menu. She was just in time to see him open and raise his own in front of his face. The action blocked him from Bill and Elaine's view, but she could see it and his expression was pinched. Sighing, she turned her attention back to her menu. The house hadn't rocked at all the last two weeks. They hadn't even had sex on Sunday night as they usually did . . . and that was her fault too.

Holly closed her eyes briefly as she recalled the first time James had tried to make advances in that area. It was the night she'd got home. Bill and Elaine hadn't been able to join them on such short notice and they'd gone to dinner alone. It was when they got home that James had tried to start something. Holly had been surprised when he'd suddenly started to kiss her in the hallway inside the front door. It wasn't Sunday after all, but she'd gone along with it.

Unfortunately, James had had a couple beers with supper and garlic Alfredo for his meal. The smell and taste of that combination as he'd kissed her had been overpowering to her new and heightened senses. Equally unfortunate was the fact that rather than offend him and gently suggest they both brush their teeth, she'd tried to suffer through it . . . and that hadn't worked out so well. After several minutes while he'd been kissing her, one hand squeezing her breast and the other fumbling at the zipper of the jeans she'd changed into, she'd had to push him away and make a run for the bathroom to toss up her own meal.

Afterward, Holly had lied and claimed that her tummy was upset and that her own meal must have been off. James had been sweet and bundled her off to bed to recover, but she'd read the disappointment in his thoughts. And what disappointment there had been. Here he'd been really interested for the first time in a long time and she wasn't up to it. It seemed that prior to her leaving on her "internship," he'd been bored to tears with their routine sex. That he only bothered on Sundays as a rule because he hadn't wanted to hurt her feelings or make her feel unwanted. Besides, he'd felt that for their marriage to work they should have sex at least once a week even if he had to imagine it was Elaine to get it up since Holly had gained those extra twenty pounds.

That last bit had left her gasping and in tears. Fortunately, James had put that down to her feeling unwell and had been even sweeter to her. But come Sunday, when he'd made the usual overtures, she hadn't been able to forget his words and despite reading his mind and knowing he wasn't imagining Elaine then, and that it was her new figure that interested him, Holly just hadn't been able to get past her hurt and work up any interest herself.

She'd tried to fake it and pretend interest, hoping that some small response might follow as they proceeded, but had felt nothing but disappointment. She'd inhaled the citrusy tang of James's aftershave, and found herself thinking she preferred Justin's more woodsy scent. And why couldn't he kiss her like Justin had? With passion and desperation instead of the wimpy nibbles he used. She wasn't even sure James knew his tongue was good for more than pushing food around inside his mouth.

Despite her pretended interest, there had been no spark at all. In truth, there had never been much spark to begin with in her marriage bed, but Holly hadn't known then what she was missing. Now that she had experienced the fireworks and passion Justin had produced in her with just a kiss, then in their shared dreams, she hadn't been able to stand the lack of it with James.

Of course, he had picked up on her lack of enthusiasm and had backed off. While she'd lain awake, feeling guilty for wanting a man other than her husband, he'd gone down to play video games through the night.

After a week of reading his thoughts and finding out other little things she really wished she didn't know, last Sunday had been a repeat of the previous. And this past week had been just more of the same. It wasn't that James's thoughts were deliberately cruel or unkind. It was stupid little things, like he suspected she was OCD because she was determined to keep the house clean. And he hated her meat loaf, which she'd always thought he liked . . . and her eggs were too runny, and her cookies were hard as rock . . .

Then there were bigger things, like while he appreciated that she'd worked while he finished his courses, James wished she'd hurry up and finish hers so that he wasn't carrying the lion's share of the burden when it came to supporting them. And why couldn't she have waited until he was making better money to switch from full-time work to part-time and start back to her classes? He felt guilty for these thoughts. After all, they had agreed to do it this way when they'd decided to marry, but he was tired of living hand to mouth. James felt her having to wait a couple years to go back to school wouldn't have been that big a deal, and they could live so much better now if she was still working full time.

Another big issue she'd discovered reading her husband's mind was that her discomfort in social situations embarrassed him and made him feel put upon. He felt he couldn't leave her alone at parties or she'd sit in a corner like a wallflower looking miserable. That had stung her and all Holly could think was that she hadn't been socially awkward at the nightclub with Justin, Gia and the boys. But then they hadn't spent the night giving her reproving looks, or censoring everything she said.

Holly had spent a lot of time the past two weeks thinking of her time with Justin and the others. Despite the situation, she'd laughed more and been more relaxed around them than she'd ever been in her life. She'd enjoyed her budding friendship with Gia, and had often found herself laughing at the twins' teasing as they trained her. She'd even enjoyed Justin's attempts to woo her. More than that she'd missed talking to the man. She kept recalling their chat on the way back from visiting his parents, and the others they'd had on their shared dream dates. They'd laughed a lot while bowling and then at the fair, at least they had before passion had overtaken them. She missed that laughter. She missed a lot of things. But mostly, she missed Justin . . . which made her feel guilty as hell and didn't help anything.

It seemed clear to Holly that unless she wanted to lose her marriage, she needed to stop thinking about Justin, banish him from her mind. She also needed to get past letting James's thoughts affect her. But it was hard. She knew she wasn't perfect and shouldn't think James would believe she was. She even had complaints of her own about him, but she still loved him, and she was quite sure he loved her despite the mild criticisms and complaints she'd read from his mind. But knowing he probably had complaints, that all husbands did, and actually knowing what those complaints were . . . well, it was two different things entirely. And Holly didn't have a clue what to do about it.

At this rate, it was looking like Gia, Justin, and the others were right and she was going to lose her marriage and her childhood sweetheart and then what would she do?

An image of Justin's laughing face came to mind and Holly forced it away. She couldn't let him affect her decision. She would not leave James for Justin. That could not be the reason. And she couldn't give up on her marriage this easily. Marriages took work. She needed to work at it. She would get past her memories of him, or find a way to block them. She had to.

"So?" Elaine said as Holly finally settled on what she would order and lowered her menu. "Tell us about New York."

Seventeen

"Bill was really weird tonight."

Holly watched the lights flickering past the car and shrugged with disinterest at James's comment. In her opinion, everyone had been acting weird tonight: Bill, Elaine, the waiter. Dear God, they'd all acted like she was Marilyn Monroe or something, fawning and sucking up to her, and hugging her too long as they'd left. Someone should have warned her about that side effect of being an immortal. She supposed it was handy when it came to feeding, but she had bagged blood to work with. Having everyone practically drooling on her was just embarrassing really when she knew she was the same person she'd been just a couple weeks ago. It had been bad enough when Bill had flirted with her lightly, but then Elaine had started jokingly suggesting that they have an orgy . . . well, Holly had been glad when they'd finished eating and could leave. Fortunately, James had seemed just as eager to go home as her.

"Elaine was kind of acting strange too. I think she was actually hitting on you," James said now.

"Jealous?" Holly muttered, glaring out the window now.

"What?" He laughed, but it didn't sound like a natural laugh. "Did you just ask me if I was jealous? Why the hell would I be jealous of Elaine?"

Holly opened her mouth, and then closed it and shrugged. "She's an attractive woman."

"Maybe. I've never noticed," he lied and Holly turned sharply to peer at him with disbelief.

"Really?" she asked dryly.

James shrugged, his attention firmly on the road ahead. "She's not my type."

"Oh, right, so you've never imagined it was her you were making love to on a Sunday night?"

"What?" he squawked with obvious alarm. "Where would you get something like that?"

"From you," Holly snarled, suddenly furious. Between classes, work, and going out it had been a really long day for her, a long two weeks actually, and while she'd tried not to be hurt by all of his little thoughts this past week, she was. They had cut her to the quick and her self-esteem was now bleeding out and turning to red rage.

"Don't be ridiculous, I would never say something like that," he protested.

"No. But you sure thought it, James."

"What, you can read minds now?" He laughed nervously and shook his head. "You're just being paranoid."

"Paranoid?" Holly asked in dulcet tones, her temper completely shredded. "Oh no, you don't get to call me paranoid, James. You can think I'm OCD and socially awkward, and you can pretend it's

Elaine you're banging to get it up, but you do not get to tell me I'm paranoid for knowing it."

"What the hell?" He glanced to her with alarm and then back to the road. "Where are you getting this stuff?"

"From you, James," she repeated grimly. "From your thoughts."

Grinding his teeth, he tightened his hands on the steering wheel and shook his head. "That's not—"

"Possible?" Holly finished for him.

"You can't—"

"Read your mind?" she finished again, and then snorted grimly. "Actually I can. You see, I wasn't away in New York at the start of the month. I was in Southern California, just outside Los Angeles, learning to be a vampire because I was stupid enough to run with scissors."

"What?" he squawked turning to peer at her. Then shock turned to anger, and he growled, "You've lost your mind."

"Really. Then what are these?" Holly asked, and opened her mouth to let her fangs slide out.

James stared, his anger slowly giving way to amazement and then fear. Before he could recover or respond, the sound of tearing metal hit her ears and Holly was thrown against the seat belt, then jerked back against the seat as they crashed into something. Even as they came to an abrupt halt, darkness was closing over Holly, dragging her into its soothing depths.

Something was dripping. That was the first thing Holly was aware of. It was followed by a damp sensation everywhere and pain. Lots of pain. Groaning, she opened her eyes and peered around, confused at first as to where she was and what had happened. A red light was glowing nearby, casting a nightmare vision across the interior of the car as it blinked on and off, briefly lighting up the man in the front seat next to her.

"James?" Holly murmured. She started to shift, to try to move closer to him, but sharp pain in her side made her halt and glance down. A tree branch had come through the windshield and impaled her, running through her right side and into the car seat.

"Nice," she muttered, and then grimaced.

A moan from James drew her attention his way, and Holly frowned and reached her left hand out to touch his shoulder. He was slumped on the deflated airbag draped over the steering wheel. He moaned again at her touch, but didn't respond otherwise and she glanced over him worriedly and then looked out at the front of the car.

They'd crossed into the oncoming lane and continued right off the road to crash into a tree, she saw. The driver's side of the car looked like a squeezebox. Her gaze dropped toward James's legs then and alarm claimed her as she saw that the metal had been pressed in and crushed his legs. She couldn't even see most of his legs from the seat down, but she could smell the blood and guessed that was the dripping she heard, it was running over the metal and dripping on the already soaked car carpet.

God, all she could smell was blood.

"James, can you hear me?" she asked, her voice surprisingly strong considering how much it hurt to even breathe.

James moaned again, and this time, started to

rouse and try to sit up, but then he cried out in agony and fell back against the steering wheel, unconscious once more.

Cursing, Holly turned her attention to the tree limb pinning her to the seat. It was a smallish branch, about four or five inches in diameter would be her guess. Gritting her teeth, Holly grasped it about six inches in front of her chest and managed to snap it in two.

"Couldn't have done that as a mortal," she muttered to herself as she tried to work herself up for what came next.

"This is gonna hurt," she grumbled, and then grabbed the end of the shaft now protruding from the right side of her stomach and yanked it out with one quick jerk and an agonized scream.

Holly sat clutching the stick and panting as she waited for the pain to ease. It was when she slowly became aware of liquid running down her stomach and soaking her pants that she dared to glance down and see that she was pretty much hemorrhaging blood.

"Crap," she breathed, and then looked around for something to at least staunch some of the bleeding until her body could repair itself. Not spotting anything right away, Holly dropped the stick, popped open the glove compartment and retrieved the half roll of paper towels she'd placed in there just last week. Pulling off wads of "the quicker picker upper," she quickly stuffed it into the hole in her stomach, wincing as she did.

"I'd never make it as a field medic," she muttered to James's unconscious form as she unrolled more paper towel to add to the first bunch. "I hope the nanos don't think the paper towel is normal and try to turn me into a big roll of it or something."

Holly laughed weakly at her own joke, and then shook her head as she pictured herself as a roll of paper towels with arms and legs.

"Must be delirious," she decided.

When James moaned in response, Holly peered at him sharply, and then eased to the edge of her seat to brush the hair back from his face. She frowned at how pale he was. The man had lost a lot of blood, and he was still losing it. Holly was no doctor, but it seemed pretty obvious that his chances of surviving weren't good if they didn't get help soon.

She peered out the car windows, looking for that help. But of course they'd crashed in one of the few stretches of uninhabited road between the restaurant in San Francisco and their home in San Mateo. James would insist on using back roads instead of the freeway. Cursing again, she turned to peer at her husband, her mind working.

This wasn't his fault; it was hers for arguing with him while he was driving. If she'd just kept her temper in reign and her mouth shut . . . How had she expected him to react when she'd flashed him her fangs? And she shouldn't have been running with scissors in the first place. If not for that, Justin wouldn't have turned her to save her life, and everything else that had happened, wouldn't have, including her husband dying on a dark back road at the age of twenty-six.

"Screw that," Holly spat, and without thinking about it, grabbed him by the hair with one hand and pulled him back to rest against the driver's seat. At the same time, she raised her other hand to her face and ripped into her wrist. If Justin could turn her to save her life, she could turn James, Holly thought grimly as she quickly placed her gushing wrist against James's gaping mouth. She wasn't sure if it was her yanking on his hair, or what, but James woke up enough to open his eyes and peer at her dazedly. He then choked and tried to back away from her wrist, but she held him still.

"Swallow," she ordered grimly. "We may be having problems, James, but I'm not going to have your death on my hands for the next millennia or however long I live, so swallow."

Much to her relief he did.

Holly kept her wrist to his mouth until James passed out again, and then took it away to see that it had stopped bleeding. The nanos had sealed it, she noted and wondered if they were doing the same to her stomach. If so, she might be able to take the paper towel out now. But Holly had other matters to concern herself with just then, and so she left the paper towel and instead turned her attention to the metal crumpled around her husband's legs. Holly eyed it briefly. She was obviously stronger now that Justin had turned her. She'd snapped that branch like a twig when she wouldn't have been able to before the turn, but breaking a branch and unbending the metal from around James's legs were not the same thing. However, she didn't see much choice here.

Straightening, Holly opened her door and got out to walk around the car. When she reached the front, she braced both hands on the uncrumpled passenger side of the hood and shoved with all her might. Much to her amazement, the car rolled back under the effort. Her confidence getting a big boost from that success, Holly moved to examine the driver's side door and then glanced into the car with surprise when James stirred. She'd thought he'd be down for the count, but he'd thrown himself back against the car seat, his face a rictus of agony. When he then began to moan in a loud voice, she quickly set to work on the door.

Holly didn't know if the blood she'd given him had perked him up a bit, or if the turn itself was already causing him pain, but James was soon screaming his head off as she worked to free him. She withstood it for a good ten minutes, before she, who had never hit anyone in her life, stopped what she was doing and punched her husband, knocking him out. It wasn't because his agonized screams were driving her crazy, which they were, but Holly just couldn't bear that he was suffering such agony. His being unconscious, to her, seemed a kindness. Unfortunately, the pain didn't let him stay under long and ten minutes later she was knocking him out again.

Sighing with relief when James fell silent again, Holly finished unbending the last of the metal pinning him in the car and then pulled her husband out of the front seat and set him on the grass at the roadside so that she could get a look at his legs. The damage was horrifying. His left leg had been nearly amputated with just a bit of tendon remaining attached at the knee. She was amazed that it had come with him when she'd pulled him out of the vehicle. His right leg was a little better. At least it was still fully attached, but it looked like someone had run it over with a lawn roller, crushing all the bones.

Mouth tightening, Holly pulled her jacket off and quickly wrapped it around both of his legs and then tied the sleeves together, hoping this way to keep from breaking the small tendon and bit of flesh that kept the lower left leg attached. She then scooped him into her arms and stood to peer up and down the road.

James had really picked a doozy when he'd chosen to use this back road. Not a single car had passed since their crash and while Holly was grateful no one had come along to see what she could do, she could use a car about now to stop and give them a lift.

Turning to the right, she started jogging up the street, hoping she'd find a busier road at the end of it and someone who could drive them home. She was nearly to a cross street as unlit as the one she was on when Holly noted the driveway on their right. Pausing, she turned to look around, relieved when she spotted the golden lights up ahead. It was a house, and someone was home. There was also a van in the driveway. Holly hurried up the driveway to the house and shifted James in her arms to hit the doorbell.

A moment later the door opened and an overweight man in a wife beater grinned out at her as he crumpled an empty beer can in his hand. "Well, hello little lady. What can I do for a pretty little thing like you?"

Holly didn't waste time on niceties, she merely slipped into the man's thoughts and took control of him. Within minutes he'd fetched his car keys and was opening the back door of his van for her. She immediately crawled inside with James and sat down cross-legged before arranging James half in her arms and half on the metal floor. Then she glanced to her chauffeur, Earl.

"Get in here, Earl, and close the door," she instructed. Holly wasn't sure if her control would hold if he was out of her sight, so didn't risk sending him around the vehicle to get in. Instead, she made him climb through the van to the driver's seat and gave him her address with instructions to drive there.

Once he'd started the engine and begun to back out of the driveway, Holly relaxed a little and grimaced as hunger immediately roared up inside her. It had been gnawing at her since the accident, but she'd managed to ignore it while she struggled to free her husband. Now though, she had nothing to distract her and it was making itself known, with a vengeance. Grinding her teeth together, she looked around the interior of the van. It looked like a serial killer's holiday vehicle. Rope, duct tape, spades, and various implements that could have been used to torture someone hung from a pegboard strapped to one side wall, while a narrow cot was up against the other behind her.

Holly considered laying James on the bed and maybe snacking a bit on Earl, but then thought again. Feeding off the man driving the vehicle just didn't seem like a good idea. And, she doubted this could be considered an emergency since it was only ten minutes to their home and the blood that waited in the fridge there. She could survive ten minutes. Besides, the bed didn't look very clean. James was fine where he was, she decided, and glanced to their driver, slipping into his thoughts to make sure he stayed on course.

Ten minutes later the van pulled to a stop in their driveway. Holly had Earl get out and open the side door, and then gave him her keys to unlock the front door. Once he'd done that, she immediately scooped up James and slid out to hurry into the house with

him. Unsure whether she'd need help or not, Holly
had Earl close and lock the front door and then
follow her as she carried James straight up to their
bedroom. She ignored the man as she laid her husband on the bed, then straightened and rushed out
of the room, barking, "Keep an eye on him."

The laundry room had seemed a good place to
keep the refrigerator of blood when they'd delivered
it, but as she rushed down to the main floor, Holly
thought the bedroom would have been handier.
Rather than grab a couple bags and have to return
later, she unplugged the refrigerator, picked it up
and hurried back through the house with it.

She would plug it back in, in the bedroom and—

Holly's thoughts died abruptly as she entered the
bedroom and saw that James had Earl pinned to the
bed and was tearing into his throat.

Cursing, she dropped the refrigerator and hurried
forward.

"Bad! Bad James!" she yelled, smacking him in
the back of the head.

When that had no effect, Holly caught him by
the shoulders and pulled her husband off Earl. It
was a lot harder than she'd expected. James was
damned strong for a man whose legs were crushed
and who'd probably lost more than half the blood in
his body, if not almost all of it. Finally getting him
off of Earl, Holly forced him onto his back and then
knelt on his chest and caught at his arms to hold
him down as he turned his attention to trying to bite
her now. Not with fangs, she noted, he didn't seem
to have those yet, he was gnashing and biting at her
with his mortal teeth, and growling like a dog as he
did it.

Holly scowled at him briefly and then released

one arm to punch him in the head again. Much to her relief, he went out like a light. Sighing, she sat back on his chest and then glanced around to check on Earl. She couldn't tell how badly he was injured, but the man was lying unconscious on the floor, his neck bleeding.

"Now look what you've done," she muttered, scowling at her unconscious husband. Shaking her head, Holly climbed off of him and went to plug in the refrigerator as she'd intended. She then opened the door, grabbed a bag and slapped it to her fangs as she counted the bags left inside the small appliance. She usually got deliveries on Monday night. James was at work then. This was Friday. More than half the blood she'd received on Monday was gone. Holly didn't know how much blood was needed for a turn, but she was pretty sure it was more than what was in that refrigerator right now. In fact, she suspected she'd need that much to make up for the blood she'd lost herself.

She needed to call the blood bank and have a delivery made. Surely they would know how much blood a turn took, right? Holly straightened and turned, her gaze landing on Earl before it shifted back to James. She couldn't go downstairs and look up the number to the blood bank and leave Earl here. What if James woke up again? He might attack the man and kill him this time.

Maybe she should tie James down. Would rope hold him or did she need something stronger?

Holly threw her hands up with exasperation. She didn't know anything about anything. She was as useless as—

Pausing, abruptly, she rushed to the bedside table and pulled the drawer open to retrieve the small slip of paper inside. Unfolding it she peered at the two phone numbers Gia had written on it, one was hers, and one was Justin's she saw. Who to call?

James groaned and started to stir, and Holly snatched the phone and climbed onto the bed and then onto her husband's chest. Dropping to sit on him, she watched his face warily as she dialed the first number. If he even blinked she was knocking his ass out again.

"And you'd deserve it," she told her unconscious husband. He was normally such a nice guy. Who would have thought he could turn into such an animal?

"I'd deserve what?" Gia laughed over the phone and Holly turned her attention to her call with relief.

"Gia, you said to call if I needed anything," Holly reminded her quickly, her gaze narrowing on James as he shifted and moaned under her.

"Yes, I did," the other woman agreed. "What do you need, piccola?"

"Help!" Holly hadn't meant to scream the word, but James chose that moment to wake and rear up at her, his mouth going for her throat. Help came out a startled yelp just before the phone was knocked from her hand and she found herself wrestling with her less than rational husband.

Holly was sitting on the floor outside the closed bedroom door, dozing against the wall when the doorbell rang. Lifting her head, she peered up the hall to the window to see that dawn was just cresting on the horizon. Day had arrived to chase away the night.

The doorbell rang again and Holly sighed wearily and dragged herself to her feet. Honest to God, this had been the longest and worst night of her life so far. She added the "so far" part in the hopes of not tempting fate. That bitch did seem to like a challenge.

"And you are suffering the effects of blood loss and so exhausted that you're not making any sense," Holly told herself as she stumbled up the hall and started down the stairs.

"You've also apparently taken to talking to yourself," she added with rebuke as she reached the main floor and staggered toward the front door. "But what the hell, there's no one here to talk back but you. James just growls and poor Earl has been curled up in a corner of the bedroom whimpering since he woke up."

Shaking her head, Holly grabbed the doorknob and—idiot that she was—opened the door without checking to see who it was first. She regretted that the moment her tired brain recognized the police uniforms the two men on her stoop wore. One had dark hair and one was blond. It was Blondie who started talking.

"Good morning, ma'am, we're . . . er . . . are you okay?"

Holly glanced down at her torn and bloodstained clothes and then back to Blondie. Her voice was as dry as dust when she queried, "Is that what you knocked on my door to ask?"

Blondie blinked, as did his partner. Apparently they weren't used to being questioned themselves. Their surprise was brief however and then their expressions both turned stern and kind of scowly.

"No, ma'am, we had a noise complaint," Blondie

said, and then completely blew the tough cop act by frowning with concern and reaching out with one hand as if he thought he might need to steady her. "Maybe you should sit down. You don't look so good. You're white as a sheet."

"That's because—" Holly paused abruptly. Blondie's scent had just reached her nose and he smelled like pot roast on Sunday. Licking her lips, she murmured, "Actually I do feel rather faint. Maybe you should help me to the living room."

They were very accommodating policemen. Concern clear on their expressions, both men stepped forward to help. As each took an arm and urged her toward the living room, Holly tried to work out the logistics of controlling them both while she fed off first one and then the other.

"Holly!"

Freezing, she turned and found she had to go up on her toes to see over the shoulders of the officers to get a look at who was at her door. Gia, she saw, and the other woman was eyeing her with rebuke. Grimacing, Holly threw up her hands and complained, "I'm hungry. I've been hungry for hours and everything hurts. I need it. This *is* an emergency."

Gia frowned and closed the front door. "Hasn't Mac delivered the blood yet?"

"No," Holly said wearily, quite sure she was going to have to let the policemen go without even a nibble. That was so unfair. She really was in pain for want of blood, agony even, and she'd been that way all night. If this wasn't an emergency, she didn't know what was.

Gia clucked her tongue as she started forward. "All right. Make it quick though. I'll see what's taking Mac so long. I called the order in right after we got off the phone. It should have got here shortly after that," she added irritably and then asked, "Can I use the house phone? I didn't get the chance to charge my cell."

"Of course." Holly waved her into the living room and then followed, pulling the officers in behind her by their hands. They were both being incredibly docile about this. She was amazed they weren't asking questions until she glanced at their faces and noted their blank expressions. Frowning, she glanced to Gia. "Are you controlling them?"

Gia nodded and gestured for her to get on with it as she pulled the phonebook out of the bookshelf next to the phone and began to rifle through it.

Sighing, Holly turned to her dinner and glanced from one man to the other. They were both pretty much the same height, which was just tall. Determination squaring her shoulders, she stepped in front of the blond, grabbed his shoulders and tried to get him to bend forward. He didn't bend. Scowling, she placed her right foot against his knee and tried to climb him instead.

"For heaven's sake, Holly, stop playing with your food," Gia snapped.

"I'm not playing. They're too tall, and you're controlling them so I can't make them bend over or anything."

"*Per l'amor del cielo*," Gia muttered and glanced to the men. They both immediately moved around Holly to sit on the couch behind her.

Instead of following right away, Holly peered at Gia narrow-eyed. "What does *por favor del cello* mean?"

"Not—" Gia shook her head and sighed. "I said per *l'amor del cielo*. It is like 'for heaven's sake.'"

"L'amor means love doesn't it?" she asked suspiciously.

"Yes."

"What is cielo?"

"Sky," she answered.

"So you said for the love of the sky?"

"Dio mio!" Gia said impatiently. "Stop stalling and feed or I will send them away."

"I'm not stalling," Holly said at once.

"Yes, you are," she said more gently. "You're nervous. This is all still new to you. But you can do this. You did it at the club."

"Right," Holly breathed, forcing herself to relax as she realized she *was* nervous and stalling. While she'd practiced feeding on mortals at the club, that had been two weeks ago, and these were cops, for heaven's sake. It was bad to assault cops.

"Think of them as blood donors," Gia instructed.

"Blood donors," Holly murmured and turned to survey her meal. The two men had settled side by side and straight backed on the couch. She considered them briefly, and then moved in front of the blond and bent over, but she couldn't quite reach his neck.

Muttering under her breath about the inconvenience of being so darned short, she climbed onto him and settled on his lap with her knees on either side of his legs. Clasping his head, she pulled him forward, and then paused to glance to Gia, who was now punching in numbers. "Are you going to control him while I feed or—?"

"I have them, go ahead," Gia said, sounding a little distracted.

Shrugging, Holly turned to the blond and urged him back against the couch again. She then leaned against him and planted her face in his neck. Hungry as she was, she had absolutely no difficulty locating the vein, and she released a little sigh of relief and let her fangs slide out.

The moment Holly's fangs pierced his skin, the man moaned and slid his arms around her waist to pull her close. She ignored that and the way his hands were now roving over her back as she concentrated on counting to thirty. This time it seemed like no time at all had passed before she reached thirty, but Holly reluctantly retracted her fangs and released the man.

Rather than go to all the trouble of climbing from one lap to the other, she then just turned and caught the second officer by the front of the shirt and pulled him closer. Burying the fingers of her free hand in his hair, she used it to control his head and quickly sniffed out his vein. Like the first man, this one moaned when her teeth slid into his throat. He also reached to embrace her, but at this angle instead of wrapping his arms around her, one slid around her front, the hand stopping on her right breast, while his other hand snaked around her back landing low enough to nearly be cupping her ass. Holly gasped in surprise and lost count for a second, but then forced herself to ignore it and quickly went back to counting.

"This reminds me of a porn my cousins once made me watch." Gia's voice was filled with laughter, Holly noted. "*Il Poliziotto Con Il Grosso Bastone.* 'The Cop with the Big Stick,'" she translated.

Much to Holly's relief she reached thirty then. Retracting her teeth, she quickly scrambled off the blond and turned to scowl at the other woman. "Ha ha. You were the one controlling them. Why'd you have him grab me like that?"

"I wasn't controlling what he did, piccola. Just what he felt," Gia said with amusement and then walked forward to give her a hug. "Is all right. You look much better already and a delivery is on its way to get you back to one hundred percent."

Holly sighed and hugged her back briefly, then stepped away and glanced to the police officers.

"I will handle them," Gia assured her. "Go upstairs and check on your husband. I will be up in a moment."

Nodding, Holly turned and slipped out of the room. She actually walked up the stairs rather than having to drag herself this time, which was nice. She even felt well enough that the idea of showering sounded pleasant rather than an exhausting trial as it had all night until now. Maybe she could grab one after Gia came upstairs. It would be nice to strip out of her bloodstained clothes and wash away the dried blood of both herself and her husband.

Holly opened the door to the bedroom and walked inside for the first time in hours. She had been in such dire need of blood before this she hadn't trusted herself alone with Earl, so had done little more than open the door and peek in to be sure her husband had not escaped his bindings. Now, she walked up to the bed and peered down at him with concern. James had stopped screaming and thrashing hours ago. He'd lain in a dead silence ever since, his face gray, and his body unmoving. Not that he could have moved much what with the—

"Duct tape?"

Holly glanced over her shoulder at that squawk from Gia. Apparently she'd been quick about handling the policemen. Noting Gia's dismayed expression as she approached the bedside, Holly glanced back to James.

"*Dio mio, cara,*" Gia said on a laugh. "What were you thinking?"

"I was thinking that I was starting to feel like an abusing spouse every time I knocked him out. That I didn't have any chain, and that duct tape is super hard to break." She pursed her lips as she peered at her husband in his silver cocoon. The only thing that wasn't completely covered was his head. She'd left him untaped from the neck to his forehead and then run several lengths of tape over him there as well. "I used six rolls of the stuff. He's not going anywhere until I cut him free."

"No, I guess not," Gia said with amusement.

A whimper from the corner made them both glance that way.

"Gia, this is Earl," Holly announced. "He was kind enough to drive James and me home tonight after the accident."

"Why is he whimpering?" Gia asked curiously.

"You can't read him?" Holly asked with surprised.

"He's panicked to the point where his thoughts make no sense. He seems to think you're some kind of sex fiend crossed with a wild dog or something." She paused and then added thoughtfully, "Or maybe he's thinking you're a bitch in heat. My English is not always perfect."

Holly gave a snort of laughter and shook her head. "James attacked him while I was down getting the blood. He got knocked out when I pulled James off of him and then he woke up while James and I were wrestling after your call," Holly explained with a grimace. "He saw my fangs."

When Gia arched her eyebrows, Holly grimaced

and shrugged. "My fangs came out while we were wrestling."

"I will take care of Earl. Why don't you go take a shower?" she suggested. "Better yet, a bath. You look like you could use a little time to yourself to relax."

"Thank you. I think I will," Holly said, turning toward the door.

"Oh, by the way," Gia said suddenly, bringing her to a halt. "While the blood got lost, they did collect your car. They said it was a wreck though. They'll handle the insurance claim and everything for you. In the meantime, they are sending you a rental."

Holly nodded slowly, but then asked, "Who are *they* exactly?"

Gia hesitated and then said, "Technically the money will come from the Enforcers. You are still under their purview. But Argeneau Enterprises handles all the details."

"Why would I still be under the Enforcers' purview?"

"Because you were mortally injured and turned on their watch due to their actions," she pointed out.

"Yes, but I'm done with my training," Holly pointed out.

"Yes, but immortals have been around long enough that they know there is a certain period of adjustment."

"They didn't cause the car accident. I did," Holly said quietly.

"You did when you flashed your fangs which you couldn't have done if you hadn't been turned," Gia pointed out.

"How do you know how the accident happened?"

Holly asked, and then rolled her eyes. "You read my mind."

"As soon as I got here," Gia confirmed.

"Oh," she sighed. "Of course you did."

"Holly, the accident wasn't your fault," Gia said firmly. "Your whole life has been turned upside down, and it's been made even more difficult because you are trying to carry on as you did before that happened. Of course things were bound to explode."

Holly smiled crookedly. "You know I find it interesting how sometimes your accent is so thick and your "English is not always perfect" and yet other times you have hardly any accent at all, and your English is just fine." '

Gia grinned and shrugged. *"C'est la vie."*

"That's French," Holly accused.

"Si." Gia smiled. "It means *questa e la vita."*

Holly shook her head and turned to continue out of the room. She needed a bath . . . and a good cry. No matter what Gia said, she felt responsible for the accident, and she always would. Turning James had been the only thing she could think to do to make up for it. But what if he hated her for it? She hadn't asked him if he wanted to be turned. How would he handle finding out what she'd done?

Eighteen

Holly stepped into the house and paused, her gaze shifting to the closed living room door as a trill of laughter sounded. It was girly and flirty and nothing like the normally husky sound that usually came from Gia. At least Holly had never heard her laugh like that before this last week as she'd taken care of and looked after James while Holly attended her classes and went to work.

Holly closed the door, a smile curving her lips as Gia laughed again, joined this time by James's much deeper chuckle. He had woken up on Sunday while she was still sleeping in the guest room. By the time she'd got up James was untaped, bathed, dressed and Gia had explained everything to him. He'd taken the knowledge that he was a vampire rather well. Better than she had, certainly, and he hadn't blamed her for any of it.

Holly moved into the kitchen and opened the refrigerator door to consider what to make for supper.

"No need to make dinner, you're going out,"

Gia announced cheerfully, leading James into the kitchen. "How was school?"

"Good," Holly assured her.

"And work?" James asked.

"Not as good, but okay," she said with a smile and then raised her eyebrows. "Why are we going out to dinner?" She tilted her head and raised her eyebrows. "What's up?"

James and Gia exchanged a glance and then James shook his head. "You'll find out. Come on. I'm hungry."

Holly fell into step behind him, following him to the door until she realized Gia wasn't behind her. Slowing, she glanced over her shoulder. "Isn't Gia coming?"

"Nope. Just you and me, Holly," James said, and added, "We need to talk."

Holly raised her eyebrows, but followed him out to the car and let him see her into the passenger seat. She wasn't sure what James wanted to talk about, but she had an idea and she didn't want to discuss it in a restaurant.

"I know," she said as James slid behind the steering wheel and pulled his door closed.

He peered at her warily. "What?"

"Gia can't read or control you. You're a possible life mate to her," she said solemnly.

James peered out the front window, biting his lip. "How did you know?"

"She's eating, James," Holly pointed out. "Old immortals who are unmated lose interest in food and regain it when they meet a possible life mate. Gia didn't eat once the entire time I was in Southern California. But she has been eating ever since you woke up from the turn."

"I didn't know that," he admitted. "About her not eating before this, I mean."

Holly shrugged. "So . . ."

"So?" he asked.

"So you want a divorce to be with her." It wasn't a question.

"How did you—"

"Why else would you want to talk to me alone?" she interrupted dryly, managing not to roll her eyes. Honestly, men thought women were so dense.

James eyed her uncertainly and then asked, "Are you upset?"

"Surprisingly enough, no," Holly admitted with a faint smile and then shook her head with a sort of bewilderment. "I knew what was happening the minute she put the first bite of food in her mouth. I listened to you guys laugh and joke. I even saw the moony eyes you made at each other, and I just kept waiting to feel the jealousy, even a little of it. But it never came, and that's when I realized . . ."

"That while you love me, it isn't like it is with Justin," James suggested with understanding.

"She told you about him?" Holly asked.

James nodded. "She didn't betray any confidences, Holly. But she told me why Justin turned you. She also told me that you were determined to be true to your marriage vows. I appreciate that," he added. "And I was too . . . mostly."

Her eyebrows rose. "Mostly?"

"I never touched her," he said quickly, and then grimaced and added, "Not while I was awake."

"Ah, the shared dreams," Holly said with amusement. "Pretty powerful stuff, huh?"

"You had them with Justin?" he asked with surprise and she realized that Gia really hadn't betrayed any confidences.

"Yes, I had them," was all she said.

James was silent for a minute and then said, "They *are* pretty powerful stuff."

"Go ahead and say it," Holly urged.

"What?" he asked warily.

"That we never had half the passion of those dreams. That what we've had was more like . . ."

"The love and affection between siblings," he said when she hesitated.

She nodded. "I suppose that shouldn't surprise us since we grew up together."

"Yeah, but you were the hottest girl around," he assured her.

She chuckled at the teasing words he'd often said to her and gave her usual response, "I was the *only* girl around."

"That too," he agreed, and then took her hand. "Holly, I don't want to lose our friendship. You've been a part of my life almost since I was born. You're family to me."

"And I always will be," she assured him, squeezing his hand gently.

"Good." He smiled with relief and then admitted, "You're taking this better than I expected. When Gia said you were so determined to stick to your marriage vows, I . . ."

"I married you in good faith, James," she said quietly. "I do love you, and if we were both mortal still, we might even have made it as a couple. The cozy home, children, growing old together and all that stuff we both dreamed of while growing up."

"But circumstances have changed," he said.

Holly nodded. "There's a reason we edit what we say. Once words are spoken, they cannot be unheard. Unfortunately, the same is true of thoughts if you can read them."

"I apologize for anything you may have heard me think that might have hurt you," James said quickly. "And really, the Elaine thing—"

"Don't even go there," Holly said with dry amusement. "You shouldn't even *have* to go there. Your thoughts should be your own, James, not something you need to apologize for." She grinned and added, "And with Gia, they will be."

James nodded and relaxed, then reached for the door handle. "Come on. Gia was worried sick about how you'd take this. She's afraid you'll be mad at her and she really likes you. Let's go give her the good news and then all three of us can go out to dinner to celebrate."

"You go ahead and tell her alone," Holly suggested. "I'll just wait here."

When he frowned at the suggestion, concern entering his expression, she pointed out, "She might feel weird about kissing you in front of me and you two are gonna want to kiss."

"You're right," James said on a laugh and slid out of the car.

Holly watched him go and then got out of the front seat and moved to the backseat instead, leaving the front for Gia. She then sat staring at the house she and James had bought together after they'd married. They'd planned to sell and move to a larger place when they were ready to have kids, but it was a good starter home.

The house suddenly blurred in her vision, and Holly blinked, and then raised her fingers to dash tears from her eyes. They were unexpected. She hadn't thought this would upset her. She really was happy for Gia and James and hadn't felt a moment's jealousy, which was just wrong. In fact, more than anything, all she'd felt was relief. Those two weeks before the accident had been impossible. She couldn't imagine trying to struggle through a lifetime of that, even a mortal lifetime. And now she didn't have to.

Still, Holly supposed she was grieving what had been. The dreams she'd had as Mrs. James Bosley. And maybe she was also crying a little because she wasn't sure of her own future. She had turned Justin away, repeatedly rejected him. What if he now did the same to her? And if he didn't, how could she be sure they could work? Until very recently, she'd been certain she and James could and that had been wrong. With Justin, she wasn't certain of anything.

"Piccola!"

Holly glanced around with surprise when Gia slipped into the backseat beside her.

"I will ride back here with Holly," the woman announced.

"Ah, you're gonna make me sit up here all by myself?"

Gia clucked her tongue. "Drive, James."

"Ha ha, very funny," he muttered, starting the engine.

"Why is it funny?" Gia asked with confusion.

Holly met James's eyes in the mirror and they both burst out laughing.

Gia merely smiled at them and then took Holly's hands. "Don't worry. Everything is going to work out. Justin will not reject you. He understood and even admired your decision to honor your vows.

And," she added firmly when Holly opened her mouth to speak, "And you do not have to trust in yourself with Justin. Trust in the nanos, yes? They will never steer you wrong. If they think you are life mates, then life mates you are, and you will work."

"Now," she squeezed Holly's hand and then turned to smile at James in the rearview mirror. "We will go have dinner to celebrate . . . in Canada."

"What?" Holly turned on her with surprise.

"Hmmm. I called Aunt Marguerite and she insisted we all come to dinner."

"In Canada?" Holly asked with disbelief.

"Hmmm. Is only a five hours flight or something like that," she reassured her. "And there are snacks on the plane."

"The plane?" Holly echoed.

Gia nodded. "It should be landing when we get to the airport. Lucian Argeneau arranged for it to come get us when I called him earlier."

Holly's eyes narrowed. "And why did you call him?"

"Because I want to be happy, but I want you to be happy too," she said simply.

"And how does flying to Canada for dinner make either of us happy?" she asked warily.

"Well . . . when James and I finally talked about everything, and he decided that he had to talk to you as soon as you got home . . ." She hesitated and then said solemnly, "I cannot celebrate and enjoy having James to life mate if you and Justin are not settled as well, Holly."

Holly bit her lip and said, "Have you ever heard the expression you can lead a horse to water but you cannot make it drink?"

Gia shook her head slowly. "What does it mean?"

"It means she's afraid you'll get her to Canada and bring this Justin guy around, but that doesn't mean he'll still be interested," James said solemnly.

Gia shook her head. "You are his life mate, Holly. You have nothing to fear."

Holly didn't say anything, but as Gia patted her hand, she worried that might not be true.

Nineteen

"Do this, Justin. Do that, Justin. We're shorthanded, Justin. Mortimer needs you, Justin. You have to come back. But where is Justin? Everyone else is out hunting a rogue, but what is Justin doing? He's delivering pastries to Marguerite's house for some damned dinner she's having. Oh yeah, we need you, Justin," he muttered under his breath as he parked the SUV in Marguerite's driveway and got out to walk around to the back of the SUV.

He retrieved the covered tray inside, then straightened, pressed the button on his key fob to close the back, and headed for the house. He was still ten feet away when the front door opened and Dante peered out at him. "What took you so long?"

"Really?" Justin asked, one eyebrow rising. "Not, 'Thank you for taking time out from your important work of hunting rogues to bring us yet more food to swallow in one or two bites, Justin.' Just, 'What took you so long?' "

Dante shrugged and stepped back for him to enter with the tray. "I don't eat pastries."

"Yeah, you do," Justin said dryly, stepping inside and turning to watch him close the door. "As far as I can tell, you and Tomasso eat everything."

"Yeah, we do," Dante admitted with a grin and then waved at the door to the living room.

Shaking his head, Justin turned and strode to the door, but stopped there as he noted all the people present. It wasn't a damned dinner—it was a party of some sort. The whole Argeneau family appeared to be here, as well as every last hunter who was supposed to be out rounding up a supposed nest of rogues Lucian had got word about. Even Mortimer and Sam were here.

"What the—" he began and then paused as Marguerite suddenly smiled at him. She took her husband Julius's arm and the two stepped sideways, revealing three people sitting on the couch.

"Holly," Justin breathed and dropped the tray he held. Fortunately, Dante was quick and managed to catch it before it hit the floor. Justin hardly noticed though; his attention had shifted to the man beside Holly. James Bosley, her husband, sat between her and Gia on the couch. That was a shock, but when he noted the silver glint in the man's eyes, he reeled back and whirled away, only to crash into Lucian Argeneau's steel wall of a chest.

"Where are you going?" Lucian asked mildly. "Aren't you going to greet your life mate?"

"She's with her husband," Justin growled. "Obviously he was a possible life mate to her too. She's made her decision. I—why the hell are you shaking your head?"

"Because you're wrong," Lucian said. "As usual."

Justin scowled at him and then hissed. "See the guy with silver-blue eyes there?"

"Justin, ninety percent of the people in the room have silver-blue eyes," he pointed out with amusement.

"The one on the couch that *isn't* related to you," Justin growled.

"You mean Gia's life mate?" Lucian asked mildly.

"No, I mean Holly's husband," he said with frustration.

"The only man on the couch is Gia's life mate," Lucian informed him.

"What?" he asked with confusion and then turned to look at the trio again. James Bosley? Gia's life mate?

"Yes," Lucian said in answer to his unspoken question.

"So Gia turned him?" Justin asked slowly, trying to absorb what he was being told.

"No. Holly turned him," Lucian answered.

"What?" Justin faced him again. "Why?"

Lucian released a long drawn-out sigh and then shook his head. "I suggest you gird your loins and ask Holly. I am bored with this conversation now."

"Gird my loins?" Justin asked with disbelief. "Who even *says* that?"

"I do," Lucian growled and strode around him to enter the room and join his wife, Leigh, by a table filled with appetizers.

"They were in a car accident. James would have died. Holly felt responsible so turned him."

Justin turned to glance at the woman who had spoken. Decker's mate, Dani, now stood on his right side.

Anders's mate, Valerie, now appeared on his left

and added, "She called Gia for help after turning him. Gia couldn't read him, so, here they are."

"Why?" he asked worriedly.

Both women laughed.

"Why do you think, Justin? Go talk to her." Valerie gave him a push.

Justin took a step, and then turned back suspiciously to the two women. "Are you guys setting me up or something?"

They exchanged a grimace and then Dani said, "The boys told us what they did in California. How they told you everything Holly hated were things she liked."

"We were pissed," Valerie added. "I mean, we get that they both wanted to pay you back for how you tormented them when they were trying to win us, but what they did didn't just affect you."

"It affected Holly too," Dani said solemnly. "And that wasn't fair. Besides, while you torment the men every chance you get, you are always sweet to us."

"Yes," Valerie agreed. "Now, get over there and put the poor woman out of her misery. She's worried sick that it's too late and you won't want her anymore."

"She really doesn't get this life mate business," Justin muttered.

"No. She doesn't," Dani agreed. "But then it's hard to comprehend when you're new to this stuff. And she has had a lot to absorb in a relatively short space of time."

"It should help now that you can tell her about life mate sex and show her what that's all about," Valerie pointed out.

"Can I?" Justin asked uncertainly, and then pointed out, "She's still married."

"Yeah, but technically the law only applies to mortals," Sam said suddenly from behind him.

"What?" Justin turned to peer at Mortimer's mate, wide-eyed. The woman was a lawyer, she would know these things.

"I read up on the law last week after you told me about your situation, and an immortal is only forbidden to use his influence on a mortal, and interfere in a mortal marriage," Sam explained, and then pointed out, "Holly, and now James, are both immortal. So, technically, the council couldn't punish you for wooing or life mate sex or—"

"But Holly was immortal almost from the start," Justin said with a frown. "I mean, she was immortal before we even exchanged a word. So the minute she was immortal, it was no longer a mortal marriage," he pointed out. "Does that mean I could have gone all out to try to win her? Used life mate sex and everything and the council couldn't have done a damned thing? It wouldn't have been breaking the law?"

"The way the law reads, yes," Sam said almost apologetically.

"Well, why the hell didn't Lucian tell me that then?" Justin asked plaintively and turned to peer at the man. Lucian Argeneau met his gaze across the room and gave him a smile a shark would admire.

"Um . . . this is just a guess," Valerie said with amusement, "But I'm thinking maybe you gave Lucian a hard time when he met Leigh?"

"Oh yeah," he muttered.

"Justin," Marguerite said quietly.

Justin turned to find the woman standing next to Dani and raised his eyebrows in question.

"It is better it worked this way," she assured him solemnly. "Holly is an honorable young woman.

Nanos or no nanos, and life mates or not, she would have suffered terrible guilt at breaking her marriage vows with you."

"Right," Justin said on a sigh as he realized that probably still held true. He could now claim her as his life mate, but claiming her physically was probably still out of the question until she was divorced.

It didn't matter, he thought grimly. She was his, and if they had to wait to celebrate their union physically, then he would wait. It would probably kill him, but he would wait.

"Go talk to her," Valerie suggested.

Nodding, Justin stopped stalling then and entered the room, heading straight for the couch.

"Holly," he said solemnly, and then quickly shifted his attention to her husband as the other man suddenly stood up.

"Justin Bricker?" the fair-haired man asked.

Justin nodded slowly, half-expecting the man to pop him in the nose for stealing Holly from him. Instead, he grinned and took his hand, pumping it in enthusiastic greeting. "I'm James Bosley, and it's such a pleasure to meet you. Holly's told me a lot about you. Gia has too. Thank you so much for saving her life that night at the cemetery . . . and for everything else."

"Er . . ." Justin glanced to Holly to see that she was biting her lip anxiously, then to Gia, who was smiling and nodding, and managed a weak smile of his own. "You're welcome. My pleasure."

James nodded, and glanced from him to Holly before prodding gently, "I suppose you two want to talk."

"Yes," Justin said firmly when Holly hesitated, and then held his hand out to her.

Smiling nervously, she accepted it and stood, allowing him to lead her out of the living room and then outside.

"So, Gia and James," Justin said as he pulled the door closed behind them.

"Yes," Holly said with a crooked smile.

"How did that come about?" he asked curiously.

Holly took a deep breath and then told him what had transpired since she'd left the nightclub and caught the bus home. She told him how right they all were about trying to live with someone when you could hear their thoughts, about the argument in the car, the accident, calling Gia and her talk with James about being Gia's life mate. Holly told Justin everything right up until Gia had announced they were to fly to Canada for dinner at Marguerite's.

"And here you are," he said with a faint smile. They had been walking as they talked, making their way around the house, and were now in the backyard.

"Well, we didn't—" she began, but he stopped walking and turned to take her hands.

"Before you say anything else, I need to tell you that Valerie told me you were worried I wouldn't still want you. Holly, you're my life mate. I want you for my life mate. I will always want you for my life mate."

"Oh," Holly breathed. "I want that too. That's why I—"

"But it's more than that," Justin continued. "At first I wanted you just because you *were* my life mate. I mean, I didn't *know* you," he pointed out wryly. "But as I got to know you, the life mate part mattered less and less. Not that it isn't really important," he added quickly. "I mean it *is* important, but I started to see you as *you* rather than just as my life mate . . . if that makes any sense at all. Jesus, I'm screwing this all up," he muttered with frustration, and then shook his head and said, "Anyway, I came to realize you really were made for me. We're both city types, we both love to dance, and taking chances . . ." He shook his head. "And there's so much I love about you. Your quick wit and ability to learn fast, your honor, your wild side, even your temper."

"I—"

"But I especially love your stubbornness, your determination to do the honorable thing and hold to the vows you made no matter the temptation," Justin continued determinedly. "So I want you to know, I will abide by your desire to stand by your vows. I won't try to tempt you to break them. I'll not touch you or kiss you or do anything that might lead to our—"

"James and I are divorced," Holly blurted almost desperately.

Justin paused, his mouth still open, and then snapped it closed and stared at her blankly. "What? How? I thought James just told you about him and Gia and that you flew here . . . You didn't fly here?" he asked when she shook her head.

"Of course, we did," Holly said softly. "But we didn't fly *directly* here. I didn't want to show up and say "Hey, Justin. We can be life mates . . . just as soon as I'm divorced." She grimaced even as she said it, and then admitted, "I wanted to come to you free and able to accept your offer, if you still wished to claim me as a life mate."

She smiled and added, "James and Gia understood when I explained it. They also were rather eager to have the divorce done and over with as well, so instead of flying straight here, we flew to New York first."

"New York?" he asked with confusion. "Why?"

"Because Lucian said Bastian could help us get a divorce much more quickly than through normal channels," she explained.

"And he did?"

"Two days," she said with a grin.

"Two days?" he asked with amazement. "Is it legal?"

"He says it is," Holly said with a shrug. "And the papers that were waiting for us when we landed two hours ago look pretty official. He's sending the originals by mail, but faxed us copies as soon as he got them so that we could see them," Holly added.

"You're divorced," he muttered, hardly able to believe it.

"Yes," she said solemnly, and stepped forward to clasp his face in her hands. "Justin, I spent so much time fighting my attraction to you while we were together that I wouldn't even let myself really see you. But then, when I got back home, all I could see was you. You were constantly in my thoughts. A song would play on the radio that had played at the club, someone would go by walking their dog, I'd pass a bowling alley, or a convertible would drive by and I'd think of you. Everything reminded me of you and I compared everything James, and every other man I encountered, did to how you would do things, and they always came up short."

She closed her eyes briefly and then continued, "And every night, I remembered our shared dreams and not only longed for more of them, but constantly wondered if it would be as good in reality." She opened her eyes, smiled crookedly and admitted, "Actually, it wasn't just at night. It was during the day too. I fought so hard to get away from you and then all I did was think of you and miss you," she admitted with a wry curve of the lips. "I don't want to fight us anymore, and while I appreciate your willingness to abide by my wedding vows and yes, I would have felt I had to . . . well," she smiled widely, "Now we don't have to."

"Now we don't have to," he echoed, and then scooped her up in his arms and carried her around the building and to his SUV.

Holly didn't ask questions until they were both in the car. But as he steered the vehicle up the driveway, she asked, "Where are we going?"

"I bought a house when I got back from California," Justin admitted, and then added quickly, "I know you might not want to settle here. You have to finish your courses in California and get your accounting license, and both our families live there too, but . . ." He glanced at her and smiled crookedly, "I was hoping someday you would come to me, and I didn't want our first time together to be in a hotel like a cheap date, or the Enforcer house with everyone there." Frowning, he quickly added, "Not, that I was presuming that we would—" He fell silent and glanced at her worriedly when Holly put her hand on his leg.

"I don't think you were presuming," Holly said solemnly. "In fact, I think that's about the sweetest thing anyone has ever done for me."

Justin smiled widely, his relief obvious. "I'm a pretty sweet guy."

Holly burst out laughing, but nodded. "And funny too. You always make me laugh. Sometimes even on purpose."

"Ha ha," he said with a smile, and then squeezed her hand as he turned his attention back to the road. It wasn't long though before they were turning into a driveway. It seemed the house he'd bought wasn't far from Marguerite's, which was nice. She'd liked the woman.

Curious, Holly peered at the house ahead, her eyes widening. It was a contemporary design, all red brick and windows. It was beautiful.

"I haven't done much decorating yet," Justin said quietly as they got out of the SUV. "I only got possession earlier this week." He glanced to her and added, "And I kind of hoped you might—I thought maybe you'd like to help," he finished.

"I'd love to," Holly assured him softly as she joined him at the front of the vehicle. Her gaze slid over the tall windows that ran the length of the front of the house. They revealed high ceilings and spacious, unfurnished rooms. She glanced to Justin though when he took her hand. She found him smiling down at her.

"Do you know how lucky I am?" he asked suddenly, squeezing her hand.

"As lucky as me," she said, but Justin shook his head.

"Luckier," he assured her solemnly as he led her to the front door. "It's very rare for an immortal to find a life mate while as young as I am."

"Young?" she asked dubiously as he unlocked the door.

"Yes." He glanced to her with surprise as he pushed the door open. Seeing her expression, he added, "Well I'm—for an immortal, I'm—God! You think I'm old," he moaned with dismay.

Holly chuckled, and stepped in front of him, to

tangle her hands in the front of his shirt and pull him close. "Maybe, but that's okay. You're *my* old man."

Justin groaned and then scooped her up into his arms.

"What are you doing?" she gasped with surprise, clutching at his shoulders.

"Sweeping you off your feet?" he offered hopefully.

Holly chuckled, and leaned her head against his shoulder, her arms tightening around him in a hug. "I do love you, Justin Bricker."

Pausing, he bent his head to kiss her gently. "And I love you Holly soon-to-be-Bricker."

"Is that a proposal?" she asked, wide-eyed.

"What? You thought you could just have your wicked way with me without buying the cow?" he asked indignantly as he started walking again, carrying her through the entry and starting upstairs to the second floor.

Holly laughed and shook her head. "You're crazy."

"About you," he agreed, stepping off the stairs and starting across a large open loft. "By the way, did I mention that while I haven't done much decorating, I did buy a bed?"

"Oh," Holly sighed. "You are a clever man."

"*Your* clever man," he assured her and she nodded.

"Yes, my clever *old* man," she teased and Justin groaned as he carried her into the bedroom.

Want more Lynsay Sands?
Keep reading for a peek
at her classic historical

ALWAYS

Available December 2015
from Avon Books

Lady Adela, abbess of Godstow, frowned down the length of the table at the nuns all seated for the nooning meal. Sister Clarice, Sister Eustice, and Lady Rosamunde were missing. It was not unusual for Sister Clarice to be late. The woman was late for everything. Most likely she had forgotten to fetch the incense for the mass that would take place after the meal, and had gone to retrieve it. Sister Clarice always forgot the incense.

As for Sister Eustice and Lady Rosamunde, however, the two were always punctual, as a rule. However, they had not been at the morning meal either. Come to that, they had not been at matins, lauds, or prime. At Godstow, it took an emergency to keep a nun from mass, and this would be no exception. Sister Eustice and Lady Rosamunde had been in the stables through the night and well into the morning, working over a mare who was having difficulty birthing her foal.

But surely they were not still at that! she fretted, then glanced sharply toward Sister Beatrice, who had stumbled over the passage she was reading. Seeing that Beatrice along with all the other women were peering up the table at her, Lady Adela arched an eyebrow questioningly. Sister Margaret, the nun seated on her right, made a motion with her hands. Margaret held one hand up, the fingers fisted but for the baby finger, which hung down like the udder of a cow. With her other hand, she imitated the motion of milking.

Adela blinked, then realized that she had picked up the pitcher of milk and held on to it, thoughtlessly, as she worried about the missing women.

Passing the pitcher to Sister Margaret, the abbess gestured to the others to continue with their meal, then rose and moved to the door. She had barely stepped into the hall when she spotted Sister Clarice hurrying down the corridor, a slightly guilty flush on her face. Unable to speak during mealtime, Lady Adela once again arched an eyebrow, demanding an explanation of the woman's tardiness.

Sighing, Clarice raised her hand and propped two fingers upward until they were inserted in her nostrils, somehow managing an apologetic look as she did so.

The action was a pantomime to announce that she had forgotten to provide incense for mass—as Adela had suspected. Shaking her head, the abbess gestured for Clarice to continue on to her meal; then she made her way out to the stables.

The building was silent but for the faint rustle of hay as various animals shifted and glanced curiously toward her as Adela entered. Gathering the hem of her skirt close to avoid trailing it through anything unpleasant, she made her way down the rows of stalls until she reached the last one. There,

Sister Eustice and Lady Rosamunde were kneeling by a panting mare. She stood for a moment, peering affectionately at their bent backs as they toiled over the laboring beast; then her mouth dropped with dismay as Sis Eustice shifted and she could see exactly *how* Lady Rosamunde was toiling.

"What in God's name are you doing?"

Rosamunde stiffened at that horrified exclamation from behind, her head whipping briefly around to see the abbess gaping at her with dismay. Then she swiftly whirled back to soothe the mare as the animal whinnied, its muscles shifting around her hands.

Leaping to her feet, Eustice ushered the horrified Adela a few steps away, babbling explanations as they moved. "The mare was having difficulty. She labored for hours before we realized that the foal was backward. Lady Rosamunde is trying to help."

"She has her hands *inside* the mare!" Adela pointed out with horror.

"She is trying to turn the foal," Eustice explained quickly.

"But—"

"Is it not the nooning hour?" Rosamunde whispered with exasperation, removing the hand she had been holding the foal's feet with to pat the mare's rump soothingly. The animal was becoming distressed by the tone of voice the abbess was using.

"This is an emergency. God will forgive our breaking silence during mealtime if 'tis an emergency," Adela responded promptly.

"Aye, well, let us hope our mare does," Rosamunde muttered, shifting swiftly out of the way as the horse began kicking its legs in a panicked attempt to regain its feet.

Sister Eustice moved at once, hurrying to the horse's head and grabbing it to hold the mare still. She murmured soothing coos at the frightened animal.

Worry almost overcame her, but Adela managed to contain herself as Rosamunde dropped back on to her knees at the rear of the reclining horse. Unlike Sister Eustice, who was garbed in the plain habit of a nun, the girl was decked out in a stable boy's pants and overlarge top, its billowing sleeves rolled back to leave her arms bare. It was the costume the girl usually wore when working in the stables. Rosamunde felt it much more appropriate than a gown, and Adela, despite her better judgment, had done little to sway her from wearing the scandalous garb. She had always been fond of the girl, and there was no one of import around to disapprove anyway. However, she had already explained to the child that she would have to shed the stable-boy clothes for good—along with many other things—once she took the veil and became a nun.

Adela's thoughts fled, her face twisting into a half grimace, half wince as Rosamunde once again eased her hands into the horse, reaching to grasp its foal and try to ease its way into the world.

"Thank the good Lord's graces that your father, the king, is not here to see this," Adela murmured, remembering to keep her voice calm. She did not wish to frighten the horse again.

"To see what?"

All three women stiffened at that deep baritone. Eustice's eyes widened in horror as she peered past the abbess toward the entrance to the stables. Her expression was enough to tell Adela that she had correctly recognized that voice. The Lord, it seemed, was not feeling particularly gracious today. The king *had* come to see what his daughter had gotten up to under her care.

Straightening her shoulders, Adela turned resignedly toward Henry, hardly noticing the men with him as she forced a smile of greeting to her face. "King Henry. Welcome."

The monarch nodded at the abbess, but his attention was on his daughter. She glanced over her shoulder at him, a bright smile replacing the anxiety on her face.

"Papa!"

Henry started to smile, but ceased as he took in the sight of her. "What the devil are you doing in the stables, girl? And all dressed up like a boy, too." He glared at Adela. "Do I not pay you people enough to hire a stable boy? Do you spite me by putting my daughter to work with the animals?"

"Oh, Papa." Rosamunde laughed, unconcerned by his apparent temper. "You know that it is my choice. We must all work at something—and I prefer the stables to scrubbing the convent floors." The last of her statement was a distracted mutter. She turned back to what she was doing.

Henry's curiosity drew him forward. "What *are* you doing?"

Rosamunde glanced up, a scowl of anxiety on her face. "This mare has been in labor for more than a day now. She is losing strength. I fear she shall die if we do not help her along, but I cannot get the foal out."

His brows drawn together, Henry peered at where her arms disappeared into the mare at the elbows. Horror covered his face. "Why, you—What—You—"

Sighing at his dismayed stammer, Rosamunde

calmly explained. "The foal is backward. I am trying to turn it, but I cannot find its head."

Henry's brows rose at that. "Will it not hurt the mare having you dig about inside her like that?"

"I do not know," she said pragmatically, reaching farther into the animal. "But both mother and foal shall surely die if *something* is not done."

"Aye . . . well . . ." Frowning at her back, Henry said, "Leave that for . . . er . . ." He peered toward the nun now moving back toward Rosamunde and the horse.

"Sister Eustice," Lady Adela supplied helpfully.

"Aye. Sister Eustice. Leave it for the sister to deal with, daughter. I do not have long here and—"

"Oh, I could not do that, Papa. It would ruin the sleeves of Sister Eustice's gown. This will not take long, I am sure, and then—"

"I do not give a damn about the sister's sleeves," Henry snapped, starting forward to drag her away bodily if need be, but a pleading glance from his daughter made him halt. She did so look like her mother. Henry had found it impossible to refuse the mother anything. Why should their daughter be different?

Sighing, he removed his cloak and handed it to Eustice, then shrugged out of his short surcoat and handed that over as well.

"Who taught you to do this?" he asked gruffly, bending to kneel beside her in the straw.

"No one," she admitted, flashing him a smile that warmed his heart. It immediately made him let go of his impatience and anger. "It just seemed to be the thing to do when I saw the problem. She will die otherwise."

Nodding, he shifted as close to her as he could get

and reached his hands inside the mare to help. "It is the head you cannot find?"

Rosamunde nodded. "I have the rear legs, but I cannot—"

"Aha! I have it. It is caught on something." He paused. "There we go."

Rosamunde felt the back legs slip from her grip and shift away. She just managed to tug her hands free of the mare as her father turned the animal within its mother until its head was at the right angle.

"The mare is too weak. You will have to—" even as the words left her mouth, her father tugged on the foal's head and front legs. Seconds later it slid out onto the straw.

"Oh," Rosamunde breathed, peering at the spindly-legged creature as it wriggled on the straw. "Is it not adorable?"

"Aye," Henry agreed gruffly; then he cleared his throat, grabbed her arm, and urged her to her feet. "Come. Time is short. 'Sides, 'tis not fitting for a girl of your position to be participating in such things."

"Oh, Papa." Laughing, Rosamunde turned and threw herself into his arms as she had when she was a child. Henry quickly closed his arms around her and gave up the reprimand as she knew he would.

"So that is the king's daughter."

Aric shifted on his feet, his gaze leaving the girl the king was embracing to glance at his friend. "It would seem so."

"She is lovely."

"Quite," Aric agreed quietly. "Unless my memory fails me, she appears a copy of the fair Rosamunde."

"Your memory fails you not. She is an exact like-ness of her mother," Shrewsbury agreed. "Except for the hair. That is wholly her father's. Let us hope she did not inherit his quick temper along with it."

"She has been raised right, my lord Bishop. With all discipline and goodness, and the disobedience worked out of her," the abbess announced staunchly, glaring at Shrewsbury for the very suggestion that the girl might not have been. Then, seeming to regain herself, she forced a smile and in a much more pious tone murmured, "It is most gratifying that His Majesty received my message. We feared, when we heard that he was in Normandy, that he might not receive the news in time to make it back for the ceremony."

Aric exchanged a glance with Robert, then asked carefully, "What ceremony?"

"What ceremony?" Adela echoed with amaze-ment. "Why, Lady Rosamunde takes the veil tomor-row."

There was silence for a moment after that an-nouncement; then Robert murmured, "The king will no doubt be a bit surprised by that."

"What!" Henry's roar drew their attention.

"I believe he just learned," Aric muttered. Turn-ing, he found Henry a sight to see. The king's face bore a furious scowl and was so red as to seem almost purple. Even his hair seemed to have picked up some of the fire of his temper and shone more red than gray. He stormed angrily toward them, hands and teeth clenched.

His daughter was hard on his heels, a startled and somewhat bewildered expression on her face. "I thought you knew, Papa. I thought you had received my message and come to witness—" Her words came to an abrupt halt when her father paused in his stride and turned on her in a fury.

"It shall not happen! Do you hear me? You are not, I repeat, *not* going to be a nun."

"But—"

"Your mother—God rest her soul—insisted on the same thing ere she died, and I could do naught about it. But I can and *will* do something now. I am your father, and I will not allow you to throw your life away by becoming a nun."

Rosamunde looked briefly stunned at those words; then, seeing the stiff expression on the abbess's face at the insult in her father's words, she allowed her temper free rein. "It is not throwing my life away! 'Tis perfectly acceptable to become a bride of God! I—"

"Will God see you blessed with children?" Henry snarled, interrupting her curt words.

She looked taken aback briefly at that, then regained herself to snap, "Mayhap. He saw Mary blessed with Jesus."

"*Jesus?*" For a moment it looked as though he might explode, or drop dead. His face was purple with rage.

It was the bishop who intervened, drawing the king's attention with the gentle words, "Your majesty, it is a great honor to become a bride of God. If Rosamunde truly has a calling, it is not well done to force her to—"

"*You!*" Henry turned on the man. "I will not hear your religious drivel. Thanks to your dillydallying, we nearly did not arrive here in time. If I hadn't chanced to hear of Aric's broken betrothal and saved a day's riding by choosing him as groom instead of Rosshuen, we would have been too late!" Whirling on the abbess, he roared, "Why was I not informed of these plans?"

The abbess blinked at him, taken aback. "We . . . I thought you knew, my liege. It was Rosamunde's mother's wish that she follow in her footsteps and become a nun. She said so on her deathbed. As you had not arranged a betrothal, I thought you agreed."

"I do not agree," he snapped, then added, "And I have been making arrangements. But what I meant was, why was I not informed of the imminent ceremony?"

"Well . . . I do not know, Your Majesty. I did send word. Some time ago, in fact. It should have reached you in plenty of time for you to attend. We hoped you might."

The king turned on Shrewsbury again at that news, eyes narrowed and accusing, but the bishop flushed helplessly and murmured, "We have been moving around quite a bit, my liege. Le Mans, then Chinon . . . Mayhap it arrived after we left. I shall, of course, look into it the moment we return."

Henry glared at him briefly, then turned on his daughter. "You are not taking the veil. You will marry. You are the only child of mine who has not turned against me. I will see grandchildren from you."

"John has never turned against you."

"He has joined with my enemies."

"That is just gossip," she argued with disdain.

"And if 'tis true?"

Rosamunde's mouth thinned at the possibility. Truly, no man in history had suffered so from betrayal as her father. Every one of his legitimate sons, her half brothers, had come to turn on him under the influence of their mother, Queen Eleanor. "There are still William and Geoffrey," she whispered, mentioning Henry's other two bastard children.

His expression turned solemn at that, and he reached out to clasp her by the shoulders. "But they were not born of my fair Rosamunde. The love of my life. I am a selfish old man, child. I would see the fruit of out love grow and bloom and cast its seeds across the land, not be stifled and die here in this convent. I would see you marry."

Rosamunde sighed at that, her shoulders slumping in defeat. "And so I shall. Who is to be my groom?"

Aric stiffened as the king suddenly turned toward him.

"Burkhart." The king gestured for him to step forward, and Aric unconsciously straightened his shoulders as he did so. "My daughter, Rosamunde. Daughter, your husband, Aric of Burkhart"

"How do you do, my lord?" she murmured politely, extending her hand. Then, grimacing apologetically as she saw its less than pristine condition—it was stained with residue from her recent work with the foaling—she retracted it and dropped into a quick curtsy instead. "I regret my apparel, but we were not expecting company today."

Before Aric could even murmur a polite response, the king announced, "You should change."

Her head whipped around. "Change?"

"Aye. You will not wish to be wed looking so."

"The wedding is to take place *now?*" *Dismay* was the only word to describe her reaction, and Aric could actually sympathize. It was all a bit dismaying to him as well.

"As soon as you are changed. I must return to Chinon."

"But—"

"See her properly dressed," the king ordered Sister Eustice, then snatched up Adela's arm and urged her out of the building. "I would have a word with the abbess."

Rosamunde gaped after them, then glanced at Eustice with a start when the sister took her arm and urged her to follow. "I am to be married."

"Aye." Eustice glanced worriedly at the girl as they stepped out of the stables. The child was unnaturally pale.

"I thought I was going to be a nun like you."

"Everything will be fine," Eustice murmured reassuringly, directing her through the convent doors and down the hallway to the left. King Henry and Adela were already out of sight.

"Aye," Rosamunde agreed, drawing herself up slightly. "All will be well." Then her shoulders slumped, and she whispered bewilderedly, "But I was to be a nun."

"It would seem you were never truly meant to take the veil."

"Oh, but I was," Rosamunde assured her. "My mother wished it so. She told the abbess. And my father never arranged a betrothal. I was born to be a nun."

"It would seem not," Eustice corrected gently.

"But what if the Lord wants me to take the veil? What if he is angered that I am not to be one?"

" 'Tis more likely the good Lord has his own plans for you, Rosamunde. Else He would have stopped your father from arriving until after it was done. Would He not?"

Frowning, Rosamunde tilted her head to consider that. Sister Eustice continued, "It seems to me that it must have been God Himself who led your father here in time to prevent the ceremony. Were your father even a day later in arriving, the ceremony would have been done by now."

"Aye," Rosamunde murmured uncertainly. "But why would God wish me to marry when there is so much good I might do as a nun?"

"Mayhap He has something more important for you to do as a wife."

"Mayhap," she murmured, but it was obvious by her tone that she was having trouble fathoming that possibility.

Sighing to herself, Eustice urged her into moving along the hall again, managing to get her to the small cell that had been Rosamunde's room since childhood. Ushering the bemused girl inside, Eustice urged her to sit on the side of her tiny, hard bed, then turned to search through the girl's small clothes chest for the dress Rosamunde had made to wear while taking the veil the next day. Coming up empty-handed, she whirled to frown at Rosamunde. "Where is your white gown?"

Rosamunde glanced up distractedly. "White gown? Oh, Sister Margaret offered to hang it for me, to let out any wrinkles."

"Ah." Nodding, Eustice turned toward the door. "Wait here. I shall return directly."

Rosamunde watched the door close behind her friend and mentor, then sank back on the bed with a sigh. She was having difficulty absorbing what was happening. Just that morning, her life had been fixed, her path a comfortable, secure one. Now events had careened out of control, changing the course of her life, and she was not sure it was in a direction in which she wished to go. It looked as though she had little choice, however. Her father's decisions were final.

So she would be married, to a man she had never

met before, a man she had gotten only a fleeting glimpse of moments ago when her father had introduced them. She should have looked at him longer, but had found herself suddenly shy. It was a new sensation for her. But then she had had very little occasion to be in the presence of men during her life. The only men she had ever even met were her father; his servant and constant companion, Bishop Shrewsbury; and Father Abernott, the priest who ministered the Sunday mass at the abbey. The reverend mother said mass the rest of the week.

She had known a stable boy, several years before. But he had not been around long. A week, perhaps; then he had cornered her in a stall, and pressed his lips against hers. Too startled to react at first, Rosamunde had just stood there. By the time she had gotten over her surprise, curiosity and the beginnings of a sort of shivery pleasure had kept her from protesting. Much to her shame, she hadn't even stopped him when he had covered one of her budding breasts with his hand.

Rosamunde had considered stopping him, knowing that anything that felt so wickedly interesting had to be a sin; everything fun did seem to be sinful, according to the sisters. But she did not know if she would have stopped him on her own, for Eustice had come upon them. One minute she had been wrapped in the lad's enthusiastic embrace, and the next he'd been dragged away and was having his ears boxed. Eustice had then dragged Rosamunde off to lecture her: she must never let a man kiss and touch her so again. It was evil. Lips were for speaking, and breasts for milking—and that was that.

The abbess had sent the stable boy away that very day.

"She did not look pleased at the news of her up-coming marriage," Robert murmured.

Shifting on the bench seat where the nuns had seated the men to eat while they waited, Aric turned his gaze from the food he was unable to choke down—despite how delicious it looked—and peered at his friend. "Nay," he agreed dismally.

"Well, mayhap 'tis just a result of surprise."

Aric grunted with little conviction.

"She is quite lovely."

Aric grunted again. He looked far from cheered by the news, and Robert sighed.

"Surely you do not fear *she* will be unfaithful? This girl was raised in a convent, man. She could not have learned the lying, cheating ways of a woman raised at court."

Aric was silent for a moment, then shifted his position at the table and murmured, "Do you recall my cousin, Clothilde?"

"Clothilde?" He thought briefly, then laughed. "Oh, aye. The girl whose mother would not allow her sweets, lest she grow in size, or lose all her teeth ere she married."

Aric grimaced. "Not a single sweet passed her lips ere her marriage, but they had a great tray of them at her wedding feast."

"Aye." Robert laughed again as he recalled the event. "She quite liked sweets once she tried them. As I recall, she nearly ate the whole tray all on her own."

"She still likes them. Perhaps more so because she was deprived of them for so long. In the two years since her marriage, she has grown to six times her original size. She has lost three teeth at last count."

Robert winced. "Do not tell me you fear your wife will grow overlarge and lose her teeth?"

Aric rolled his eyes, then sighed. "What is missing in a convent?"

"Well, I realize they can be strict in these places, but I am sure they have an occasional sweet or—"

"Forget the blasted sweets!" Aric snapped. "*Men*. Men are missing in convents."

"Aye, well, but that is the very reason behind their existence and—Oh!" A chagrined look on his face, he shook his head. "I think I see. You fear that having been deprived of the company of men all these years, your wife soon will find herself overly fond of their company."

Aric muttered under his breath and turned away with mild disgust at the length of time it had taken to get his point across. Surely his friend had not always been so dense?

"Aric. Friend. Do not allow Delia's behavior to color your views. She was raised by her uncle, Lord Stratham, the most notorious reprobate in the land."

"Yet my mother was not."

"Ah." Robert sighed.

"She was raised most strictly."

"Yes, but—"

"And *she* could not contain her passions."

Robert shook his head. "I can see you will not be easily reassured, but 'tis not as bad as all that. If you fear she will become overfond of the company of men, you merely have to keep her away from court. Keep her in the country, where the only men she may meet are peasants and serfs. Surely she was brought up with enough sense not to dally with one of *them*." He clapped his friend on the back encouragingly.

"Oh, aye. The king would most likely be very pleased should he never see his daughter again," Aric muttered. Robert frowned.

"Oh, there is that. He will most likely wish her at court on occasion."

"Most likely," Aric agreed dryly.

"He appears to hold great affection for her." Robert's frown deepened as he thought on that. "That could be a problem, could it not? Jesu! A king for a father-in-law," he marveled in horror as he realized the full significance of it. "Should you not make her happy, he might have you drawn and quartered. What a spot to be in!"

"Robert."

"Aye?"

"Stop trying to make me feel better."

Rosamunde's fretting ended abruptly at the opening of the door. Sighing, she pushed herself to a sitting position as Sister Eustice reentered with the gown she had fetched lying carefully over her arm.

"The creases are all gone, fortunately enough," the nun informed her and started to push the cell door closed, but paused when the abbess's voice sounded in the hallway. By the time Adela arrived at the door, both Rosamunde and Eustice were waiting curiously. Adela took one look at Rosamunde's expression and hurried forward.

"Oh, my dear child," she murmured soothingly, seating herself on the cot beside the girl. She embraced her briefly. "All will be well. You will see. God has a special path for you to follow and you must trust in him."

"Aye, 'tis what Sister Eustice said," Rosamunde whispered as tears welled in her eyes. Oddly enough, the small droplets of liquid had not threatened until the very moment that the abbess offered comfort. It had always been that way. While both Eustice and the abbess had taken the place of her mother on that beautiful woman's death, it was the abbess to whom Rosamunde had turned to bandage her banged-up knees and soothe her hurts. And it never failed that Rosamunde could stand absolutely anything with a stiff upper lip and grim smile until the abbess came around; at the first sight of Adela's kind face, though, she always broke down.

"Oh, now. Shh, my child. Do not cry. You must have faith in the Lord. He chose this path for you. Surely there is a reason."

"I am not crying out of fear of what is to come. Well . . ." she corrected honestly, "mostly I am not. Mostly I am crying for what is ending."

Bewildered, the abbess shook her head slightly. "What is ending?"

"I will have to leave you all, the only family I have ever known. Aside from my father," she added loyally.

Eustice and Adela shared a dismayed look, their own eyes filling with tears at the realization. They had been too distracted to consider that truth.

"Well . . ." Sister Eustice glanced desperately around, everywhere but at the young woman who had been her student in the stables since being a small child—young Rosamunde had latched onto Eustice's voluminous skirts and trailed after her the moment she had gained her feet and been able to walk. The nun had taught her everything she knew, and the look on Eustice's face conveyed her misery at their separation.

"Aye," Adela murmured unhappily, her own watery gaze on the floor. She had been taken with

Rosamunde from her birth. The baby's red curls and sweet smile had melted her heart as nothing else ever had. Contrary to tradition, she herself had overseen the girl's lessons in the schoolroom. She had spent hour after hour feeding the child's expanding mind, encouraging patience, and curbing the temper that seemed always to come with redheads. The rewards for her effort had been great. Rosamunde was everything she had ever wanted in a daughter. With a grimace of pain, the abbess rose to her feet.

"Every bird must leave the nest one day," she said practically. She moved to the door, only to pause and glance back uncertainly. "I never thought you would leave us, Rosamunde. I was not warned." Adela sighed unhappily. "Thinking you would not need the knowledge, there was much I neglected to teach you about marriage and the marital bed."

"The marital bed?" Rosamunde frowned worriedly as she noted the sudden stain of embarrassment on the older woman's cheeks.

The abbess stared at her, at a loss for a moment, then turned abruptly away. "Sister Eustice shall enlighten you," she said abruptly. She started to slip out of the room, then paused to add, "But quickly, sister. The king is most impatient to have this business done."

The door closed, leaving Eustice staring at it in stupefaction.

MORE VAMPIRE ROMANCES FROM
NEW YORK TIMES BESTSELLING AUTHOR

LYNSAY SANDS

UNDER A VAMPIRE MOON
978-0-06-210020-7

Christian Notte has seen enough of his Argeneau relatives taken down for the count, but he never imagined he'd let himself fall in love—until he meets the enthralling, charmingly skittish, and oh-so-mortal Carolyn Connor.

THE LADY IS A VAMP
978-0-06-207807-0

When Jeanne Louise Argeneau left work, she never thought she'd end up tied down—kidnapped—by a good-looking mortal named Paul Jones. More attracted than annoyed, she quickly realizes there is more to her abductor than meets the eye.

IMMORTAL EVER AFTER
978-0-06-207811-7

Anders felt a connection to the green-eyed beauty from the moment he cradled her bruised body in his arms. But before he claims Valerie Moyer as his life mate, he must destroy the vampire who almost stole her from him forever.

ONE LUCKY VAMPIRE
978-0-06-207814-8

Secretly playing bodyguard to sweet, sexy Nicole Phillips is turning out to be the wildest ride of Jake Colson's immortal life. He's barely had time to adjust to his new state when he must stop whoever's targeting her.